Highest Praise for
NO TIME TO DIE

"Breathless thrills and pace, but real substance too: a perfect mix of nail-biter and thought-provoker, from a writer to watch. Highly recommended."
—Lee Child

"An intelligent, exciting tour de force. The story is tight, the characters are fascinating, and the twists are terrific and totally unexpected . . . A crackling good read . . . Has the magic touch."
—Michael Palmer

"*No Time to Die* takes a terrific, original premise—What if someone literally could not age?—and turns it into a heart-pounding thriller that keeps its surprises coming to the last page. Fans of Michael Crichton will love this."
—Joe Finder

"A fast-paced thriller with sound, cutting-edge science that explores the fundamental mysteries of aging. *No Time to Die* may be fictional, but it vividly evokes the most exciting aspect of my research to date."
—Dr. Richard Walker, editor-in-chief, *Clinical Interventions in Aging*

"Defeating aging may be far harder than *No Time to Die* suggests, but it's definitely possible. By highlighting in fiction aspects of this tragedy that are all too real, Peikoff may just save some."
—Aubrey de Grey, Ph.D., chief science officer, SENS Research Foundation

LIVING PROOF

"Kira Peikoff's imagination is a wonder to behold and an amazing place to visit. *Living Proof* is not only thought provoking, it's an all-too-believable premise that makes for some high drama. You have to check this one out."
—Steve Berry

"Taut, energetic, and imaginative, *Living Proof* is a near-future page-turner that asks vital questions about the value of human life. Kira Peikoff bursts on the scene with style, offering readers a tight and suspenseful thriller that will not only keep them up past their bedtimes, but also have them pondering its life-and-death issues long after the book is closed. A remarkable debut!"
—Lisa Unger

"Kira Peikoff gets suspense and how to write it. This is a terrific read—tightly woven and tense as a coiled snake. I was a decade older than Kira Peikoff when I wrote my first thriller . . . I'm jealous. Do yourself a favor and buy this book."
—Michael Palmer

"A thriller that keeps you turning pages; a novel of suspense fraught with danger; a fascinating look at a serious moral issue. Kira Peikoff belongs to a very small cadre of writers to watch—who have something important to say and are hell-bent about entertaining you at the same time. I cannot wait to see what she writes next!"
—M.J. Rose

"First-time novelist Kira Peikoff comes out of the gate with power, grace and insight. This is a brilliant debut thriller!"
—Jonathan Maberry

"A tremendous debut—smart, savvy, and suspenseful. Kira Peikoff is a writer to watch."
—Alafair Burke

ALSO BY KIRA PEIKOFF

Living Proof

NO TIME TO DIE

KIRA PEIKOFF

PINNACLE BOOKS
Kensington Publishing Corp.
www.kensingtonbooks.com

PINNACLE BOOKS are published by

Kensington Publishing Corp.
119 West 40th Street
New York, NY 10018

All Kensington titles, imprints, and distributed lines are available at special quantity discounts for bulk purchases for sales promotions, premiums, fund-raising, educational, or institutional use. Special book excerpts or customized printings can also be created to fit specific needs. For details, write or phone the office of the Kensington special sales manager: Kensington Publishing Corp., 119 West 40th Street, New York, NY 10018, attn: Special Sales Department; phone 1-800-221-2647.

ISBN-13: 978-0-7860-3489-5
ISBN-10: 0-7860-3489-0

First printing: September 2014

10 9 8 7 6 5 4 3 2 1

Printed in the United States of America

First electronic edition: September 2014

ISBN-13: 978-0-7860-3490-1
ISBN-10: 0-7860-3490-4

To M.J. Rose

and in memory of
MICHAEL PALMER

PART 1

Every Night and every Morn
Some to Misery are Born.
Every Morn and every Night
Some are Born to sweet delight.
Some are Born to sweet delight,
Some are Born to Endless Night.
—WILLIAM BLAKE

PROLOGUE

Washington, D.C.
Thursday, March 7

The echo down the hallway didn't surprise him. Not at first. The old industrial warehouse creaked whenever Eli stayed late to work in his lab. *His* lab: he could say that finally, after two decades of toiling away in this windowless steel complex, where his most important colleagues were the half dozen chimpanzees in cages lining the side wall. They were the first to try whatever new multimillion-dollar drug was being developed for human use by the research team at Panex Pharmaceuticals—the team that was now officially led by Eli himself.

He was peering through his microscope, reveling in his recent promotion, when the faint echo down the hall assumed the distinctive pattern of footsteps. Usually the researchers wore sneakers, so their movements were announced by squeaks of rubber against the floor. But now the rhythmic slap of a man's dress shoes struck the ground, drawing closer.

Eli glanced up with a frown. He'd thought he was

alone—it was 10:15 P.M. on a Thursday after all. Everyone else had left hours ago. Even the security guard went home at ten o'clock.

"Hello?" he called. Across the room most of the chimps were sleeping, but an elder one with a crown of silvery fur perked up with a grunt, curling his massive finger around the wire of his cage.

"Not you, Jerry," Eli muttered. He had affectionate names for all the chimps—Jerry and Elaine shared a cage, next to George and Kramer, Larry and Newman—even though he knew theoretically not to get attached to animals who sometimes had to suffer and die for the sake of the research.

The footsteps were louder now, nearly encroaching on the lab.

Eli slid off the stool and nervously tore off his latex gloves.

"Who's there?" he called.

A lean older man crossed into the doorway. He wore wire-rimmed spectacles and an elegant gray suit that matched the color of his thinning hair. His alert eyes lit up at Eli as if in recognition, though Eli was sure he'd never seen him before. His face was all edges: a pointy nose, jutting chin, bony cheeks. A leather briefcase hung off his left shoulder, and he was double-fisting crystal champagne flutes, each one filled with bubbly golden liquid. One glance at his sharp looks told Eli that this man was shrewd, dignified, respected. He was *someone*.

Eli felt himself relax as his curiosity piqued. Any brief worry about a trespasser vanished. In any case, Eli cut an imposing six-foot-three figure, albeit more bulk than brawn. He could take care of himself. The man smiled at him.

"Dr. Eliot Shipley?"

He nodded. "Just Eli. And you're . . . ?"

"Mr. G. I'm on the board at Panex. We're all very excited that you've been promoted to head of R&D." He walked toward Eli and extended the champagne flute in his right hand. "At our dinner earlier tonight, the board agreed you deserve to be congratulated in person, so I came to surprise you with a little toast on their behalf. We heard you usually stay late."

Eli took the fancy glass, grinning. He ran a hand through what remained of his sparse blond hair—which, at age sixty-seven, wasn't much. It was about time the corporate bigwigs sat up and took notice of him, after years of his toiling in practical obscurity to help put the cheapest, most effective drugs on the market for their bottom line. Sometimes too cheaply produced, in Eli's opinion, though to the execs there was no such thing, so he did as he was told.

"Wow," he said. "I'm flattered. You didn't have to—"

The man lifted his own champagne. "Please. The pleasure is mine. Cheers."

They clinked glasses and drank. Eli recognized the sweet, smooth flavor. It was the good stuff, Dom Pérignon, the kind he bought his wife last year for their thirtieth anniversary.

"Delicious." He took a few more hearty sips to show his appreciation.

A strangely satisfied smile tugged at the man's lips. "You've done so much, it's only fitting that you finish on top."

"Oh, I'm not planning to retire anytime soon."

The man was still smiling that same odd way, in almost ironic glee.

A vague uneasiness settled over Eli. "In fact," he added, "I'd rather die than ever retire."

The man's smile widened ever so slightly. "I'm glad to hear that."

There was nothing unfriendly about the way he said it, yet Eli felt a chill of hostility as sure as if he'd delivered a blow.

Eli lifted his leg to take a step back—and that's when he noticed the sudden heaviness in his foot. Moving it was like trying to uproot a tree. He uttered a little gasp; fear shot through him.

"What's happening?" he demanded. Then, as if without permission, his fingers loosened around his glass. It slid through his grip and shattered at his feet, splashing the remaining drops of champagne on his white coat. He stared from his weakening hand to the man, terrified. "Who are you?"

"I told you," the man said calmly. "You can call me Mr. G."

He racked his brain trying to remember the names of the company's board members—was there anyone whose last name started with *G*?—but Panex had been acquired by a major conglomerate, and the management at the highest levels had never interacted with him before.

Now the rest of the chimps were awake, anxious, scratching at their cages. Eli glanced over to them as if for help. Through their cages, six pairs of glassy black eyes were trained on him, set deep in heads the size of globes. His eyes darted to his microscope ten feet away, its light still shining on a petri dish. On the counter nearby, a tray of chrome instruments gleamed under the fluorescent lights.

His eyelids drooped, but he forced them open, his head lolling forward. Then his knees buckled, the walls appeared to shift, and he found himself sprawled on his stomach in the middle of the lab. A pleasant fogginess rolled in, spooling around his brain like cotton candy; it dissolved his fear and his urge to fight. Somewhere far away an inner voice was shrieking at him to run, but all he wanted was to rest his cheek against the cool tile floor for a moment. Just one little moment, and then he would get up. He allowed his eyes to close. God, that felt good.

An acute sting at the base of his neck snapped him awake.

"Ow!" he cried, reaching up to swat away whatever it was.

His fingers brushed against a thin needle as it was being pulled out of his skin.

His mouth opened to scream; a whimper came out instead. His breathing grew shorter as he rolled onto his back. His muscles were turning to concrete, solidifying him from within.

Before, he had imagined death as a distant concept in relation to himself, something that mainly happened to the old and the sick. But now he wondered if he was about to die. He wondered if it would hurt. He wasn't a religious man, but through his mental fog he sent up a quick prayer to any and every deity he could think of: Jesus, God, Allah, Buddha.

He raged at his body to sit up. He flexed his core, his arms, his chest, yet when he expected to move, nothing happened. He felt utterly limp, a puddle where once there was a man. Struggling to keep his eyes open was like trying to lift a car with his lids. He became aware of a shadow above him. With great effort, he looked up.

The man was sipping champagne, regarding him with a look of amusement, as though Eli had only pretended to lose control of himself for their mutual entertainment. Eli tried to communicate a look of entreaty—*I'll do anything, anything at all*—but even his brows had frozen. His throat seized up, choking off his air. He was a statue. He would suffocate in a few minutes if something didn't change fast.

The man inhaled an indulgent breath. "So, Dr. Shipley, how does it feel to be locked-in?"

Eli could feel his face turning purple. That was when the chemist in him realized what had been plunged into his neck. Succinylcholine. Nearly untraceable, with a quick half-life, the drug was used to paralyze anesthesia patients before they were intubated.

"Don't worry," the man said, as if reading his mind. "It'll wear off real fast."

Eli tried to wrestle his lips into one question: *Why?*

"The worst is the surprise, isn't it? Thinking you're doing well, better than ever, actually, when out of nowhere your world is destroyed."

What the hell have I ever done to you, Eli wanted to shout. *I don't even know you.* His mouth merely twitched.

A twitch! That meant the drug really was wearing off already. He felt a loosening in his throat, all the way down to his diaphragm.

The chimps were aggravated now. He couldn't turn his head but he could hear the commotion coming from their cages—the restless pacing and scratching at the bars, the high-pitched shrieks and taunts that sounded like a fight about to break out.

Just as he was able to force a tiny gasp of a breath, the man unhooked the two gold clasps on his briefcase and pulled out a pocketknife. When he flicked it open, a shiny blade popped out. Eli's eyes widened. The hand and the blade came closer until his whole visual field was a glint of light on a silver edge.

Let it be fast, he thought, bracing his neck for the pain.

But the blade sunk into his cheek. Its point cut across his flesh, ear to nose, in one deep horizontal gash. He cried out as warm blood oozed down his face. Since he couldn't lift a hand to wipe it away, it dribbled down his lips, over his teeth.

The man crouched down to appraise his handiwork, his impassive face close enough that Eli could smell the alcohol on his breath. Apparently satisfied, he clicked the knife shut, slipped it back into his briefcase, and turned away. Eli felt a jolt of hope. As if it were an afterthought, the stranger threw a glance over his shoulder and remarked, "They like the face."

They?

The man retreated, but instead of heading for the door, he veered left, toward the chimps.

Eli sucked in a ragged breath, trying to thrash his legs; they moved an inch.

Time seemed to slow as he heard the slide of a metal lock and the squeal of a cage door opening wide. Two of the beasts lumbered out, attracted by the scent of his blood. He braced himself as they stampeded on all fours toward him, their longtime captor. George and

Kramer came into view, the two youngest and most aggressive males. He tried to scoot away, but his muscles were too weak.

They tore into his cheek wound with astonishing viciousness. The pain was stunning. But it wasn't until their teeth sank down to his bone that he knew agony.

Before he lost consciousness, he caught a glimpse of the man sauntering toward the door. He was waving good-bye with a postcard in his hand. On the front was a picture of the Earth revolving around the sun, and on the back, some kind of scrawled message that Eli couldn't make out. At the bottom was a signature in large cursive, one that meant nothing to him, but that would come to evoke radical feelings everywhere.

It was a single name: *Galileo*.

CHAPTER 1

Dr. Helen McNair was weeping when the doorbell buzzed. It was after midnight on a sweltering June night, and unless her boss was coming to give her back her job, she wanted to see no one. Not even Natalie, the only person who knew about her soon-to-be infamous resignation from Columbia. No doubt her friend was waiting ten floors below, probably with a bouquet or baked goods, insisting on consolation.

She grabbed a tissue and rose from bed, pressing the button on the intercom. Her studio apartment, decorated with paintings of colorful flowers, failed to cheer her as it usually did.

"You really didn't need to come over."

"Actually," said a deep male voice, "I did."

She felt her body stiffen. "Who's there?"

"I've come to help you, Helen."

"Who are you? How do you know my name?"

"I know what happened today and I can fix it. Come downstairs, but hurry—we don't have long."

"What do you know?"

"All of it. Your secret experiment. How the dean caught you and flipped out."

The hair on her arms prickled. "But that's impossible! It hasn't been announced."

"It doesn't need to be."

She glanced up at the ceiling as if there might be a hidden camera in the corner, but saw none. "So—you're stalking me?"

"Not stalking. Recruiting you. I'm the person who can give you back what he took away."

Her finger hovered next to the intercom. "Excuse me?"

"A lab of your own. No one to bother you. Isn't that what you want?"

Her voice rose angrily. "Okay, now you're mocking me and it's not funny."

"We're extremely serious."

"We?"

"You have allies you don't even know about."

"Right." She rolled her eyes. "Leave me alone or I'm calling the cops."

A second man's voice piped up—a gruff voice that sounded oddly familiar. "No! Helen, don't. We're here to get you out of this mess."

There was no way it could be Professor Adler, the chair of the Biology Department, who had contributed to the mess by recommending her expulsion to the dean. More likely, her grief over the sudden death of her career—the four-decade love of her life—was causing auditory hallucinations. She stuck a finger in her ear as if to reset any faulty wiring.

"Just come downstairs," urged the first man. "If you

don't like what you see, you don't have to open the door."

He was right. She had no doorman, but the front door to her apartment building was glass; she could take a peek without letting anyone inside, and then she would have a description to tell the police. She could even try to snap a furtive picture on her cell.

She pressed the button on the intercom again. "Wait right there."

Then she pulled a terry cloth robe tight around her slender figure, padded into the hall, and rode the elevator downstairs, clutching her phone. The lobby was deserted. As she walked by its oval mirror, she barely noticed her mussed gray bun and puffy eyelids. All her attention was focused on the front door, trying to discern the forms in the shadows. Two men were standing on the stoop. The one on the left was tall and powerfully built, with a gleam of mischief in his eyes and a jaw sharp enough to cut ice; the other was older, stout and bald. The first man she didn't recognize; the second, she most definitely did.

She let out a gasp and yanked open the door. "So that *was* you!"

Adler only nodded. "Now will you let us in? There's a lot to explain and not much time."

Her gaze darted to the tall man. Something about him seemed vaguely familiar, as though she might have seen him from a distance, but she couldn't place when or where. "Who are you?"

"You don't know me," he said, extending a hand. "I go by Galileo."

She hesitated, glancing back at Adler.

He smiled apologetically. "I know you think I work for the dean, but I don't."

"You don't?"

"Not ultimately."

"But we were just in your office—?"

"It's a good front, isn't it?"

"Who do you work for, then?"

He tilted his head at the striking stranger. "Him. And now—so can you."

CHAPTER 2

Zoe Kincaid wrenched the sweaty quilt off her legs and threw it to the floor. Adrenaline ample for a racehorse had been pumping through her since midnight, practically spinning her mind faster than the Earth itself. For what felt like the hundredth time, she glanced at the orange numbers on her alarm clock: 7:59 A.M.

Sixty-one minutes.

She wasn't sure if she was ready.

Her grandfather's voice sprung to her mind: *If there's a job to be done, just do it.* The first step was to get out of bed. Then, endure the next hour until her secret appointment with Dr. Carlyle. Together, at 9:00 A.M., they were going to reckon with the only enemy she feared: her own body. Time was short—though how short, it was impossible to know—and he was her last chance at a real diagnosis.

Light crept through her window like an intruder,

dampening the clock's glow. She winced when the numbers morphed to 8:00 A.M. A sledgehammer of high-pitched bells assaulted her ears, insolent in their cheerfulness. She tapped the alarm off. Then silence, except for the city noises seeping in from the street: cars speeding down Broadway, doors slamming, the occasional honk. Morning as usual for everyone else.

She looked around the room that had been her sanctuary for twenty years—at the oak desk where she had spelled her name for the first time; at the pink beanbag chair gathering dust in the corner; at the faded rainbow wallpaper she still loved. How simple it used to be to seek relief from her woes, in a lollipop or a Band-Aid or her mother's arms. Today, not even the most elaborate fort of her childhood could shelter her from the doctor's imminent news. With a shiver, she realized that one outcome was certain, no matter what he said: Later this morning, she would be returning home distraught—either vindicated but ill, or healthy but ruined. There was no other option.

Outside her bedroom, footsteps fell softly at first, and then louder. She darted to her door and heard a slow shuffle marked by the regular plunk of a cane. Opening the door a crack, she peeked out to make sure no one else was around and whispered, "Gramps."

In the hallway, he caught her eye and smiled. She beckoned for him to come in, to hurry. Her heart swelled as he tried to speed up. His arthritic grip on his cane tightened and he sank it into the carpet like an oar, pushing off. Despite the effort, his creased face betrayed no hint of strain. A narrowing of his eyes showed his acceptance of the challenge, offset by a slight grin that told Zoe he took pleasure in conquering it. Once an Olympian, always an Olympian. In 1948, he had broken the world record for running the 400 meter dash in 46.2 seconds. After aging out of the sport, he'd carried that determination into medicine, becoming a renowned physician who had never given up on a single patient for being too sick or not sick enough.

He was the only one who had not given up on her.

When he reached her, she put an arm around his frail waist and ushered him into her room, then closed the door.

"I was just coming to check on you," he rasped, sinking onto her bed. "Are you all right? You look flushed."

She shook her head, too tired to feign bravery. "I couldn't sleep."

"I'm not surprised."

Her dainty brow creased. "What if it's bad?" She looked into his watery blue eyes. "What if I'm dying?"

He shook his head. "Come here, darling."

"Why could no one ever explain my seizures?" she demanded, standing. "Or why I look like this?"

"You're small for your age."

"Stunted," she corrected. "Thin and short doesn't even cover it." They stared at her reflection in the full-length mirror next to her bed. When he spotted the ugly purple bruise inside her elbow, a look of pain crossed his face, but he said nothing. She folded her arms. Gramps was unflinching around any wounds except for hers.

Underneath her tank top and shorts—size 00—was

a slight rounding of her hips if she squinted. Beneath two mosquito-bite breasts, her torso was a flat slab of skin and bone, her legs sticklike; she couldn't gain weight, even eating a diet rich in butter, cheese, and whole milk. Yet her cheeks looked cherubic from a persistent layer of baby fat. With her fine blond hair and freckled sloped nose, she looked on the wrong side of twelve, impossibly far from the woman with high cheekbones and full breasts she had yearned to become for a decade.

"At least you're proportional," he pointed out.

"To a ten-year-old boy. Why didn't the growth hormone do anything? All those shots for nothing." She turned away from the mirror to look at him.

He frowned. "That was unusual."

"And why did I have so much trouble at school?" She crossed her arms.

"That's a different issue, dear. Adjusting to college can be very trying. You were living away from home for the first time—"

"But what if some virus is killing off my brains?"

He ventured a smile. "You're going to Northeastern. A very respectable university."

"Not like it's Harvard," she declared, reddening at the thought of the professors who had ripped her apart like hyenas over prey, and with the same enthusiasm. Her flush deepened at the other, worse humiliation she'd suffered there, one too unbearable to relate to anyone, even Gramps. "Plus I only got in because of Dad's legacy. Anyway, that's over."

"For now," he allowed.

"Whatever. The point is, I can feel something is really

wrong. I don't care if Mom and Dad are ignoring it." She strained past the lump in her throat. "I just don't want to die."

He pulled her into a hug, and despite herself, she slackened against his arms. "I'll tell you a secret," he murmured. "Everyone is afraid to die. Every single person. And when it's your own kid's life at stake, you're even more scared. That's why your parents would rather act like everything is fine."

"But you agree with me, don't you? That's why you haven't said anything about giving me the blank check?" She didn't add that the check was ripped up; that despite his generous offer, she couldn't bring herself to take a penny from his savings, which her late grandmother's illness had drained.

Silence for a moment, then: "Yes," he said. "We can't let them stop us."

She pulled away from his embrace. "I don't want to leave you, ever."

"Death is inevitable, darling." He looked her in the eye, but the warmth of his gaze did nothing to dull the sting of his words. "Mine before yours, I'm sure. But once you get to be my age, it's not so tragic. I've had a long wonderful life—"

"Stop!" she cried, pressing her temples. "I hate talking about this."

"It's reality," he said, clasping her delicate hands with his knobby ones. "We live, hopefully a nice long time, we get old, and then we die."

"How are you not scared? I thought you just said everyone was." Her heart pounded the way it always did when she was forced to confront the idea of vanishing—*poof*—for all of eternity.

"I used to be, when I was your age," he replied. "But eventually I realized there's nothing you can do to escape it, and by the time it happens, you won't even know. So the more time you spend thinking about it, the less you spend living."

She relaxed slightly. He always made her feel safer around her worst fear, like an animal tamer caging a vicious beast.

"Are you afraid of anything?" she asked.

He looked away. The top of his head caught a ray of light and she could see purple veins snaking across his bare scalp. She glanced at the clock. It was already 8:25 A.M.

"That's a yes," she said impatiently. "What is it?"

"I'm afraid of lots of things," he admitted. "I know you don't want to think of me that way, but you're old enough now to know your old gramps isn't superhuman."

"Of what most?" she pressed, already conscious of the answer. But she needed to hear it from him, to know she wasn't a hypochondriac.

"Of anything happening to you," he said, looking at her. "Will you let me come with you?"

"No, I want to go alone." It was a lie, but she could detect exhaustion in his face.

Before he could react, there was a hard double knock on the door. As her mother bustled in, Zoe spun around to open her dresser, hiding the bruise in the crook of her arm—evidence of the secret blood tests. Luckily there was no stamp of the MRI or X-ray.

Her mother's wavy auburn hair fell over her shoulders, framing her smooth face. She was proud to still sometimes get carded, and insisted that Zoe's youthfulness was a genetic blessing she would one day appreciate. "Dad! What are you two doing in here? I've been calling from downstairs. Breakfast is on the table."

"Thank you, dear. I was just giving Zoe a little pep talk, that's all."

"A pep talk?" She hovered in the doorway. "For what?"

"An interview," Zoe blurted over her shoulder, grabbing a collared pink shirt from the drawer. Then she turned around to face her mother, noticing how her fitted dress emphasized all her perfect curves. "Excuse me," she said, stepping past her into the walk-in closet and closing the door. After putting on the shirt, black pants, and flats—all purchased, to her chagrin, in the kids' department at Macy's—she inhaled a shaky breath. *Half an hour,* she thought. *I can wait thirty more minutes.*

She walked back out, stretching her lips into a carefree smile. But the characteristic dimple in her cheek, that barometer of sincerity, was missing. Her mother glanced at Gramps and then at her.

"If you're too sick to stay in school, then why are you looking for a job?"

Zoe shrugged. "To keep me busy. It won't be too demanding."

"Who is going to hire a college dropout in this economy?"

Zoe looked at Gramps; from behind her mother's back, he glanced at her bookshelf.

"A bookstore," she replied. "A Barnes & Noble

downtown. I've got to run." She breezed past her with an air kiss, amazed at her own sangfroid.

Just as she reached the door, her mother's manicured fingers clamped around her forearm. "A long-sleeved shirt, Zoe? In the middle of this heat wave?"

"It's formal," she snapped, wincing as her tight sleeve constricted around the bruise. She yanked her arm away.

"Good luck, darling," Gramps called after her, though the forced lightness in his tone betrayed his worry. She wondered if her mother noticed.

She looked over her shoulder, compelled by some force within her that cried out not to leave him. His whiskered chin had sunk to his chest, helplessness incarnate.

"Bye," she whispered, and hurried down the corkscrew wooden stairs. They lived in a rent-regulated duplex that cost the same paltry sum as when her parents had moved in two decades earlier, before the neighborhood became gentrified.

As she rushed toward the front door, a pile of mail on the counter caught her eye. One envelope had a blue circular logo next to the words *Chase Bank*. It was addressed to her father. Across the top, in bold capital letters, were the words: ***IMPORTANT—DO NOT DISCARD.***

Zoe felt the blood drain from her face. She looked around, slipped the envelope into her purse, and ran out.

For a Monday morning in June, the streets of New York were bustling. Though Zoe had lived on the Upper

West Side all her life, she had only recently begun to appreciate how Manhattan invigorated her. After living on the Northeastern campus for those eight stifling months, trapped in a slow-moving sea of popped collars and red sweatshirts, the caffeinated pulse of Manhattan made her eyes open wider and her heart beat faster.

Dr. Ray Carlyle, the city's foremost medical geneticist, was located across Central Park on Fifth Avenue and 68th Street. She could make it there on foot if she scrambled.

Finding Dr. Carlyle had felt to Zoe like meeting the Wizard of Oz at the end of a yellow brick road paved by a sadist. The first brick was laid six years ago, when at age fourteen, she still had not gotten her period like all of her friends, nor sprouted breasts or grown an inch. When a prescription growth hormone failed to effect any change, her endocrinologist wrote off her condition as "idiopathic"—one with no known cause—and told her she might never bear children.

But the longer the status quo persisted, the more left behind she felt, especially when her high school peers began to revel in their nascent sexuality. The extent of Zoe's own experimentation was listening to their gossip. Some of her friends even fell in love, and that was what hurt the most. More than breasts or height, she longed for movie-ending, Imax-sized love. She wasn't sure where sex fit into her fantasy, though. She was ashamed to admit that she found it more embarrassing than erotic—all those bodily fluids and weird noises her friends spoke of with self-conscious laughter. Not that she had to worry. Guys only stared at her blankly, if at all.

During her lonely adolescence, Gramps had been a

lighthouse of optimism. He told her the stories of his Olympic failures before winning the gold, and of his relentless courtship of her late grandmother before he finally won her over, too. That he existed, that a man so tender and debonair *could* exist, powered her through those aching years.

Then one day near the end of high school, the road unexpectedly twisted. She suffered a seizure, and more than one top neurologist couldn't pinpoint a cause. The seizures got out of control, until after months of trial and error, a rare combination of antiepileptic medications silenced them. As life settled into an uneasy routine until high school graduation, she tried to ignore the mysteries of her body as easily as everyone else did.

When the fall rolled around, she hadn't felt ready to leave Gramps or her parents, and at the last minute deferred college for a year. She couldn't really explain her attachment to home, when all her friends were desperate to move up and on. She just knew she strongly preferred to stay put, where she was comfortable and accepted. But once she finally started at Northeastern, with hundreds of new faces staring at her in dismay, she began to focus on her otherness once more.

On her first day in the dorm, her roommate asked what would become a common question around campus: "What are you, like, twelve? Some kid prodigy?"

It was almost easier to act the impostor than to explain the unexplainable.

With the same refrain constantly circling her, soon she found it was all she could focus on, even as her grades slipped. College had not just magnified her underlying sense of defectiveness, but lit it on fire. Then, two months ago, it burned her alive. All semester, she'd been working up the nerve to talk to her crush, a popular sophomore who played first violin in the school orchestra. Figuring they shared a love of music, she approached him at a frat party to ask him to a concert, the Boston Symphony Orchestra.

He took one look at her and raised an eyebrow. "Aren't you a bit young for me?"

A brunette standing next to him smirked. "Maybe her babysitter's off."

Their drunken friends cracked up. The joke spread, innocuous teasing for everyone else, but a torch of humiliation for her. The following weekend, she showed up at her parents' brownstone with two suitcases. They had no choice but to accept her decision to drop out, however disappointing.

At home with time to spare, her uneasiness morphed into an obsession, and then a quest, unceremoniously launched late one night in her bedroom with the Google search: "undiagnosed disease help."

That was how she found Dr. Carlyle, a legendary diagnostician in genetic disorders. He was a consultant to the National Institutes of Health's Undiagnosed Diseases Program, an arm of the federal government that aimed to tackle the cold cases of medicine, with a limited acceptance rate of fifty people per year. Though it seemed impossible to gain entry into such an exclusive program, Dr. Carlyle himself was right in New York City, with a private practice that accepted new patients. When Gramps corroborated his famed status, her excitement was propelled to stratospheric heights.

If there was anyone on earth who could diagnose the mysterious, disparate problems she could only term *her condition,* Zoe felt certain he'd be the one. But her parents hadn't been quite as thrilled. Years ago, they had encouraged her to see plenty of specialists, then became wary after many futile visits; then accepting of the repeated diagnosis "idiopathic"; and finally, adamant that she accept it, too.

"Accept the things you cannot change," her mother quoted from the Serenity Prayer with the regularity of rain.

And have the wisdom to know the difference, she always thought in response. But her father was convinced that her obsession with her health had become neurotic.

"Enough," he had commanded. "You're a perfectly capable young woman, and you're just using these symptoms as an evasion."

"That's not—"

But he held up a hand.

"As a condition of living at home until you sort this out, you're going to a therapist, but *no more doctors.*"

It was 8:49 A.M. Zoe cringed as she hurried through Central Park, recalling the memory of her father's piercing eyes, his shame at her for being a college dropout. A warm summer rain pelted the grass under her feet, turning the dirt soggy. She squished across the lawn, not caring as the soil muddied her pants and slid between her toes. The only thing that mattered was Dr. Carlyle's diagnosis. After that—

Time ceased. Her whole life, every desolate and bewildering moment, was compressing down to this one hour, this 9:00 A.M. appointment. The magnitude of it flattened her focus to a point, and beyond that, the future skewed like light through a prism, breaking off into infinite directions.

But one thing was real, regardless of how the morning's events would play out: inside her purse was the envelope that could ruin her. Inside was her parents' credit card bill—a sum total of over $10,000 for her recent full body X-ray, MRI, tissue analysis, and genetic screening. Their family's Scrooge-like health insurance plan had denied coverage for the tests after she had already gotten them, so she had no choice but to charge the card. Would she face her parents with remorseful trepidation or calm conviction when they opened the bill?

She let out a nervous breath as she stepped from the mushy lawn to the wet concrete of the sidewalk. As Dr. Carlyle's nondescript office building came into view, she worried for the first time if she could have been wrong about her own motives. What if, as her parents believed, she was using her health obsession to conceal some more profound psychological distress?

No. She shook her head defiantly, whipping her wet blond hair against her cheek. The rain was pounding the ground with increasing intensity, and passersby scrambled under the awnings of the nearest buildings. Already drenched, she stopped and turned her face to the sky. The warm drops felt like tears that wouldn't come—tears for herself, for her parents, and for the river of betrayal that separated them.

Since stealing the credit card, her first morally questionable act, her idea of growing up had taken on a new meaning—not the reckless fun of unsupervised independence, but quite the opposite—a crushing responsibility for every choice she would ever make. Was this what it really meant to get older?

Every step in her soaked pants felt leaden as she crossed the final block to Dr. Carlyle's clinic, to answers. She squinted at the slick asphalt of Fifth Avenue, which glowed red in the taillights of passing cars. Maybe she was searching for a neatness that didn't exist, but she was counting on one explanation to tie everything together, from her size, to her seizures, to her inability to fit in. *There can be a simple answer to a complicated problem,* she reassured herself. *Newton proved that three times over.*

As she walked up to the clinic's door, the sound of the rain drowned out the world, leaving her worst fear the loudest noise. *What if there is a simple answer— but it's a death sentence?* The door stood inches away, gray as the sky. A gold plaque next to it read: Ray Carlyle, MD.

She froze. *This is happening,* she thought.

It wasn't too late to turn back, go home and admit her mistake, and work tirelessly to pay back every penny. She could return to Northeastern next semester and get on with her life, without ever learning the results of the tests. Ignorance, bliss. Throw in some drinking and drugs to dull her unease, and she might almost feel like everyone else. It would be so much easier than hearing Dr. Carlyle speak words like *survival rate* or *terminal.*

Her head throbbed at the base of her skull as she considered which choice would be the true evasion. She looked back at the road, at the cars splashing by, and beyond the trees, at the glistening path home.

A vibration near her elbow startled her: the appointment reminder on her cell phone. It was 9:00 A.M.

If there's a job to be done, just do it.

She pushed open the door and walked inside.

CHAPTER 3

Les Mahler hated coming to the southeast quadrant of D.C. The vacant-eyed homeless roaming the neighborhood for food and drugs, the shabby apartments with half-broken shutters, the litter strewn over the streets like dirty confetti—all reminded him too well his own humble origins, the Bronx. With his dual doctorates in biology and philosophy and his prestigious title—chief of the Justice Department's Bioethics Committee—he wondered if his colleagues would ever believe that he once belonged to a place just like this. That for years he was a terrified blue-collar kid whose daily concern was to hide from the gang that ruled the streets.

He walked faster, sweating in the warm morning air, as if to distance himself from the ugly recollection. *Focus.* The official investigation into Helen McNair's disappearance had yielded no clues so far, and he was getting impatient. The police had been treating it like a missing persons case until a few days ago, when Les opened his official mail at the D.C. headquarters to find a notorious postcard: on one side was a picture of the Earth revolving around the sun, and on the other, Helen's name in black ink and the signature *Galileo*, the leader's brazen moniker for himself. These postcards were how the enigmatic organization known as the Network always claimed responsibility after an innocent person vanished into their secret ring. Allegedly the Network exploited their victims to carry out illegal science experiments, far from the prying eyes of any government oversight; the postcards appeared to be a way to mock the impotency of Les's committee, which was responsible for overseeing human experimentation nationwide. Its open investigations were highly confidential. The public had no knowledge of the Network or Galileo, and Les planned to keep it that way until after the whole gang was found and dismantled. But so far it had proved impossible to track down a group whose only appearances came through a string of disappearances. It was like trying to locate a black hole: you knew it existed, but only because of what it sucked away.

Helen McNair marked the twenty-seventh person—all scientists, doctors, or very sick patients—who had vanished. None of the victims had ever been found, except for one who disrupted the pattern: Dr. Eliot Shipley, a researcher found mauled to death in his lab by his own chimpanzees. His death was glossed over in the press as a tragic accident. He had died alone, there were no fingerprints anywhere on his shredded body, and only a harmless amount of alprazolam had been detected upon autopsy, but the committee knew not to be fooled when the heart-sinking postcard arrived a few days after his death.

Les knew that some of his staff were troubled that Dr. Shipley's body had been left behind, whereas all the other victims had disappeared. It appeared oddly messy and random in the context of Galileo's carefully orchestrated world, but then again, as Les reminded them, who could expect consistency from a maniac?

The investigation into Shipley's death was futile. Helen's disappearance on top of it was the tipping point that galvanized Les to start cutting corners. The proper system was slow and inefficient—search warrants, subpoenas, paperwork. If Les had learned anything during his years of government servitude, it was that taking matters into his own hands was the only way to get a job done fast.

A familiar housing project came into view one block away—a graffiti-covered brick building five stories tall. Three lanky teenage boys were slouched in front of it, the pungent scent of marijuana emanating from their lit joints. As he passed by, Les felt their eyes on his expensive suit. His grip tightened on his tan leather briefcase—not in fear, but alertness. No one could intimidate him anymore, least of all a couple of punks. Walking by, he met their menacing stares with a cold smile. It amused him to think of how ordinary his briefcase must appear to them. He maintained eye contact until they looked away, and then walked unchallenged into the building, whose door was propped open. Inside the deserted foyer, an emaciated cat mewed, brushing up against his ankles. Even through his pant legs, he could feel the sharp ridges of its ribs.

Inside his pocket was half of a bagel and lox, wrapped tightly in deli paper—his breakfast still waiting to be eaten. He tore off the paper, inhaling the smoky salmon scent, and placed it on the floor. Then he quickly climbed the stairs two flights, marched to the last door on the left, and knocked twice.

" 'S open," came a voice.

A wave of disgust hit him as he stepped inside the studio apartment. Rotting food, empty Coke cans, and cigarette butts lay on the floor in front of a faded cloth couch, where an obese, bearded man was lounging with a laptop. He wore torn sweatpants and no shirt; his hairy chest glowed as white as his screen. He turned to face Les a beat late, as if he had been deep in concentration, and blinked a few times. His mouth opened, exposing two rows of yellow teeth, but no sound came out.

Les closed the door and leaned against it with a smile. "Miss me, Cylon?"

"What—what are you doing here?" The man's spine flattened against the couch as if to back away. Though his real name was John Westfield, he was known online as Cylon, his computer hacker alter ego. Busting him was a fond memory from Les's days in the FBI's Science and Technology unit. At the time, it had been one of the biggest stings of his career, allowing the FBI to recover thousands of Social Security numbers Cylon had stolen from ultrasecure bank websites. The crime had cost him more than three years of hard time. Les knew he had practically nothing left of his wealth or reputation.

"What did I do?" he demanded, putting his hands up. "I just saw my probation officer yesterday."

Les ambled to the couch, wading through the trash,

and perched on the armrest opposite him. "Nothing, I just wanted to talk to you in person."

"How did you know I would be here?"

"You never leave this shithole."

He shrugged. "Not much, I guess."

"Looks like you're having a tough time getting back on your feet."

"I can too." He swung one leg toward the floor.

"Not literally," Les soothed. "I mean, life after jail is never easy, but especially now. Who's going to hire an ex-con? Even if you cleaned yourself up, your record is the kiss of death."

Cylon squirmed. The MacBook Pro on his knees rocked like a drunken boat. "You came here to tell me what I already know?" It was as close as he had ever come to confrontation, and still he couldn't look Les in the eye, or anyone for that matter.

"No, I came here to help you. I work directly under the President now. I closed a big case for him recently and he owes me one. He told me so himself."

"Okay . . ."

"So here's the deal. I need you to do me a favor, and in return, I'll ask him to pardon your felony."

Cylon gasped. "You would do that?"

Les smiled at his gullibility. "It's a pretty big favor."

"I'll do it."

"Let's see if you can. I need you to hack into Columbia University's servers and get me the e-mail account of an ex-professor named Helen McNair. She was kidnapped by a dangerous gang. But privacy laws are slowing down the release of her account, which could contain crucial clues. We need it ASAP if we want to find her alive."

Cylon's pupils dilated as he assessed the challenge. His mind seemed to be whirring like a hard drive.

"Well? Can you do it?"

He looked down, his voice a whimper. "I don't want to go back to jail."

"You won't," Les assured him. "Remember, I've got all the connections you need. You're safe working for me."

"Really?"

"Yes." Les tried to look him in the eye, but it was like trying to connect two same-side magnets.

"I dunno."

Les sighed. He would have to sacrifice the briefcase after all.

"As a bonus to get you started, I brought you this." He unhooked the two gold clasps on the case and flipped it open to reveal a row of tight green wads. "Two thousand bucks cash. Off the books."

Cylon stared at the crisp bills. His lower lip trembled. "I dunno," he repeated.

"What don't you know?"

"I'm s'posed to be done hacking."

Les snapped the briefcase shut and stood up with a regretful smile. "Okay, but I don't think your probation officer will be very happy to hear that you're hiding drugs."

"What! I am not!"

"Does it matter?"

Cylon's eyes closed. "Fine. When will you talk to the President?"

"As soon as it's done. I'll make it my top priority."

"How d'you know he'll pardon me?"

"I'm positive. Now, when you have the info, copy it onto this blank drive and then call me with this phone."

Les handed him a thumb drive and a disposable cell. "I'll come pick it up. You don't even need to leave." He turned to go, briefcase in hand.

"Wait, what about the money?"

"Oh, of course." Les opened it and shook it out, watching Cylon's rapt face as the wads rolled to his feet. The earthy scent of paper money filled the room. "And remember what I said about time?"

"Uh-huh," Cylon grunted, still transfixed by the cash.

"You have twenty-four hours."

He snapped to attention. "But what if—"

"You don't want to find out."

New York City
9:00 A.M.

Zoe's heart flapped like a panicked bird as the door to Dr. Carlyle's office shut behind her. A dissonant chime jingled. *I am here,* she thought. *I am really doing this.*

In the waiting room, rows of black plastic chairs were stationed like sentries on either side of a center aisle. At its far end a receptionist waited behind a tall wooden desk. About a dozen people were scattered throughout the room, paging through worn-out magazines or plugged into headphones.

Zoe ventured a few steps down the aisle as if she were walking a plank, but her steely mouth and defiant chin concealed the struggle behind each step. No one watching her would have guessed the extent of her terror. At the front desk, she stood on her tiptoes and smiled up at the bored young woman on the stool, who looked to be about her own age. Probably a college student killing time for the summer, doing what Zoe ought to be doing—making money, not just spending it.

"Hi." She hated the way her voice came out—small and questioning like a child's. She cleared her throat. "I'm here for a nine a.m. with Dr. Carlyle."

"Your name?" the girl asked, barely glancing away from her computer screen.

"Zoe Kincaid."

The girl typed a few words, paused, and then looked Zoe full in the face. The corners of her mouth twitched down, though it was hard to read her expression. Was it pity? Fear?

"What's wrong?" Zoe asked.

The girl's face smoothed into a professional smile. "Dr. Carlyle will be right with you, sweetie. Come this way." She walked around to the front of the desk, towering in her heels above Zoe, and extended a hand out to her.

"It's okay, I'm not a kid," she said wearily. "I'm probably older than you are."

The girl drew back her hand with a frown, looking her up and down. Zoe could only shrug.

They walked down an antiseptic hallway to a tiny room, where she soon found herself alone under the glare of fluorescent tube lights. She climbed onto the examining table and kicked her heels against the strip of translucent paper stretched across it.

She had lied to the receptionist out of grown-up duty, but to herself she could admit the truth—she did want a hand to hold. As the doctor's knock loomed, all she could focus on was the emptiness of the chair in the corner. Its white plastic sheen radiated loneliness like heat. She closed her eyes and pictured Gramps sitting there, inevitably distracting her with an off-color joke—*Maybe he'll help you fill out. Better late than never, right?* She looked around the room at its starchy white walls and desk covered by an array of plastic gloves, tubes, cotton balls, and the harsh orange soap that carried an aroma of despair. The one photograph on the wall showed a sepia image of Half Dome, the gigantic rock at Yosemite. Zoe was reminded of her favorite ride at Disneyland, Indiana Jones, where in its climactic finale, the car lurches toward an oncoming massive boulder. Trapped inside a cave with no apparent exit, all seems lost—and even on second and third rides, this hopelessness had overcome her—when at the last moment, the bottom of the cave drops out to reveal the road to safety.

Stuck inside this room now, with no apparent trapdoor in the ground, Zoe knew that this time, she really was about to be steamrolled. Was it too late to slip out unnoticed? To cling to the safe notion that she was simply an obsessive hypochondriac? Rather than gravely ill, perhaps fatally—

A loud rap on the door startled her. She stiffened, bracing for Dr. Carlyle's face. His expression would tell her everything. The door pushed open and he walked in, carrying a hefty file under his arm. Reserved, serious, he briefly made eye contact and nodded hello. His lips formed a curt smile, without showing teeth. The permanent wrinkle between his gray eyes looked deeper than ever. This was all wrong. She waited—hope dropping off by the second—for his cheerful welcome or buoyant handshake, but his earlier confidence that had so reassured her was gone. He turned around to face his computer and spoke with his back to her.

"Zoe, how are you?"

In her mind, fire engines blared a five-alarm emergency through every neuron. *I'm dying. It's over.* She wondered if she could find her voice, but then reminded herself that she had chosen this route. *Reality.* After so many years in hiding, she was going to claim it.

"I'm here," she said.

Dr. Carlyle turned to face her and sat down on his black swivel chair. He glanced down at her encyclopedic file, licking his lips.

"Please, just tell me now if it's curable," she pleaded. "Whatever it is."

"I—I'm afraid not." His apologetic tone was a death sentence. "Not that we know of, but—"

She felt her jaw sag, saw his image blur like a funhouse hologram. All that registered was skin-prickling horror—her body's blanket of dread ignited with an acid torch. His next words barely penetrated.

He touched her arm. "Zoe, did you hear me?"

"What?"

"It's not what you think," he said.

"I have a brain tumor, don't I?" she choked out. "I knew it."

"Your brain is perfectly healthy. It's not what anyone thought."

She wiped the tears from her eyes. "What does that even matter now? How long do I have?"

"Let's back up a second." His tone was firm, but not unkind. "I want to go over your test results. Are you with me?"

"Can't you just give it to me straight?"

"There's no name for your condition, Zoe. Not yet. That's why I want to go over everything with you very carefully, so you understand what we're dealing with."

"Huh?" This was so far afield of her expectations that she almost laughed. "What are you talking about?"

"Let's go over your tests one by one. The MRI of your brain showed that your corpus callosum is not perfectly formed, lacking some of the posterior body and splenium that we would expect in a twenty-year-old woman, but your cognitive functions have remarkably continued to develop, if a bit slower than normal, due to the plasticity of the neurons and neuronal circuits."

She let his words hang in the air, struck by the bizarreness of using her frazzled brain to process news about her brain. Her head began to throb. "So? What does that mean?"

"In an otherwise normal adult, it could be meaningless. Statistical deviations from the general population happen all the time. But"—he shuffled his notes to a new page—"your full-body X-ray shows that your growth plates never closed."

"Growth plates?"

"The soft parts at the end of each of our bones that help contribute length to the bones as we grow. In females, the plates usually close after puberty, around age fourteen to seventeen."

She shifted on the examining table, her feet twitching with a desire to run, run away as fast as she could. "But I never really hit puberty."

"Right. The question these results all boil down to is, Why not? You've been the same height and weight for years and you've never menstruated. We also analyzed your recent radiographic dental scans and compared them with similar tests that Dr. Harrington performed when you went to see him for the growth hormone treatment. When you were fourteen."

"I remember," she said. "It did nothing."

"No one could have guessed at the truth then, but now enough time has passed so that the results are quite shocking." Dr. Carlyle looked bewildered, but also strangely hyper. She noticed that his hands were trembling.

"Your teeth," he went on, "normally change from childhood through adolescence. But yours haven't changed since you were fourteen."

"I'm . . . I'm not sure I get it."

"One final result," he said. He leaned back and crossed his legs in an imitation of composure, though his knuckles were white around his pen. "Anthropometric measurements show that your weight, height, and body mass index are less than the second percentile for a typical twenty-year-old woman. So now you see what I'm getting at."

"No." Her fingertips tingled with anxiety. "What?"

"Zoe." He stared at her in open awe. "You stopped aging six years ago. You're physiologically fourteen years old."

CHAPTER 4

New York City
9:25 A.M.

Zoe didn't know how much time passed before she spoke again.

"That's ridiculous," she breathed. "I'm twenty." Though instantly, she knew he was right. She closed her eyes as nausea bloomed in the pit of her stomach, spreading upward.

I'm still a kid.

She looked down at her arms and legs, touched her face. Her skin felt cold. She dug her nails into her cheeks to see if they were still hers. Pain bit. She pulled back her hands in surprise, staring at her rounded nails. Child-sized nails. Finally she looked up at Dr. Carlyle, speechless. He reached for her hand, pressing it between his own. The unexpected kindness hastened fresh tears. She clutched him like a lifeline, letting go of all propriety. He squeezed back.

"But how?" she managed to choke out. "Why?"

"We just don't know. My hypothesis is that it might stem from a disruption of the master regulator gene, which no one's identified yet, but which is thought to exist."

"What?" It was hard to comprehend anything outside of her shock.

"It's an idea that was first proposed in 1932 by a British marine biologist, who proposed that there's a master gene that guides organisms through development, aging, and eventually death. But if this gene were disrupted, a chain reaction would occur throughout the body—which could explain your failed growth and seizures. Needless to say, this is only a guess. It merits much closer study, of course."

An astonishing thought swept through her with such force that she sagged against the wall. "Wait, am I not about to die?"

"I was just getting to that." A smile crept onto his lips. "I see no evidence that your body is breaking down. In fact, quite the opposite. Your heart, lungs, and bones are in peak condition."

"My God." She closed her eyes again. "I was about to . . . I don't know what . . ."

"I understand. This is all very overwhelming." He paused. "But once things settle down, I hope you'll realize how valuable a contribution you could help make. You're nearly unprecedented, Zoe."

She withdrew her hand from his and wiped her tear-stained face. "Nearly?"

"There's only one other case in the literature that comes close. A girl, Victoria Janzen, born in 1980 in Australia, whose growth stopped completely at around nine months old. She lived eighteen years as a baby, and no one could figure out why. Just like you, the only things that grew were her hair and nails. They called it

Syndrome X. Unfortunately she passed away after a sudden seizure in 1998, about two years before the first human genome was sequenced. They didn't have the antiepileptic medication then that you're taking today. But many of my colleagues today believe she was the one and only recorded case of a disruption of the master regulator gene."

Zoe exhaled a deep breath she didn't know she was holding. Dr. Carlyle watched her, allowing her to absorb the full weight of his words.

"Why did Victoria stop aging as a baby, and I stopped at fourteen?"

He shrugged. "It's a good question. I would guess that the idiopathic metabolic disorder that prevented you from reaching puberty somehow partially turned off your master gene."

"Only partially?"

"Your cognitive growth has not been severely affected, so whatever mutation you have, it's pretty much just compromised the physiological part of the gene's expression. In other words, your mental age has been able to advance somewhat beyond your physical age."

"But not Victoria's?"

"Right. I'm guessing she had a mutation that turned off the entire gene. But I can't say for sure."

A more pressing concern was already spilling out of her lips. "If they had the medicine, could Victoria have lived forever?"

"Forever is a very long time," he said, rubbing his chin. "What we do know is that there's no known upper limit of human longevity. Every generation pushes the boundary. There's nothing in nature that says we have to age."

She balked. "So you're saying I might live to be a thousand?"

"I wouldn't necessarily go that far. Even if you're not susceptible to aging, there's still a million other ways to die—sicknesses, injuries, et cetera. It's not as if you're immortal. And anyway, we don't know what effect this condition will have on your organs long-term"—Zoe opened her mouth to interrupt, but he beat her to it—"though how long is long-term, I really can't say."

"How could I be only *fourteen*?" She squeezed her throbbing temples with the heels of her hands. "I have a driver's license, a high school diploma. I just babysat a girl that age last week!"

Dr. Carlyle tilted his head, eyes widening. "What was that like?"

The girl, Bethany, was the daughter of her parents' friends, and Zoe had been doing them a favor by staying the evening while they went out. But it had felt less like a chore than a get-together—watching *Harry Potter* on Blu-ray, baking brownies, and paging through a titillating copy of *Seventeen* magazine. Zoe had felt so comfortable that night, never once feeling self-conscious about her lack of alcoholic tolerance, political interests, or a boyfriend—the triple threat of grief in college—but thought little of it afterward.

"It was fun," she admitted. "But . . . still . . . this is crazy. I can't wrap my head around it."

"Take your time," he said gently. "I have a psychologist on staff who would be happy to see you whenever you'd like . . ."

"What am I supposed to do with my life now?" she blurted out. "What about college?"

"That can be sorted out later. First, go home, talk to your family, spend some time taking this in."

"All I want to do is grow up," she whispered. "That's all I've ever wanted."

Dr. Carlyle faltered for a moment. "I'd be happy to schedule your first session with—"

She shook her head. "Do you think, if you study me, you could figure out a way to make me age?"

He smiled as if at a child's amusing remark. "You know, most people would ask the opposite."

She was in no mood for irony. "Could you?"

"Well, if we can first learn what's stopping it in you, the goal would then be to manipulate the genes to turn them on or off at will. So it's possible, but it could take a long time, a very long time."

"Centuries?"

"Maybe not that long. Could be decades, unless some genius gets us there faster."

"Aren't you a genius?"

He smiled. "I don't specialize in aging research, but I have brilliant colleagues who do. They would want to sequence your entire genome."

"Will it hurt?"

"Not much. It's only drawing blood."

"And a genome is like all my genes together?"

"Sorry, I should have explained." He leaned back in his chair and folded his hands over his knee. "Yes, your genome is the entirety of all the information you've inherited, encoded in your DNA. At Columbia, I teach my students to think of a genome like a book. It has twenty-three chapters, which are your chromosomes, and in each chapter there are roughly forty-eight to two hundred fifty million letters. Those letters spell out all your genes, which determine your characteristics. The whole book fits into a cell nucleus the size of a pinpoint, and there's a copy of it in pretty much every cell in our bodies. So when we sequence a genome, we examine about ninety-eight percent of those three billion letters to see if we can find any unusual spellings—any clues unique to your body at the molecular level."

She took a deep breath. "I see," she said. Though she didn't, not really. The scale was impossible to grasp. How could *billions* of letters fit into a single cell that you couldn't even see? Even though she'd taken biology as a one-semester requirement in high school, the subject had never felt real or urgent until now. "So," she said, wanting desperately to understand, "you think I have misspellings, right?"

"Exactly, called mutations."

"And—and how would those affect your overall hypothesis? About the master gene?"

"The master regulator gene," he said, smiling. "Well, today, we think of genes as ripples in a pond, not as isolated entities. So if the master regulator gene was disrupted, it could set off mutations in other genes that affect aging, which could cause other mutations, and so forth. They can also just happen randomly. So finding mutations in you wouldn't necessarily prove my hypothesis. The key is to locate mutations that lead to the master regulator gene itself."

"Okay," she said. "I think that makes sense."

He reached into his briefcase at the foot of the desk, pulled out a well-worn hardcover book, and handed it to her. On the bright blue cover were the swirly letters

A, T, G, and *C,* and a title: *The Genomics Age: How
DNA Technology Is Transforming the Way We Live and
Who We Are.*

"It's a primer I assign undergrads in Intro to Genetics," he explained. "You're quite precocious, Zoe. Listen to me, don't underestimate yourself because of a
number. Read this book and you'll get a better idea of
what I'm talking about. I can tell you want to."

She hugged the book to her chest gratefully. " 'Why'
was my first word," she said. "My grandpa is forever
proud of that."

Gramps. She couldn't wait to go home and collapse
into his arms. He would be the air above water.

"I should go," she said, sliding off the examining
table. Her feet dropped to the floor with a shaky thud.

"Call me when you're ready to go forward, or if you
need anything at all," Dr. Carlyle said, handing her a
card emblazoned in black with his personal contact information, including his cell phone number. "I'm
going to recommend your case to my colleagues at
NIH. The Undiagnosed Diseases Program—you might
have heard of it."

She smiled. "That's how I found you. I did my research, too."

"Then we're a good team." He patted her shoulder
as she walked to the door. "I'm looking forward to
hearing from you," he said. "Assuming you do want to
proceed," he added. "You do, don't you?"

She turned around to face him, but he held up a
hand.

"Don't feel pressured to answer just yet," he said.
"What you choose to do with your body is obviously
up to you."

"Is it?" she asked. "If I'm really only fourteen?" Every time she spoke the number felt like an aftershock.

His frown deepened. "That's a good point. There's no legal precedent . . . I suppose your parents would need to sign off going forward . . ."

"Forget that," she declared, straightening her spine. "I'll set the precedent. I'm still my own person and I'll make my own decisions."

Dr. Carlyle raised his white eyebrows. "Well then . . ."

She grabbed the doorknob, still facing him. His eyes shone with worry as his mouth opened, then closed.

"My whole teenage life," she said, "I've wanted nothing more than to get to the bottom of this. You think I'm going to stop now?"

He exhaled. "Even if your family . . . ?"

"Leave them to me." The strength in her own voice stunned her—she hadn't known any was left. She pushed open the door, still holding the textbook close to her chest.

"Take good care," he said. "Call me anytime."

"I will," she promised, stepping out into the deserted hall. "Bye."

They shook hands, his palm swallowing hers. Her grip was firm nonetheless. Then she walked down the hallway on wobbling knees, trying not to stumble. As she rounded the corner, she glanced back. Dr. Carlyle was watching her like a starstruck pedestrian, mouth partly open, his eyes ablaze.

He smiled sheepishly when she caught him, making no attempt to hide his fascination. A prick of nervous excitement struck her then, similar to the feeling she got before boarding a plane. Whenever apprehension about flying overcame her, she'd think of Gramps's favorite poem—Tennyson's "Ulysses"—and remember to summon her sense of adventure for the trip ahead. *"I will drink life to the lees,"* she'd tell herself. *"To follow knowledge like a sinking star, beyond the utmost bound of human thought."*

There was no better time to apply it. She mustered up a smile for Dr. Carlyle, absolving him of embarrassment. He grinned back, electrifying the hallway with a tacit message that made her shiver, for she knew it could be true. Tucked into her body, inside her bones and skin and muscle, was a secret written in a language as universal as it was cryptic. Not just any secret, but one sought for all of time—the answer to the primeval mystery of why we age and die.

CHAPTER 5

Les's cab crawled across town from Southeast back to the committee's headquarters in Northwest for an hour, more than double the time of his little errand. Because he founded the committee from scratch five years ago, he felt he had tacit authority to cut any corners necessary in pursuit of his goal. Being the boss felt good after the suffering he had endured earlier in his career. The worst experience by far had been his position heading up the FDA's division on drugs for rare diseases. Later, after that job spectacularly backfired—the memory of it still evoked horror and rage a decade later—he'd quit and defected to the law enforcement side: the FBI's special unit on science and technology crimes.

There, he became increasingly upset by the fact that no good federal oversight existed to regulate human experimentation in labs nationwide. Sure, there were local institutional review boards that were supposed to approve experiments, but who reviewed *them*? Officially it was the job of the Office for Human Research Protections within the Department of Health and Human Services. But that office was a joke. Les knew that their lax oversight had allowed corrupt review boards to get away with egregious acts like hiding industry financial ties, ignoring risks to human subjects, forgoing informed consent. The whole thing was an invisible public disgrace—and vulnerable people were getting hurt.

And so, five years ago, with the President's blessing, the Bioethics Committee was born. A specialized agency within the Justice Department, it was the optimal convergence of Les's passion with his credentials and his Washington connections. No one else could have gotten it off the ground. Now, all researchers whose clinical trial applications were approved by local review boards had to gain secondary approval of their desired study by the federal Bioethics Committee—an extra level of regulation. The committee then maintained stringent oversight of the local boards responsible for ensuring that each study was carried out according to the rules. Sure, it could take twenty years and $800 million to bring a new drug to market this way, but that was the cost of getting it done right.

Not only had the committee reformed the hierarchy of ethics oversight, it also had the power to investigate and police any suspected violations, with all the resources of the FBI at its disposal. As Les liked to say, it was a one-stop shop for protecting human subjects. No one else was better equipped to take on Galileo's Network. Les had recruited many of the twenty committee members personally, but some, like Dr. Benjamin Barrow, had ingratiated themselves with the right political staffers on the D.C. social circuit and lobbied hard for a place in the elite group. Ambition could be just as dangerous as depravity, and Les thought he saw too much of it in Barrow. That man acted like he wanted to be chief—he was already second-in-command—and if Les didn't break the Network soon . . .

But of course he would. He had to. His heart pumped in anticipation—no challenge in his life felt quite as worthy of the formidable power he knew lay inside him, waiting to be tested.

He cursed under his breath as the cab finally pulled up to his office. He was late for his morning briefing with Barrow and disliked giving his would-be rival any reason to fault him. Skimping on the tip, he jumped out and endured the elevator's climb to the tenth floor. He was racing down the empty hallway toward his door, ignoring the hot coffee sloshing over his cup, when a voice stopped him.

"Dr. Mahler."

He turned around, his back straightening. Barrow stood a few feet away, watching him with an inscrutable expression. He was broad-shouldered and tall, probably a former linebacker, with impeccable posture and a thick head of white hair that contrasted with his tanned face. Les wondered which parts of his appearance were by design—the tan, certainly, but possibly also the hair and the wrinkle-free forehead. They were about the same age, but Les wore it proudly. He wasn't afraid to get old.

"Dr. Barrow, good morning." Of all twenty members of the committee, Barrow and he had the least friendly rapport. Les suspected that the coldness between them was due to Barrow's rumored desire to displace him, but the irony was that Les was actually grateful to have him around. As a top internist and well-published activist against unregulated human experimentation, he was practically born to be on the committee. It was just too bad that he had refused to socialize like a normal human being after he secured his position several years ago, skipping out on many of the important cocktail parties and dinners and galas that the average person would kill to attend. Sometimes he didn't come into the office for days at a stretch. There were whispers of depression. But he was so competent at his job that no one cared to confront him. It became tacitly agreed that he could work from home whenever he needed to. No one knew much about his personal life except that he was divorced and lived alone—something else he and Les had in common, along with their shared passion for their work. Yet a friendship seemed impossible between them.

Barrow squinted at him. "I thought we were meeting fifteen minutes ago."

"Sorry, I had a personal matter to attend to. Come on in." Les opened the door and Barrow brushed past him, carrying a sturdy black box under his arm—the evidence. They sat on the executive L-shaped white couch near Les's desk, which was already cluttered with too many notes and files to allow a visitor any space.

"I don't have much time, so let's get down to business." Barrow unlocked the airtight box and Les scooted closer to peer into it. This was the closest they could come to the Network and its infamous leader.

Inside was an array of identical postcards individually encased in clear plastic.

Each one showed the same stock photo of the Earth circling the sun in space. Twenty-seven times now, Les had received a postcard with the victim's name written in clear cursive. Then there was the strange phrase, handwritten in black ink: *And yet it moves—again.*

Beneath it, the signature: *Yours, Galileo.*

Les sighed. "The whole thing is bizarre."

"The nut thinks he's Galileo reborn or something. Classic megalomaniac."

Les flipped over several more—they were all identical, except for the time stamps and postmarks—Cleveland, San Diego, Jacksonville. All likely stops on the so-called Galileo Underground, the Network's rumored cluster of safe houses across the country that allowed them to transport people undetected—but *to where*? The location of their headquarters was unknown.

These postcards were the only proof of Galileo's existence—whoever he was. The handwriting experts thought it was almost certainly a man. Something about the backward slant of the loops. Of course, it could have been someone else writing on his behalf, or he might not exist at all. One theory was that he was just an idea propagated by the Network to make their followers feel part of something historic, something legendary.

"There is something about the handwriting that's been bothering me. Look at this one." Barrow fished out one from the pack, the one sent after Eliot Shipley's death, postmarked in D.C. "See this?"

"What about it?"

"It's slightly off. Look at the loops in the *o*'s. They're more narrow than the others. And this dead body doesn't fit the pattern of all the disappearances."

"So? What can we do about it now?"

Barrow shook his head. "It's just odd. I checked with the handwriting experts and they agreed. They think a different person wrote this one."

Les frowned. "Okay, so a lemming might have written it for him. What's the difference? There might not even *be* a Galileo. It might just be a bunch of maniacs working together."

"I disagree. For the Underground to be so well organized, someone's got to be running things. Any group that effective must have a leader who's the real deal."

Les eyed him. *Jealous much?*

Barrow plastered on a smile, more a poorly concealed sneer.

"Well, we can't prove it one way or another. And Shipley's long dead. There's nothing we can do for him now, but this woman—" He grabbed the most recent postcard from the stack, the one received after Helen McNair's disappearance. "There might still be hope."

Everything about the postcard was predictable—the handwriting, the message, the fingerprints from multiple people all over it, a tactic surely meant to obscure the source. The postmark was from New York, dated four days earlier. If she wasn't dead already, she probably would be soon.

"So," Les said, "she was fired from Columbia on Wednesday, vanished on Thursday, and this postcard arrived at our office on Friday."

"Yep." Barrow's nostrils flared, as if he were annoyed by the return to obvious facts.

"What were the circumstances of her firing?"

"We already went over—"

"I want to hear the *exact* circumstances again."

Barrow didn't hide his exasperated tone. "She was found to be exploiting her lab on campus for unauthorized research. Attempting to create synthetic life. The dean found out after a security guard caught her there in the middle of the night. She confessed and he let her go immediately on Wednesday."

"And then?"

"And then she disappeared the next day from her apartment in Manhattan. There was no evidence of a struggle or break-in, but she's sixty-seven, so figure she didn't put up much of a fight. Then on Friday, this postcard arrived here."

Les found himself pacing, though he didn't remember rising from the couch. "Was her termination announced in any way before she disappeared?"

"No. The dean was embarrassed by the whole thing."

"So no one else knew?"

"Not that we know of. It was a very quiet affair. Of course, we're still waiting to access her private accounts. She has no husband or kids, but maybe there's someone she was close to. It will be important to determine those contacts and talk to them, if any exist. In my experience, women tend to spill secrets. I'll follow up with the Justice Department today."

Les suppressed a smirk. *I'm two steps ahead of you, buddy.* "The timing is interesting, isn't it?"

"How so?"

"This nut job only targets scientists or doctors, right? We can agree on that being the common denominator?"

"That, and people with serious medical conditions."

"So McNair disappears *right after* she was fired. How did Galileo know to target her the very next day?"

Barrow grimaced. "That's the question."

A loud chime interrupted them from Les's front pocket—his cell phone. He tried not to betray any excitement when he read the caller ID.

"Excuse me," he said. "I have to take this."

Barrow seemed in a momentary trance, eyeing Les with his upper lip slightly curled. His long legs stayed planted.

"It's my ex," Les lied. "Sorry."

Barrow hopped to his feet, taking the box with him. "I'll see you at the next meeting, Chief." His emphasis on the last word sounded almost pointed, but not enough to merit a reaction. *We'll see which of us knows how to get a job done,* Les thought.

When the door closed, he hissed into the phone. "Well?"

"I got in." Cylon's nasal voice sounded proud. "Just now."

"Already? You're a genius!"

"It wasn't that hard. I have her e-mails right here."

"Can you tell if there's anyone she wrote to often? Friendly seeming?"

There was a pause. "I'm scrolling. Here's e-mails from students, a couple from the dean . . ."

"Anyone else?"

"Someone named Natalie Roy. Says on her signature that she's another professor, same department. They seem pretty friendly." Les heard clicking sounds. "Looks like there's more from her than anyone else."

"Don't move. I'm coming over."

Les slipped the phone back into his pocket with a

smile. Too bad Barrow couldn't know. Les hated to admit that he liked him for his coldness, his skepticism—the very qualities that would have repelled anyone else. Les felt drawn to people whose respect was a prize, not a party favor. With time, Barrow would come to recognize that Les deserved to be chief, and that propagating a rivalry would only hurt one of them. But Les was forgiving. He wanted to keep the best men on the team after all. So with every move, he would chop away at Barrow's icy exterior and thaw him into an ally.

Until then, he knew just where his next meeting would be—New York.

New York City
10:20 A.M.

No one spoke right away. Zoe looked from her mother's stunned horror, to her father's angry disbelief, to Gramps's quiet amazement. Her blurted announcement hung in the air. She imagined it sinking down into their skulls like a gas, paralyzing them on impact. Ripped open in her father's lap was the dreaded credit card bill. Everything was out.

Seconds ticked by like drops of Chinese water torture. Her mind was an overblown circuit. She thought nothing, felt only the rubbery burn of her calves from sprinting the mile and a half home from Dr. Carlyle's office. A tinny ringing in her ears filled the living room's silence. Then her father's voice burst out in a snarl.

"So this isn't a joke, Zoe? You've spent ten *thousand* dollars on medical tests without our consent?"

"I had to know," she whispered.

"What kind of quack doctor did you find on the Internet?"

She blinked. "Dad, he's one of the leading diagnosticians in New York."

"This is an outrage! I didn't raise you to be a thief!"

"But the tests—"

"Forget the tests!" he snapped, tearing shreds of the envelope apart like tinsel. "I thought we raised you to be more sensible than this!" He turned to his wife, who was sitting beside him on the faded beige sofa's edge. "What did we do wrong?"

Zoe watched her mother's face. A tear slid from the corner of her eye along the thin bridge of her nose. She met Zoe's gaze as if seeing her for the first time in months—not just as a reminder of her own failings, but as a human being, a daughter in distress.

Sitting in his shabby leather recliner, Gramps was watching them all. Behind his head hung a framed portrait of the four of them grinning in beach chairs and sunglasses, shot during last summer's vacation to the Outer Banks. The peacefulness of their family on that trip struck her now as unbearably distant. Gramps noticed her grimacing and shot her a glance of compassion, but said nothing. She wondered if his silence was a sign of his agreement with her father, or merely his reluctance to be burned in the fray. It wasn't like him to shy away from a fight.

"Stephen," her mother said. "Can't you see she's hurting? Her health is more important than the money. Maybe there is some truth to what he told her. I mean, we've never had a proper diagnosis all these years."

Zoe gave her a grateful look.

"Pam, please. To claim she is still fourteen years

old—who's ever heard of such a thing? I'll have my firm file for malpractice before he knows what hit him. No asinine doctor is going to mess with my kid"—he turned his fiery gaze at her—"even if you did ask for it."

She jumped to her feet, clenching her fists. "You think I asked to be born this way?"

"Enough," came a voice, low yet so steadfast that everyone froze. Gramps was standing without the aid of his cane, holding his palms out to signal quiet. Zoe had never seen him with such a severe expression, like that of a prison guard toward a delinquent. He spoke slowly to her father.

"How you raise your daughter is not my business—until you cross the line. I tried to respect your parenting, Stephen. I tried to back off like you wanted—" Her father made a motion to interrupt, but Gramps's eyes narrowed. "Stop. Yes, I know I'm a guest in your house, but you know what? I don't give a damn. That's who I am, and if you don't like it, throw me out. But over my dead body will I stand by and let you bully either of my girls."

He spoke with the authority of a judge, even as his hands were quivering, reaching for the steadiness of the couch. Pam rushed to hand him his cane and Zoe felt a sob rise up in her throat. Endless love poured through her. She looked at her father: He was sitting completely still, his lips pressed hard together.

Gramps lowered himself back against his recliner. "Now that that's out of the way," he said, "we can get to the real issue. What you have failed to recognize"—he paused, looking at each of them—"is that Ray Carlyle is no fraud. Zoe, you're a medical marvel."

Her mother looked frightened. "How—how can you be sure?"

"Every doctor knows his name, Pam. He's a legend in the medical community. If this is what he told Zoe, I'd hang my life on it." He looked at her with a small smile. "Darling, we weren't expecting this, but what a relief! You're not ill, you're not dying." He held out his arms and she rushed into them from her lonely perch. She buried her face against his shoulder and he wrapped his gaunt arms around her. It felt ineffably good to be held.

Pam cleared her throat, taking her husband's hand. Her face had drained to ashen pale. "So this is for real?"

Zoe pulled away from Gramps and nodded. "He said only one other girl in recorded history had a similar condition, but she died before they could research why."

"No wonder you had such a tough time at Northeastern. I feel terrible!"

"If this is really true, we've been awful to blame you," her dad conceded. But then his expression hardened again. "So they probably want to drag you into some lab now, don't they?"

Pam pressed her husband's hand. "Honey, we've all had quite a shock for one day. Why don't we talk about that later?"

Gramps smoothed Zoe's silky blond hair. "What do you want to do, dear? Do you want to go up and take a rest? We don't need to figure anything out today."

"No," she said, staring at her father. "Let's be clear. I will never be a pawn of a bunch of scientists, okay?"

"Amen!" he said, looking relieved.

"I *want* to go to the lab," she went on. "It's my body, my choice, and I choose the truth. Dr. Carlyle said he would refer me to the NIH so I could get into their program on undiagnosed disorders."

"Oh Jesus," he muttered, holding his forehead. "Do you know what these guys are after, Zoe? They don't care about you. They just want money, power . . ." he gestured wildly, slicing the air with his palm. "They're cutthroat."

"You just think that because you spend all day suing doctors," Zoe retorted. "Admit it. You think they're mostly bad. But you don't really know."

"And neither do you," he shot back, standing up. "You want to be one of their lab rats? You want to undergo tests and procedures you won't understand, just so they can get a bunch of statistics and cold hard cash from new grants? They don't care about you, the human being—only you, the DNA!" He tugged at his stiff white collar and sat back down with a sigh.

"Your dad has a point," her mother remarked. She rubbed a fraying thread on her blue cotton dress. "We just want to protect you, sweetie. Who knows what you'd be getting yourself into?"

Zoe shook her head at the room's soft Oriental area rug, the rug that had padded many a fall during her earliest years. "But I don't believe it. I can't believe Dr. Carlyle and his colleagues are bad."

"You're still so innocent," her father said. "Just like a child. You don't know any better."

A cold sweat came over her. She looked at Gramps.

"I don't think you're hearing her," he cut in. "What did Dr. Carlyle tell you, dear? What would the next steps be?"

"He said they would sequence my genome," she whispered. "That they could maybe figure out the cause of aging once and for all, and then possibly be able to control it at will."

Gramps raised his eyebrows at her parents. "That's a pretty solemn statement. Are you prepared to turn your nose up at it?"

"Silas," Stephen said. "Cut the hype. Zoe can't be trusted to make these kinds of decisions for herself. Our job is to protect her."

"Your job," Gramps corrected, "is to respect her. She may still biologically be a child, but she has more years under her belt than any fourteen-year-old I know. She's not disabled. She should be allowed to make up her own mind."

"Thank you," Zoe muttered, looking to her parents. "Are you going to physically restrain me?"

"Look, it's not that we want to stop you from being independent," her father said, getting up again to pace. "We just want you to be safe. Who knows what will happen if all the wackos out there find out about this?"

"I'll be fine!"

"I wish we could believe that. And I'm sorry this is happening to you. It must be terrifying. Your mother's right. The money doesn't matter. *You* do."

"My health matters, but so does my happiness. Please, Dad. All I want is to grow up and be normal. This research is my only chance."

"But do you realize what a can of worms you'd be opening? You're talking about scientists trying to fundamentally alter our genetic makeup. Like Frankenstein. This isn't something to mess around with."

"But don't you see it could be a good thing? Maybe you could live longer, postpone your old age—"

Her mother shook her head. "We're supposed to get old and die, to clear out for the next generation. That's the natural order of life."

"So you'd choose death over life, just because living longer is unnatural? So is chemo, but that saved your ovaries!"

"That's different," her mother said sharply. "Cancer is a pathology. Aging is normal."

"Aging is the leading cause of death in the civilized world," Gramps interjected. "Just because it's always been that way doesn't make it desirable."

"The way I see it, nature made you special," her father declared, ignoring him. "It's not up to us to go against it, or to question why."

"But it is, Dad. Otherwise how can we ever make any progress?"

"Smart girl." Gramps patted her hand and Zoe noticed the pained look in her mother's eyes, which had nothing to do with nature and everything to do with a jealousy she would never admit. Gramps noticed it, too, for he whispered in her ear: "Go give your mother a hug."

She stood and went to her parents on the sofa opposite Gramps, where her father stood fuming.

"Don't worry so much about me. I've gotten this far." She bent down and hugged her mother tightly. Then, just as she was turning to her father, he walked over to Gramps, who pushed himself up from his recliner and stood again without his cane, staring up at his formidable son-in-law.

"I don't appreciate," said Stephen through clenched teeth, "any further interference in our family matters."

"Stephen—" Pam interrupted, but he ignored her.

"I will act as I see fit," Gramps replied.

"He was just looking out for me, Dad," Zoe interrupted, hurrying between them. Her small body barely reached to their chests. "Relax."

Stephen did not break eye contact with him. "You've insulted me and encouraged my daughter down a path I regard as dangerous. Now, I'm giving you one last chance. Unless you agree to back off, I'm going to have to find you another living arrangement."

"No!" Zoe cried. "You can't do that! Please!"

"Stephen," her mother pleaded, "that's really not necess—"

"That's okay." Gramps held up a hand. "I've ruffled a lot of feathers. I'll stay out of it from now on." He looked down at Zoe, and only she caught the mischievous smile in his eyes. "It's about time I excuse myself."

Stephen gave a curt nod and stepped aside. Gramps shuffled toward the stairs, squaring his shoulders just as he'd taught Zoe to do whenever the boys at school taunted her. As he approached the foot of the stairs, she noticed, in his path, a pair of sandals that she had mindlessly kicked off. Before she could even shout, his foot had hooked into one of the glittery silver straps, shifting his already precarious balance a notch off center. Oh God, it was too much—he pitched forward, arms flailing to find the cane he had left behind.

"Here!" she screeched, racing toward him, holding it out like a sword two feet in front of her. Why, oh why had she been so careless with her shoes, after all her mother's nagging—

He tried to spin around to meet her, but the effort clinched his fall. Her sandal slid out behind him across the slick wooden floor, thrusting him face forward at a sickening speed. His hands barely rose up in time to greet the crashing ground. As he splayed across it, Zoe heard an unmistakable crack, like a hollow branch splitting in two. She screamed and rushed to his side, dropping the cane. Her parents were beside them in an instant.

"My wrist," he moaned, twisting into the fetal position and holding his right wrist to his chest. Dizziness overcame Zoe when she noticed its angle—it was bent all the way backward, the back of his hand touching his forearm.

"Go call 911," her mother instructed. "Hurry."

She obeyed, rising in disbelief. "But it was just a slip," she murmured. "I trip all the time . . ."

A heavy arm draped over her shoulders. "His bones are frail," her father said, as they turned away from Gramps's writhing. "I shouldn't have been so harsh. I just forget how old and fragile he is."

Hours later, after Gramps had checked out of the hospital with a bright white cast from knuckles to elbow and a bottle of painkillers, after he had settled back into his favorite recliner and waved off Zoe's heartfelt apologies for the fifth time, she snuck upstairs to her bedroom. Thunder rumbled overhead as she locked the door behind her, cell phone in hand, dialing a number already memorized. She endured several rings, her desperation climbing, as the rain outside smacked against her window.

Finally a man answered in a monotone professional voice.

"Dr. Carlyle?" she said quickly. "It's Zoe. Zoe Kincaid."

"Zoe, hello! I didn't expect to hear from you this soon."

"Yeah, listen, remember when we were talking before, how you said the goal was to control the aging genes, so I could grow up one day?"

"First we need to figure out how they work."

"But once you do that," she continued, "if you can speed up my aging, won't you also be able to slow down someone else's?"

"Not just slow it down—we'd be able to stop it altogether. If the theory proves correct, and if we can figure out how to chemically replicate your body's way of turning off the master regulator gene, well—then aging could go the way of polio."

"That's a lot of ifs. What are we waiting for?"

"You."

"I'm ready. Let's do it."

"Are you sure? You've had less than a day to think—"

"Yes," she broke in, thinking of Gramps. "We don't have much time."

CHAPTER 6

Natalie Roy was deep in concentration when a knock on her office door startled her. She looked up from the sixteen-page report on her desk, eyes blurry from hours of cross-checking every chemical name, number, and comma. Next to its red-marked pages—the promising results of her latest experiment in her quest to extend the lives of fruit flies—was a list of prestigious journals with names like *Rejuvenation Research* and *Molecular Genetics*. If she was going to have any chance of beating out that supercilious suck-up Mitch Grover for tenure, publishing her research was key.

Of course, the contest shouldn't have been this close a call. Her scientific contributions were more significant than his overall. But no matter—when contemplating that elusive *T* word, Columbia's world-renowned Department of Biological Sciences harbored a dirty secret—quantity trumped quality. And Mitch had more publication credits.

Natalie shook her head, rubbing her eyes. The shortsighted faculty board would probably vote down Watson and Crick if the famous duo hadn't published enough after discovering DNA. And not just any passion project would inspire grant money. It had to be one that aligned with a review board's agenda.

Everything was so goddamn political, far from the unvarnished search for truth she had envisioned as a teenage wannabe researcher twenty years ago. Of course, Mitch got all the federal funding he needed for his trendy projects, while she'd had to struggle to raise private capital after getting turned down multiple times. Her life's mission of increasing human longevity wasn't too appealing to a bloated government that depended—ironically—on the death of its citizens for survival.

She blinked at her office's bare white walls, the standard-issue wooden desk and simple black lamp, her one window overlooking the redbrick campus below. She was too busy to care about decorating her space and had only two personal items: a gardenia plant on the windowsill, and the photograph on her desk that always restored her good spirits. It was of the most beautiful child she had ever seen. Her son.

In it, Theo, then eight, was proudly holding a soccer ball under his arm. His hair was a mop of messy brown curls, his eyes jade green. The picture was a decade old, but she kept it for his smile. His joyful exuberance at that age reminded her of the true spirit alive beneath his tense adolescent exterior. Lately he was worrying about how she, as a single mother, was going to afford his college tuition. He was planning to start community college in the fall to avoid going into debt at a fancy school, but this kind of talk crushed her. She desperately yearned—above all else—to give him the world she had raised him to believe in, a world where greatness was possible. She couldn't give him back his absent dad, but she could give him a shot at free Columbia tuition and proof that you could successfully pursue a dream. If only she could get tenure.

What if her efforts weren't enough? Due to cost-cutting measures, the department had just one spot available, and Mitch was already in good favor with Professor Adler, the department chair. If only Helen would return her calls! Her closest friend, who up until last week had been a fellow professor in the department, would know just what to say—but she'd been impossible to reach since her resignation. As if to add insult to injury, Adler had announced that no one would be hired to replace her in the department—another casualty of the grim economic forecast—so Natalie and Mitch were forced to continue battling for the only tenured spot available.

Someone rapped on her door again, this time harder.

"Natalie, are you in there?" a gravelly voice demanded.

She recognized it and jumped up to open the door.

"Dr. Adler! I didn't realize that was you—" She broke off when she saw Mitch Grover and several other faculty members standing behind him, looking apprehensive. "What's going on?"

"We have an unexpected meeting in 14-L," Adler said. "Right now."

Mitch met her confused expression with a shrug: *I know nothing.*

"We?" she questioned.

"The whole department. Come on."

She locked her office and joined the procession

down the austere white corridor, falling into step behind the others, only mildly curious. Odds were it would be another bureaucratic time-waster. After they quickly rounded up the rest of the fifteen-member staff, they filed into the largest conference room on their floor, which looked out over Columbia's cobblestone campus and magnificent domed library. Inside, the walls were adorned with framed clippings of past and present staff members' accomplishments—prizes won, discoveries made, patents granted. A long rectangular table of polished mahogany took up most of the room, surrounded by black leather executive chairs.

Two stern-looking men sat at the head. One was stout, bald, and typing on a BlackBerry with two agile thumbs. The other was lanky, gray haired, and exuded dignity as if in a conscious effort to appear authoritative. His sharp chin was lifted high, his posture erect, his navy suit expertly tailored. Natalie watched him watch everyone trickle in and sit down. She noticed how carefully he assessed each person without seeming obvious. Their eyes met when his rested on her. His steely gaze felt more like a challenge than a greeting. She stared back, refusing to be intimidated.

He looked away to address the room, clearing his throat. "Good afternoon, everyone. Thank you for coming on such short notice. My name is Les Mahler. I'm the chief of the Justice Department's Bioethics Committee, and this is my colleague . . ." He looked to the man on his right.

"Bud Pinter, FBI," he said, briefly holding up a gold badge in a black case. "Executive assistant director of the Science and Technology branch."

The room was as quiet as a cemetery. Natalie felt

her heart quicken. What in the world could these men want with Columbia's Biology Department? She looked around and saw that the other professors also seemed concerned, shifting in their seats and glancing at each other. Seated up near the men, Adler looked grim. What did he know?

"Of course, you all are wondering why we're here today," Les Mahler continued, his voice deeper than Natalie had expected out of his slender frame. "I'm afraid we have some upsetting news about one of your former colleagues. As you probably all know by now, Dr. Helen McNair resigned from her position last week after an internal controversy." Les looked at Adler, who nodded his permission. "Dr. McNair was engaged in attempting to develop the first synthetic life-form in her laboratory, a project she had kept secret from the rest of the staff for fear of a backlash."

Around the room swelled questioning murmurs and surprised expressions. Natalie pretended to look shocked, but she'd known for months. She and Helen were each other's confidantes, which made it all the more hurtful and surprising that her friend had failed to return a single phone call, text, or e-mail since the dean's unfortunate discovery. Natalie assumed she just needed some space to privately grieve the loss of her career. Surely she would call soon.

"Why did she resign?" asked a young male adjunct.

"The dean caught wind of the project," Adler replied, "and asked her to." Natalie pressed her lips hard so her mouth would not betray her. The school's unfairness was truly appalling. Rather than uphold Helen's work as a model of innovation, the cautious Dean Loren was skittish around any scientists "trying to play God" and "overstepping ethical lines of inquiry." His cautious attitude was exactly what had prompted Helen's secrecy in the first place, to no avail. But why was the FBI involved?

"As it turns out, she didn't just resign," Les Mahler said, looking straight at Natalie. "She's disappeared. No one has seen her for six days. She lived alone, and her apartment is vacant. Her relatives have not been able to contact her, and her credit card shows no activity."

Natalie's lips parted in shock, her mind racing. Helen had never mentioned wanting to go away. She hated leaving Manhattan, even used to joke that it would take a funeral to get her out—her own.

"Now, normally, this would be treated as a missing persons case by the local police department, but we do not believe this to be a regular case." Mahler turned to his colleague. "Bud, do you want to . . . ?"

Bud Pinter opened a black file on the table and pulled out what looked like a postcard encased in clear plastic. Without removing the plastic, he held it up for the room to see, pinching it between thumb and forefinger. The focal point of the postcard was a photograph of the Earth moving around the sun in space.

"This," Pinter said, "is a postcard that was mailed to our headquarters the day we believe Dr. McNair disappeared. On the flip side"—he turned it around to show a short loopy scrawl on the white back—"is her name and this message:

" 'And yet it moves—again. Yours, Galileo.' "

Everyone stared. Pinter's tone carried a gravity that assured them this was no joke. Natalie frowned. The sentence reminded her of a famous line uttered by the real Galileo Galilei back in the sixteen hundreds, when the Church had forced him to recant his heretical belief that the Earth revolved around the sun. He'd cooperated, but then said under his breath, "And yet it moves." Four words that would come to forever signify rebellion against dogma—now hijacked by a madman.

"This will come as a shock," Les Mahler said, "but the person who calls himself Galileo runs a covert network of radicals who pose a serious threat to scientists, doctors, and even patients here in the U.S. You won't likely have heard of him because we've kept his profile extremely low, under the radar of the media and the public. But his cult is disturbingly entrenched across the country, from what we have been able to glean, and so far has proved impossible to penetrate or track."

He paused, looking at each stunned face around the table.

"This group is extremely dangerous," he went on. "Their crimes have a pattern—they always involve someone in a medical or scientific field who suddenly goes missing. Then, like clockwork, a postcard arrives just like this one, sometimes even on the same day, as if to boast that the abduction was premeditated, and the postcard was mailed in advance of the crime. By the time we get it, it's too late. There's always the victim's name, the same message, the same signature. The only thing that changes is the postmark, which comes from a different city every time, from Burbank to Anchorage to Des Moines. All over the country. We don't know where the victims go or what happens to them."

Natalie felt warm tears sting her eyes as a surreal image popped into her mind—Helen, bound and gagged, in the clutches of a felon. It didn't seem possible. The last time they had seen each other, right after her forced resignation, Helen was a woman in mourning. Her spouse of forty-five years was her career, and its sudden death had knocked her sideways. She'd gone straight home to be alone. Natalie was certain she hadn't known of any impending danger.

She raised a shaky hand. "How many have been targeted?"

Pinter answered. "Twelve scientists, eight doctors, and six patients—and now Dr. McNair."

"Just—vanished?"

"It seems that way. In many of the cases, we've recovered suicide notes, but these victims had no reason to end their lives. We think their captors must have forced them into it, so it seems like they're disappearing of their own accord."

"Have any . . . remains ever been found?" Adler asked.

Mahler paused, his face grim. "Only once. The man was a top industry researcher doing drug development, found mauled to death by a couple of lab chimps that had escaped their cages. His death was ruled accidental, but Galileo's postcard arrived shortly afterward."

"We don't know why he was left behind to die instead of abducted like all the other victims," Pinter added. "It's another mystifying aspect of this case."

"So the other victims—they could still be alive?" Natalie asked.

"It's possible," Mahler said. "But not probable. The committee's mission for two years has been to track down this Galileo and uproot his Network, but it's been much more difficult than you can imagine. They seem to be very well connected, with rampant safe houses across the country, known as stops on the Galileo Underground. But it's impossible to prove."

"Leading to where?" Mitch Grover asked. For once, Natalie noted, the smug smile was wiped off his face. He looked nervous.

"We don't know. That's the question."

Natalie raised her hand again. "What's the motive? Why abduct these people in particular? Why Helen?"

"We can only speculate," Pinter replied. "What the victims have in common is a history of controversy—they're all scientists and doctors who have gone against the grain in various ways. Except for the patients, who all had mysterious or late-stage illnesses before they were abducted."

"It's possible that they're being punished or exploited somehow," Mahler added. He didn't elaborate.

"So how can we help?" Adler asked. He leaned forward. "Anything you need, Columbia is at your disposal."

"Be vigilant," Mahler said. "Don't hesitate to call if you have anything suspicious to report. There's also a number where you can anonymously call in tips if you're worried about retribution." He passed out cards with contact information. "Everything said here must remain strictly confidential. If this story gets out, a media circus will make Galileo burrow down somewhere. We need him to be up and active, not hiding. Also please clear your schedules for the rest of the afternoon. We're going to need to question each of you privately regarding Dr. McNair. Even the smallest thing you tell us could prove significant. Time is of the essence if we have any hope of finding her alive."

Natalie choked back a sob. How could this be happening? And to Helen of all people—the most passionate and daring friend she'd ever had, the only one who shared her courage to try to push humanity forward.

"One more thing," Mahler said. "I apologize for what this will do to your working environment, but it must be said. From now on, each of you needs to be very careful whom you trust. As you know, Dr. McNair's controversy and resignation was an internal matter. The only way Galileo could have known to target her so soon after the fact is if his Network relayed the news back to him."

Adler looked taken aback. "What are you saying?"

Mahler turned to answer him, but before he opened his mouth, Natalie realized why his initial observation of the staff was fraught with suspicion.

"Dr. Adler, I'm afraid your department has a mole."

CHAPTER 7

"**Z**oe?"

She pressed the phone hard against her ear to get closer to the voice. "This is she," she said into the mouthpiece, barely above a whisper.

"It's Dr. Carlyle."

She held her breath and raised her eyes wide at Gramps, who was resting in bed on a spread of pillows she had fluffed. His cozy room had its own personality apart from the rest of the house—the walls were decorated with vinyl records of Frank Sinatra and Tommy Dorsey. On his night table was an old black radio that he still used to listen to baseball games. Across from his bed, a floor-to-ceiling bookcase was lined with leather-bound classics, medical textbooks, and dime-store paperbacks. Next to the open window, Zoe sat in a wooden rocking chair and hugged her knees to her chest.

Gramps's half-sleeping eyelids whipped open. Though only one full day had passed since her diagnosis and his accident, she had never been more conscious of losing precious hours to the wasteland of unproductive time—time without any progress toward a solution to Gramps's aging. Nor had she ever been so aware of how advanced his frailty had become. Before, she had never really noticed his cane, or his labored movements, or his faint wheezing when he climbed the stairs. After she watched his wrist snap like a pencil, the frightening truth had become clear—he was old. Old in a final way that she might apparently never know, in an irreversible way that took all of her courage to admit, unless she could get to the scientists fast enough, as fast as possible.

"Zoe, are you there?"

"Hi! Hi, I'm here." All day they had been waiting for his call, like shipwrecked sailors for a boat.

He cleared his throat. "I'm afraid I have some bad news."

"What?" The hair on her arms spiked, meeting the chill that flowed down from her neck. "What do you mean?"

"I spoke with the director of the NIH program this morning and told him about your case. And, well, even though he was personally fascinated, he said the program could never accept you."

"Why not?" She clutched Gramps's pale green bedspread, unable to look at him.

"It's quite maddening, I'll be honest. The National Institutes of Health is an arm of the government, so their research mandates come with an agenda. Antiaging research is specifically not on it, because if people were to live longer, many of the major federal programs like Social Security and Medicare would be severely overburdened. The economy could crash, and then there's the government's concerns about overpopulation and limited natural resources. Not that I agree; I'm just repeating what I was told. I'm sorry, Zoe, but the NIH won't touch your case with a ten-foot pole."

Panic rose in her throat like a fist, choking her. "I can't believe this! Don't those people want to figure out how to live longer?"

"It's not up to them, unfortunately."

"This is ridiculous!" she moaned, and the childlike whininess of her own voice grated on her. She spoke again, more evenly. "There must be someone else I can see."

"There is. I made some other calls for you, and there's a prominent biogerontologist up at Columbia who can't wait to meet you. I've taken the liberty to arrange the introduction for today at three, if that's okay. His name is Dr. Mitch Grover."

Two hours later, Zoe found herself in a small office whose walls were papered with gold-framed diplomas— a BS, MS, and two PhDs—as well as various certificates of honor and recognition. On the wide desk in front of her lay neatly organized stacks of reports, journals, and class syllabi next to a bronze paperweight statue of *The Thinker*. The real-life thinker behind the accomplishments was younger than she would have guessed, probably in his midthirties, which dazzled her all the more. So what if his smile carried an air of pretension? He shared her eagerness to unlock her body's secrets. He was going to help her help Gramps, and that knowledge filled her with warmth.

Before she could stop herself, she had poured out her entire story to him, from her failed development right up through Dr. Carlyle's shocking diagnosis and the NIH's stunning rejection.

"I just can't believe that something as insignificant as politics could come before real *life*," she finished tearfully. "But it doesn't matter now, does it?"

Dr. Grover handed her a tissue. "It can be very disruptive to mix science and politics," he agreed. "We just want to get after the truth, and then they go and set all these restrictions based on some bureaucrat's notion of what's worth studying."

"I don't know how you can stand it."

"I'm lucky enough to work in a private institution." He smiled, showing a row of unnaturally white teeth. "I only work on projects that I find important, not the trend of the day. And you know what? It's their loss, because we're going to make history."

"How soon can we get started?" she asked, nearly bouncing in her chair. "You'll want to sequence my genome, right?"

"Definitely. But before we talk further I'll need you to take a look at these consent forms." He handed her a few sheets of paper. "To participate in scientific research, you're required by law to agree to any possible risks and consequences, and to release Columbia from all liability . . ."

"Fine, fine." She waved a hand, skimming the pages. "Where's a pen?"

When he didn't give her one right away, she looked up. He grimaced, seeming embarrassed on her behalf.

"I know this is annoying," he said, "but I'll need your parents to sign off. Because of your unusual case—your true biological age—you're still technically a minor."

"That's bull. I can decide for myself."

"I'm sorry, but I spoke with Columbia's lawyers as soon as I knew you were coming. In order to move forward, we need your legal guardians' written and verbal approval. Otherwise we could be exposing ourselves to a major lawsuit."

She felt her stomach clench. "And verbal?" Written was one thing—she'd seen her parents' signatures enough times to copy them blindfolded.

"Yes, I'll need to speak with them both to confirm that they've read and understood the forms."

"But—they'll never agree! They don't even know I'm here!" In a few stumbling words, she explained her father's cynical position on the scientific establishment—along with his status as a high-powered attorney—and her mother's hands-off concurrence.

"Oh," he said. "I had no idea."

"But I'm over eighteen!"

"I'm sorry. The lawyers . . ." He trailed off, looking crestfallen.

"So what are you saying? I can never escape my parents' control?"

"I don't know." He paused, gritting his teeth. "I don't see how we can move forward without this right now. In other circumstances, I might be willing to bend the rules a little, but . . ."

"But what?"

He eyed the open door behind her. She got up to close it.

"But what?" she repeated.

"I can't really go into it with you." He sighed. "Look, my department is going through some internal issues, and the last thing I want to do is stir up a controversy."

"What about making history?" she said.

"Things are touchy around here right now. I can't go into detail." He fidgeted with a rubber band on the desk. "I can't afford to get myself in trouble."

She shook her head. "So that's it, then? Just because of a stupid form?"

"I don't expect you to understand. I'm sorry—this is very disappointing for me also. Extremely disappointing."

She jumped to her feet, marched to the door, and swung it open. She could picture Gramps at home in bed, nursing his broken wrist and eagerly awaiting every crumb of the meeting. *Now is when the magic starts,* he'd predicted as she walked out the door.

She threw a final withering glance at Dr. Grover and steadied her voice, despite the anger and desperation trembling through her. "Thank you for your time, but I'll find someone whose hands aren't tied by fear. I don't expect you to understand."

Peeking out of her office, Natalie watched the defiant girl storm down the hallway. Her knobby knees brushed together with each stride, while her long braid flicked back and forth like a puppy's tail. She looked no older than twelve or thirteen, but had Natalie over-head correctly? Mitch's door had been open for most of their meeting, and if what the girl told him was true—

As Natalie debated whether to run after her, the ele-vator at the end of the hall opened and the girl stepped inside. In a split second, Natalie was on her feet, knocking back her chair, just as the doors slid closed. Catching the briefest glimpse of her face, Natalie saw that she was wiping her eyes, her thin shoulders heav-ing. Then she was gone.

Natalie's sense of maternal anger overpowered all else. She strode into Mitch's office, where he was sit-ting behind his desk, looking dazed.

"What the hell was that?" she demanded, stopping in the doorway. "Why did you make that poor girl leave crying? Who is she?"

Mitch shook his head. "Such a damn shame. Zoe Kincaid, possibly only the second person ever to have Syndrome X. And parents that want to keep her under a rock."

"My God. Are you sure?"

"Ray Carlyle made the diagnosis, so I'm pretty damn sure."

"My God. I never—Mitch, the chance of being born with that must be one in a trillion! Let alone to have it happen to someone during our lifetime."

"I know. But what can I do? She says they'll never consent, and I'm not going to be the one to cause prob-lems, not with that lunatic Galileo on the loose and Helen probably dead, and"—he looked sharply at her— "a spy roaming the halls."

"Don't talk about her like that," Natalie snapped with such ferocity that he winced. "And don't you *dare* look at me that way."

"What way?"

"Come on, Mitch." Since yesterday, when Les Mahler had spent double the time questioning Natalie as everyone else, a tacit suspicion had sprung up around her like a foul mist. It was ludicrous. If she had any information that could help find Helen, the feds wouldn't be able to keep her away.

"I'm sorry," he muttered. He became bothered by a coffee stain on the desk and rubbed it with the heel of his hand.

"Anyway, lightning's not going to strike in the same place twice." Natalie plunked herself into his guest chair and leaned toward him. "Don't you realize that girl is like a walking fountain of youth?"

His hand froze. He stared at her. "So you want me to get the school sued?"

"Do you really think that would happen? It's not like you'd be hurting her. You just need a DNA sample to start the process."

"I can't, her father is a partner at Powell Kincaid." His eyes narrowed to charcoal slits. "Oh, I get it. I get what this is all about. Well, aren't you clever."

"What are you talking about?"

"You want tenure just as much as I do. If I screw up, you're golden."

"Jesus Christ, Mitch." She shook her head in disbelief, about to skewer him, when a rousing thought struck her. Her expression took on a shade of contrition. "You know what? Forget it. You're probably doing the right thing."

"I know I am. Now, if you'll excuse me, I have a class to teach."

Without a word, she returned to her own office and locked the door.

It was quiet, save for the faint chatter of students exiting a lab down the hall—wisps of laughter, trilling cell phones, the scuffle of retreating footsteps. Then silence.

Her heart thumped against her chest. She was acutely aware of the scent of the gardenia plant on her windowsill, a gift from Helen for her thirty-seventh birthday just a few weeks earlier. Now it was in full bloom. The velvety white blossoms burst from the leaves, throwing off an intoxicating sweetness. What would Helen think of walking away from the chance of a lifetime out of fear? Helen, who had risked her career—and maybe her life—for work she believed in, for the possibility of greatness.

She was—is—no coward, Natalie thought, *and neither am I.*

What a blessing it seemed not to age, yet she could see how it would also be a curse. To be forever trapped on the verge of womanhood, waiting for a maturity that would never transpire. To be left behind by time, so that the gap between her spirit and her body grew ever wider. No wonder Zoe was seeking help from science, no wonder she had left in tears. So what if her parents wouldn't agree—she was twenty years old, and perfectly mentally able. In fact, from what Natalie had overheard, she was one of the most articulate girls around. Her parents deserved neither to own her nor to ruin the incredibly rare home run that nature had set up. If Natalie stepped up to the plate, no one would have to know. It was reckless, to be sure, but what would be the cost of inaction?

Could she live the rest of her life knowing she'd let her greatest opportunity slip away? Her heart was racing as though it had made the decision before her mind.

She'd need Zoe's case history and a blood sample to get started. Her lab was ready and waiting. Those years of research on the drosophila flies would prove necessary much sooner than she'd ever hoped. Already she was thinking of the particular chromosomes that she'd analyzed as promising locations for a master regulator gene or group of genes, if they existed. Her fingers twitched for a microscope. Zoe's DNA was the ultimate answer key to the test she had been studying for all her adult life.

Natalie found that she was pacing the length of her office, clenching her fists. Tenure was about as crucial as lipstick in comparison. Mitch's sense was shriveled by his competitiveness. What was the real point of tenure, unless to have full jurisdiction over your own experiments? To stick out your neck for knowledge and truth without retribution? Only she cared enough about the work to deserve it, even though Mitch would probably be the one to triumph with the faculty in the end. But that was beside the point now; if she did make a breakthrough as Nobel-worthy as she imagined, every biology department the world over would be begging to appoint her, no matter what technicalities she'd bypassed in the process. Theo would never have to worry about their financial stability again—and what was more, he'd have a confident hero in her, not a mother embittered from her dual failures at both love and work.

Either she could sit around and wait for defensive lawyers and illogical parents and bureaucratic faculty to bicker it out for months or years. Or she could act. She turned on her heel for the tenth time and gazed across the room at her desk.

The shiny black phone gleamed. She ran to her computer, did a quick Google search, and dialed a local number. It rang once before a recorded message picked up.

"You have reached the medical office of Dr. Ray Carlyle. To make an appointment, please press one. For prescription refills, press two. For the billing department, press three. For all other inquiries, please stay on the line."

She waited, inhaling the thick scent of gardenia.

Soon a woman's voice came on the line. "Dr. Carlyle's office, how can I help you?"

"Yes," she said in a higher-pitched voice than usual. "Hi. I'm the assistant to Dr. Mitch Grover at Columbia. You referred a patient to our lab earlier, Zoe Kincaid?"

"Oh yes, what can we do for you?"

"Dr. Grover needs another copy of her records faxed over. It hasn't come through yet."

"Oh, I'm sorry about that. I know I sent them earlier, but I could have gotten the number wrong. Can you give it to me again?"

Natalie smiled. "Of course."

In just a few minutes, she'd have what she needed to begin.

* * *

Fifteen minutes later, at 4:45 P.M., the phone rang inside a locked and empty office nearby. When no one picked up, an answering machine beeped and a woman's deferential voice punctured the stillness:

"Hello, Dr. Grover, this is Nancy calling from Dr. Carlyle's office. I'm so sorry about the missing fax, but I've sent it again at your assistant's request. I didn't catch her name, but could you please have her call me back to confirm receipt? Thanks so much."

CHAPTER 8

New York City
4:45 P.M.

The mechanical beeping of the fax in the department's common room was a beautiful sound. Natalie had the room all to herself—the water fountain, the Keurig coffeemaker, the bulletin board papered with outdated announcements, the vintage sofa—but most important, the dusty old machine in front of her. She watched with growing excitement as page after page of Zoe Kincaid's medical history cranked out of it. Could this be a historic moment, she wondered—could these very pages make it into a museum one day? With a smile, she envisioned future people exploring an exhibit titled "The Age of Agelessness." It would be about the twenty-first century's advances in discovering and eradicating the biological causes of aging. Perhaps Theo's kids would tour it, balking at pictures of sagging elderly folks, just as her generation had once balked at the fearsome scars of smallpox—a dangerous scourge of a bygone era, responsible for the deaths of countless victims.

Perhaps she would still be around to tour the exhibit

with them. Oh, how joyful it would be to know her child's children, and theirs! Not as a bedridden grand-mother, too weak like her own nana to answer the door-bell, but as a still-vigorous woman, immune to time, continuing to work, to love, to live. Life stretched ahead in her mind like an open highway, the horizon only a trick of the eye, with humanity riding not just into the sunset, but beyond it. With the time to gain more wis-dom and experience, how many individuals whose lives could be fulfilled, how many couples whose love could thrive long past a brief flash of decades, how many gen-erations who could enjoy one another, living bridges to history and culture and art?

A statistic came to her that she had read recently in the journal *Biogerontology*—worldwide, 100,000 peo-ple died of aging every day. In the industrialized world, almost 90 percent of *all* deaths were attributable to age.

She thought of her mother's grim descent into senil-ity during her last years, and her father's heartbreaking deterioration from a lively, youthful man to a frail skeleton before his death. How much incalculable suf-fering could be avoided! Yet so many people blanched when Natalie told them about her mission. They al-ways threw out the same predictable arguments about overpopulation and strained economies. But if more healthy years were added onto life, that would mean a massive growth in global productivity, leading to in-evitable increases in technology and quality of life. If history proved anything, it was that human beings were brilliant at solving complex challenges. Her research was about taking the reins of control from nature and giving it over to individuals to decide about their own lives and deaths. Ultimately, she felt, no one could make those decisions for anyone else, nor ethically have the right to do so.

The fax machine was sputtering to a halt. She seized the warm stack of paper from the tray and leafed through it with the eagerness of a disciple holding the Holy Scripture, then ran back to her office and locked the door. She couldn't wait to scour every detail, but first things first. On the final page she found it—Zoe's phone number. Underneath it was her emergency contact: a Mr. Silas Gardner, whose own number happened to be a digital palindrome: (917) 333-3719. Her math-minded brain was always spotting numerical patterns like that without trying. Before she could consider his possible relation to Zoe, a knock on her door jolted her.

Her visitor twisted the doorknob hard, but it wouldn't budge. She jumped up, uneasy, and shoved the stack into her top desk drawer. "Who's there?" she called.

"Natalie, open up," a familiar male voice said.

She clicked aside the lock and opened the door. Behind Professor Adler stood Mitch. They both looked furious. Her breath caught as if on a hook in her throat.

"What—what can I do for you?" she asked.

"Is this true?" Adler demanded. "Have you gone behind Mitch's back to pursue a project that could provoke serious legal consequences?"

She stared from him to Mitch, who was shaking his head as if in shock at her audacity. How could they already know?

"What? I—" She licked her lips, calculating fast. Each second that lapsed was a testament to her guilt.

She had to say something. "I was fascinated by the girl's case," she began. "Almost no one has seen Syndrome X. I just wanted to look into it a little."

"What do you mean *a little*?" Adler asked. "Mitch tells me the lawyers still consider her a minor, and her parents are uncooperative. Do you realize what your involvement could mean?"

"You could screw up the whole department's reputation!" Mitch cried. "And that means mine! Why don't you ever think of anyone besides yourself?"

"Funny, I could say the same to you," she snapped.

"All right." Adler's tone was irritable. "I'll take it from here," he said to Mitch. Natalie stepped aside as Adler walked in alone and shut the door.

"Look," he said. "Let's be straight. I don't have illusions about what you were doing, and I understand the draw of the case, I really do."

She swallowed, aware that her entire career rested in his hands.

"But you have to realize that recklessness is not a virtue. It's only going to get you fired."

She pursed her lips, still not trusting herself to speak, for the bubble of anger that was rising threatened to explode. *By recklessness,* she wanted to counter, *you mean the pursuit of truth in this esteemed institution of higher learning?*

"I could take this up to the dean right now," he continued. "I know he doesn't have much sympathy for those who endanger the school's well-being, no matter the cause." He turned to gaze out the window, as if contemplating the worth of the majestic campus below. Catching his regal nose in profile, Natalie was reminded of a king surveying his empire. Then he looked back at her.

"But I'm not going to do that."

"You're not?"

"No." He smiled magnanimously. "You're a brilliant scientist, Natalie. I knew when I hired you that you were no ordinary mind, and that you'd probably go against the grain as all unconventional thinkers do. I've been waiting for this day to come."

She gaped at him, unsure if she had just imagined his words, the greatest professional compliment she'd ever received.

"It would be a real loss to let you go now," he went on, "when your career is heading toward its prime. I've had you in mind for tenure all along."

"You have?" She clutched the edge of the desk to steady herself. "What about Mitch? You're always talking to him."

"He's always talking to me," Adler corrected. "As a researcher, he doesn't have half the vision you do." He pointed a stern finger. "And that stays between us."

The affection in his eyes granted her permission to smile. "Of course."

"So we're going to ignore this ever happened on the condition that you immediately drop this case. Do not contact that girl. Is that understood?"

She hesitated. "With all due respect, it would be a travesty to let her DNA go to waste. She's over eighteen, she wants this—"

He held up a hand. "It's too risky right now, Natalie. You have to wait until after the courts figure out her legal status."

"That could be years!"

"Then so be it." He stared hard at her. "The last thing the dean wants is another scandal coming out of this department, with all of us already watching our backs. Am I making myself clear?"

There was only one correct answer. "Yes."

"So we're agreed?"

She nodded forlornly, bemused at how an act of mercy and one of torture could be the same.

"Where are the files?" he asked. "Mitch said you called her doctor to get them. The receptionist left him a message."

A sigh of frustration escaped her. How could she have known to prevent that? Not that it mattered now. "Here," she admitted, retrieving them from her desk drawer and handing them over.

"I'll keep them for you." He snatched the papers and dropped them into his briefcase. "Trust me, it will be easier this way. And if you need them in five years, come talk to me."

Her throat tightened. She bit her tongue to prevent protest, knowing his goodwill stretched only so far. He reached out to shake hands, which she did reluctantly, and then he opened the door and left without another word. Soon after, she followed him out. There was no more work to be done tonight.

As she locked up her office, she was surprised to see Mitch standing nearby, as if he'd been waiting for her to leave. He sidled up to her, his breath hot on her neck.

"Hey, assistant," he crooned. "That was a cute little trick."

She glanced around the hallway. It was after five o'clock. No one else was around. Her hand burned to slap him. "What you do want, Mitch?"

"A better question is what you think you're going to get by playing dirty?"

"I'm not playing at all," she replied, stepping away from him. "I just want to be left alone in my lab."

"And you still have one after today? I can't imagine Adler is very happy with you."

"We've settled it," she said icily. "So yes."

"Really? That's a shocker." He frowned. "You go behind my back and nothing happens?"

"You ruined the best chance I've ever had, that's what happened." Her voice was shaking. "If you can believe it, I'm not out to spite you, Mitch, I was only making up for your loss. Trying to do the world some good. You might consider it sometime."

Ignoring his livid expression, she whirled around and marched into the waiting elevator. She kept her back to the door until it slid closed.

"Sweetheart," Gramps said, "I hate to see you so upset."

Zoe burrowed her face into his shoulder, having just recounted her failed meeting with Dr. Mitch Grover. Gramps sat up taller in bed and put his arm around her. The late afternoon sun shone through his bedroom window, illuminating the yellow gold of her hair.

"It's just so unfair," she lamented, her voice muffled by his arm. "I want to be my own person again."

"It's very frustrating," he agreed. "If only we could get your mom and dad to come around, but you know how stubborn they can be."

Zoe sat up and sniffled. "They'll never listen to me

now if I'm just a kid. And Dad's fed up with you; I don't think you should push him."

"Not if I still want to live here."

"So where does that leave us?" She tossed her arm in the air. "All the scientists who would want to work with me will have this legal problem."

"Not to mention," Gramps added in a resigned voice, "there are very few researchers local to New York who are even qualified. It's not as if we can relocate. So unless we can get your parents on board, you'll exhaust your options pretty quickly."

"So you're giving up?" she cried. "That's not like you!"

He opened his mouth to respond, but coughed instead, a dry hacking that rattled his lungs, and she sprung up to fetch him a glass of water. Immediately she regretted scolding him. When he reached for the glass, still coughing, she noticed the tremor in his hand.

"Thank you, dear," he managed after a few sips. "Now, I'm going to tell you something that will be very hard to hear, but you need to be strong."

She froze. "What?"

He looked at her with a sad smile. "I know why you're so desperate. It's not just about wanting to make scientific progress, or even finding a way to grow up, am I right?"

She glanced down at the bed. He was getting uncomfortably near the topic she most dreaded.

"It's really about me, isn't it?" he said gently. "You want to help me stop aging. You think your body holds the key to my salvation."

Her head snapped up. "It does! Dr. Carlyle said they just have to find my mutation, and then they'll figure out how to turn it off and on!"

Gramps paused, as if searching for the least painful words. "That may be so," he said. "But that kind of sophistication is most likely years away. It's all right, don't cry. I've had lots of years of love and happiness, and I couldn't ask for more. But I know you won't stop trying to make this happen, even after I'm gone. You're destined for greatness, sweetheart. Not because of your body, but your mind. You're independent and fearless, and you've never given up on a thing in your life."

"No," she whispered, clutching his hand as if her grip could keep him stationed to Earth. Raised purple veins crisscrossed his arthritic knuckles, but still his fingers felt solid, reassuring, smelling of his favorite lemon soap. It was impossible to imagine the world without him—stripped, horrific, like a world without sight. Darkness would reign forever after.

She curled up next to him and let his warmth flow over her. "I won't stop, I won't, I won't," she murmured until the words blurred together and lost meaning, and all that remained was the certainty in her mind that bowing down to fate was a fate worse than death.

CHAPTER 9

For what seemed like the fiftieth time in two days, Les pressed PLAY on his computer. The DVD on his office computer whirred, and then the image of Natalie Roy sitting cross-legged in a black mesh chair filled his screen. Her face was feline, angular, with high cheekbones and a puckered mouth. Brown hair fell to her chin in a sleek bob, showing off her slender white neck. She licked her lips and glanced at a gardenia plant on her windowsill, just offscreen. He heard his own authoritative voice begin.

"Please state your full name and position for the recording."

"Natalie Elizabeth Roy. Assistant professor in the Department of Biological Sciences, Columbia."

"How long have you known Helen McNair?"

"Approximately four years, since I first started working here."

"And what is the nature of your relationship?"

"We're colleagues and friends."

"How close of friends? Be more specific."

"Pretty close. I don't know how you want me to quantify it. It's not a scientific measurement."

"You talked every day?"

"No. We're both busy. That's why I didn't think much of it when we didn't speak for several days last week."

"We'll come back to that. Did you socialize outside of work?"

"Yes, sometimes we would grab a bite to eat or catch a movie."

"Was your age difference ever an issue?"

"That's an odd question."

"Was it? She's old enough to be your mother."

"I don't see how the private details of our friendship are relevant to her being abducted."

"Just answer the question, Dr. Roy."

Watching it, Les thought the menace in his tone came off perfectly—just enough to sound threatening, while still within the realm of composure.

She crossed her arms. "I don't know what you're getting at. Sometimes she tends to mother me because she knows I'm raising my son alone, trying to be as good a mom and a scientist as I can be. I have my dark moments, and she gets that. But that's the only way the age difference has ever played a role."

"Have you ever had a fight?"

She didn't answer right away, and Les paused the video to rewind a split second. He zoomed in on her mouth until her pink lips filled half the screen, and pressed PLAY again.

"Have you ever had a fight?"

The muscles in her chin tensed. "No. Never."

Liar. "So you never got angry with her or disagreed with anything she did?"

"Isn't that what a fight is, Dr. Mahler?"

"Let's reiterate, then. You and Helen McNair were quite close. She intimately knew about your life outside of work. She comforted you during tough times and you confided in her and vice versa. Is that correct?"

Natalie nodded.

"Did you know, prior to my announcement in the meeting just now, what she was doing in her lab?"

Her lips formed the word as he spoke. "No."

"No? Did you ever suspect that she could be capable of performing a secret, potentially dangerous experiment?"

"No. She never told me anything about that. I still can't believe it."

Natalie's lips pressed together. She regarded the camera with a blank stare.

"Listen, Dr. Roy. If you have information to share but you're worried about repercussions, don't be. Anything you say here will be kept entirely confidential."

"Unfortunately I have nothing else to add."

Pure bullshit. Les shut off the video in disgust. There was nothing more insulting than being lied to, point-blank. It was the moral equivalent of being spat on. But if she was hiding vital information, how could he prove it? Despite his determination, he could find nothing concrete in her personal e-mail exchanges with Helen, no way to root his suspicions in fact. All that cash sacrificed to Cylon for nothing.

But *someone* was working for the Network through

Columbia, relaying information back to Galileo, someone who was close enough to Helen to know about her
secret project. And Natalie knew something that she
wasn't letting on, that much seemed clear. How could he
force her to cooperate before it was too late? Helen had
already been missing for a week now, with no trace of—

A sudden, urgent knock on the door interrupted his
thoughts.

"Who's—"

Before he could finish, Benjamin Barrow charged
in, red-faced and waving a newspaper.

Les stood up at once. "Excuse me, but—"

"Have you seen this?"

"Seen what?"

Barrow dropped the newspaper onto his desk and
jabbed at the page. *"This."*

New York City
7:30 A.M.

Natalie's bedroom door burst open, flooding the dark
room with light. She buried her face in her pillow as the
memory of the previous day's near-firing punctured her
consciousness like shrapnel. Clinging to sleep was useless. She heard footsteps pattering over the carpet and
soon a bony hand squeezed her shoulder. "Mom."

"What's up?" she asked groggily, feeling for her
glasses on the nightstand.

"What have you done?" Theo's face appeared a blur,
but there was no mistaking the anger in his voice.

"What?" She sat up and slid on her glasses. He was
glaring at her with suspicion, as if she were an impos-

tor of his real mother. Her hand flew to her palpitating chest. "What are you talking about? You're scaring me."

"This." He thrust his laptop onto her knees. "I've already gotten three e-mails about it."

She peered down at the screen, at a headline that screamed in bold:

TIME OUT ON MAD SCIENTIST'S ILLICIT EXPERIMENT
COLUMBIA PROF CAUGHT TRYING TO SNEAK AGELESS CHILD INTO LAB

Under the subhead was a thumbnail reprint of her official faculty photo from Columbia's website. In it, her chin-length brown hair was neatly straightened, framing her sharp features. Her green eyes beheld the camera proudly, reflecting her elated smile. The picture had been shot the day after she was hired. Next to her picture was a headshot of Zoe smiling tentatively against a blue background, as though for a school portrait. The slight chubbiness of her cheeks and her large guileless eyes made her look like a young tween, though the picture was dated last year.

She looked at Theo in shock. "Are you kidding me? What the hell is this?"

"The *Post*. It's a mistake, right? They messed something up?"

Speechless, she looked again at the glowing screen, where the article was posted under the local news tab. Its time stamp was 6:36 A.M.

NEW YORK—A Columbia University assistant professor's attempt to smuggle a child with a rare disorder into her lab was intercepted Wednesday, according to a source with knowledge of the incident who spoke on condition of anonymity.

Dr. Natalie Roy, 37, was caught impersonating another professor's assistant in order to obtain confidential medical records and contact information of the girl, Zoe Kincaid, who was recently diagnosed with a nearly unprecedented condition called Syndrome X. According to her doctor, Ray Carlyle, chair of the National Association of Medical Genetics, Kincaid's body stopped aging altogether when she was 14 years old. She is nominally 20.

"It's possible that her body contains a mutation that could hold the key to the mystery of why we age," he said, when reached at his office Wednesday evening. "Sequencing her genome could prove a very promising step in unraveling this mystery, which is why Zoe went to Columbia to meet with researchers."

However, the legal issues surrounding her case are complex and require caution, according to Columbia's lawyers. General Counsel Mark Whitman said that since her brain stopped development so young, she could technically be considered a minor, and as such, cannot be considered her own agent. Her parents have not consented to the research, which is why her case was turned down before Dr. Roy attempted to secretly pursue it. What lies at the root of Dr. Roy's actions, according to the source, is her zealous desire to make a scientific breakthrough no matter the human cost.

It remains unclear what repercussions she will suffer for her missteps, but Columbia's administration is aware of the situation, the source confirmed. Dr. Roy has been an assistant professor in the Department of Biological Sciences for four years and has had no prior history of offenses, according to the school's records. She was unable to be reached for comment before press time.

"Sometimes we have to put our research interests

aside and focus on what's right," the source concluded. "Above all else, protecting a child comes first."

Natalie blinked at Theo in a daze. He was staring at her. A lock of curly brown hair fell over his eyes, but he didn't push it away.

"You did it, didn't you?" he whispered.

"That little—" *prick*, she wanted to say, but stopped herself. "This is unbelievable." Seeing her own face next to such a slanted story was surreal, like a vicious prank. But it *was* real—and it was appallingly public character assassination.

"So it is true?" Theo pressed. His disappointment bordered on disgust. She felt as though one look at his face could split her into a thousand broken shards.

"Zoe's over eighteen," she protested. "She wanted this, she came to us! If the guy I work with wasn't such a—"

"But the lawyers?"

"Oh, screw the lawyers! All they care about is not getting sued. They'll make any story up to cover their butts. But Zoe has two decades of experience, more than any minor I know! She should be allowed to think for herself. The lawyers are the ones who are so *zealous* that they don't consider the *human cost*!"

Natalie slammed the laptop shut and reached for her cell phone, which she always left on silent during the night. She had eleven missed calls, five that she recognized as Adler's office line.

"Oh my God, I have to go right now." She leaped out of bed and ran past Theo into the bathroom, pulling the door closed behind her.

"But what's going to happen?" he called. She could

tell his cheek was right up against the door. "What will we do if you lose your job?"

She nearly gagged at the words, and was glad he couldn't see her.

"Mom?"

"It'll be all right, honey," she heard herself say. Somehow her tone sounded competent and reassuring—the secret weapon of mothers in emergencies. She wished her own mother were still around to tell her the same. A powerful maternal force overcame her. She opened the door and scooped Theo into a tight hug, holding the back of his head with her palm. His tall and lanky body was rigid in her arms.

"It'll be okay," she whispered.

He didn't respond.

Forty-five minutes later, she was walking into Adler's corner office with an escalating sense of trepidation. Other faculty members and students she passed in the hallway stood in clusters, whispering and glancing at her with unmitigated contempt. Anonymous hate mail was already piling up under her office door with accusations like "child abuser" and "child hater." The lies made her eyes burn. She yearned for a friend, but without Helen—the one person who would have understood—she was alone.

Surprisingly, Mitch was already sitting in Adler's spacious corner office when she entered. He refused to make eye contact with her, instead staring out the floor-to-ceiling window at the treetops swaying below. She wondered if he was at all ashamed of obliterating her career, or if he was just poorly avoiding awkwardness. She ignored him, fighting the torturous urge to scream, and instead sat in the black leather chair at his side. Together they faced Adler, whose usually placid expression was the epitome of fury. He acknowledged Natalie's presence with a glare, then shifted his attention to Mitch.

A copy of the *Post* lay open on his desk.

"What the hell were you thinking?" he barked. "We had settled this privately yesterday. Of all the asinine things to do, you called a *reporter*?"

Mitch glowered. "I wasn't the one who called him. Someone else leaked it."

Natalie stifled a bitter laugh. "You never cease to amaze me."

"Mitch, we're not total idiots," Adler snapped. "Give me a break. You did this. You have single-handedly brought the worst press to our school at the worst time possible. Admit it."

"Fine, I talked to the stupid reporter. But he called me first!"

Adler rolled his eyes. "Sure he did. He divined that you wanted to throw Natalie under the bus."

Mitch squirmed in his chair. "You weren't even going to punish her! I was just doing the right thing." His face was growing redder, Natalie noticed, and he kept pinching his collar away from his neck.

A vein popped up on Adler's forehead. "By doing the *right thing,* you have probably cost us thousands upon thousands of dollars in lost grants, not to mention the priceless cost of disrepute. Do you know how long it's going to take for this to wear off?"

"It's her fault!" Mitch cried. "None of this would have happened if she hadn't done that."

"Yes, but you never should have *ever* spoken to the media!" Adler roared. "Those damn reporters are going to be all over us like flies, right when we're trying to keep the FBI investigation under wraps." He shook his head. "Thank God you didn't say anything about the mole and Helen! But still, what is the Bioethics chairman going to think? If Les Mahler wasn't already going to put the department on probation, I bet he will now!"

Mitch paled. Probation by the Justice Department's Bioethics Committee meant that all the Biology faculty's experiments would indefinitely need to be monitored and approved by a federal representative to ensure that no ethical lines were being crossed. It was worse than a hassle. It was an insult of the worst order, akin to branding the department with a scarlet letter. Often it led to an exodus of the faculty and an inability to attract new talent.

"Neither of you thought through the consequences of your actions," Adler said. "You're both very talented"—he looked sadly at Natalie—"but I'm afraid that's not going to be enough to save you. On direct order from the dean, your terminations are effective immediately."

The commotion downstairs roused Zoe from sleep—yelling, scuffling, the house phone ringing and ringing unanswered. A prickling sweat came over her as she heard Gramps's voice rise above it. She jumped out of bed and ran down the stairs in time to see her mother blocking the front door, clutching Gramps's arm, in an apparent standoff with her father, who was shaking a newspaper at them.

"I didn't do anything," Gramps was shouting. "Stephen, calm down!"

Zoe raced up to them. "What's going on?"

Her father turned to her with rabid eyes. "You! Going behind our backs to Columbia!"

"Dad, I told you, I wanted the research. It's my body," she said, trying to stay calm.

"You should have told us first," her mother scolded. "Look what happened. You almost got caught up in some crazy scientist's web! And now the media's made a circus of it!"

"What?" She looked anxiously from Gramps to her parents. "What are you talking about?"

"That," her mother said, motioning to the newspaper in her father's hands. He handed it to Zoe. When she finished reading, her face was white.

Her secret plan had backfired. But who was this Natalie Roy who wanted to help her?

"You led her straight into the tiger's lair," her father was bellowing to Gramps in the foyer, "and it's only lucky that someone found out before she got hurt! She wouldn't have gone this far if it weren't for your encouragement." He shifted his gaze to his wife. "Pam, I can't put up with him anymore, that's it."

"Don't you dare accuse him of anything," Zoe interrupted, standing as tall as she could, though even with her shoulders thrown back, she only reached up to her father's burly chest. "I went to Columbia all by myself. And *I* was the one who called the *Post*. I just didn't tell them the story they printed."

"What?" her parents screeched in unison. Gramps's eyes widened as his eyebrows shot up. It took a great deal to surprise him, but Zoe saw that this was enough.

"I needed you to take me seriously," she told them. "I thought if I appealed to the media, they would print my story and put pressure on you to consent to the research. I knew you would never agree on your own. I mentioned Mitch Grover, the scientist I met at Columbia who turned me down, so I guess they called him, and then somehow things got all twisted. The article was supposed to be about the fact that I can't age, and how I'm looking for science to help me—not that I'm a little girl being exploited! I don't know what happened."

Gramps sighed. "They'll always go for the more sensational story if they can find one."

Her father blinked, while her mother crossed her arms, looking hurt. "You should have just come to us. I didn't know you were that serious."

"It wouldn't have mattered, and you know it. You and Dad would never have signed those forms."

"I don't know what to say, Zoe," her father said in a quiet voice, which alarmed her more than his shouting. "You're totally out of control. You've ignored our warnings not to open this can of worms, and look where it's gotten you. Your mother and I will need to spend some time discussing a proper punishment, but until then, you're grounded. No cell phone either."

"Seriously?" she replied in disbelief. "So I really am fourteen all over again?"

"You're living under our roof, and you will respect our rules, no matter how old you are. Now give me your phone."

"It's upstairs. I'll go get it—but only if Gramps stays. You have to promise nothing will happen to him." Gramps looked at her, and she could tell he was touched.

"He isn't going anywhere," her mother said, still holding on to his right arm to keep him steady. His left hung by his side in the white plaster cast.

When her father reluctantly agreed, she turned around and hurried up to her room, knowing she didn't have much time. Finally there was a scientist who wanted to work with her—if only it wasn't too late! She shut the door and anxiously searched online for Columbia's number. She would delete the call history afterward.

An operator answered after one ring. "Columbia University, how may I direct your call?"

"I'd like to be connected to the office of Professor Natalie Roy," she whispered. "In Biology."

"One moment, please."

The line clicked, and the on-hold music came on, a gorgeous violin concerto that she recognized as Tchaikovsky's. It was one of her favorites because its joyful melody always made her feel more happy and alive, more herself. She hummed it under her breath, her hope rising with each bar.

Then the music abruptly cut off.

"Miss, are you still there?"

"Yes, hi," she said quickly.

"I'm very sorry, but Dr. Roy's line has been disconnected. She's no longer employed."

CHAPTER 10

Les stared at the picture of Zoe Kincaid on his laptop, trying to wrap his mind around the very fact of her existence.

Biologically frozen.

Her smiling cheeks puffed out with remnant baby fat, framed by long blond hair that fell over her nonexistent chest. How could she be a college freshman? She seemed straight out of *Ripley's Believe It or Not!*—a sleazy late-night television show his ex-wife, Darcy, used to enjoy.

Their two-bedroom apartment was quiet since she'd moved out. Now it contained only what he needed and nothing more. Minimalist white couches, a glass table, a stainless steel kitchen. He enjoyed standing next to the wall of windows in his bedroom, thirty stories high, surveying the roofs of the lesser buildings. He wasn't the type to get lonely. There were always women to call, if the itch needed scratching. Of course, that was the root of his problems with Darcy in the first place, but he was better off living his own life. Calling all the shots. He had never been good at compromising, not with his peers growing up, not with his nightmare of a father, and especially not with Darcy.

The only person who had ever truly mattered to him was his mother. The thought of her pierced him still, the decade since her death having done little to dull the loss. He would never allow himself to forget the big picture nor the small details of their life together: Not just the fact that she had rescued him at age eleven from his abusive father under cover of night and then started over—first in a homeless shelter, then in a dirty old studio apartment, working long hours on her feet as a waitress at Denny's to support them both on her meager income. She never asked his father for money and never asked Les to work—just wanted him to enjoy what was left of his childhood, though his innocence had disappeared long before.

He never could bear to tell her about the bullies at his new school, always explaining that this bruised eye came from a basketball game, those bad scrapes from a skateboard accident. It pained him more though to think of the secret *she* had been keeping from him during those difficult years. He'd been too absorbed in his own daily battles to notice her progressively jerky movements, her unsteady gait, her difficulty chewing and swallowing.

But then one day when he was seventeen, he'd come home from school to find her lying on the couch, instead of at her shift at the restaurant.

"What are you doing here, Stanley?" she yelled at him. "I told you to leave us alone!"

"What? Ma, it's me. Dad hasn't bothered us for years."

Her glazed-over look cleared, and she seemed to awake to her surroundings. Her inevitable confession soon followed—she had Huntington's disease, a rare inherited illness that manifested itself in midlife. There was nothing the doctors could do to prevent her eventual death. After learning of her diagnosis, Les did everything he could to make sure she never had to work again. He held down three part-time jobs in college, living at home to take care of her, and earning scholarships all the way through. Once he graduated with his PhDs and got his first assistant professorship, he had scraped enough together with his savings, her disability checks, and his income to hire full-time help for her.

She was a fighter. Even on the days when she didn't remember him at all, when she was writhing in her wheelchair, her eyes roaming back and forth, Les knew her benevolent spirit was still there, pure and alive underneath the disease. All he wanted was for her to live the rest of her life in peace and comfort, and what he'd ended up doing to her instead—

He wrenched his thoughts away from the horror as his body clenched, the way it did every time his brain vomited up the memory.

After composing himself, he focused again on Zoe. There were so many scientists like Natalie Roy who were frothing to get at her, now that her case was public. He felt nothing but hostility toward them, even though he'd come from their ranks long ago. Of his desire to research, little remained. Many years had passed since he'd been in a lab, practically another lifetime ago, but he remembered dissections the most—the singular feeling of taking a knife to skin and splitting it open to reveal an animal's organs inside, like hidden jewels.

Les stood up and went to the kitchen to retrieve a steak knife out of the wooden block on the counter. It had been so long since he'd dissected anything. He missed it.

The search for treasure had compelled him since he was a little boy. It was an instinctual urge to dig below the surface, to peel away layers and unveil whatever was concealed. In biology, you could go ever deeper. It was the quintessential search to find the secret stuff at the heart of life itself. Inside the skin, the organs, the blood, the cells and their nuclei lay DNA, the master coder, the wizard behind the body's curtain. Within Zoe Kincaid's DNA lay perhaps the biggest secret of all. It was a secret that should never be found.

A secret that made her the biggest prey.

He ran his index finger over the edge of the knife.

New York City
9:30 P.M.

The worst part of Natalie's day was not getting fired, despite the horror of watching Adler speak the word "terminations" with the glum finality of a doctor calling time of death. She had pictured a fishhook gutting her career, spewing the bloody entrails of the scandal across her spotless resume, leaving stains that would never fade. Numbness overcame her, a strange tingling sensation crawled down her arms and into her fingertips. It had taken all of her grace to stand up, thank Adler for the best four years of her life, and walk out, suppressing her undignified urge to argue. She'd said nothing to Mitch and took little satisfaction in their shared fate. Justice served was only limp consolation for her own distress.

Even when Nick, her college sweetheart and one-time husband, had announced his affair all those years ago—while Theo was still in diapers—her sense of loss then did not compare to what she felt today. Not that she ever could have imagined a more painful loss, from the vantage point of a twenty-three-year-old mom just starting graduate school. But in retrospect, she saw that the fabric of her life had remained intact, in a way that now seemed impossible. Without a cheating husband, she still had the real love of her life—her son. But without her work—and without the prospect of any job in her field—she was an outcast.

Yet getting fired still wasn't the most agonizing moment of her day. It was telling Theo that his worst fear had come true.

She suspected he knew what had happened as soon as she returned home that morning armed with boxes and Helen's gardenia plant, the salvaged remains of her office. That was ten hours ago, and she still wasn't over her shock at his reaction.

"It pisses me off that they fired you," he told her. "I've been thinking about it. That article was totally biased and makes you out to be a monster, but I know you would never hurt anyone."

She dropped to the couch beside him, flabbergasted. Their 32-inch flat-screen television was showing a baseball game, and Theo had his feet propped on the leather ottoman, a soda in hand. Not the posture of someone about to scream at her.

"I mean, come on," he went on. "You're the most caring person I know. You always used to worry about the city corrupting my innocence. And now you stress about whether you're overworking your students or tipping cabbies enough. It's crazy to think *you* would exploit someone, no matter the reason."

She closed her eyes, picturing the vicious notes she had received that morning. "You don't know how much that means to me."

Theo turned to her. His wide green eyes had retained the sweetness of youth, in spite of the manly stubble dotting his chin. "You've always been obsessed with defeating aging, and then this miracle girl shows up, so how could you just walk away? I get it."

"You do?"

He touched her arm. "I don't blame you, Mom. You're always telling me to go after my dreams and take risks. So you took a big one and it didn't work out. Things don't always, do they?" His face darkened, and she knew what—whom—he meant.

She smiled through tears of gratitude. "I'm afraid not."

Then he grinned. "I never knew you had such balls."

"Theo!"

"Well, it's true. Posing as an assistant? That's pretty badass."

She rolled her eyes, noticing how tall and handsome he had become almost overnight—gone were the acne and braces of his early adolescence, replaced by clear skin and straight teeth. His light brown hair looked thick and soft, and she wished she could still run her fingers through it like the old days.

He was smiling at her, and she wondered if he was trying to project strength for her sake, in spite of his own disappointment. At eighteen, he really was becoming a man.

"I'm still out of a job," she reminded him. "I don't know what I'm going to do, but my savings will last us a little while. And I will find a way to keep putting money in your college fund, even if I have to flip burgers."

"Actually, don't sweat it." His smile brightened. "There were a few college recruiters at my track meet right before graduation, and I just found out one's scouting me. If I train hard enough this summer, I could get a full ride to USC. No community college."

Natalie gasped, throwing her arms around him. All of her anger and frustration melted before his happiness. "Honey, that's fantastic! I can't believe it!"

"Me either." He grinned, bouncing his knees. "So don't worry too much about me. I'm going to make this happen. I already ran five miles this morning."

His words soothed her like a balm. She trusted his determination as much as her own. If possible, she would have kissed the recruiter who had given him hope when he needed it most.

"And I'll make us lemonade," she vowed. "Just you wait." It was their shorthand for turning an unfortunate circumstance into something worthwhile.

"It's a deal," he said, extending his hand.

She shook it.

* * *

Now that he was finally in bed asleep, she had some time to think. A plan was hatching in her mind to follow through on her vow, but its window of possibility was quickly closing. She would have to act—fast.

It was audacious, to be sure, more so than anything she had attempted before. But great rewards often came at great risk. And what more did she have to lose? Theo was less reliant on her than ever. She could see clearly, for the first time, that he was capable of taking care of himself. In a way it saddened her that their shared daily life would soon come to an end, but it was also liberating. All she'd have left in life was her work, and of that, nothing remained to her except one thing. Her ongoing experiments in her lab would be shut down or divvied up among the remaining staff, her papers would go unpublished, her classes would be reassigned.

Nothing was left except her ardent desire to meet Zoe Kincaid.

The chance to conquer aging—and to spare millions of people tremendous suffering and death—beckoned to her like a time machine would have to Einstein. How could she ignore it? Pretend as if a major moment in scientific history wasn't within reach? The temptation was more than she could bear. Even failure would be more acceptable than apathy.

There was also the tantalizing fact that her access pass to the lab was still in her purse, tucked in an inner pocket. It was Columbia property that she should have returned. Tomorrow, someone would surely notice, and she would have to hand it in.

It was already 9:30 P.M. All she needed was a blood sample containing Zoe's precious DNA to store on slides until she could find another lab to carry out the experiments. But finding that next lab could take years, and in the intervening time, Zoe could move or get sick or fall out of reach. So tonight was like a rare eclipse: When else would she, Zoe, and a lab perfectly align again?

She pulled her computer onto her lap and typed Zoe's name into Facebook, but her profile was private. Of course, her cell phone number would not be listed in a public directory, and Natalie couldn't exactly call her parents' house, even if she could track down their number.

She clutched her own cell phone, willing herself to recall Zoe's number. Squinting, she could almost picture the digits—but was it (917) 479-7302 or (917) 479-2703? Damn Adler for taking the files! If only she'd known to memorize it. What else—

She bolted upright, nearly knocking her computer to the floor. The number of Zoe's emergency contact was a palindrome. Yesterday, she had smiled to herself for inadvertently recognizing its pattern, and now the pleasing digits returned to her like a boomerang: (917) 333-3719. His name was Silas, she remembered.

Before she could contemplate what she might say, she dialed the number and held her breath. After three rings, she started to exhale. Another ring passed. She pulled the phone away, about to hang up, when she heard an old man's voice.

"Hello?"

She clutched the phone to her ear. "Hi there! Is this Silas?"

"Speaking. Who's this?" He sounded tired, and she realized how late she was calling.

"I'm"—she faltered, thinking of the *Post* article—"I'm a biogerontologist who'd very much like to meet Zoe. I'm so sorry if I woke you."

"Not at all." His voice perked up. "How'd you get my cell? No one except my family knows it."

"Well, I . . . saw her files. You were her emergency contact."

There was a pause. "Is this Natalie Roy?"

She detected wonder, but no hostility, which encouraged her frankness. "Yes it is. I didn't know whether to say so. Look, I'm not some evil scientist like I was made out to be. I would never hurt Zoe in any way. I'm just genuinely fascinated by her case and would love to sequence her genome, if she's still open to research. I know she was yesterday."

He chuckled. "Hang on a second."

She waited, unsure if she was making a terrible mistake. Could one phone call constitute harassment? But thirty seconds later, a high-pitched female voice chirped on the line.

"Hello?"

"Hi," Natalie said. Her heart ricocheted against her chest. "Is this Zoe?"

"Yeah. Is this really Natalie Roy? From Columbia?"

"Yes, well, not anymore, unfortunately."

"Oh my God! I tried to call your office before, but they said you were gone."

"You did? You called me?"

"I knew about you from reading that article. No one else wants to study me but you. And I didn't know how to find you. I can't believe you called Gramps! But we have to hurry."

"You're in a rush?"

Natalie heard a door faintly close, and Zoe's voice dropped to a whisper. "Gramps is so old. You have to figure out how to stop his aging before it's too late. Dr. Carlyle said the secret could be in my body."

Natalie closed her eyes, feeling her chest squeeze with sympathy. So that was why she had rushed out in tears. What pressure she had put on her own small shoulders! Yet she was helpless without science, as helpless as Natalie herself had been when her own parents crumbled from old age. All the love in the world could not stop the march of death.

"You must really love your grandfather," she said.

"I'd do anything for him. Can you help us?"

"Well, it's true that there could be a very important mutation in your DNA—but it could be a long time before any practical applications come of it, if we can even find it. You know that, right?"

"Well, what are we waiting for?"

"The first step is for me to obtain a blood sample."

"How? Let's do it!"

"I could pick you up right now in a cab. But, Zoe? We need to go to my old lab, where all the equipment is. I have to warn you, I'm not supposed to go there anymore. We need to be careful."

"Is there no other lab we can go to?"

"Not that I can access. I'm afraid this is our only shot. After tonight, I won't be able to get back in."

"So how will you do the research?"

"I'll do whatever it takes to find another lab. I may need to move out of state, so that's why I'd like to get the sample from you now, while we're both still here and I can get in one last time."

Zoe's voice held no fear. "I'm ready if you are."

"I'll leave right now. I can't wait to meet you." Natalie didn't add what else she was thinking: a true fourteen-year-old could never sound so brave.

Zoe crept as quietly as she could down the wooden stairs, avoiding the creaky spots. Her parents were asleep in their bedroom on the second floor. Gramps followed behind her, taking care to step exactly where she did, holding the banister for support. Her excitement mounted with each step, but she knew she couldn't rush and leave him stranded. They didn't speak until they reached the bottom. He clutched her arm as he trudged beside her toward the front door.

"I want to go with you," he whispered. "We don't know this woman. Let me come."

Zoe shook her head. "It's too much for you. I can take care of myself. I took karate, remember?"

"But you're so small." He winced as if he might have offended her. "You're the boss, though." It was his affectionate kid nickname for her—one that had now taken on a new significance. She smiled. It wasn't lost on either of them.

Through the window, she saw a yellow cab roll to a stop in front of their door. She could make out the silhouette of a woman in the backseat.

"I'll be fine," she whispered. In case she was threatened, Gramps was the last person who could defend her, but she didn't say so. She wondered if somewhere, deep down, he still saw himself as a young Olympic hero, merely contained in the shell of a crippled old man. Like Ulysses—made weak by time and fate, but not in will. She and Gramps shared flip sides of the same tragedy, she realized—both were trapped in bodies that belied their souls. She grabbed his hand and steered him to his favorite recliner in the den.

"Wait here," she instructed. "I'll be back soon."

He sat down with a look of defeat. "But how will I be able to reach you, just in case?"

"You think I didn't think of that?" she said, pulling her cell phone out of her purse.

He raised his eyebrows. "I thought your father took it."

"He did. And hid it in the toolbox, where he hides his extra key." She shook her head with a smile and leaned down to kiss his cheek. "Don't worry, this is going to be awesome. I love you."

"I love you, too," he whispered. "Please be careful."

She held her index finger to her lips and tiptoed to the door. Opening and closing it was the trickiest part, but she managed to slip out just as Gramps gave a few coughs for good measure.

Outside the quiet night was cool. She should have brought a jacket, but it was too risky to go back inside. She skipped down the brownstone steps, inhaling the scent of the pink and white magnolia trees that lined the block. As the sweet fragrance filled her with a sense of possibility, the cab's rear door popped open for her. She grasped the cold metal handle, glancing over her shoulder at the apartment's second-floor window. Its light was off, so she climbed inside and shut the door. The cab lurched forward, its headlights stabbing the darkness.

Natalie twisted to face Zoe full on, smiling and extending her hand. "It's so nice to finally meet you."

"You're so young!" Zoe exclaimed, and then blushed.

"I just imagined you as way older. I read your CV online, and you've done so much."

Natalie was prettier than she'd imagined, too, but didn't say so. With her sleek brown bob, prominent cheekbones, and shapely breasts under her cashmere sweater, she looked more like a hip news anchor than a nerdy scientist. Though Zoe would never admit it, she always noticed the size of other women's cheekbones and breasts before anything else, and judged their femininity accordingly. Already, Natalie's ranked about ten times greater than her own, and Zoe felt a deep-seated envy stir, admiration of a womanliness that could so far be matched only in spirit.

Natalie chuckled at her surprise. "Thank you. I may look young, but I've been doing research since I was your age." She cleared her throat. "Since college. So I've had a lot of years to build up my CV."

Zoe could tell she was being modest. "Yeah, but it's what's on it that's impressive. All that stuff with the genes you found that relate to aging . . . didn't you get a MacArthur genius grant?"

A proud smile tugged at her lips. "About five years ago. It was given to me with the hope that I would work on targeting the location of the master regulator gene. The gene that's believed to underpin the entire aging process."

"Dr. Carlyle told me about it," Zoe said. "I'd never heard of it before."

"Most people haven't. It's still only a theory."

"So what happened?" she asked eagerly. "What did you find?"

Natalie glanced out her window at the shuttered storefronts zipping by on Broadway. The usually busy road was deserted at this hour, and the green lights seemed to last an eternity.

"I didn't find it," she replied. "But I came closer than anyone ever has. That is, I found several possible locations on certain chromosomes that I think could hold the gene, or group of genes. I just haven't been able to dig much further. It's very hard to separate out the cause and effect when you don't have a picture of what the gene would look like turned off—without that, we can't begin to reconstruct the chain of events that kick in to accelerate aging. It's impossible to know which chemical reaction causes which, like dominoes that are all falling. We can see they're being knocked down, but we can't tell where it started." A smile spread across her face. "Not yet, at least."

Zoe couldn't help picturing a perpetual collision of dominoes inside of Gramps's body, one striking the next, and the next, involuntary as a heartbeat and just as finite. She wondered how many more he had left.

The cab slowed, and she saw that they were in a grittier neighborhood than her own. Few people ventured onto the shadowy streets, and those who did walked with hunched shoulders and quick strides. She felt the first clip of fear, but brushed it off. Something about being with Natalie made her feel safe.

After paying the driver, they climbed out on the sidewalk next to Columbia, right at the threshold of the cobblestone campus. Near the black gate stood a sleepy security guard, who barely moved when Natalie flashed her blue faculty ID. Before he could decide to inspect her picture, they strode past him and onto the university grounds. It was as awe-inspiring as its surroundings were not. Zoe wanted to stop and admire the imposing dome supported by columns that formed the centerpiece of the campus, and the statue of a bronze lady on its steps, but Natalie took her hand and pulled her along. A few students sauntered by them, loudly talking and laughing, but otherwise, the campus was empty.

They walked past the domed building and a great wide lawn, then sharply turned to the left and stopped before a smaller, rectangular building. It looked to be about ten or twelve stories high. Etched above the door were the words: FAIRCHILD CENTER, DEPARTMENT OF BIOLOGICAL SCIENCES. Natalie reached into her purse to retrieve her access pass, and Zoe noticed a gleam of sweat on her upper lip, despite the breezy night.

"Are you okay?" she whispered, standing in front of her, in case anyone should pass them.

Natalie flashed her a reassuring smile. "No one's here. Let's go in."

She held her magnetic pass up to the door's black sensor and a green light flashed. As she opened the door, Zoe went in first, ducking under her arm. All the lights were off. The door closed behind them with a soft thud.

"Stick by me," Natalie said. "I don't want to turn on the lights in case someone notices." Zoe reached for her hand, but grasped her elbow by accident in the darkness. Natalie's pace was brisk, and Zoe had to take extralong strides to keep up. The faint blue glow of her cell phone gave them a few precious inches of sight. She tried not to imagine a rat scurrying over their feet.

"I'd know my way around here in my sleep." Natalie's voice seemed disembodied, bouncing off the walls like an echo. Zoe could tell the hallway was narrow and she sucked air in, warding off claustrophobia. The air smelled like a janitor's scrubbing fluid, pungent with cleanliness. They blindly rounded a corner and walked down another hallway, their rapid footsteps tapping the floor in tandem.

"Almost there." After a few more steps, Natalie stopped and unlocked a door, then led Zoe inside a darkened room.

"Close your eyes."

She obeyed. Fluorescent lights switched on with a buzzing sound and her hands flew to her face.

"Sorry," Natalie said. "But we can use the lights now. This is an internal room, no windows."

When Zoe opened her eyes, she saw that they were in a lab about twice the size of her bedroom. All kinds of exotic equipment filled the room. Many were items she didn't recognize, but some she did, like computers, microscopes, test tubes and slides, which sat on a long counter in the back of the room. Wonder overcame her, as if she had landed on an alien planet far more advanced than her own.

"Welcome," Natalie said. "This was my lab."

"I'm sorry. It's beautiful."

"I don't think most people would call it that."

"Well, I think it is. In a way that trees and mountains could never be, even though they're beautiful, too."

"Funny, I know just what you mean." Natalie tilted her head, contemplating her with a smile. "Okay, let me tell you what I'm going to do and why, and then let's do it and get out of here."

"Sounds good."

"To sequence your genome, I'll need to study your DNA, which is in the blood sample you're about to give. I'll start off the process here, tonight, by breaking your DNA down into small pieces, using my hydrodynamic shearing device, and then I'll store it on glass slides called flow cells. Keeping it on slides is a better way to preserve the DNA than to just save your blood in a test tube."

"Why do you have to break it into small pieces?" Zoe asked, climbing onto a stool next to a tray of empty vials, syringes, and rubber gloves.

"That allows the sequencing machines to analyze the base pairs in manageable chunks—it's like reading a book one page at a time. Imagine if all the words were smushed together onto a single, gigantic scroll—it would be far too long to read at once."

"I see." Zoe extended her arm and Natalie dabbed the inside of her elbow with a cotton ball. The scent of rubbing alcohol permeated the air.

"When I find my next lab, I'll begin the process of unveiling your genetic code. Using the slides, I'll run many chemical reactions with colored dye to reveal several hundred of your DNA bases at a time. It's a painstaking task, far too complex to explain on the spot. But in order to look for mutations, I'll compare what I find to the known human genome, which was mapped by scientists in 2003 and is 99.99 percent accurate. I'm especially planning to focus on the certain locations I told you about."

"Where you think the master regulator gene might be."

"Yes." Natalie's green eyes shimmered with intensity. "Finding that gene is the key to my theory about aging."

"Which is?"

"I had a paper published last year explaining it. In my view, aging is progressive disorganization resulting from postmaturational expression of genes that continue to cause developmental changes after development is complete."

Zoe raised her eyebrows. "One more time in English."

Natalie smiled. "In other words, once we're grown up, that master regulatory gene is still telling our bodies to keep changing even after we've matured all the way. That gene causes what I call development inertia—a persistent reorganization of the body's parts. That normally occurs during development but it's coupled with genes that coordinate the complex changes that occur in our bodies. The information in those genes is exhausted when we reach maturity, but developmental inertia continues, progressively disrupting the internal order of our bodies—and that's why we eventually break down and die."

"So if you can find the gene . . ."

"Then we can silence it in young adulthood—at peak physical health—and become biologically immortal."

"Like me, but grown up."

"Exactly. Let me show you my favorite passage from a textbook that sums up my whole life's work—and then you'll have a better idea just how exciting this is for me." She dashed over to a shelf stacked with thick hardcover books and pulled down one with a black spine that read: *Gerontology Perspectives and Issues,* 3rd Edition. She brought it over to Zoe, leaned down for her to see, and opened it to a dog-eared page. "Look here."

Standing, Zoe read the highlighted passage over her shoulder:

> Perhaps the richest treasure of all in the hunt for longevity genes will be finding the genes responsible for the differences in life span between different species. To date, none have been identified. However, it is believed that this approach will likely lead to the discovery of pacemaker genes— a small collection of master regulatory genes that controls the tempo of age-related erosion of homeostasis and organismal decline across species.

"A treasure hunt," Zoe breathed. "That's so cool."

"I know." Natalie glanced at her watch. "We better hurry, though. I want to get you back home as soon as possible. Why don't you sit down again." She motioned to the stool next to the counter and Zoe hopped up onto it. "This'll be quick and pretty painless," she added, as she slipped on latex gloves and went about preparing a needle and tube.

"That's okay, after all the tests I've had, I'm not squeamish."

She held out her arm again and Natalie instructed her to make a fist. "Such tiny veins!"

"I always get that. Too bad guys aren't impressed," she blurted, and then flushed. She hadn't meant to say that, but was so at ease.

As Natalie chuckled, they heard an unmistakable rumble. The needle was inches from Zoe's arm.

"What was that?" she asked.

"I don't know."

"Wait, listen."

The rumble was getting louder, more measured—footsteps. A group of them, coming closer. Natalie glanced nervously from Zoe to the room's only door.

"There's no way out," she murmured. "No windows."

Zoe jumped off the stool. "What do we do?"

Natalie was already running to turn off the lights. "The supply closet, over there," she said, pointing. "Hurry."

The lights flickered off as Zoe rushed to the left side of the lab, knocking over a chair in the total darkness. It clattered loudly to the floor.

"Damn it," she muttered, but it didn't matter. The lab's door was already opening, letting in a stream of light from the hallway. She heard Natalie gasp and whipped around by the force of her own curiosity, despite knowing that she ought to duck.

In the doorway stood two stern-faced policemen— next to her horrified mother and father.

"Oh, Zoe!" her mother cried, rushing to bombard her with a hug. "You're okay!"

Her father charged up to Natalie, who stood helpless in the back of the room. "You're going to be put away for a long time," he snarled. "No one lays a hand on my daughter."

Natalie's face had drained to a sickly white. "How did you find us?" she whispered, as the two policemen approached her. She tried to retreat, but found the wall right behind her.

Mr. Kincaid's gaze swung from her to Zoe, who was squirming out of her mother's hold. "You think you're so smart, taking your cell phone. You didn't know I installed a GPS tracker on it just in case. I was worried you would pull a move like this."

Zoe felt her stomach drop away.

"We heard you sneak out," he said, "and wanted to see where you were going."

Her jaw hung open. No words could form.

One of the policemen clicked a pair of handcuffs into place around Natalie's slender wrists, while the other one spoke in a grim voice accustomed to commanding hardened criminals.

"You're under arrest for trespassing and child abduction."

"But my son!" she choked out, straining against the handcuffs. "What's going to happen to my son?"

"You have the right to remain silent," he warned her. "Anything you say can—"

"I wasn't abducted!" Zoe screamed, hurtling herself toward Natalie. But her mother's arms locked around her like tentacles and the policeman droned on, barely glancing in their direction. Her father shot her a warning look.

"Anything you say can and will be used against you in a court of law. You have the right to speak to an attorney. If you cannot afford an attorney, one will be appointed for you. Do you understand these rights as they have been read to you?"

Natalie gave a dazed nod. The men grabbed hold of her biceps and roughly escorted her toward the door.

"I came here on my own!" Zoe shouted at their backs, ignoring her parents' dismay. "I didn't mean to get her in trouble!" But they paid no attention. Natalie craned her head around, and despite her shell-shocked expression, Zoe caught her lips mouth the words: *It's not your fault.*

Then she was yanked out the door.

CHAPTER 11

Les spoke into the phone, his voice grave. He was in his office ripping up sheets of printer paper, unable to keep his hands still. The white shreds looked as though a blizzard had let loose over his desk.

"Stephen Kincaid?"

"Yes?"

"This is Les Mahler, chief of the Justice Department's Bioethics Committee. I was very concerned to hear about your daughter's abduction last night."

"Thank you." There was a long pause. "Sorry, I'm still a bit in shock—what can I do for you?"

"Listen, we've decided on the need to disclose something to you on behalf of the committee and the FBI. You understand that this is extremely confidential and privileged information, requiring your utmost discretion."

"Absolutely." His tone took on a nervous edge. "You have my word."

"We believe your daughter is in great danger. Her

condition primes her as the perfect target for a group of wayward scientific activists collectively known as the Network. They prey on individuals who might be suitable for experimentation. Twenty-seven people have already been targeted."

Kincaid gasped. "How could I not know about this?"

"The President has kept it highly classified so as not to spook the public."

"Of course. I see. So how can we protect her?"

"Make sure you know where she is at all times, no matter what. Don't let her leave without knowing exactly where she's going."

A deep sigh came over the line. "But she's very strong willed and doesn't get scared easily. Even if we tell her about this, she might not take it seriously."

"Try to get her to understand the danger she's in. The Network is viciously efficient: we haven't been able to recover a single victim out of the twenty-seven, except for one they killed and left behind."

"Jesus."

"In the meantime, we're working around the clock to infiltrate it. I'll update you if and when I have news to share."

"Is Natalie Roy . . . Oh my—could she have been recruiting Zoe . . . ?"

"That's what we're working to find out. But either way, we can rest a little easier knowing she's in jail."

"Thank you. Thank you so much for telling me."

"No problem. We just want your little girl to stay safe."

Les didn't add the rest of his thought: *from science*. Not only was Zoe Kincaid *in* danger—she *was* a danger. If Natalie Roy or someone similar from the Network actually did get to plumb the depths of her unique DNA, the result could be disastrous: a fundamental manipulation of the human line that would alter the species forever after. If ageless freaks were to dominate the planet, then what? There'd be a population explosion leading to a catastrophic lack of resources. Natural death was desirable—not only that, it was necessary. Death wasn't up to individuals to control—only to submit to when their time came. God help everyone if some lunatics in the Network tried to change that.

Now that Natalie was out of the way, the extent of her menace to society was a moot point. After Galileo, it was Zoe Kincaid who worried him the most.

New York City
2:00 P.M.

The Metropolitan Correctional Center was a scab upon downtown New York City, a squat building the color of grime. Inside, the air reeked of hopelessness. Natalie's holding cell was home to a family of cockroaches that scooted around the dirty floor, indifferent to human disgust. In adjacent cells, other women's moans echoed like a howling wind. Natalie sat on a ragged cot hugging her knees to her chest, as if compressing her body would allow her to be less than fully present.

Her booking and arraignment had passed in a blur—in less than twenty-four hours, she'd been photographed and fingerprinted, and had appeared before a judge to enter her plea of not guilty. He was notoriously harsh on any charges involving children, so he set her bail impossibly high for her to post at $250,000. With a smirk, he had announced the date for her preliminary hearing—two months away—and struck his gavel, calling "Next!" without hesitation.

Now she was wearing a brown jumpsuit, devoid of all possessions, identity, and purpose—and of her son. She rocked back and forth on her heels, softly muttering his name, looking up every once in a while as if an escape path might materialize in her seven-by-nine-foot cell. But the walls were solid cement, the black bars as hard as bone. Wan daylight eked through a slight rectangular window. Its glass seemed designed to filter out radiance and warmth.

Her life was ruined. Her dreams of ceaseless toil in the lab, unraveling the mystery of aging one DNA strand at a time, were over. Part of her wondered if this was all just a mistake, if she would be released when the authorities realized Zoe wasn't truly a child. That she and Natalie had the luck to coexist on the same planet was staggering. That they were now being forced apart—it was like finding two halves of a ripped lottery ticket and burning both.

A uniformed guard strode past her and she cried out for his attention. She was cold, hungry, thirsty—and helpless. But he walked past, barely shooting her a glance. Across the way, in a cell facing hers, a stocky female prisoner snickered.

"Help," the other woman mimicked in a high-pitched tone. "Ain't one gonna help your ass here."

Natalie turned her face to the wall to avoid eye contact.

Instead of her own plight, she thought of Zoe's. Poor Zoe—to be treated as a second-class citizen, completely denied the voice she thought she had. Natalie wondered how she was coping with the indignity, and with her dashed hopes. As for her own, nothing could salvage them. If she thought she was a pariah after one transient newspaper article, then serving jail time was like a tattoo on her face. When she got out, she would be relegated to the blackest of blacklists. Never again being able to look through a microscope was akin to a musician going deaf overnight. Yet it was a risk she had chosen to take, and she would suffer the consequences, however unfair they were.

But Theo had not chosen his grief. What would happen to him without her? Not just practically and financially, but emotionally? He was staying at a friend's house in the short-term, until a more permanent solution could be found. It was harrowing to accept that there was nothing she could do to help him, the baby she had cradled, the one person for whom she would gladly lay down her life. And she was worse than powerless—she was the perpetrator of his agony.

He had not come to see her yet, and she was both dreading and craving their initial visit. Even if he were enraged, she would be able to drink in the sight of his face. She would preserve his image in her mind with all the care of a fine curator, examining every detail to keep the memory intact. One glance, she felt, could sustain her for a year.

And after that?

Closing her eyes, she lay down on the rigid mattress and tried to make sense of how one bad week could annihilate everything she held dear.

* * *

"Dr. Carlyle," Zoe nearly shouted into the phone. She was sitting alone in her bedroom with the door closed, while outside a gaggle of reporters huddled on the doorstep. News of the previous night's arrest had traveled from the police blotter to the local media, who were salivating for firsthand details of the "abduction." To the tabloids, Zoe was learning, people fell into only two categories, victims and villains. When both seemed clear-cut, the story fit the template of sensationalism to perfection.

"Dr. Carlyle," Zoe repeated. "Are you there?"

"Yes, are you okay? I heard—"

"Please, I'm fine. I chose to go. But no one will listen to me, and now Natalie's in jail! What can we do?"

There was a pause. "I'm sorry. There's not much anyone can do at this point."

She paced over her sheepskin rug. "What if you tell everyone I'm not really a child?"

"I—I can't afford to get in the middle, Zoe. I understand that you feel older, but it's up to the courts to decide whether and when you can become your own guardian."

"But you know that could take years! You're just going to let Natalie rot in jail for a crime she didn't commit? Plus she's the only person who might be able to help my grandfather!"

"I'm sorry." He sounded crushed. "I really am."

"You can't just give up. That's not good enough. I'm telling you, she's innocent. They might listen to you and let her go."

"I'm afraid the system doesn't work like that. Even if I agreed to testify, the trial could take a long time. And there's no guarantee she'll be exonerated."

Zoe racked her brain for a galvanizing reply, but realized he was right; they were backed against a corner as tight as Natalie's cell. "So that's it, then. It's just over? No last resort, no nothing?"

"Well." He cleared his throat. "Zoe, you're a brave girl, I know that. The question is how brave."

"What are you talking about?"

"There is still one thing that could be done."

"Well, why didn't you say so!"

He paused. "Have you heard of the Network?"

She stopped midskip across the room. "You mean, the crazy group my dad says is out to kill me?"

"We're not killers," he said. "Far from it."

CHAPTER 12

Natalie awoke to the screech of her bars swinging open. A prison guard's leathery face peered down at her, the closest she'd come to human contact all weekend. He usually just slid her half-edible meals through a flap and marched away.

"What's going on?" she murmured, raising herself onto her elbows.

"Bail was posted. You're free to go."

She stared up at him, dumbfounded. His formidable figure stood in silhouette at the entry to her cell. "What?"

"You heard me." The hint of a smile tugged at his lips, but his eyes remained stoic. "Get out of here. Go."

"I—I don't understand," she stammered. "I don't have the cash—who?"

"Said his name was Mr. Roy. Your ex-husband?"

"Nick?"

"Yeah, that was it."

She shot upright, swinging her legs out of bed. "But

I haven't heard from him in a decade!" Once he remarried and started another family, he had stopped sending Theo birthday cards. After that, she'd wanted nothing to do with him or his money, even if he was a successful venture capitalist. "How would he even know what happened?"

The guard shrugged. "Maybe he saw the papers. Here's your stuff." He handed her a plastic bag containing the cashmere sweater, jeans, and low-slung heels she'd been wearing the night of her arrest, as well as her purse with her wallet, phone, and keys. "I'll leave, you get changed, then I'll show you out. He's waiting for you."

"He's here?" Her mouth hung open as she tried to picture what Nick might look like. Would his curly blond hair be receding? Would he still be slender and athletic, or paunchy around the middle?

"Out front," the guard said. "Hurry up. I don't got all day."

He stepped out, and she ripped off her jumpsuit and slipped into her soft, familiar clothes. The scent of her gardenia perfume still lingered on them and reminded her of Helen. Natalie had never missed her friend more.

The guard was waiting as promised when she stepped through the bars. With a smile, she handed him her barely touched breakfast of peanut butter on toast, picturing the lox and bagels she would never take for granted again.

"It's all yours," she joked.

"Ha." He patted the EpiPen in his front pocket. "I don't do nuts. But for prison food, it don't look half bad."

"Can't say I'm going to miss it."

They walked down the corridor to jeers and catcalls of the incarcerated women whose cells lined the long stretch. Natalie kept her head down until they turned the corner into an administrative holding area, and through that, to the heavily watched lobby. Cameras were stationed in all corners. Burly security officers stood by the door, eyeing her. Fresh air was just steps away. She was practically bursting to run out, but waited for the guard to clear her as he entered notes into a computer.

He turned to her and announced what sounded like a script. "You're to return to court for your hearing date on August seventh, and on condition of release, you're to have zero contact with the victim. Failure to comply will lead to your immediate arrest."

She nodded vigorously.

"Okay, then you're free to go. But just so you know, some reporters are waiting to hound you out there. News travels fast."

"Thank you," she said. "Thank you."

She spun around and charged through the metal detector, out the wide double doors, and into the windy early morning, with the guard trailing behind her. Five strangers swarmed her and thrust black recorders into her face, cameras clicking.

"Tell us why you did it."

"Do you regret it?"

"Do you think you deserved to get caught?"

She stumbled backward, waving them away, but they continued to buzz around her, snapping pictures and yelling.

"What would you want to say to Zoe's parents?"

"No comment," she muttered. "No comment."

They showed no signs of backing off, so she elbowed through the cluster to the edge of the sidewalk. Cars whizzed by on the busy street, honking, and well-dressed men and women walked to work clutching briefcases, oblivious to the dark world just out of their sight. The racket of voices and traffic thudded against Natalie's eardrums, sensory overload after days locked in a cell. She glanced upward, breathing in deeply. The sun was inching up into the sky—the sky!—and at first, she didn't notice the tall bearded man standing a few feet away, watching her.

A man she had never seen in her life. He was wearing aviator sunglasses and a baseball cap over short black hair. His plain gray T-shirt and faded blue jeans revealed a tanned, muscular physique, but his age was impossible to tell. He could have been thirty-five or sixty.

He approached her and smiled as if they were sharing a private joke. The reporters noticed him, and ceased shouting to watch her reaction.

"Natalie!" he exclaimed. "I know you weren't expecting me, but when I saw on the news that you were in trouble, I had to come."

She froze, too confused to move. The reporters waited. He reached out his arms and enveloped her in a hug before she could say a word.

"Play along," he whispered in her ear. "I've come to get you out of here."

He pulled back and she suppressed a gasp. Up close, she noticed the faint blending makeup around a prosthetic nose masking his own.

"I've thought about you and Theo every day," he said. "I picked him up. He's waiting in the car."

"He is?" She saw that a blue sedan with tinted windows was parked along the curb.

"Yes, now let's get you home." He took her hand, but her feet remained planted. "I know I have a lot of apologizing to do, but I've missed you both more than you can imagine," he said. "Won't you give me the chance?" A strange urgency in his voice prompted her to respond, before she'd had a chance to think.

"Oh, Nick," she said, the lie sounding shrill to her ears. "I've missed you, too."

He kissed her hand and led her to the car, as the reporters snapped pictures. Like a gentleman, he opened the front passenger door. With no time to stop and ask the torrent of questions clamoring for release, she climbed inside. One question rose above all else. She twirled around to inspect the backseat.

Theo was there.

He was not alone.

PART 2

The only free road, the Underground Railroad,
is owned and managed by the Vigilant
Committee. They have tunneled under the
whole breadth of the land.
—HENRY DAVID THOREAU

CHAPTER 13

The call came while Les was finishing his six-mile run on the treadmill at the local gym. Without slowing, he plucked his cell phone from the plastic holder and eyed the number. It was a 212 area code. New York City. He wiped the sweat off his ear.

"This is Les."

"Les? Stephen Kincaid." The words tumbled out as if they couldn't be spoken fast enough. "Zoe's father. We talked last week?"

"Of course." Les continued to jog, pumping his free arm. "What can I do for you?"

"She's—she's disappeared. We woke up this morning and she was gone, her backpack was gone. We've already called the police. Please, you have to do something!"

Les jabbed the treadmill's emergency stop button and slid backward off the machine.

"You weren't supposed to let her out of your sight!"

"She must have left in the middle of the night—What could we do? Lock her up?"

"You said she's very independent, right? Could she have run away on her own?"

An irritated sigh came over the line. "I can't believe she wouldn't tell anyone, not even her grandfather. They're bonded at the hip."

"And he doesn't know anything?"

"That's what he says, but he's a bit of a rebel, my father-in-law. I wouldn't be surprised if he had something to do with this." Les heard a woman's angry shout in the background. "Sorry, my wife thinks I'm just being paran—"

"Hello? Les?" interrupted a panicked female voice. "It's Pam. Is there anything you can do to help us?"

"Everything in my power." He was having trouble keeping his voice even. "But first we have to try to rule out the most serious scenario."

"The Network? Do you really think they could have—?"

Les clenched his teeth. "I'm afraid it's possible."

Her shriek pierced his eardrum. He glanced around, searching for privacy. The joggers on the treadmills were plugged into their headphones, paying him no attention.

"Listen to me. I need you to stay calm while I look into this. I'll call you when I know more."

As they hung up, snatches of images bombarded him—Zoe Kincaid's cherubic face, the splashy headlines that would be all over this story if she wasn't found stat, the map of the U.S. on his wall, with its twenty-seven red pushpins from coast to coast, where each prior victim had vanished. *Still twenty-seven,* he thought. *No more than twenty-seven.*

For the rest of the morning, he waited in dread, going in a blur from the gym to his office, hoping that any second Stephen would call back to say she had come home. No call came. Finally, just after 11:00 A.M., the mail arrived. He quickly scanned the pile of letters, memos, packages. And then he saw it—a post-card of the Earth revolving around the sun. On the back was Zoe's name, the same cryptic message—*And yet again it moves*—and Galileo's bold signature. It was postmarked from D.C. yesterday, when she was still safe at home—which meant her abduction had been carefully planned and executed. There was no telling where she was now.

The next moment the phone was in his hand, Stephen Kincaid on the line.

"Don't move," he instructed. "I'm getting on the next flight to New York."

This day was getting worse by the hour. When his flight landed, Les received a message from Benjamin Barrow at the committee with more bad news—Natalie Roy had been bailed out of jail, and now she and her teenage son were nowhere to be found. A mystery man had posted every last penny of her $250,000 bail, which the FBI had already traced to an offshore Cayman Islands account in the name of G.I. Joe—an insult and a mockery, in Les's opinion. Exactly the kind of stunt the Network prided itself on.

The New York media was reporting that the man

who had come to Natalie's rescue was her ex-husband, with a picture of their embrace on every outlet's home page, but Les was informed that her actual ex-husband had been tracked down in Oregon and knew nothing of her plight.

The close-ups of the man at the jail proved no help. His baseball cap and black aviator sunglasses covered half his face. What was left—a slightly hooked nose and overgrown stubble—was not enough to positively ID him against any other photos on file, though the FBI was trying to find a match. Les felt certain there would be none. Because if he was working for the Network, he was a clean specimen—an agent sent to do Galileo's dirty work. Rounding up targets. Natalie. Her son. Zoe.

Now where was he taking them, and why?

By the time Les arrived in his chauffeured car at the Kincaid brownstone on a tree-lined Upper West Side block, he had received yet another disturbing update—one that he guessed would not go over well with Zoe's parents.

Her mother ushered him inside, all pleasantries forgotten. From the look of the home, one would have thought a violent crime had occurred. Yellow police tape marked off Zoe's upstairs bedroom. Police had clearly combed the entire house for evidence of an intruder. Furniture was out of place. Sofa cushions littered the floor of the living room, a chair was overturned in the kitchen, cabinet doors haphazardly flung open.

Pam, a curvaceous woman with auburn hair, showed Les to a spacious office in the rear of the apartment, which took up the first two floors of a brownstone. She halfheartedly apologized for the chaos. Behind them trailed Stephen, a big-boned, imposing man whose expression Les recognized. It was the realization that you were in hell. Last into the office came a slow, elderly man who wore a cast on his left arm and carried himself with the majesty of an older era. The grandfather. He also appeared concerned, though his body language lacked the anger of Stephen's, Les noted. No one seemed relaxed enough to sit down.

Stephen crossed his arms. "Do you know anything we don't already know?"

"We're dying for information," Pam said. "Please, anything at all."

Les glanced at the old man, wondering if he knew what was coming. Was that why he was so quiet?

"In fact I do." He cleared his throat and sat down in a black chair next to a large wooden desk. No one else moved. "I assume by now you've heard about Natalie Roy."

"We've been watching the news nonstop," Pam said. "Do you think the man who bailed her out is the same guy who took Zoe?"

"It is our suspicion, unfortunately."

"If I could get my hands on that maniac—" Stephen began. He dug his fingernails into his palms.

"We're doing everything we can," Les said. "We've set up an AMBER Alert to find the car, and we're tapping the phone records of those who could have even the slightest involvement. What we've found already is . . . startling."

"What?"

Les leveled his gaze at the grandfather. "You received a call on your cell phone from Natalie Roy on the night she took Zoe into her lab. At 9:37 P.M. It lasted five minutes and twenty-two seconds."

"Dad!" Pam exclaimed, whirling on him. "Is this true?"

"You checked into *my* records?" His eyes widened. "I barely even use the cell phone."

"I knew it!" Stephen shouted in his face. "Goddamn it, Silas!"

"Honey, stop, let him explain. I'm sure there's an explanation?"

"So you don't deny it," Les said. "You spoke to Natalie Roy that evening?"

"She called me," Silas said.

"And what did you discuss?"

"Nothing really. I can't remember that well."

"Dad, you have to tell us," Pam implored. "Come on."

"Silas, Zoe's life could be at stake. We absolutely need your full cooperation." Les's omitted threat hung in the air.

Stephen looked ready to explode. Pam put one hand on his back.

Silas shot his son-in-law a withering glare, then looked at Les. "I didn't do anything. She called me and asked to talk to Zoe, so I let her. She was no criminal then. I went to sleep. The next thing I knew, Zoe was coming home in a police escort. I had nothing to do with it."

"You facilitated it!" Stephen snapped. "What else do you know that you haven't told us?"

"Nothing! I swear it!" His wrinkled hands flew up, and right then, Les noticed a crinkly bulge in the front pocket of his shirt. When Silas caught him staring at it, the guilt on his face was unmistakable.

You're a terrible liar, Les thought, extending his hand. "Mind if I?"

"I'd rather not."

Pam clutched his arm. "Dad, please. No one will be angry with you if you just cooperate."

"Bullshit," he muttered. But he stuck two fingers into his shirt pocket, withdrew a folded piece of paper, and reluctantly handed it to Les. "I found it this morning, under my pillow. I swear on my father's grave, that's the last thing I know."

Les snatched it and read the bubbly handwriting aloud, the obvious script of a young teenage girl.

Gramps—Don't come after me. I'm doing this for us. Destroy this note as soon as you find it. I trust you. ♥ *Z*

Pam clasped a hand over her mouth. "No. No."

"They've brainwashed her!" Stephen cried. "How could we have let this happen?"

"Silas," Les said. "What is 'this' she's referring to? 'For us'?"

He shrugged. "I can only guess. She's been obsessed with this antiaging research ever since we found out about her condition. I know she's desperate to try to help me live longer, and if she has a unique genetic mutation . . . which seems highly probable . . ."

Les shook his head, chilled by a sense of foreboding. If some mercenary scientists unlocked Zoe's DNA for future generations to exploit—it was the beginning of the end.

He thought with disgust of the back alley near his childhood home in the Bronx. The place was teeming with cockroaches, their flat shiny shells skittering in all directions and spilling out into the street. Was that a microcosm for human life on Earth if too many people survived for too long? He thought of his mother, whose life had been marginalized already from poverty and disease, though she had deserved so much more. With even more restricted resources, what would become of all the people like her?

"I've got to get to work," he declared, rising to his feet. "We haven't got a minute to lose."

"I wish I could help more," Silas said. "That girl has a real mind of her own when she gets an idea in her head."

"Did she keep a diary?" Les asked. "Or anything that might give us some more insight?"

Pam was wiping a tear from her cheek. "The police tore the house apart and couldn't find a thing. Her laptop and cell phone are gone. We even broke the lock on her jewelry box, but there was nothing—"

"Wait!" Silas grabbed her wrist. "Has anyone checked her medicine cabinet?"

"Yes, Dad. Nothing was out of place, all her—" She broke off with a gasp. "Oh my God."

"No! It was there?"

"What?" Les demanded, glancing between them. "What was there?"

"I can't believe I didn't notice before, I was just so frantic. She must have forgotten it."

"She has a severe seizure disorder . . ." Stephen started, trailing off and shaking his head.

"A complication of her condition," Silas added. "She requires a special pill every day, or else . . . and . . ." He seemed on the verge of crying. His arthritic hands were trembling.

Les shifted his focus to Pam. The sight of the dignified old man so upset made him uncomfortable, a reminder of how carefully constructed his own composure might be.

"Could she have taken another bottle?"

Pam shook her head. "Our insurance only covers one bottle at a time. The pill is a combination of two antiepileptic drugs that are mixed in a specific ratio just for her. It's the only thing that works. And right now, it's upstairs."

CHAPTER 14

New York City
8:45 A.M.

"Theo! Zoe!" Natalie exclaimed, as the strange man jumped into the driver's seat next to her and slammed on the gas. "What are *you guys* doing here?"

Before anyone could answer, she reached out to touch her son's arm to make sure he was real. The sight of his handsome face seemed like a magic trick her deprived soul might have conjured up.

"Honey, are you okay? Are you hurt?"

"I'm fine, Mom." Any anger he was harboring toward her seemed to have melted away. "We're getting you out of here."

Next to him in the backseat, Zoe's indignation flashed in her eyes. "Did you think I was going to just sit back and watch them do this to you?"

"You're behind this? But how did you—?" She twisted in her seat to stare down the driver, who was navigating the city's narrow streets with the slick mastery of a native. She noticed they were rapidly heading northwest, toward the West Side Highway. "Where are we going? Who *are* you?"

"Galileo," Zoe said, "tell her."

Alarm spread through Natalie like a brushfire. She stared at him. "You're not really—?"

He was still wearing the Yankees baseball cap, sunglasses, and the prosthetic nose, and upon closer inspection, she could see that his trim black beard was also a guise. The stubble appeared just a little too even. But his lips were real—and they were smiling at her.

"It's great to meet you, too." His words carried a hint of an accent she couldn't quite place, faded British with a hint of something grittier, like Brooklyn.

Her fingers closed around the door handle. They were going sixty now, flying down the highway, much too fast to roll out. She glanced back at Theo and Zoe, examining them for signs of abuse or coercion. There seemed to be none—so far.

"Who are you?" she shouted. "And where are you taking us?"

"Mom," Theo said, "calm down."

"I will not calm down. What is going on?"

"It's pretty simple, actually." Galileo tore his eyes off the road to glance at her. "First off, anything you've heard about me is a lie."

Les Mahler's announcement in the meeting at Columbia last week came back to her. If he was right, this man was a dangerous radical who led some kind of shadowy cult that had claimed dozens of victims, all science-related, including—

"Where's Helen?" she demanded. "What have you done with her?"

"Oh, she's settling in wonderfully. I know she can't wait to see you."

Arctic cold prickled her arms. She whipped around to the backseat, her pulse racing in her fingertips. "Guys, we're going to jump out of this car the second it stops, *do you understand?*"

Theo rolled his eyes. "Come on."

"You're coming," Zoe said. "We're fine."

Appalled, Natalie fumbled to extract her cell phone out of the plastic bag of her possessions from the jail and jabbed at the power button.

The battery was dead.

"There's no need for that," said the man who called himself Galileo. "If you want to get out, I'm happy to let you off. In fact, I'll turn around and drive you back to your apartment, where you can wait out the summer without a job until your court date. Given the severity of your charges and those police witnesses, I'd say odds are good you'll do hard time." He grimaced, as if it pained him to think of her returning to prison. "Or you can hear me out."

"But you can't go back!" Zoe protested, leaning forward against her seat belt. "Not after all we've gone through to get you out."

Natalie, still clutching the door handle, stared from her to the man. "You better talk fast."

"I should correct myself," he said, a slight smile returning to his lips. "You do know one true thing about me—my name."

"Your parents named you Galileo?"

"Our given names are irrelevant. It's how we identify ourselves that counts."

Outside, the gleaming gray river snaked by along

the highway. Now they were doing seventy-five. How come, the one and only time she wanted it, there was no traffic?

"As you seem to be aware," he went on, "I'm the leader of a grassroots movement that's in the midst of waging an underground scientific revolution."

"Oh," she muttered, "I'm aware."

"Let me guess. In a meeting at Columbia, Les Mahler told you we're a cult?"

She raised her eyebrows. "How could you know that?"

"Well-placed sources, my dear."

Then she remembered. "The mole!" It was probably Mitch. No one else in the department could match his spirit in ugliness. "I know just who it was, too."

Galileo chuckled, not at all insulted. "First off, the Network is no cult. We're a band of volunteers that have gotten together to accelerate progress."

They were about to exit Manhattan, speeding toward the Lincoln Tunnel. At least, she thought, they might pass through a tollbooth on the other end—maybe she could wave down an attendant somehow. But unless they hit congestion in the tunnel, she'd only have a split second . . .

"All of the people who've appeared to vanish," he was saying, "actually sought out my help or someone on their behalf did. Our mission is to give experts like you the total freedom required to pursue biomedical advances as quickly and efficiently as possible. No board-required approvals, no drug companies or bu-reaucrats pushing agendas, no byzantine FDA regula-tions. We started several years ago, funded by venture capitalists in Silicon Valley, with one specific project in mind—and that's multiplied as more and more scientists and doctors have escaped their traditional careers to join our movement." Darkness descended as they raced into the tunnel. Galileo paused as he switched lanes to avoid an aggressive driver who was riding his tail.

"We now have about six hundred allied members in strategic locations around the country, who enable us to privately transport our crew and supplies. In return, they and their families are first on the list for our innovative therapies currently under development. It's like the Underground Railroad for science. This time the slavery is less obvious—though no less insidious."

She frowned. "Who's enslaved?"

"You."

"Me?"

"You. And other unconventional, risk-taking scientists like you."

"By whom?"

"Good old Uncle Sam."

"How do you figure?"

"Les Mahler's Bioethics Committee is a great example. They're just a bunch of glorified policemen with fancy degrees and a fear of change."

She opened her mouth to retort, but realized she didn't disagree. The way Les Mahler had studied her and the other scientists at that meeting, it was as though they were a bunch of wayward tinkerers who required his close watch, lest their experiments upend society. It was worse than a lack of respect, it was disdain.

"And a million other ways that come together to inhibit brilliance and risk and innovation," Galileo added. "Maybe it's refusing your grant requests, or your tenure, or cutting off your funding, or pulling your clinical trial, or delaying approval of your drug, depending on the politics and the powers involved." He did a quick check over his shoulder and switched lanes again, accelerating into a spot ahead of a slow driver.

"Or maybe it's big pharma," he went on, "only funding research that will help their bottom line, not necessarily the real revolutionary work that's crying to be done, but that won't yield a profit for years or decades to come. That's where the Network comes in. At our headquarters, we've now got refugees from the system researching stem cells, cloning, memory manipulation, synthetic life, 3-D organ printing, and our biggest project of all. The project that united the movement with a single vision, that got us our funding, and that I believe will change the world as we know it."

Natalie's heart was pounding. She was no longer aware that they had passed through the tunnel, out into the bright open sunlight. "Which is?"

"To finally address the question people have asked since the beginning of time—*Why are we mortal?*" He took off his sunglasses and looked at her, and in his blue eyes, she was surprised to detect a profound sadness. "You and Zoe are the two people we need to help us find the answer."

"See?" Zoe piped up in her girlish voice from the backseat. "This is totally legit, it's the best thing that could have happened to us!"

Natalie closed her eyes, her mind reeling. "So what you're telling me is, there's a secret lab somewhere in America where you want to take us to research the cure for aging?"

"Not just *a* lab. We've got forty-five of them, mostly

underground, with a whole team in place who can't wait to meet you. Geneticists, biostatisticians, physiologists, radiologists, endocrinologists. I have to say, your paper from last year in *Rejuvenation Research* on the developmental theory of aging is very popular in the compound."

She snorted. "If you're trying to lure me to my grave, that's a good one."

"Ever the skeptic, aren't you?"

If anything, her doubt seemed to please him.

"What scientist worth her weight isn't?"

He nodded, keeping his focus on the road. Now they were in New Jersey, and the spiky skyline of Manhattan was little more than a box of matchsticks through the rear window.

"Helen warned me you were stubborn. Here." He reached into his pocket and tossed a silver cell phone into her lap. "Call her."

Natalie's mouth fell open. "Really?"

"Of course. I was going to lead with that, but you kept cutting me off. Not that I blame you."

"What if I just called the cops right now?"

"You could. But I'm not worried."

"Why not?"

"I think you know why."

She held the phone, glancing again behind her to make sure Theo and Zoe were okay. They were watching her calmly. Of course they were. Teenagers always took the least amount of convincing to join rebellions.

But that was what she prided herself most on at that age, too. She recalled her college protests against communism with other so-called activists, who were really just kids with a penchant for going against the grain.

She'd always been attracted to other nonconformists, whether they were celebrated or misunderstood or maligned, as long as they were fighting for principles she could respect.

Principles like Galileo's.

If he was sincere. But there was a nagging feeling in the back of her mind—if only she could bring the thought to the surface.

She closed her hand around the phone, noticing her knuckles were white.

"Did you find her?" he asked, his eyes on the road. "She's the only Helen."

She stared at the number listed for her closest friend, a number with an area code she'd never even heard of, hoping this wasn't a trick born of a madman's cruelty. On top of all else, she didn't think she could bear to hear Helen sounding desperate or tortured—if she was even alive.

"Well?" he said.

"Found it."

She pressed the phone to her ear and waited.

CHAPTER 15

A familiar voice answered "Hello."

Natalie's throat tightened. "Helen?"

"Nat?"

"Hel, oh my God. Is it really you?" Hot tears spilled over her lids, tumbling down her cheeks. It was the first time she had allowed herself to cry. "Are you really okay?"

"I'm better than okay. I wanted to call you, but by the time I got here, you'd been arrested. Guess inmates can't accept collect calls . . . Are *you* okay?"

Natalie laughed through her tears. "I've been so worried about you. I'm . . ." She trailed off. How could she communicate, in Galileo's presence, that she wasn't sure if he was a clever rebel or a dangerous lunatic? And that two innocent kids—well, people—in the backseat, whether they knew it or not, were depending on her judgment for survival?

"You're . . . ?" Helen prompted. "You must be with Galileo?"

"Right." She snuck a peek at him to see how closely he was listening. But he was craning his neck to say something to Theo and Zoe. In the rearview mirror, she caught them smiling at him.

"I know exactly what you're thinking," Helen said. "And you know what? You don't have to worry one bit. Wait until you see what he's created."

"So you really are fine?" It was difficult to shake the chilling image that had been haunting her, of Helen gagged and bound, or worse. "You're safe?"

"Safer than I've probably ever been. I have my own lab. Everyone here does. We're all doing our own cutting-edge thing, hands free of IRBs and the FDA and all that. I actually fit in for once in my life, and so will you."

"I want to," she admitted, feeling her internal wall of skepticism start to crumble. She hadn't realized how badly she wanted to believe Galileo. Yet her scientist instincts were like iron girders, keeping the wall intact. She doubted the appearance of truth unless it could stand up against rigorous testing. Helen's cheery voice alone wasn't proof of her well-being. What if, right now, she was being force-fed her words by one of Galileo's henchmen?

Through the window, Natalie noticed a billboard off the highway advertising a botanical garden. An orchard of cherry blossoms was pictured.

"Hey, remember the gardenia plant?" she said, thinking fast. "The one you got me for my birthday?"

"Of course, why?"

"Are there any gardenias where you are? Or would you say daffodils are more common?"

There was a pause. "Um . . ."

"Ballpark guess." She cleared her throat. "More daffodils or gardenias? Lilies or roses? You know me with flowers."

Come on, she willed, *remember the poisonous house-plants.* Daffodils and lilies were toxic if consumed, while gardenias and roses were harmless. It was a cryptic attempt, but Helen had gotten her bachelor's degree in botany before turning to molecular biology.

Another pause. Then Helen burst out laughing. "God, I miss you. There's nothing but fields of gardenias here. And roses."

"Whole fields?" Out of the corner of her eye, she noticed Galileo glancing at her quizzically.

"As far as the eye can see."

"So where is this fairyland?"

"Ask him. We're not supposed to discuss it over the phone. But you're in good hands, okay? He'll get you here safely, you just have to trust him."

After they hung up, Natalie's shoulders loosened and she sank back into the passenger seat. Their conversation was aloe, fading her sting of suspicion. It seemed that she and the kids really were safe. She handed the phone back to Galileo. Blue sky stretched for miles overhead, hardly a cloud in sight. Through the window, the sun's rays were warming her shoulder like a caress, a tangible reminder of her freedom—thanks to this man.

"Feeling better?" he asked. "I can still turn around, if you want. No one who comes to the compound is ever forced, and I plan to keep it that way."

A nagging feeling popped through Natalie's consciousness—a body had been found. A scientist murdered in his own lab. Les Mahler had told them so.

Her heart began to pound. Casually, so as not to spook the kids, she turned the dial on the car radio to the first music station she could find, one blasting classic rock. She inched the volume up and opened her window to the roar of the wind.

Galileo grinned. "There we go."

His smile vanished when she looked at him. It was hard to reconcile how a man with such kind eyes could be evil. She could see how Helen could have gotten sucked in. She kept her voice low, so only he could hear.

"Don't scare the kids, but you're going to get off on the next exit and drop us off at the first place we see. No screwing around. Is that clear?"

"Whoa, what happened?"

"You almost had me, too." She shook her head. "It's like you know just what I wanted to hear. And then you come off all righteous. You're unbelievable."

He seemed confused. "What are you talking about?"

She spoke through gritted teeth. "You killed that man in his own lab. You let his animals maul him to death! How could you?"

A look of realization—and fury—crossed over his face. "I didn't," he said. "Someone framed me. I'd never even heard of the poor guy until word got back to me that *I* was the one responsible for his death."

"Come on."

He lifted his right hand from the wheel as if taking an oath. "I swear on my life. I was at the compound when I first heard about it. Hundreds of miles away from D.C."

"How can you expect me to believe that? What about the postcard you sent?"

"I never sent it. Those are dollar-store postcards anyone can find. We have our reasons for using them.

But the thing I don't get is—how could anyone copy my exact message unless that person had seen an example before? And we only send them to the headquarters of the Bioethics Committee."

"So you're saying someone there framed you? That's crazy."

He shook his head. "I really don't know. I wish I could explain it. All I know is the actual murderer wanted to get rid of that scientist for some reason and blame it on me so he'd never be suspected."

She raised her eyebrows. "That the best you can do?"

"That's the truth."

The way he said it, without adornment or apology, made her believe it.

"So you aren't a killer, then."

"Never." He briefly took his eyes off the road to look at her. His face was dead serious. "My mission is recruitment and productivity, not torture and death. If I'd known that guy was in trouble I would have gotten him out of there. Why do you think he was the only person whose body was left behind?"

"True. It doesn't fit the pattern." She was surprised at how relieved she felt by his explanation. Her head rested against the cool glass of her window.

"Everyone else has come into the Network of their own accord, thanks to my help. As I told you, it's always their choice—there's never any struggle. Sometimes they leave behind a suicide note so no one will come after them, but that's their choice, too."

She exhaled. Either she could believe him, and Helen's account of him—or Les Mahler's. An exit on the highway was fast approaching.

He motioned to it. "Do you want me to get off? It's up to you."

"No," she said. "No, I think we can go on."

She turned around to check again on Theo and Zoe. Oblivious to the anxiety that had gripped her moments before, they were playing a game on an iPad.

"Where did that come from?"

"I got it for them. We've got a long drive ahead of us."

She smiled. The fact that he had considered the happiness of the kids, even if it seemed like a minor detail, reassured her of her decision. She let herself relax against the seat.

"So how did you find my son? And Zoe? Where are we going? And how long are we planning to stay there?"

"One at a time," he said with a smile.

The radio was still blaring, and despite the obnoxious volume, she was thankful for the privacy it afforded them.

"Theo's supposed to start college in the fall," she said. "I can't just keep him cooped up in some secret research compound forever."

"Of course not," he said, matching her lowered voice as a Bon Jovi song poured from the speakers. "I thought you'd want to have him near you at least at first. But let's see how things go. Most of our researchers work and live there full-time, though you can leave at any time. If you choose to stay, we can always send him to live with a nearby member until he goes off to college. Once you're part of the Network, you're family."

The last word resounded in her mind. For years, it

had meant one person only—her son. How she longed to give him the brothers and sisters who never materialized, the aunts and uncles who didn't exist, the grandparents who had died of old age, the father who might as well have died. To be welcomed by strangers into a whole thriving community—it made a lump grow in her throat. She had always been conscious of the need to treat others well, but this was on another level entirely.

"But wait," she said, as another question occurred to her, "if my theory on aging is so popular, then why haven't you sought me out sooner?"

"Adler didn't want to lose you."

"*Adler?* As in, my former boss, *Professor* Adler?"

"The one and only."

"I don't understand. How could you—? Oh my God, are you saying that *Adler*—?"

"Is the mole?" He grinned. "I'm afraid so."

She shook her head, thinking back to when Les Mahler had announced to Adler that his department was harboring a mole connected to the Network. So his horrified expression had been feigned. He must have been hiding his amusement at the irony. She turned down the music to process this surprise.

"I can't believe this. I just can't believe this."

"Adler's been one of us since the beginning. He tipped me off to Helen's plight, and then yours. I wanted to come for you last year after I read your paper—I knew we needed you badly—but he said you were getting groomed for tenure and you could already do your research there. But then we found out about Zoe, and that changed everything. We knew she could be walking proof of your whole idea of developmental inertia, and that you two had to link up. So when Columbia didn't go for it—nice try, by the way—and Adler was forced to fire you, he knew your work was far from over. That it's only just beginning."

She was unaware that her mouth was hanging open. "Did you guys hear that?" she said, craning around to the backseat.

"I already knew all that, Mom," Theo said, without taking his eyes off the iPad. "Adler called me to explain everything when you were in jail."

"And Dr. Carlyle told me," said Zoe. "That's how I knew it was legit."

"We just didn't count on you getting arrested," Galileo said. "You couldn't give up, could you?" Despite his tone of mock annoyance, his voice carried an overtone of admiration.

"If only I'd known!"

"I was already on my way the night you went to jail, so then I had to go back and wait until your bail posted. An unfortunate wrinkle, but we managed to straighten it out, didn't we?"

She couldn't stop shaking her head in disbelief. "All this trouble you went to, all this money, for me?"

"We need you, Natalie. Together with my team, you and Zoe might just set the world on fire."

Her heart was racing again. "Where is this place?"

"Tonight we're headed to Ohio. But that's just our stop for the night. It's one of our safe houses along the Underground."

"And then? The end goal?"

"The last place on earth where you would expect to find a world-class research center." He switched hands on the wheel and flashed her a grin. "Any guesses?"

"No. Just tell me."

"Not even one guess?"

"Oh, I don't know. The lost city of Atlantis?"

"Nope."

"Carved into Mount Rushmore?"

"Nope, but you're getting closer."

She frowned, more bewildered than ever. "I give up."

A high-pitched shriek from the backseat interrupted them. He slammed on the brakes and Natalie's arms flew to block her face. A delicate hand closed around her shoulder and shook it.

"No!" Zoe shouted. "Look!"

CHAPTER 16

Zoe clutched Theo's hand when she saw the words in amber lights flashing ten feet above the highway:

CHILD ABDUCTION

BLACK HONDA CIVIC

NY LIC: ADL 4671

Theo, eighteen years old with a runner's long-legged physique, was the kind of guy who exuded charisma—exactly the kind who never looked twice at her. But now his hand felt clammy in hers and his face was pale. Despite her own fear, the tingly sensation of their palms together surprised her. She had never held hands with a guy before.

"How could you let this happen?" Natalie demanded, nearly screaming at Galileo. "Now we're both going to jail!"

He didn't answer right away. Zoe watched his precision multitasking as he typed a rapid text message on his phone while navigating the four-lane highway. So far, he had the unflappable disposition of an army commander, without the sternness.

"Not to worry," he said. "Just a slight blip, that's all."

"Someone is probably calling the cops right now!"

He glanced over his shoulder as he switched to an emptier lane. They were doing eighty, the clear afternoon sky evoked calm, and the road was pretty deserted. How many people even paid attention to those signs?

Zoe sought eye contact with Theo to gauge his level of concern, but as soon as she looked at him, he turned toward the window and released her hand. A little stab of hurt pricked her.

"Are we going to get caught?" she asked, hating how childish her voice sounded. She wondered if that was why she didn't feel as afraid as Theo and Natalie were—she was naive. Her father's hurtful words flooded back to her. *You're just like a child. You don't know any better.* But Gramps had never said that. Oh, Gramps! One teeny tiny part of her felt that it would be fine if they did get caught. She could run home into his arms and tell him she tried. But no—that wouldn't do either of them any good. He was looking older by the day.

"Leave it to me," Galileo said. "I've—"

They all heard the distant wolflike howl that cut him off.

Natalie pressed her face to the window. "What was that?"

Zoe felt her stomach lurch. There was no mistaking the sound of a siren. The howl grew sharper, louder, soon becoming an all-out wail. She reached again for Theo, but he yanked off his seat belt and hurled himself onto the floor.

"Get down!" he shrieked at her. "Hurry!"

She obliged, nearly toppling onto him before falling behind Galileo's seat into the fetal position.

"Let me do the talking," she heard him say to Natalie.

Their car slowed and pulled over to the shoulder. Red and blue lights danced through the rear window, their glare reflecting off the vinyl floor mat near her face.

"What can you possibly say?" Natalie hissed. "It's over!"

Zoe curled her limbs in tight like a fist. Her whole body was quivering as the car rolled to a stop. Her mind raced—*handcuffs, jail, Gramps, death.*

She heard Galileo's window slide open.

"Hello, Officer." He sounded as relaxed as if he were greeting a friend. "Did you find us all right?"

Did he what?!

"Sure did," came a stranger's Midwestern drawl. "I left as soon as I got your text. The calls are already coming in."

"What will you do with our car?"

"Leave it down by the junkyard. I'll destroy the plates."

"And you remembered the radio?"

"Got it right here. The dispatcher won't know the difference."

"Fine. When does your shift end?"

"Midnight."

"So can you make it to Columbus and back before then to make the trade?"

"No prob."

"Then I'll text you the address. Please get us a rental

sedan for one week. Nothing flashy, no red. Here's the ID, and the card to bill."

"You got it."

"Sorry for the last-minute emergency."

"I'm happy to help. I didn't know if I'd ever get the chance."

As Zoe's spinning brain tried to make sense of their exchange, her door swung open. A warm breeze drifted into the car. She peeled her hands away from her eyes and gaped at the man standing two feet away. He was a muscular young officer with a shaved head and intelligent brown eyes.

"So you're the wonder kid," he said.

"I'm not a kid," she retorted. "And no one's abducted me. There's been a big misunderstanding."

"I don't think so," he replied, reaching in to grab her hand. She kicked him away and scooted back, leaning up against Theo.

"Whoa there, little miss. I'm not gonna hurt you."

Galileo edged him aside and poked his reassuring face into the backseat, hovering inches above her. "It's fine, Zoe. Let's go."

She took his hand and hauled herself out of the car just as the officer got into their car's driver's seat. Standing on the side of the highway, with her long hair slapping her face, she felt as exposed as if she were naked.

Galileo ducked his head back into the car. "Guys, get out. Hurry."

Natalie and Theo complied without argument, springing out of the car and joining them on the road's narrow shoulder. They lined up along the metal fence that separated the highway from a field of swaying grass.

"Where are we going?" Zoe asked, trying to keep her balance. Every time a car zoomed by, the hot wind gusted hard enough to blow her sideways.

"This way," he yelled over the roar of the traffic. He led them toward the police car parked behind theirs. It was empty.

"Get in." He motioned to the scary-looking backseat, which was cut off from the front by a solid plank of glass. Zoe obeyed, and Theo climbed in after her. Natalie went around to the front and jumped in as Galileo took the wheel and shut the door. Up ahead, Zoe could see their old Civic pulling into traffic.

Their new car jumped forward with the ferocity of a lion on the prowl. In seconds, they had gotten up to full speed and passed the Civic. Zoe watched it disappear in their wake and then turned to Theo, openmouthed. This time, he acknowledged her sentiment with a dazed shrug. Static noises of the police radio were sputtering in through the dashboard up front, but Galileo hit a switch and silence filled the car.

"What the hell?" Natalie said. "Do you have some kind of superpower that was invented on the compound?"

He chuckled, leaning back with one hand on the wheel. "Just quick thinking. The Underground is strategically spread out along a few special routes we've carved out, like this one."

"We're on a route right now?"

"Yep. Besides recruiting scientists, we've concentrated most on establishing allies in law enforcement. We've made sure to have at least one in every precinct along our routes, just in case of an emergency like this. This plan was made and rehearsed long ago."

Zoe tapped on the glass that divided the backseat from the front. She could still feel the adrenaline pounding through her body and was pretty sure Theo could, too. His palms lay flat against the seat and his upper lip was glistening with sweat. Natalie must have noticed as she slid the glass open.

"Are you all right, honey?"

He exhaled. "Better than ever."

"What's wrong?"

"Oh, nothing, just that you almost got arrested again and I've got no money and nowhere to go. Everything's great!"

"But she didn't," Galileo said. "Don't worry, Theo, nothing bad will happen to you or your mom as long as I can help it."

Or to me, Zoe thought. *Right?*

Natalie looked at him. "Thanks. But how can you trust a cop? What if he's playing you?"

"I was just going to ask the same thing," Zoe chimed in, even though she wasn't. Now that she was away from home, she silently vowed to put more effort into thinking like the grown-up she wanted to be, no matter her age. To start, she'd learn from Natalie's example and try to think of smart questions. Out the window, a suburban strip mall passed by with the typical big-box stores. It was hard to believe that this mundane landscape was actually an elite organization's top secret route.

"The short answer," replied Galileo, "is, I can't. So I've developed a system that tests loyalty and sincerity. There are no requirements of race or class to be in the Network, which I feel very strongly about. Freedom should never discriminate. But members are initiated only after they pass certain tests, and even then, no one outside the compound knows enough to endanger it. Which is why, I hope you'll understand, I haven't been totally forthright about where we're going. Not until we get there, just in case we get separated and you're questioned."

"So you're like the spider in the web," Natalie said. "You weaved it and now you're holding it together."

"I'm sure that's how Les Mahler thinks of me. To him, I'm a tarantula."

"So what if something happens to you?" Theo asked. "What would we do?"

"Yeah," Zoe said. "Then what?"

"Well"—Galileo's blue eyes met Zoe's in the rearview mirror—"you've found the Network's Achilles' heel."

She swallowed hard. "You?"

"The truth is, it all depends on my expertise and connections. I do have safeguards in place that I can't disclose. But if anything did happen to me, things would be very difficult."

"Then what are you doing driving us out in the open like this?" Natalie snapped. "Can't you hire someone to do this kind of thing?"

"I often do. But this time is different. You and Zoe are the two people the Network was born to recruit. Our whole central mission is to figure out and defeat the cause of aging. So how could I let anyone else be in charge of transporting you? I know all the ins and outs of the Underground, every ally in every city, every backup plan by heart."

"He's kind of a control freak," Theo whispered to Zoe. "Don't you think?"

"Yeah, and I'm glad," she whispered back with a

smile—too big of a smile, but she couldn't help it. He'd acknowledged her again, and this time, let her in on his own private observation. She wondered if it was possible—in spite of her freakishness—that he could find her the slightest bit attractive.

"But there's one other thing," Galileo was saying to Natalie, "that you need to know."

"What?"

"I assume you're familiar with the Archon Prize?"

She snorted. "That's like asking a physicist if he's ever heard of the Nobel."

"I don't know what it is," Zoe said, embarrassed but too curious to resist.

"It's a competition that was developed a few years ago by a bunch of old, really rich guys to incentivize progress in finding the cause of aging," Natalie explained. "The goal is to submit breakthroughs by the deadline, and then a bunch of experts are going to get together and assess which is the most promising. The prize is twenty million bucks for further research."

"And," Galileo added, "you can submit anonymously. We've identified this competition as a way to pull in significantly more funding for the Network, which has expanded so fast that we need the capital desperately. But combined with the bad economy, we're headed for trouble. Our investors are shrinking just when we need them the most."

Natalie cocked her head at him. "So you spent a quarter million bucks to get me out of jail?"

He switched hands on the wheel and looked at her. "I've read every paper you've published. It's the smartest investment we've made."

In the backseat, Zoe saw Theo smiling proudly on

his mother's behalf, though Natalie threw her outstretched palms into the air.

"But you're betting the house on me! What if it's all for nothing?"

"You know what they say in Vegas," he said. "Go big or go home."

"When's the deadline?"

"December thirty-first."

Her mouth hung open. "That's six months away!"

"That's right."

"Impossible!"

"Nothing's impossible when you have the kind of talent and resources I've gathered."

She buried her fingers in her glossy brown hair. "And if we don't make it in time?"

"Then we don't make it. But right now," he said, "you and Zoe are our best hope."

I'm needed, Zoe thought with a sense of awe. *I'm needed by something so much bigger than myself.* She turned her wrists over and studied the blue-green veins intertwining under her delicate skin. It was amazing to think that the blood coursing through her thin veins might contain the secret to human longevity.

Theo was watching her. When she looked up, he smiled too quickly at her—an attempt to mask his morbid fascination. She could see in his eyes the visceral urge to recoil.

"I'm still human," she said.

He opened his mouth, looking guilty, but said nothing. She turned away with a pang in her chest. Even if she did contribute to some paradigm-shifting breakthrough, would she always remain an unloved freak? And how many years of loneliness was she looking at?

For all the awe and specialness she felt, nothing could overpower the tragedy she knew was hers and hers alone.

Exhaustion set in. This had been one of the most eventful days of her life, and the hum of the engine was lulling her to sleep. She laid her head against the window and closed her eyes. No one bothered her, even when they pulled off at a deserted rest stop to stock up on food and stretch their legs.

When she woke, twisting her neck back and forth uncomfortably, the sky was deepening to a violet dusk. Their surroundings had changed. Rather than a highway through a dense forest, they were passing through a small town with an upscale main street filled with small boutiques and restaurants. Beyond it, roofs of suburban houses sprawled out in rows. She wondered where the brown-eyed police officer was, and how soon he would come to meet up with them. Uneasiness plagued her. What if he really was untrustworthy?

"We're almost there," Galileo announced. "Tonight we're staying at the home of Julian Hernandez, a wonderful friend of the Network who's volunteered to host us. Once we arrive, we'll all eat and shower and rest. We've got another big day of driving tomorrow and will be starting out at dawn."

"Not in this cop car, right?" she asked.

"No, the officer needs it back, so he'll be dropping off a clean rental later tonight. No one looking for you will have any lead to it."

She didn't protest, despite her anxiety over going somewhere unknown. Last summer, it had been intimidating enough to make the move to Northeastern, only a few hours away. But she wasn't a little girl. She could handle it.

She lifted her arm to roll down the window for some fresh air—

Her arm stayed still.

She tried again, but it was as stiff as cement, and the stiffness was spreading rapidly. She could feel it propel through her like venom, the all-too-familiar symptom of her worst nightmare.

Help, she gasped. *Get my pills!*

The thoughts were clear, but no words came out. Her tongue flapped uselessly as her limbs started to flail. She tried again, struggling against the blackness that was engulfing her.

My pills!

Theo's distorted voice reached her ears from far away, as though he were shouting into a well.

"She's having a seizure!"

His hands clamped down on her wild arms.

Then the world went dark.

CHAPTER 17

Les knew something was very wrong. After he'd landed back in Washington, D.C., he'd learned that the black Honda Civic, NY license ADL 4671, had been spotted along Interstate 70, near Wheeling, West Virginia, at 5:15 P.M. A cop car left the nearby station at 5:18 P.M. to find it—and hadn't been heard from since. The Civic had also vanished—no other sightings had been reported, even though the AMBER Alert continued to flash on every major highway along the East Coast.

It was now just past 8:00 P.M., and the sky was darkening along with his mood. The sunset he normally enjoyed through his office's west window now seemed repulsive, as if the sky's colors were bleeding upon the open wound of the horizon.

He couldn't stop pacing across his office in the committee's headquarters. Zoe and Natalie were in that Civic, he was sure of it, along with the mysterious driver who had to be one of Galileo's underlings. Where could they have gone? He'd lost track of how many times he'd called the police dispatcher to check on the missing cop car, but there was no news. It frustrated him that the small-town precinct in West Virginia—from which the cop had originated—had not yet retrofitted their squad with internal GPS trackers, so that missing car could not be traced. The more time went by, the farther away the fugitives were getting.

His only hope was the clue Zoe's parents had given about her medication. Her mother guaranteed, with tears in her eyes, that she would suffer a seizure within hours unless she took it. Les had spent the entire day spreading an alert, with the help of the FBI's Science and Technology division, to every major hospital and pharmacy within five hundred miles to watch for either the admittance of a girl matching Zoe's description or the prescription call-in of the rare medication she required.

Every time the black phone on his desk rang, his heart leaped. Every time, he pictured the face he now knew well, though had never seen in person—her cornflower blue eyes, her freckled nose, her pink lips. Was she wise enough to be afraid, he wondered, or clueless about the dangers that awaited her in the grip of the Network? Despite her restricted capacity, she had to know that the potential for exploitation of her body was staggering.

He was her only hope of rescue. But as to what he was planning to do when he found her—a grim possibility was already crossing his mind. This was war; not just between Galileo and him, but between man and nature, hubris and restraint, future destruction and present salvation. Sacrifices would have to be made. He thought of all the future people whose lives would turn freakish, who would suffer untold consequences for agreeing to try an experimental drug if one were wrought by Zoe's DNA. It shocked him when he really thought about it, the suffering that scientists could carelessly inflict on others under the auspices of good.

It would be simple to divert the blame.

The phone jingled, piercing the stillness of the office. He sprinted to it and pounced before the second ring.

"Hello?"

"It's me." Benjamin Barrow, the committee's second-in-command. "Any news?"

Les sighed. "I'd call you."

"Still no sign of the Civic?"

"Not for almost three hours."

"It doesn't make sense." Barrow's tone was irritable, bordering on disapproval. The subtle note piqued Les's fury—as if he wasn't doing everything possible, flying to New York and back, meeting the girl's family, making every damn phone call he could think of. And where was his esteemed colleague? Attending some fancy bioethics conference in California, enjoying a bunch of free food and adulation, in the midst of the most serious case of their careers.

"They're going to have to stop for gas at some point," Les said through clenched teeth. "All area stations have been alerted." He didn't add the part about the hospitals and pharmacies as well, in case Barrow decided to demean his strategy before it had a chance to work. "When will you be back?"

"As soon as I can. My talk is tomorrow night. Try to keep things under control until I get there."

"Thanks." Les didn't even try to conceal his sarcasm. *Jerk.*

He hung up before he said anything he would regret.

It was agitating how quickly the phone rang again, as if touching its cradle triggered the ring.

"What?" he snapped, assuming it was Barrow calling back.

"Uh, is this Les Mahler?"

"Speaking."

"This is Officer Laughlin calling from the Thirteenth Precinct in Columbus, Ohio. We just got a call from the CVS pharmacy on Parsons Avenue that the medicine on the special alert was called in about five minutes ago."

"Columbus, you said?"

"Yes. You want us to send a SWAT team?"

With a few nimble clicks, Les brought up a map of Ohio on his 27-inch monitor and zoomed in. If the Civic had continued on Interstate 70 going east after passing through Wheeling, West Virginia, at 5:15 P.M., it could feasibly be 150 miles away, placing it right around—*yes!*—Columbus, Ohio.

"Get them there *ASAP*," Les instructed, "and I'll send in reinforcement if need be."

"You got it."

Les stared at the map. "You're four hundred miles northwest of D.C.?"

"Thereabout."

"Change of plans. Let's keep this quiet. I want you to send an unmarked car. Plainclothes cops. Have them trail whoever picks up the drug. One little bee could lead to the whole hive."

"So no arrests?"

"Not right away," he said, thinking of the FBI's air fleet at his disposal. "Not until I get there. I'm on my way."

"You got it."

Les smirked as he hung up: a certain condescending partner wouldn't learn the news until it was too late for him to share in any of the glory.

CHAPTER 18

Zoe awoke to the sensation of a cold wet compress against her sweaty forehead. Her mother's arms tightened around her from behind, hoisting her up. Wait, not her mother. The arms were covered with brown hair, strong and muscular. And then she remembered: Galileo.

"You're back," he said, in a voice filled with relief.

She struggled to sit up, fighting nausea. She was stretched out against him in the leather backseat of the cop car. Theo and Natalie were in the front, watching her through the divider.

"Slow," Galileo commanded.

She sank back against his arms, closing her eyes. "What happened?"

"You had a seizure. We couldn't find your medication."

"Oh my God." In her mind, she could see the bathroom cabinet where she had forgotten the bottle. A lump clogged her throat. *Stupid, stupid, stupid!* Why was she so absentminded? Why couldn't she be more responsible?

"I have to go back," she said. "I'm so sorry." Now everything was ruined. Natalie wouldn't get to do the research, and Gramps would be stuck with his advancing age.

Under her chin, Galileo's hand opened up, revealing an oval blue gel capsule. She gasped and turned to face him. This close, she could see that the worry lines around his eyes ran deep, but he was smiling.

"Look familiar?" he said.

"Did we go home?"

He shook his head. "We're still in Ohio."

She looked out the window. They were in some kind of shopping center parking lot. Across the lot was a wide gray building with a red roof. The words CVS/PHARMACY were splashed across its façade. "So how—?"

"I called Dr. Carlyle and he told me what medication you needed. I called it in to the closest pharmacy under a phony registration, and here we are."

"Wow." Just the sight of the blue pill rejuvenated her. She took a swig of water from a bottle he handed her, and downed it.

"So I don't need to see a doctor?"

"I am a doctor."

"You are? For real?"

"Boarded in internal and emergency medicine. I'm taking good care of you, don't worry. Do you remember what day it is?"

"Tuesday?"

"Good. Do you remember how old you are?"

She started to say *twenty* but then her eyes narrowed. "Trick question! Not fair!"

He chuckled. "My dear, you're going to be just fine."

She smiled, shaking her head. "Now what?"

"We go to the safe house for the night, as planned. We'll continue our journey tomorrow after we all get some rest."

As drained as she was, a thrill zipped through her. Their adventure could continue after all.

"We're so glad you're okay," Natalie said. "I was really worried."

Theo didn't say anything. She wondered if he was too freaked out to go near her now, let alone speak.

Soon Galileo was driving them again on a busy road lined by small businesses—a funeral center, a Chinese restaurant, a nail salon. The sky was dimming to a purple twilight. Inside, the car was silent. Zoe was too embarrassed to look at Theo. *So much for a good first impression,* she thought.

The car accelerated and swerved off the main road, pulling into a tree-lined block filled with upscale two-story houses. Zoe caught Galileo's eyes in the rearview mirror as he glanced back. He looked tense.

"What's wrong?" she asked.

"Nothing. I thought maybe there was a strange car behind us."

She and Theo turned around at the same time to look, but no one was there. Galileo made a U-turn and pulled again onto the main road. They drove for about a mile before passing a gray sedan that had pulled off to the side of the road.

"That car again," Galileo muttered. "I don't like it one bit."

He swerved again onto a smaller road that led to another cluster of middle-class homes. Sure enough, the gray car soon appeared, crawling several hundred feet away.

Natalie squinted into the rearview mirror. "Who is that?"

"I don't know, but I don't want to find out. And that's the house." Galileo pointed out her window at a well-maintained split-level home with its lights on at the end of a cul-de-sac. Running perpendicular to it was a white wall that separated this block from the adjacent one.

"What are we going to do?"

By way of answer, he swung around in a violent U-turn and sped down the street, then turned right, left, right in quick succession, getting farther away from the car and deeper into the suburbs. After three more right turns and two lefts, Zoe felt lost, but Galileo apparently knew his way around. They came to a stop at the end of a block that looked identical to the other one—large houses, manicured front lawns, nice cars parked in driveways. The weird gray sedan was nowhere to be seen.

For a minute, they waited. Zoe chewed on her lip until it bled. Natalie and Galileo kept craning their necks around to inspect all windows and mirrors. Theo's eyes were intent on the rear window, not meeting hers.

"Now," Galileo said, "let's go."

They lunged out of the car as if it were on fire. Zoe clutched her backpack close to her chest. Inside the front pouch was a tiny bulge where Galileo had put her pill bottle.

"This way." He tilted his head to the white wall that

was now on their left side. "We jump over and go in through the backyard. Just in case."

"Do you tend to suffer from paranoia?" Natalie asked, only half joking.

He grimaced. "A hazard of the job. But usually it's nothing."

Crickets chirped in surround sound and twigs crunched underfoot as they approached the wall, which was dwarfed by the dense tall trees that rose up on either side of it. First Theo lifted himself up and hopped over with no trouble. Galileo hoisted Natalie over, and then Zoe. She felt safe and weightless in his arms, but when he set her down on the wall, its stucco scraped against her calves. To help her jump down, Theo extended a hand and she took it.

Once Galileo scrambled over, he led them through a dense maze of trees and shrubs to a short wooden fence about her height. Even she found it easy to hop over without much help, but she did have to suppress a grunt when her feet landed hard on the dirt. Soon the others were by her side in a private backyard surrounded by rustling trees. The full moon cast their elongated shadows across the grass. Before them stood the two-story safe house, its windows illuminated but obscured by heavy curtains.

"This is it," Galileo whispered. "Let's go in. But first, a precaution: Everyone turn around."

CHAPTER 19

They traversed the yard backward. Galileo explained that inverting the direction of their footprints was an easy way to mislead anyone who might come poking around. To Natalie, it was another example of either his paranoia or ingenuity; she wasn't sure which. But they obeyed. He stayed a few feet out ahead, his reverse stride purposeful, his spine erect.

In the glow of the moonlight, Natalie could see the tense muscles of his back underneath his T-shirt and the corners of sweat that darkened his armpits. Her breath caught when she also noticed on his head of black hair the strands of white that glistened in the light when he moved. Was it possible that he could be ten or fifteen years older than she'd suspected? The thought reminded her just how little she knew about him—and how quickly she had extended her trust.

He turned around to motion them to wait. Then he took off jogging across the backyard toward the house next door. At first Natalie's stomach lurched. Could he be deserting them? But when he crept back over his footsteps in the grass, she understood. More misdirection. He joined them again as they made their way to the back door, Zoe taking huge reverse steps to keep up.

Galileo knocked six times in a strange pattern of emphasis, every other knock a stressed beat. "It'll take a minute, but don't worry. He's expecting us."

Theo kicked a fallen twig away from the door. Zoe sighed and scanned the yard. Except for the swaying trees and a distant rumble—probably thunder—the night appeared still.

When Natalie's impatience was reaching its peak, she heard plodding footsteps inside the house coming closer. Galileo smiled as if to say, *See?*

The curtain was pulled back on the sliding glass door and an elderly olive-skinned man peered out at them. His face seemed molded from ancient clay. Cracks ran from the corners of his dark brown eyes and around his mouth.

A latch clicked and the door slid open. The four of them squeezed through, Galileo leading the way. The scent of spices hit Natalie first—cumin and coriander and pepper. She saw that they were standing in a cheery kitchen decorated with yellow tiles and a painting of tulips in a geometric-patterned vase.

Before them, the man stood hunched over at the waist, his hands clasped behind his back, beaming up at them. Natalie wondered if this was his way of showing respect. If so, it made her very uncomfortable. How could Galileo require this kind of subservience? The poor man was overweight, and as he stretched out his arms and leaned forward, she worried he might topple over.

"Galeeleo!" he exclaimed in a thick Mexican accent. "I am so happy to see you!"

"And you, Julian!" Galileo said, crouching down to embrace him.

"How was de trip?"

"Well, we made it." He gestured to Julian's back. "How've you been?"

Natalie winced as she watched his futile efforts to strain against his back and stand tall. That was when she realized that he wasn't purposefully hunched over—he was disabled, his body frozen in a permanent bend. Her spine ached just looking at him.

"Good," Julian said with a smile, and Natalie could see he was forcing cheerfulness, despite what must have been great pain.

"Why don't we sit down," Galileo suggested, "and then—"

"No, no I am fine. Introduce to me your friends."

Galileo obliged with a round of introductions. Theo and Natalie each shook his hand, which carried a surprisingly firm grip. When Zoe reached out hers, with a delighted grin he pinched her cheek instead.

"You are *muy bonita, señorita*. Just like my little girl."

"Who's not so little anymore," Galileo said. "His daughter, Nina, works at the headquarters. You'll all meet her, she's lovely."

"What does she do?" Natalie asked, more to be friendly than out of real curiosity.

Julian's grin deepened into the proud smile of a man who'd gambled everything and won. "She is—how you say—a virologist."

"Cool!" Theo exclaimed.

"She's one of our best researchers," Galileo said. "We're very proud to have her."

"What's wrong with your back?" Zoe asked.

An awkward pause ensued, during which Natalie shot her a chastising look. Any adult ought to know better. Julian raised his eyebrows.

"Sorry," she mumbled. "I was just wondering."

She's still uninhibited, Natalie thought with fascination. *Still like a child.*

Galileo patted Zoe's back as if to reassure her. "That's okay. He had a bad accident at work last year."

"I was elevator repairman," Julian said. "One day I fell into shaft. From de seventh floor."

Zoe wrung her hands, clearly regretting bringing it up. "I'm so sorry."

"It's okay." His face brightened. "The Network save me."

"What's a little extra construction," Galileo said, winking at Julian. Then he caught Natalie's eye. "We take care of our own."

"What did they do for you?" she asked, intrigued.

"I show you." He motioned with a hand to follow him, trudging out of the kitchen through a short hallway that opened up to a living room furnished with an old boxy television and beige fabric couches. He stopped at the base of a steep green-carpeted staircase, leaned on the handrail, and pointed. *"Aquí!"*

Carved into the wall, to Natalie's surprise, was an elevator. Zoe pressed the button, which lit up. A moment later, the doors slid open to reveal a blond wood–paneled interior, straight out of a luxury hotel.

"Whoa!"

"So I no have to move," Julian explained. "After, I couldn't take stairs but I live here forty-six years. I no want to leave."

Galileo patted his shoulder. "I'm so glad it's working out. Why don't you go upstairs to rest and I'll make us dinner?"

"Oh, but Señor Galeeleo, you drive all day!"

A car door slammed—loud enough to come from his driveway. Natalie felt her heart palpitate. Galileo rushed to the front door and peered through the peephole. Natalie reached for Zoe and Theo and pulled them close.

"I expecting no one," Julian said, frowning.

"Well?" she called.

When Galileo turned around, his eyes had gained the hardness of a soldier.

"Julian, it's time. Don't be afraid, you know what to do. Guys, follow me."

Natalie felt her stomach shred itself. "Where?"

Zoe's lips started to tremble. "I don't like this."

The knock came. It sounded as grim as a gunshot.

"Hang on," Galileo said, running to grab their backpacks from the kitchen.

The knock gave way to a pounding that lacked any charade of politeness. The doorknob jostled.

"*Ay, Dios,*" Julian breathed, sinking onto the bottom stair.

Natalie felt a suffocating helplessness set in around them like quicksand. There was no way out. A vision of her desolate jail cell flashed before her, and of the promised lab that might have been. Galileo was pulling her by the arm, toward the staircase.

A gruff voice yelled through the door. "FBI, open up!"

Before she could further contemplate their peril, she felt Galileo's hand on the small of her back shuttling her, Theo, and Zoe upstairs. They tripped over each other, scrambling to move quickly, no time for questions.

"We know you're home!" shouted the voice outside. "Open up!"

As they reached the top of the stairs, Natalie glanced around wildly. There were only three modest rooms—two bedrooms and an office. Where could four people hide?

"They're going to find us!" she whispered.

"No." Galileo turned to look her in the eye, as though he had all the time in the world. "You forget who's really running this show."

"Who?"

A mischievous smile broke across his face. "Me."

CHAPTER 20

"If you don't open this door," Les shouted, "we'll have to break it down!" His blood was pumping at his temples. He hadn't felt this alive, this intense, since the day he founded the committee five years ago.

"Are we really going to?" asked the anxious cop standing next to him on the doorstep. "You know, break it down?"

Les smiled at him as at an angel. In spite of the AMBER alerts, the forensics work on the postcards, and the coordinated effort to man interstate checkpoints, it was this scrawny plainclothes cop who had saved the day by trailing the car—*a stolen cop car*. In fact, Les knew he himself deserved all the credit—the brains behind the operation always did. But he was feeling charitable.

A blockade had been stationed for reinforcement at the neighborhood's artery to the main highway, and two helicopters were hovering above—the FBI chopper that had flown him in and one from the Ohio State Police—beaming around white spotlights like the moon's rays on steroids. The fugitives were cornered up, down, and sideways.

"We have a SWAT team for that," Les told the cop. "Chill out."

"But what if it's not this house?"

"The whole damn block has been searched. It has to be."

Inside, they could hear someone shuffling to the door.

Les fingered the pistol in his holster, tangible proof of his control. *I got this,* he thought. How satisfying it would be to see the smugness wiped off Benjamin Barrow's face when he found out.

The door opened a crack and a short, elderly Mexican man poked his face out.

"Hola, señores," he said. "Can I help you?"

The audacity, Les thought. "We've been banging on your door for five minutes, sir. What took you so long?"

The door swung all the way open in answer. The man wasn't short, he was disfigured, hunched over as if his back were supporting an invisible stack of bricks.

"I'm very sorry. I am slow to get around, you see."

"Oh. And your name is?"

"Julian Hernandez."

"I'm Les Mahler and this is my colleague Dave Wood." He flashed his shiny federal badge with the seal of the Bioethics Committee—an eagle standing atop a microscope. "I'm sorry to inform you there's a suspected kidnapper in your neighborhood. We have to inspect every house on this block."

The man's brown eyes widened in horror. "Of course! Please, have a look."

Les stared at him, challenging him to flinch or look away. But his face was placid—either the blank look of an innocent or the practiced blankness of an accomplice.

"Come in," he added. "Take your time."

"Thank you." Les charged past him inside, sizing up the territory. It was a modest house that showed its age in its fixtures and furnishings—faded fabric couches and dusty bookshelves in the living room to the left, and to the right, an antique wooden table surrounded by old chairs.

Les directed the cop to check out the upstairs, while he staked out the downstairs, hurrying through a wall-papered hallway and into the kitchen—the only room so far that looked lived in. Pink and yellow and blue tiles brightened the space as if it were a carnival. Water was boiling on the stove and the pungent scent of taco spices permeated the air. Julian followed at a distance, lagging behind.

"Why so much food?" Les asked, eyeing the counter-top, which was covered with shredded cheese, diced avocados, tomatoes, and an open can of beans.

His eyebrows shot up. "What?"

Les swept an arm over the counter. "Seems like you're having guests."

"No, señor," he replied. "I make a lot at once to save for the whole week."

"You live alone?"

"*Sí.*"

"For how long?"

"Oh, more years than I can count *en inglés.*"

Les noted the flicker of fear in his eyes when he noticed the gun, but that wasn't tantamount to guilt. He brushed past the old man into the living room. To tuck away four people in a house like this could not be easy. The fireplace was too narrow, the kitchen cabinets too small. There were no crevices or shielded corners that he could see. He walked through each room, including the sparse two-car garage, looking underneath couches, opening cupboards, peering behind curtains, under counters, in the washer and dryer. But the few rooms that comprised the downstairs were frustratingly devoid of hiding spots.

They had to be upstairs. He was heading to the staircase when he noticed, carved into the wall on his left, what looked like an elevator. Curious, he jabbed the button and the doors slid open. The interior was like a tight wood-paneled closet, so tight that only a few people could fit at a time. Four, no way.

The cop scurried down the stairs then with his palms upturned.

"Nada. Just two empty bedrooms and an office."

"No attic?" Les asked Julian, who shook his head.

"I checked," the cop said. "Nothing."

"You looked down the elevator shaft?"

"Empty."

Les shook off his disappointment. He expected Galileo to be slicker than that.

"But every other house has been searched!"

The cop shrugged. Julian glanced between them, his expression impartial—almost bored. Les could feel his certainty dissipating. He wanted to punch a hole in the wall. How the hell could four flesh-and-blood people vanish into thin air?

"Let's check outside," he snapped, leading the way to the back door.

The yard was about a half acre of patchy grass with a humble row of potted plants and flowers near the door. The roses were wilting in the heat, scattering white and pink petals over the ground. There was no outdoor pool or other potential hiding spot out here. But the property did back up onto a dense bunch of trees and shrubs just past the fence. Taking heart, Les shined his flashlight over the grass. He squinted, dropping to his knees. Distinct patches were crunched into the lawn, bending the blades of grass sideways. Were they—footsteps?

"Hey," he called to the cop. "Check this out."

Together they aimed their flashlights over the suspicious sweep of grass, tracing the indentations across the yard. At a patchy spot with only soil, Les noticed something strange. One of the footprints was smaller than the others, only about eight inches long, and its imprint was a crisscross pattern of interconnected squares.

He knelt down, examining the marks. With a little analysis, they'd be able to determine the type and size of shoe, but to him it was obvious—these footprints belonged to a kid. He thought back to the house and made a mental note to go check more closely for this specific print on all floors and carpets. If Zoe and the fugitives had been in this yard, they could very well have been in the house, too—which would mean the old hunchback might be an accomplice.

He examined the lawn further. At a certain place in the middle, the cluster of steps appeared to diverge. One set of large footprints trailed off to the left, leading all the way to the neighbor's backyard. In the thrall of discovery, Les followed them up to the short dividing fence between the two houses and then ran back to the center, where the cop was calling him over. Here, the side-by-side indentations—some big, some small—were pointed toward the back fence. Toward the forest. So they weren't in the house after all. They had split up and gone on the run. Les smiled. *Gotcha.*

With the reinforcements he was about to call in, they would be captured in no time—pathetic ripples crushed by his tidal wave.

He thought of the veneration he would garner back at the Capitol. Benjamin Barrow would have to concede his effectiveness, and together they would use this hook to reel in Galileo and destroy him.

But in the service of humanity, before the celebrating could commence, there was still one unfortunate but necessary chore for Les to tackle. The girl was too dangerous, even if freed from the Network. At any point in her life—and who knew how long it might otherwise be—some deviant scientist could get hold of her DNA and wreak havoc. He thought of a chilling quote that had always stuck with him, from Gore Vidal, about what human beings were doing to the planet already. *Think of the Earth as a living organism that is being attacked by billions of bacteria whose numbers double every forty years. Either the host dies, or the virus dies, or both die.*

This particular virus was like a superstrain. All he had to do was isolate her once and for all.

Then he would be freed up to concentrate on his biggest prey—the scum who made the experimentation possible.

CHAPTER 21

Zoe's legs dangled around Theo's neck. She was sitting on his shoulders inside the dark crawl space that Galileo had revealed to them, behind a fake wall in Julian's bedroom—one that slid open only at the touch of two thumbs placed on invisible sensors. But the space was hollowed out for only two people, so she had to scrunch herself atop Theo's shoulders. Natalie leaned against Galileo, her knees balled tight, and he lay contorted around her. It was the only way the four of them could fit.

Before, a second had never registered as a unit of time in which experience could dwell. Now Zoe knew better. Each one mounted a struggle against sound, against movement, against panic. It was frightening how elongated time became when you were trapped with the catastrophes roaming like wolves through your mind. You could age years in a minute. Well, she supposed someone else could.

It seemed that hours were passing without any change. Her thighs and rear tingled. She was desperate to stand, to stretch, to take her pill. She didn't want to think about what would happen if she were to have a re-peat seizure. The cool smooth walls confined them. The only way out was to move the wall and expose everyone.

Don't seize, she told herself. *Don't panic.*

Her breath was coming in short gasps. She squeezed her eyes shut, summoning the spirit of Gramps. His raspy voice, his playful smile. His eyes that seemed to see past all her inadequacies straight through to her soul. She hoped that he understood why she had to leave, and that he would forgive her for the first real secret she ever kept from him—for his own benefit.

What would he do if he were here right now? Proba-bly turn this hell into a silly game to pass the time—*first one to twitch loses.* Why was it that some people had the power to improve a horrible situation with their presence alone?

In the midst of her yearning she heard someone tap on the wall. Six light taps. Her whole body braced. Galileo's hand flew to her leg with a tacit command, *Freeze.* Theo's shoulders tightened, lifting her an inch.

The voice came through muffled but distinct.

"All clear. You can come out now."

It was Julian's.

Her first instinct was to cry. Usually she repressed feelings of weakness in front of strangers—so often was she trying to be a strong adult—but now she let all her tension flow out, unchecked. The relief was monu-mental. Theo chuckled, not unkindly, when her tears dripped onto his face. It was still too dark to see, and she wondered if he was shedding a few himself.

When the wall opened, they scooted out one by one. It was all she could do not to race through the house flipping cartwheels. All that glorious space! She tried to contain herself as Galileo restored the wall to its original position. Natalie hugged Theo, as Zoe danced in circles around them.

Galileo turned to Julian and put a hand on his shoulder. "How are you? Okay?"

Zoe stopped twirling to listen, chastising herself. How could she not have asked him that right away? Part of behaving like an adult was showing empathy to others, unlike kids, who tended to be interested only in themselves.

"Fine," Julian said, smiling. "They leave to look in forest."

"Then I wish them luck," Galileo said. "They'll need it."

"It was tight fit, *si*?"

"You might say. But it served its purpose. See, you thought we'd never need it."

"You should have seen us," Natalie added, beginning to chuckle.

"Good thing no one farted," Theo said to Zoe. "Especially you."

She giggled, smacking him. "Gross!"

Galileo let them indulge their amusement, but he didn't crack a smile. Instead he typed away on his cell phone.

"Oh, lighten up," Natalie said, poking his arm. "You can't be above a fart joke."

"Maybe if we were off the hook. But they're just going to search even harder. Next time we might not be so lucky."

Zoe's giddiness evaporated. She didn't like the severity of his expression. It reminded her of the look on her father's face when her mother received her diagnosis of cancer—a look that had been indelibly seared into her memory.

"So what do we do?" Natalie asked.

"Get out of here ASAP." He waved his cell phone. "Remember our cop friend? He's parked in the garage right now in a rental car, waiting for us."

"Great! What are we doing? Come on!"

"There's apparently a police blockade at the exit to the main road. Every passenger is being checked for ID."

Zoe felt her face crumple. Why did things have to be so hard? This was all her fault. If she hadn't forgotten her pill at home and had a stupid freaking seizure, no one would have been able to track them. All she wanted was to get to the compound so Natalie could get on with the research. Gramps couldn't wait forever.

"Now what?" Natalie said in a low voice.

He hesitated. "There's a way, but I don't want to force it on you"—he looked at Zoe—"especially not in your condition."

"I'm fine," she declared, annoyed. "Try me."

He seemed reluctant to explain, rubbing his temple as if it ached. "You've already had a seizure. We could take our chances and spend the night, wait it out."

She shook her head. "I'll feel so much better if we can just get out of here." Then she remembered how she had been insensitive to Julian, so she turned to him. "No offense, you know."

He waved a hand. "Better for me. I no want to get in trouble."

They all looked at Galileo.

"Well," he said, "you three would have to squeeze into the trunk. It should be less than five minutes altogether, but it won't be pleasant."

Zoe closed her eyes. The thought of entering another dark, trapped space made her want to sob. When she opened them, she saw that Natalie was shaking her head. Theo looked too exhausted to react, or maybe he was just the type of guy who didn't show fear. It was after midnight. They had been traveling for some fourteen hours.

"And where will you be?" Natalie asked.

"In the passenger seat. I have a federal badge."

She raised her eyebrows.

"Friends in high places," he said, as if that were a satisfying answer. Zoe stared at his angular face in profile, wishing she could crack even one of the mysteries that surrounded him. Who was he, really? Why was he risking so much? And how did he cope with the pressure? Maybe the Network had already invented some kind of drug to help normal people become extraordinary. If so, she could pretend she'd taken it, too.

"Can you even breathe in a closed trunk?" Theo asked.

"It won't be totally closed. I've done it before. The trick is to stay calm and not hyperventilate."

"I don't know," Natalie said. "It seems risky. What if they search it?"

"What if they search the house again? Next time they'll be more careful. I don't know what prints we might have left around here."

"I'm in," Zoe announced, surprising everyone with her sureness, herself most of all. She forced a smile. This was no time for cowardice or indecision. *If there's a job to be done, just do it.*

Galileo shot her a grateful look, and she could tell he understood the level of bravery she'd had to summon from deep down, where Gramps's soul had left its imprint on hers.

"All in?"

Theo eyed her with a new respect. "If she is, so am I."

Zoe tried to contain a grin as a warm flush crept into her face.

Natalie put her arms around them both and narrowed her gaze at Galileo.

"There's nothing on this earth more precious than these kids." At the last word Zoe stiffened, but Natalie didn't seem to notice. Her voice was trembling with emotion—and menace. "I'm trusting you to understand that."

CHAPTER 22

In the trunk, Natalie's breathing quickened as the car slowed.

The checkpoint.

She was lying in the fetal position with Theo and Zoe scrunched on either side of her. Their warm bodies pressed against hers, making pools of sweat at each point of contact. Theo's knees bent into her back. Zoe, being spooned, had pulled her elbows in tightly at her sides. They jutted into Natalie's ribs like tiny spears. The ceiling of the trunk loomed several inches above their faces, so close that she wondered if a coffin would be spacious in comparison. Unlike the cool crawl space, the air here was stuffy and reeked of gasoline fumes from the tailpipe.

It was dark except for a razor-thin edge of light visible around the perimeter, the broken seal that allowed them to breathe. From the outside, it was impossible to tell that the trunk wasn't fully shut. She knew that if they started to suffocate, she could push it open all the way—but that would mean instant capture. Not a last resort she wanted to use.

The car stopped, jolting them into one another. She felt Theo's hot breath on her scalp and Zoe's waif-like body tensing against hers.

The trick was to stay calm.

"Almost there," she whispered. If being a mother had taught her anything, it was that comforting others was the most soothing way to comfort yourself. She tightened her arms around Zoe, drawing her even closer. The sweet scent of her hair was an antidote to the noxious odors of gas and sweat, like cherry blossoms on a spring day. Innocence, youth, beauty. She concentrated on imagining a world in which those precious attributes were sustainable, a world she was determined to make real. A sharp ache pinched at her temples. If only she could endure a little longer. *How bad do you want it,* she goaded herself. All the years of studying, the thousands of hours in the lab, the lack of complete attention to Theo, the loss of her marriage—yes, Nick had cheated, but hadn't she pushed him away?—all in the service of her relentless search for that powerful gene.

And—as far as she could tell—the proof was an inch away.

Sweat dripped from her cheek onto Zoe's hair. Natalie didn't know how much longer they could hold out. The oxygen in the trunk seemed to be thinning. Each breath was less and less effective. She gulped, expanding her lungs with fumes, then choked out a cough, tried again, choked again. Why were Zoe and Theo able to breathe so steadily? In a surreal moment of detachment, she saw what was going to happen— she alone was going to suffocate. *Unless.* All around, the fresh night air was seeping in, taunting her to throw open the trunk and inhale a greedy breath.

But how could she devastate Theo? Her returning to jail and outing Galileo in the process would leave him with nothing. It was getting harder to think straight. Her brain throbbed, thoughts blurred. Lucidity receded like a tide, washing away all but the immutable pearl of her soul, her love for her son. No lab and no gene in the world could tempt her to abandon him.

She was moments away from giving in to the blackness when his arms wrapped around her.

"Breathe, Mom," he whispered. "You're just panicking."

I love you, she wanted to say, but didn't have the breath. All she wanted to do was stand in a wind tunnel and suck in the coldest, freshest air of her life. Instead she inhaled the stuffy gas fumes, trying not to choke. Why wasn't the car moving?

"That's right," he said. "Nice and easy."

The authorities were probably searching the car. Soon they would open the trunk and then the whole charade would be over. It was taking too long. Something was wrong. Had Galileo been caught?

Then the car lurched forward, picking up speed with each turn out of the neighborhood. No sirens could be heard, no signs of pursuit. The whine of the engine crescendoed until all they could hear was the roar of the car, as if they were encased in its very core. They accelerated until Theo and Zoe were rolling and jostling her at every bump, but she wasn't bothered. By the time they reached peak speed, she knew they were on the open highway, a straight shot through the unsuspecting night to freedom.

* * *

They emerged from the trunk at a rest stop in the middle of nowhere. No houses could be seen in any direction, just wide open fields under the starry night sky. Zoe clutched Galileo in relief, her short arms barely reaching around his back, while Natalie looked on with tenderness and a hint of envy. How she wished to fall into a man's arms and be held. But propriety dictated that adults didn't give in to such whims.

As if reading her mind, Theo pulled her close, and with a slight shock she noted that he was not so young anymore. He was a head taller than she was, and broad through the chest, his shoulders muscular and strong. What had happened to the scrawny teenager she knew? Was there no end to his growth spurt? It hardly seemed possible that this handsome man-child had come out of her body eighteen years earlier.

"You saved me," she confessed, leaning on his shoulder. "I was freaking out in there."

"I just got you out of your head," he replied. "I never knew you were claustrophobic."

"You weren't supposed to." She gave an abashed smile. "I've tried so hard not to pass my quirks on to you."

He raised an eyebrow. "Are there more?"

"Oh, you have no idea," she joked. Galileo shut the trunk and turned to them, with Zoe beaming at his side. The car was a silver Nissan sedan with Ohio plates, utterly ordinary. Through the passenger window, Natalie saw the officer friend of the Network sitting in the driver's seat, still wearing his cop's uniform. She shuddered to think where they might be without his cooperation. "I can't believe you pulled it off."

Galileo smiled; the lightheartedness had returned to

his eyes. "We should be fine now." He looked down at Zoe, who was hanging on to his arm. "You got your pills with you?"

"Right here." She held up her backpack.

"Good girl."

"How much longer will it take to get there?"

"About three days. But I'm going to drive through the night and see if we can't get there faster. I'm guessing you guys would like a rest already."

They all nodded. Even Theo, who was such an adrenaline junkie that he had once gone skydiving without Natalie's permission.

"What about our friend?" Natalie asked, sticking a thumb at the driver.

Galileo sighed. "That part of the plan's ruined. He was supposed to return to the station in his cop car, seemingly unable to find us. But now I'm sure it's been towed away as evidence. They'll think we stole it."

"So what's he going to do?" She checked her watch. It was after midnight. "Isn't he due back now?"

"Yep. So we're going to play into their version of events."

"How so?"

"We'll drop him off near a gas station somewhere back along our route between Wheeling and Columbus, where he'll go and call the station. He'll say he blacked out after a struggle with me before I took off with his car, and then he later woke up in a ditch near the highway with all his personal effects missing. He'll say he walked until he found this gas station and called. It would be consistent then that his car was discovered where we left it, miles west of where we allegedly dumped him."

Natalie balked, horrified. "But you're taking the hit for something you didn't do!"

"So what? To them I'm already a monster. But he's a real person who's going to have to face a lot of questions. This way, he'll seem heroic and victimized and nobody will hold him accountable." Galileo paused as a single car sped past them on the otherwise empty road. Natalie thought they probably looked like a regular American family, a husband and wife and two kids pulling over to stretch their legs. He lowered his voice. "It's absolutely critical that he and Julian and everybody else who put their lives on the line for the Network are protected at all costs."

"But why do they go to so much trouble?" she blurted, before she could stop herself. "Their lives would be over if anyone found out."

"The reason is always the same. To help a loved one." He lifted his chin toward the officer in the car. "His mom is at the compound, in our hospital. Acute myeloid leukemia. We're trying a radical gene therapy that's years away from federal approval—and so far it's working."

Natalie's lips parted in awe, and she caught a glimpse of the way Theo was watching him. There was no mistaking the admiration in his eyes—and the longing. Zoe seemed to have already claimed Galileo as a surrogate father figure and he appeared to be enjoying the role, or at least was humoring her. Just as Natalie was wondering whether his affection was sincere, Zoe tugged on his sleeve.

"Can we go to sleep in the backseat now? I'm tired."

"Of course you can, darling," he said. "Of course."

Zoe didn't see the shadow that crossed his face then,

but Natalie did. It was a split-second shift from his guise of composure, a flicker of the heart chafing against some pain it wishes to forget.

When Natalie woke up in the backseat the next morning, the kids—or rather Zoe and Theo—were still snoozing on either side of her. She had started to think of them together as *the kids,* even though Theo was officially an adult, and so was Zoe, at least nominally. The girl plainly craved respect, even if she did at times slip into childlike patterns of speech and behavior. But her bravery and rebellion were the hallmarks of late adolescence, and her intelligence was precocious for her physiological age. No, Natalie was sure she did not deserve the label *kid*—this whole journey was predicated on that notion, after all—and resolved never to let it slip anymore in her presence.

Galileo was driving up front alone, humming along to a Beatles song on the radio—"When I'm Sixty-Four." She couldn't help smiling at the irony as she wiped the crust of sleep from her eyes. Ahead in the distance, the sun shone on a great white arch that rose gracefully into the sky, dwarfing the buildings below it.

"The Saint Louis arch!" she exclaimed.

"Yeah, we're going to pass right by it."

How fitting, she thought. The arch was the famous Gateway to the West, erected as a monument to westward expansion and discovery. A celebration of the new world that lay at the feet of the pioneers, waiting to be explored.

"You must be exhausted," she said. "How long have we been driving?"

"About nine hours since you fell asleep back in Ohio. I had to backtrack to Pennsylvania to drop off our friend. But he's out of danger now. His story went over well. And we're just about a day and a half away."

"You have to sleep. I don't understand how you can still be driving."

He explained that they were going to stop at another safe house in Springfield, Missouri, for a few hours so he could nap.

"Why don't we just spend a whole day there?" she suggested. "It's fine, really. No one's following us now."

"I wish we could. But in this job there are no days off. I have to leave on another mission as soon as we get to the compound."

Their time at the safe house in Springfield came and went. Galileo slept in the bedroom of the family's absent son, who was a computer tech at the compound, while Theo and Zoe kicked around a soccer ball in the backyard and Natalie sipped iced tea. After taking turns showering and filling up on hearty home-cooked barbeque, they loaded into the car again for the final thirteen-hour stretch.

Green grasslands passed by, and stretches of wide-open desert in which nothing surrounded them for miles but red sand and rock outcroppings. Night fell. The heat outside barely eased—the barometer said 95. It was different than the sweltering summers of New York that she was used to; this heat was dry and breezy, devoid of suffocating humidity. Desert heat. She had never experienced it before.

Despite her exhaustion, sleep was the furthest thing from her mind as they crossed the border into New

Mexico. No one had spoken for some time, so Galileo's voice nearly startled her.

"We're just about there."

Her heart hammered as she leaned forward to peer out the windshield. In front of them were the outlines of tall, jagged mountains set against a twinkling black sky. In the backseat, Zoe sat up and shook Theo, who had been dozing.

She pointed out the left-side window. "Look!"

Natalie saw, too. Glittering neon lights in the distance. A tan castlelike building nestled against the foot of the mountains. It seemed like a majestic Native American palace of some kind.

The lights grew brighter as they approached the sprawling, glittering castle and pulled into its parking lot. Rising directly behind it, the mountains soared like arrowheads, blotting out the low-hanging moon. In the front splashed a fountain, lit from beneath with pink and purple lights. A billboard above it read in neon yellow—DANCING EAGLE CASINO. Next to it was a rendering of a fierce-looking warrior with feathers protruding from his head and a braid hanging by his ear. On the sign in the lower right-hand corner were the words PUEBLO OF LAGUNA INDIAN RESERVATION.

"This is the secret lab?" Zoe asked in disbelief.

"Come," Galileo said, turning off the ignition. "Just follow me."

They jumped out, grabbed their backpacks from the trunk, and walked past the fountain through two heavy doors. A blast of cigarette smoke and air conditioning greeted them. Natalie felt a rush of unease as the sights and sounds of the casino hit them—clattering coins, shrill beeping noises, rows of colorfully blinking machines. A few older men sat huddled around a roulette table in the center of the floor. No one paid them any attention, and before they could absorb the atmosphere, Galileo was leading them into an empty carpeted hallway. They wound around four corners, three lefts and a right, until coming to a stop in front of a black door that read AUTHORIZED PERSONNEL ONLY.

Natalie traded looks with Zoe and Theo. They stared at her, bewildered. Had Galileo lured them here after all? Had she been a fool to trust him? Who the hell was he, anyway? She would never forgive herself if anything happened to them.

But it was too late to second-guess anything now. Only jail awaited back home.

Galileo pressed his index finger against the door's metal lock. After three seconds it clicked and opened. He ushered them into a compact elevator and the door slid shut behind them with a metallic whir. Immediately the floor dropped. It seemed like minutes passed. Natalie was sure they were going to hit bottom, but their descent continued, slow and measured. Her heart knocked against her chest at an alarming rate.

They stopped with a thud. A door that she had thought was a wall opened onto a dank, pitch-black tunnel. There was no saying how long or deep it ran. She tightened her arms around Theo and Zoe. Neither resisted.

"Welcome," Galileo's voice reverberated down the narrow passage. "On the other side, your new life awaits."

PART 3

All truths are easy to understand once they are discovered; the point is to discover them.
—GALILEO GALILEI, 1564–1642

CHAPTER 23

The walk through the tunnel was brisk. With a flash-light, Galileo led single file, trailed by Natalie, Zoe, and Theo. The comfortable mood of the car ride was gone, replaced by tension as thick as fog. Though they had been traveling together for almost three straight days, Zoe knew that the balance of power had shifted completely to him. It was too late to turn back. Not that she wanted to.

As they trekked deeper, their footsteps scuffing the concrete floor, she found herself thinking of the first man in space. He of all people would understand her electrifying mix of terror and anticipation, the two strange traveling companions that accompanied a journey into the unknown. She was grateful not to be alone.

The air smelled like cool packed dirt. Galileo's flashlight shone brightly, illuminating the sheer jagged rock walls that bordered their path. Her thighs burned as they trudged along, and soon she realized that they were climbing up a long, subterranean slope. After about twenty minutes, the path dead-ended at a door. He turned to face them, and she could just make out the outline of his sharp jaw moving in the dim light.

"It's after three a.m. but people don't keep normal hours here."

He pressed his index finger against the lock and twisted the knob.

Zoe planted her feet, bracing herself. She didn't know she was squeezing her eyes shut until Theo gave her a little tap on the back. Stumbling across the threshold, she inhaled the freshest air she had ever breathed.

And opened her eyes.

She found herself in a circular concrete courtyard measuring about an acre, surrounded by a series of connected, short brown buildings. Beyond those, the mountains stretched to the sky, blocking out any sign of the casino and its flashy lights. The only light here was the silvery gleam of the moon and a few irregular yellow glows emanating from different rooms. In a window to her right, Zoe could see people bustling about, walking back and forth carrying some kind of equipment. In windows to her left, people were lying in white beds, reading or watching television. She recognized the blinking monitors and cluster of wires at their sides. They must be patients, she thought. In hospital beds.

Next to her, Natalie and Theo were looking around in awe. Galileo checked his cell phone, giving them a minute to get their bearings.

Natalie shook her head. "I don't understand. How is this possible? How could you get away with having this whole place carved out?"

Galileo gave her a mischievous smile. "Reservations are considered domestic dependent nations. The tribes have territorial sovereignty to rule their own land, so the government can't touch it."

"How did you get it?"

"Through a special arrangement with the Laguna Pueblos. We share some of our funding with them and they don't ask questions. It's win-win."

Zoe traded a glance with Theo, impressed. This was a man who knew how to pull things off.

He gestured to the courtyard, which was empty except for a few scattered benches and a rectangular spread of grass that resembled a small park. "We call this the quad. It's where we hold meetings of the entire compound. To our right are the labs. Natalie, yours is waiting and ready. I'll show you down there in the morning."

She frowned. "Down where?"

He seemed pleased. "There's always more than meets the eye, isn't there? That building goes five stories underground."

Her eyebrows lifted. "Oh. With how many labs?"

"Seventeen in use. Another ten waiting for new recruits." He shifted his attention to the row in the next section of the circle, straight in front of them. The squat buildings were constructed of tan adobe bricks, an oval window carved in each facade. "Those are the living quarters. You'll each have your own private apartment with a bedroom, kitchen, and bathroom. They're tiny, I'm afraid. But you're all used to Manhattan."

"I get my own place? Sweet." Theo jogged a few yards ahead to scope out the apartments, and Zoe couldn't help admiring the cut muscles of his calves.

She tugged Galileo's shirt. "Will we be next to each other?" It was weird to think of living in her own apartment, but then, what about any of this *wasn't* weird?

"You and Theo will be," Galileo said. "Natalie, we have a place for you closer to your lab and next to Helen. But don't worry, it's just a short hallway away."

Natalie frowned. "When can I see her?"

"I'll tell her we're here, but she's probably asleep. Which reminds me. There are intercoms wired in every room, which you can use to reach each other. We don't have phones."

Zoe hugged her elbows tight, thinking of Gramps. "So no call to the outside?"

He shook his head as the three of them watched Theo jog back toward them, grinning. "We have some pretty strict rules, as you can imagine. If any information slipped about our location, it could endanger all of us."

She crossed her arms as Theo reached them. His smile vanished when he saw her frustrated expression. "But how can we contact people, then?" she demanded.

"We have the Internet on two computers up there." He pointed to the tallest point on the compound—a slim, windowed tower set on the roof of the lab building. "That's the Brain, our center of command. You can write e-mails there as necessary, which our 24/7 IT security team will review and anonymize to send through proxy servers and obscure our IP address."

Zoe watched Theo to see if he understood this. To her surprise, he was nodding.

"How many servers do they bounce it off?" he asked.

"About ten. By the time it reaches the recipient, the outbound server is completely masked."

"Badass. Do you think I could talk to the IT guys sometime? I want to study computer science in college."

"I'll arrange it. Maybe we can get you a head start here."

Theo widened his eyes at Zoe as if to say, *Doesn't this place rock?*

She scowled. Gramps didn't use e-mail, never had. How was she supposed to contact him? Later she would ask Galileo what to do. He seemed to have a solution for everything.

"Let's continue our orientation," he said, gesturing to a barnlike structure next to the apartment section that reminded Zoe of her high school gym—a wide, low-ceilinged box. "That's the cafeteria. Three meals are served a day, between seven and nine, noon and two, and six and eight. It's nothing fancy, but it's better than your typical mess hall. There's also a small fitness center with some treadmills and weights, open all the time. But most people get their exercise here with a hike." He waved toward the mountains. "Back there's a trail with some good hills. It's isolated and inaccessible except from here, so don't worry about being seen. Be alert for wildlife, though. We have had a few rattlesnake sightings."

"Awesome!" Theo exclaimed, looking at Zoe. "We should check it out."

"Yeah," she said. "Sure."

Ever since she had insisted on sneaking out in the

trunk back in Ohio, the dynamic between them had changed. Theo seemed friendlier, less freaked out. She hoped it had something to do with gaining his respect, and nothing to do with pity.

"Just be careful, you guys," Natalie said. "Don't go looking for trouble."

"Mom," he groaned.

"Sorry, but as your mother, I have a biological obligation to tell you that." She exchanged a smile with Galileo, and Zoe thought she saw a strange look pass between them. She was sure Natalie held his gaze a second too long.

"Can we see the Brain center?" Theo asked. He was like the typical kid in a candy store, she thought. A total techie nerd, not at all the shallow jock she had assumed on first impression. A hot nerd, no less.

Galileo chuckled. "Another time. I think your mother and Zoe would probably rather get some sleep before tomorrow."

Zoe knew she was too hyper to sleep, but Natalie agreed.

"Almost done here," he said. "I want you to know your way around." He motioned to the final section of buildings on their left side, where the patients were housed. "That's the hospital and rehab center. Right now we have six patients receiving experimental treatments. We try to keep up their quality of life as much as possible, so please, go introduce yourselves sometime. They love getting visitors. It boosts their morale."

"Will do," Zoe promised. And she meant it. Even if she wasn't sick in the traditional sense, she wasn't so different from them—struggling to break free of her physical limitations, with the future hazy and unpredictable. But then, she wondered, who *wasn't* in that boat? Everyone "normal" was stuck in the booby trap of their own bodies too—but rather than be frozen like her, they were fighting to stave off deterioration. Her mom had a whole cabinet of antiaging products that did nothing, while her wrinkles and her worries deepened.

But if—and it was a big if—Natalie could find her mutation, it would mean a whole new paradigm for life—and death. Her aging process could be switched on until she reached the perfect age, like twenty-five, and then switched off in Gramps and her parents. Then her whole family might all be at peace with their bodies at last.

A thrill rocketed through her as she surveyed the circle once more. After that harrowing journey, they were here, this place was real, and the work that might change their lives forever could finally begin.

The next morning, upon entering the cafeteria, the four of them were greeted with thunderous applause. Beneath the low ceilings, about thirty people stood up as though giving a standing ovation. Next to rows of plain wooden benches and tables straight out of a summer camp mess hall, they whooped and cheered. They looked evenly split between men and women, roughly thirty to seventy years old. Zoe traded a glance with Theo, aware for the first time that they were by far the youngest people here.

He seemed amused, flashing a thumbs-up at the small crowd. But she couldn't help feeling caught off guard, nervously tucking a lock of hair behind her ear. Overwhelmed by homesickness the previous night, she hadn't slept more than an hour in her strange new bed, resulting in a lingering feeling of unease.

"Sorry," Galileo whispered in her ear. "It's the tradition to welcome new people."

Zoe looked at Natalie to gauge her level of embarrassment, but she was cupping her hand over her mouth. "Helen?"

A petite, grinning older woman with a gray bun emerged from the crowd, rushed toward them, and threw her arms around Natalie.

"You made it!" she said, turning to Galileo. "You did it!"

"I told you we would."

Natalie clutched her friend's hand. "It's really you."

"Who did you expect?"

She shook her head with a smile.

"Wait till you see the labs. You're going to flip out."

Helen turned to Theo, gazing up at his lanky six-foot frame. "Sweetie, did you grow *again*?"

He shrugged. "Nice to see you."

They hugged, then she crouched to Zoe's height. "And you must be Zoe Kincaid."

She stuck out her hand and Zoe shook it, aware of the other woman's inquisitive once-over. The whole room, she noticed, was watching her. Studying her. She wasn't sure whether to feel creeped out or delighted.

"I'm happy to be here," she said loudly, as much to the room as to Helen. "So when do we get down to business?"

The crowd laughed, and another burst of applause broke out. She smiled, starting to enjoy the spotlight. Here, she didn't need to explain, shield, admit, or deny her condition. On her own terms, for the first time, she could belong.

"Without further ado then," Galileo said, "let me introduce you to the aging team. Guys, do you want to come forward?"

Eight researchers stepped apart from the crowd— men and women, young and old, white, black, Asian, and Latino. All wore expressions of pride and gave a little bow or nod as Galileo called out their names and expertise.

"Dr. James Wong, genetics of aging with a focus on gene expression at specific developmental stages.

"Dr. Karen Rosenstein, genetics of aging with a focus on temporal order and physiological integrity.

"Dr. Susan Holmes, neuroendocrinology with a focus on the role of neurotransmitters in hippocampal function.

"Dr. Nina Hernandez, immunobiology with a focus on systems maintenance and function.

"Dr. Peter Daley, biochemistry with a focus on molecular measurements and metabolic status.

"Dr. Terrance Crouse, radiology, for MRI and CT scans.

"Dr. Richard Lee, biostatistics, for modeling and evaluating the data.

"Dr. Gina Patterson, medical anthropology, for anatomical measurements."

Zoe watched in awe, trying to take it all in. Their individual specialties sounded like Chinese to her, but Natalie's jubilation grew with each one. At the end Galileo gestured to her.

"And as you all already know, Dr. Natalie Roy. Genetics with a special interest in antagonistic pleiotropy and aging. Together, with Zoe, our dream team is finally complete."

More thunderous applause. They were certainly an enthusiastic group, Zoe thought. Not much like her image of scientists as antisocial and repressed. When the clapping died down, Galileo addressed Natalie. "What are your first steps going to be?"

She cleared her throat, looking down at Zoe. "To collect your blood sample. I suggest we start chromosome testing using karyotyping analysis."

The two geneticists, Dr. Wong and Dr. Rosenstein, raised challenging hands.

"I know," Natalie acknowledged, "it's unlikely we'll find anything that way." She turned back to Zoe, translating the unspoken exchange. "Because karyotyping visualizes only large chromosomal abnormalities. Probably your mutation is very small and requires another way to be detected. So next I would do CGH microarray, yes?"

Dr. Wong seemed pleased. "That's what I was going to suggest."

Zoe was desperate to keep up. It was hard to fathom the level of knowledge that these superhuman people possessed. "Which is?"

Natalie sighed. "You won't get this, but microarray works by exploiting the ability of a given mRNA molecule to bind specifically to the DNA template from which it originated. By using an array containing many of your DNA samples, we can determine in a single experiment, the expression levels of hundreds or thousands of genes within a cell. The amount of mRNA bound to the spots on the microarray is precisely measured with a computer, generating a profile of gene expression in the cell."

Zoe almost laughed. *That* was supposed to make sense to her?

"And if that doesn't yield anything," piped up Dr. Rosenstein, "we'll sequence your genome looking for partial point mutations." She raised her eyebrows at Natalie for confirmation.

"That's right," Natalie said, pinching her index finger and thumb together as if she were squeezing a grain of rice. "Those are subtle changes in single genes—the smallest changes and the hardest to find. If you have a weird variant around genes that control developmental rate, that might be meaningful and will give us a locus to investigate further."

"So basically," Zoe said, throwing her arms wide then drawing her palms closer together, "you're looking for the biggest stuff first, then going smaller and smaller."

"Exactly." Natalie turned to the team. "She's a bright one, so watch out."

Eight people shot her smiles as they gathered around Natalie, chatting about their experiments. In no time, the whole group swept out the door toward the labs, leaving behind cooled plates of eggs and toast on the cafeteria's long wooden tables.

Galileo hung back with Zoe and Theo. "You guys going to be okay without me?"

"Why?" she demanded. "Where are you going?"

"Other business. I won't be back for a while."

She tried to hide her disappointment, but apparently

did a poor job because Theo's arm fell around her shoulders, weighty and reassuring.

"No biggie," he said. "We'll stick together."

She gave him a shy smile, her pulse quickening. Maybe this land of possibilities had even more in store for her than she was counting on.

CHAPTER 24

The brick house was a one-bedroom wedged in among a row of look-alikes on a forgettable suburban block in Queens, New York. As soon as he drove up, Les could tell that it was a lower-class neighborhood, filled with patchy front lawns, cheap old cars, and broken bottles in the gutter. He was all too familiar with this kind of living—the kind where drunken screaming fights were rampant, where the neighbors hardly bothered to call the cops if a brawl broke out.

The sky was dark. He got out of his car, walked to the door, and knocked, holding his briefcase under his arm. After a few seconds, a beefy man opened the door a crack and poked his tan face out. His hostile expression appeared to soften as he sized up Les's elegant suit and tie.

"Who're you?"

Les said his name. "Chief of the Bioethics Committee. Pleased to meet you." He flashed his badge inside his jacket. "And are you Jasper Haynes, prison guard at the downtown Metropolitan Correctional Center?"

"Yeah. What can I do for you?"

"Mind if I come in and ask you a few questions about one of your former inmates?"

"Not at all. The place is kinda dirty, though."

"No prob."

Les walked in and found himself in a dining room that smelled of McDonald's fries. A red and white bag sat crumpled on the table next to a half-eaten cheeseburger and a large soda. Behind the table stood a kitchen with checkered wallpaper, outdated appliances, and a sink full of dishes. It opened onto a carpeted living room furnished with a sagging couch and a cluster of video game consoles at the base of a flat-screen TV, which was currently blasting a baseball game. On the wall above it was a framed poster of Muhammad Ali standing triumphantly over a prostrate opponent.

Les cleared his throat as he sat down on one of the dining table's wooden chairs. "Sorry to interrupt your dinner. This won't take long."

"It's cool. Want something to drink?"

"Water would be great, thanks."

As Haynes turned and headed to the kitchen, Les slipped the plastic lid off his host's soda cup, dropped in two small white tablets and replaced the lid, then sat back against his chair and fiddled with his BlackBerry. When Haynes returned with his water, Les took the glass with a smile. "Cheers," he said, touching it to the soda cup.

Haynes lifted his cup and took a swig. "So, what's this all about?"

"I want to talk to you about Natalie Roy."

"The woman who checked out a couple days ago?"

"You mean, was bailed out?"

"From my little hotel." The guard grinned, showing

off a row of crooked bottom teeth. "Except instead of paying to stay, you gotta pay to get out."

Les's warmth vanished. "So this is all a joke to you, huh?"

"What?"

"You think it's funny that now she's on the run?"

"No, I—"

"Do you know who she is?"

The guard squinted and rubbed his forehead. "Sorry, I suddenly don't . . ."

His eyes lost focus as he stared into the distance, his face draining. Les was sure he was going to pass out, but instead he laid his head down, cheek to the table. His eyes closed and his fleshy lips parted. A thin trail of drool slid out the corner of his mouth. Through his open mouth, he inhaled deep, slow breaths.

The television was still blaring the baseball game. It was obnoxiously loud. And just what Les had in mind. He flipped open his briefcase and surveyed its contents with satisfaction. Then he pulled on latex gloves, selected a coil of twine, and went to stand next to the sleeping guard.

"She's evil," Les said softly in his ear. "And you let her go free." He coaxed the guard's limp arms behind his chair and worked the twine around his wrists, then his ankles. His prisoner offered little resistance, just a few impotent grunts. It wasn't until Les stuffed a cloth gag into his mouth and fastened silver tape over it that his eyes fluttered opened—and registered terror. He tried to thrash his limbs and scream, but Les tapped him on the shoulder with something cold and sharp. A single glance at it made his body go still.

It was the blade of a pocketknife.

Les plunked it onto the table and spun it hard, so its blunt edge cut circles through the air. He stopped it when the point was aligned with the guard's chest.

"I want to play a little game," he said. "But it won't be fun if you don't play along, so I'm counting on you, okay?"

The guard tried to form a few muffled words.

"Just nod your head, idiot."

He nodded, his pupils dilating.

"Good. Now here are the rules: When I remove your gag, you *will not scream.* Otherwise . . ." He ran his gloved finger along the blade. "I really don't think you want that. You with me so far?"

The guard nodded again. His eyes were bulging now, forcing his heavy lids open. Les was having fun. He pulled his briefcase within reach.

"I brought a little picnic for you." Inside was an array of food and drink—a single-serve carton of milk, a bag of mixed nuts, a plastic container of shrimp, a hard-boiled egg, and a cup of strawberries.

"I couldn't help noticing your EpiPen sticking out of your shirt when you were photographed outside the jail," he went on. "You know, when you let that bitch off. And now no one can find her, or the guy who picked her up, or the girl they kidnapped. Which left me to wonder, what are you so *deathly* allergic to?"

The guard shook his head wildly and thrashed again, nearly knocking himself—and the chair—over.

"Remember our rules," Les said, stroking the blade. He wrinkled his nose. "No one wants a mess. Now, I hope you're still hungry after that Big Mac. What should we try first?"

The guard had given up struggling and was staring ahead, refusing to look at the food.

"You don't want to play? Fine. I'll choose." Les opened the container of shrimp and curled his lip. "I can't stand that fishy smell, can you?" He sniffed it. "I think this might have gone bad in the heat. Sorry about that."

He ripped the tape off the guard's lips and removed the cloth to stuff in two pink, wilting shrimps. Before the guard could spit them out, Les forced his mouth closed and kept his hand over it.

"Now chew."

With a disgusted look, he did. Then spat all the pieces into Les's hand. Les shoved them back inside and pinched his nose closed. "Swallow, God damn it!"

Haynes obeyed, muttering curses into his gloved hand.

"What was that? You want to wash it down with some milk? Here."

Again Les pinched the guard's nose as he brought the carton to his lips, forced them open, and poured. The milk spilled onto his chin and coated his tongue white. Les pressed his lips closed as he swallowed. They stared at each other. His prisoner regarded him with a look of pure hatred. Nothing happened.

"You're not the first person I've had to punish," Les said. "But you are just as idiotic as the last guy. Do you want to hear how he died?"

The guard scrunched up his face and shook his head almost imperceptibly.

"No? I'll tell you anyway. His name was Eliot Shipley." Les paused as a smile of amusement came to his lips. "I've never told this to anyone before. But I feel like I can talk to you. Trust you." He spun the knife around on the table again, enjoying its flash of silver.

The guard averted his gaze and focused instead on his lap, where drops of milk had left dark wet circles on his shorts.

"So this guy," Les went on, "he was a pretty big jerk. A research scientist who made drugs that ended up killing innocent people. Like my mom."

He swallowed hard as the recollection assaulted him. How could he have known then, back when he was in charge of the FDA's division of drugs for rare diseases, that the drug he himself approved for a clinical trial to help her would actually end up killing her? And not just killing her, but torturing her. She had suffered for years hoping for a cure, and when a new drug application came along claiming to neutralize the mutant gene responsible for Huntington's disease, Les had jumped at it. He should have known to look for the cheap shortcuts that Panex Pharmaceuticals might take to serve its corporate interests—the bottom line drove them like a steamroller over any measly human lives that stood in the way. But he had been naive approving that trial, and even pulling strings so his mother could take part.

For twenty-three days after trying the drug, she had lain paralyzed but conscious, a panicked prisoner of her own body. Those weeks would haunt Les for the rest of his life.

Thanks to his mother's death and a few others who had suffered a similar fate in the early trials, the FDA had mandated that a warning label on the bottle would list possible "rare side effects," which made Panex happy because the drug still got approved over Les's objections. He came to see that the whole enterprise of drug development and clinical trials was a corrupt machine, favoring exploitation of the poor and vulnerable who could never really understand what they were getting into, nor whose ends they were there to serve.

"The point is," Les said to the guard, "someone had to pay for what she went through. It was only fair. So Eliot was mauled to death by his own chimpanzees. Left alone overnight while they shredded his body to pieces. The mess of blood and guts was so bad the next day that the police could barely tell his remains were human."

The guard thrashed against his twine with wide-eyed terror. Les grabbed the knife and pointed it at his neck. He grew still.

"Don't worry," he said, "yours will be much, much cleaner. Let's keep things moving. Shall we try the nuts?" Les opened the ziplock bag and selected a few peanuts from the almonds, walnuts, and cashews. "My personal favorite," he said as he parted the guard's lips once more. "Nothing like a good peanut butter sandwich, right?"

The guard moved to chomp down on his fingers, but Les was too quick. He dropped the peanuts in and shoved his jaw closed. The guard squirmed with all his might, trying to spit and kick and bite. Still Les managed to keep his mouth shut with the peanuts inside.

It was enough.

First his lips expanded as if an invisible pump were inflating them. Then he coughed violently, his eyes filled with panic. Les stepped back to let nature take its course. It didn't take long, only a minute more of struggling and wheezing, gasping and choking. His face turned a deep shade of blue. Tears ran down his cheeks. He gurgled at Les with pathetic urgency, his eyebrows lifting up and down as if they were flailing. Soon the whimpering eased, the struggling against his restraints subsided. A few incoherent sounds escaped his obscenely swollen lips. Then his head dropped to the table and was still.

"Someone had to take the fall," Les said.

The fugitives had embarrassed him by escaping from that suburb in Ohio, and if Natalie hadn't been let off so easily, none of it would have happened.

Someone always had to take the fall when Les was wronged.

And he could think of no better person to take the *blame* for the fall than Galileo—the man who thrived off illegal human science experiments. When the Network came on the scene two years back, Les realized he had the perfect setup at last to extract his revenge for his mother's death. One simple copycat postcard arriving at his own office, and bam!—everyone on the Bioethics Committee believed Galileo was taking responsibility for the vicious chimp incident.

This one would be just as easy.

After taking one last look at Mr. Jasper Haynes's slumped body, Les went to work untying the twine around his ankles and wrists. The body was still warm. Les lifted it to the floor and splayed out his arms, so it looked as though he had fallen after the tragic strike of anaphylaxis. Then Les cleaned up the remains of their little picnic, returned the pocketknife to his briefcase, spilled out the cup of soda and his own glass of water into the sink of dirty dishes. Within five minutes of Haynes's last breath, Les was driving away.

By the time a postcard signed by Galileo and bearing the name of Jasper Haynes arrived in the committee's D.C. headquarters, his death would already have been declared accidental, his body long disposed of, and the crime scene disturbed by who knew how many people. It would be too late to figure out the truth.

But it wouldn't be too late to let Galileo live with the consequences.

CHAPTER 25

A week later, the escape of the fugitives in Ohio was gnawing at Les with the sickening omnipresence of a parasite. Still no trace of them had been found. As if that weren't shameful enough, now he faced the task of recounting the incident before twenty scornful faces—the entire Bioethics Committee. The stunning escape, combined with a new postcard from Galileo claiming responsibility for the death of Natalie Roy's prison guard, had prompted the committee to demand an emergency meeting. Now here they were: all twenty members convened around a lacquered wood conference table to join forces on the single case that trumped every other. The case that Les apparently couldn't handle alone.

Ever the professional, he stood and recited the facts about the escape without emotion, hiding his own exasperation as if to balance out theirs. The black Honda Civic abandoned in a junkyard off I-70. The Ohio state trooper knocked out cold, his vehicle stolen and later found empty in the Columbus suburb of Worthington.

The search that proved futile despite the helicopter patrols, despite the police blockade, despite the sheer avalanche of manpower that had descended on the neighborhood.

He passed around the latest postcard that "Galileo" had apparently mailed to the headquarters a few days earlier, with the standard message and signature. It looked authentic, if he did say so himself. At home, before sending it, he'd practiced on eighteen other postcards to get the slant of the loops exactly right. Then he burned all except the best one in his fireplace, drinking a merlot as he watched them blacken and crumple in the flames.

His colleagues examined what they didn't realize was his handiwork. They passed the postcard from one to the next around the table with the solemnity of doctors studying a deadly bacteria. Les noticed that Benjamin Barrow spent a minute longer than everyone else scrutinizing it, but at last he gave up and passed it along.

"I don't get it. Why would he target a prison guard this time?" asked the man next to Barrow. "All the others were science related."

"That's a good question." Les paused for good measure, though his answer was prepared. "Maybe the guard found out something about whoever posted Natalie Roy's bail—or maybe he learned something from her—and Galileo had to eliminate him before he spilled the beans."

"That would make sense," said a woman halfway down the table. "I mean, the poor guy was found dead right after Natalie Roy got out."

Les nodded at her for reasons she would never know. "What's become quite clear," he said, "is that we're dealing with an organized criminal gang that has never existed before in the history of bio-crimes. They're clever, prepared, and vicious, and they stop at nothing to get what they want."

He glanced around the table, hoping that his aggrandized statement would soften their judgment of him. It was true, anyway. The Network was too shadowy and too vast for one man to take on. But deep down, he didn't believe that excuse. If one man was strong enough to run it, one man was strong enough to destroy it.

Seated to his left, Barrow wagged a slender index finger and addressed the room. "I believe our chief has left out an important part of the story."

Les shot him a look. "Excuse me?"

Barrow's cold blue eyes were mocking. "Before this postcard. Back when the fugitives got away."

"What are you talking about?"

"Oh, just the part where they stopped at a pharmacy and you were notified." His attention shifted to the whole group. "Our chief could have closed in right then and there, but no. Instead he decided to let them get away."

The committee expressed their collective disapproval with a hurl of knife-gazes.

"Is this true, Les?" asked a dour woman who was known to act cliquey with Barrow and the other most senior members. She peered at him through brown tortoise-shell bifocals.

Assholes, he thought, glaring at Barrow. "At least I was here working."

Barrow pushed his white hair back with the infuriating sigh of a victim. "Apparently not well."

"So now we've got nothing?" asked a man with a goatee, exchanging a dismayed look with Barrow.

"Not *nothing*," Les said through clenched teeth. "I was getting to that. First of all, let me clarify that I didn't just 'let them get away.' I ordered an undercover car to track them so we could get more intelligence. It was not my intention for that car to lose them."

"Oh no?" the man muttered.

Les ignored him. "During our investigation of the neighborhood, I came across some fresh footprints in the backyard of an old immigrant named Julian Hernandez. These have now been analyzed. One sole, smaller than the others, had a unique pattern with interlocking squares. It's been identified as a size five Converse sneaker. We've contacted Zoe Kincaid's parents and confirmed that she happens to own this very shoe. And that it's missing from her closet."

His colleagues stared at him, unimpressed. On the lacquered wood walls, their individual framed headshots—each one the grave epitome of authority—appeared to double the severity of their judgment. Les felt a prickle of sweat under his armpits.

A blond-haired woman with a pointy nose voiced their frustration. "But we still don't know where they went."

"Without anything else to go on," he said, "I agree this would be unhelpful. But get this. After the search of the neighborhood and the woods, I personally went back to Hernandez's house and scoured every inch of the floor, upstairs and downstairs. And I spotted a print in the thick carpet of his bedroom that seemed to me just like that one. Forensics confirmed today that it was a size five Converse sneaker."

Now he had their rapt attention. Even Barrow perked up, watching, waiting.

"Hernandez denies having anything to with it," Les went on. "He says they could have entered through the back door when he was in the living room watching TV. But I don't know. For one thing, his sliding glass door creaks pretty loudly. Of course he says he's hard of hearing. We can't indict him because his involvement is impossible to prove. But we *can* still question him, as long as he agrees to cooperate. I'm flying back to Columbus today to see if I can trap him into spilling something."

"Have you looked into his history?" Barrow asked, twirling a rubber band the way he often did when he got excited.

"Of course." Les ticked the facts off his fingertips. "He was an elevator repairman for thirty years. Emigrated from Mexico in 1972, became legal in '78. Owns his house. But most interesting, I think, is that he has a daughter named Nina born in 1980. The mother died in childbirth."

"Let's talk to her, too," Barrow said. "What does she do now?"

"That's the thing." Les paused. "She's a scientist. With a doctorate in immunobiology from the University of Arizona. And as far as we can tell, she hasn't been seen or heard from in two years."

Les relished the surprise that registered on their faces, and the subsequent realization.

"Two years ago," said a man in a tweed jacket. "Wasn't that when the Network allegedly formed?"

"That's right."

Barrow tapped his fingers across his mouth, eyeing Les with something akin to respect. "You might be onto something. But when you go to question this guy, you can't come on too strong. If he shuts down, you're out."

Les gave him a tight-lipped smile. "I'll handle it."

A red-haired woman spoke from the far end of the table. "Who thinks someone else should go, too? Do good cop, bad cop?"

Inwardly Les moaned. All he wanted was to be left alone to confront Hernandez, not worrying about a colleague who might deviate from the script. But to his chagrin, everyone around the table was nodding.

Barrow flashed him a guileless smile. "I'll go."

Les closed his eyes. *Of course you will.*

Six hours later, after hammering out their approach on the flight from Reagan to Columbus, they pulled up to Julian Hernandez's two-story home. It was 8:30 P.M., still early enough to call, and Les was feeling pretty good. Barrow, in spite of his haughtiness, had proved to be a supportive partner, praising his aggressiveness and suggesting new ways to harness it for maximum effectiveness. While Les hated to admit it—and never would aloud—he found himself the tiniest bit grateful to have Barrow at his side, shouldering some responsibility for the task ahead. *The enemy of my enemy is my friend,* he thought as they knocked on the door, federal badges in hand.

"We got this," Barrow said. "Remember the line about the cult."

His ribs expanded with anticipation. The old man had no idea what was coming. While they waited for him to answer, Les was distracted by an unnerving thought. Hernandez was an elderly, decrepit seventy—and only fourteen years his senior. Les had never thought of that stage in life as a reality. It had always been a vague theoretical proposition, made more distant by his physical robustness and mental energy. But suddenly it struck him that he *was* going to be old one day.

And one day, he was going to die, most likely of aging.

His mind went blank. The words he had recited so many times in lectures filled him, at once soothing and blistering. *Death is a necessary and desirable end. An important part of the cycle of nature with which we should never interfere.*

The door opened, wrenching him back to the present. Julian's coffee-colored face thrust through the gap. Beholding Les with a flicker of recognition, he pressed his lips together and glanced at Barrow. Disbelief and fear crept into his eyes, but his accented voice came out steady.

"Señor, I tell you before, I don't know nothing."

"Mr. Hernandez," Les said, "this is my colleague Benjamin Barrow on the Bioethics Committee. We need to ask you a few more questions."

"Can we come in?" Barrow asked, one black boot already through the doorway.

Julian hesitated as if trying to remember his rights.

Les took advantage of his uncertainty by elbowing the door open a little more.

"This will be fast," he promised. "We appreciate your cooperation."

Julian stepped aside, leaning on his cane. Barrow and Les followed him to the living room, taking seats on the faded beige sofa. The house no longer smelled of taco spices, Les noted. Now it reeked of lime cleaning spray. The layer of dust he remembered—on the coffee table, the mantle, the wood floor—was gone. He felt a beat of pity for the old man. If Julian were innocent, as he claimed, the ordeal must have been traumatizing. Fugitives breaking in and taking cover in your house. Trampling over your floor, touching your things. No wonder the place was scrubbed clean.

Or cleaned of evidence.

Les traded a quick look with his partner. *Ready?*

Barrow gave a slight nod. Les looked Julian in the eye, remembering the lines they had rehearsed all afternoon. "Mr. Hernandez, we want to remind you that these people who found cover in your house kidnapped a young girl. As long as she's in their grip, her life is in serious danger."

"Her parents are beside themselves," Barrow added, his tone grave. "She has a severe medical condition and could die without the proper medication."

"It may already be too late." Les allowed a meaningful pause. "We have no other leads except her footprint. In your house."

Julian sat stonily, his mouth shut.

Les propped his arm up on the couch, his tone switching from ominous to matter-of-fact. "This is simple. You tell us what you know so she isn't dead by the time we find her."

"But I no have information," Julian said, turning his palms up.

Barrow crossed his ankle over his knee and leaned forward. "Mr. Hernandez, you seem like a nice man. You've worked hard your whole life. You're proud to be an American, right?"

He nodded.

"Well, Americans tell the truth. We stand by our country in times of need. Your service to us, here, now, would be the greatest way you could repay this country that has given you everything."

Les leaned in. "Not just you, but your daughter, too."

Julian started. "You know about Nina?"

Barrow stared at Les for a long moment. His eyes burned with provocation, the tacit challenge hovering in the air between them. This was the part in the script they had debated the most—whether to take a risk, improvising more than they really knew, or to play it safe and truthful.

Les turned to Julian as the lie escaped his mouth. "Mr. Hernandez, we know all about your daughter."

"You do?"

Barrow chipped in, careful to conceal any hint of accusation. "We know she's working for Galileo's Network in secret."

Julian shook his head, looking back and forth between them. "How you know that?"

Dead giveaway, Les thought, biting his lip to kill his smile. Very few people in the public knew about the

Network's existence, so the reaction of an innocent man should have been bewilderment.

"Whatever you know about the Network is wrong," Les declared, ignoring Julian's question. "They dupe good people into following them, claiming all kinds of impossible-to-promise rewards."

"It's understandable why a bright girl like your daughter would get sucked in," Barrow said. "But no matter what she might have told you, it's a lie. The people who run it are the worst thugs on Earth. Tricking brilliant scientists like her into running horrible experiments."

"Once you get in," Les said, "it's almost impossible to get out. Mr. Hernandez, this cult has sunk its fangs into your daughter. She needs you now more than ever. Please, help us help her. We're the good guys. Tell us what you know."

Julian looked down, wringing his hands.

Barrow reached out and touched his arm. "The sooner you talk, the sooner we can work on getting your daughter out of there. But if we've got nothing to go on—"

"If she's even still alive," Les threw in.

"As long as you cooperate, there won't be any repercussions for you," Barrow added. "But we can't extend that generosity much longer."

Julian squirmed, his gaze darting between them.

"We're the good guys," Barrow repeated with a smile. "You can trust us."

The seconds passed as they stared at him, thawing his resolve. His face was grim. There was a tortured look in his eyes. When he muttered his assent at last, Les wanted to pump his fist in the air. Keeping his tone stern, he hurled questions from the script before Julian could second-guess himself.

"When was the last time you saw Nina?"

He held up two stubby fingers. *"Dos años."*

"Where did she tell you she was going? Or did she just disappear?"

"She say . . . ah . . ." He paused, struggling to find the right words. "You speak *español*?" he asked.

Les shook his head, but to his surprise, a flow of perfectly accented words left Barrow's mouth. *"Sí, un poco. Tengo familia en España."*

Julian's face brightened. The two of them exchanged a few sentences that Les couldn't translate. Then he launched into a rapid-fire monologue, wagging a finger and frowning as if he were warning someone, then shrugging and shaking his head. Les watched him, latching on to a few words here and there—*"mi casa"* and "Nina"—but was mostly lost. Barrow tilted his head in an encouraging manner, asking questions without appearing to judge. Their rapport seemed to improve as Julian shifted to speak only to him. Les felt annoyed, invisible, until he saw Barrow's eyes widen.

"What?" he demanded.

Barrow fired off several more questions and Julian looked down as he answered, his tone recognizable in any language. It was shame.

"What's he saying?" Les asked, his hands growing cold.

"Muchas gracias," Barrow said, inclining his head. He turned to Les, but his expression was difficult to read. Les wondered if he was tempering his reaction for the sake of the old man.

"There's good news and bad news."

"Bad first."

"He has no clue where his daughter is, or where the girl could have been taken. And he still claims he had nothing to do with them sneaking into his house."

Les sighed. "Great."

"But listen to this. He has diabetes, and his daughter wanted to help cure him. That's how she got sucked into the whole crazy Network in the first place. She told him she'd have to disappear for a while and he couldn't tell anyone or risk putting her in danger. He didn't like the sound of it, said he argued with her, but she insisted. He hasn't heard from her since. Now he thinks she was the one who told the fugitives where he lived so they could go after the gold stashed up in his bedroom."

Les frowned at Julian. "You think she betrayed you? After leaving to supposedly help you?"

The old man shrugged. "I not explain it."

"They must have brainwashed her. Was anything stolen?"

He shook his head. "They not find it."

"Why didn't you tell me this before? Why did you deny knowing anything?"

A frightened look came into his eyes as he mumbled a few sentences in Spanish.

Barrow interpreted. "He didn't want to out her in case it gets her in trouble. But now he's so worried that he doesn't care. He just wants us to find her again."

"Which we will," Les said.

"But wait." Barrow's words came tumbling out. "The last time he talked to her before she left, she tried to convince him to offer his house as a safe house. He refused, but she told him he could change his mind anytime. All he'd need to do is display the secret sign of the followers outside, and then they would know they were welcome."

"Which is?"

"A mailbox decorated with a painting of the sun."

Les gave a disgusted snort. "What the hell does that mean? Galileo thinks he's the center of the universe?"

"Who cares?" Barrow's tone was slick with contempt. "We alert the post office right away, and the next thing we know—"

Les finished his thought with a smirk. "The leads will come pouring in."

CHAPTER 26

Galileo's return to the compound after a two-week absence changed the mood of the place, and Natalie could feel the difference in the air. His presence was like a hearth, restoring both warmth and energy to the isolated valley. People smiled at each other more and walked faster. When he was away, as Natalie had discovered, their morale was subject to the daily frustrations of experimentation. A communal misery sometimes united them more than any lofty shared goals.

But on the day that he came back—clean-shaven, in a linen suit, his tan faded and his wavy black hair growing out—the place buzzed. Beyond the speculation over his recent whereabouts was an eagerness to reunite with the man who made their passion projects possible. Natalie accepted that they celebrated him as the architect of the grand scheme in which they lived. They told her of his genuine interest, not just in their work, but in them as human beings—each with a family and a home left behind in order to join the compound. It was a choice to stay, a choice he never seemed to take for granted, and that was what endeared him to them the most.

She couldn't help wanting to cut through the rejoicing with a few pointed questions. Yes, he was bold and brilliant and gracious. Yes, he had pulled off a feat of stunning complexity. But who was he? Why did he do it? And was there *anyone* on earth who really knew him?

No one could tell her the answers.

Over the past three weeks, between grueling days in her state-of-the-art lab, she had discovered that it was everyone's favorite late-night topic. Even Theo and Zoe enjoyed staying up to discuss it, attending the nightly gathering in the quad, a kind of town square ritual that Natalie had come to anticipate. To her delight, they appeared to have overcome their initial awkwardness and become friends. While she literally burrowed down to work, they spent their days hiking through the mountains, reading to the hospital patients, and amusing themselves with the iPad's reserve of television shows, books, movies, and music.

Three times a week, Galileo had arranged for Theo to study computer science with the tech guys in the Brain. Neither he nor Zoe had been to sleepaway camp before, which this place somewhat approximated, and Natalie could tell they relished their daily freedom. If Zoe was homesick, as any actual fourteen-year-old would be, she didn't show it.

Every night, Natalie felt grateful for their newfound contentedness, even as she knew it couldn't last. The long summer days would inevitably turn colder and darker, signaling the time for Theo to start college and

Zoe to return home and embrace whatever future lay before her. Even if Natalie wouldn't mind staying forever, engrossed in productive work, living alongside Helen and the others, she knew the kids could not. That was partly why she was rushing to run the experiments as quickly as possible.

The eight-person team had welcomed her with so much enthusiasm that she wondered if they were overcompensating, given the typically hostile competitiveness among scientists. But when they recounted for her all of their prior experiments, displaying the models and results, she understood that their reaction was genuine. Trying to find the master regulator gene was a random shot in the dark depths of an organism's entire genome, like searching for a single piece of seaweed in an ocean. You needed someone like Zoe, with that gene fundamentally changed—akin to making the seaweed glow—and an enterprising specialist like herself to figure out where to look.

The less-than-humble truth was that she and Zoe were the best thing that could have happened to the project. But she made sure never to act like she knew it, or risk their goodwill becoming resentment. Her lifetime in labs had not yet solved biology's biggest mystery, but it had schooled her in fragile egos.

As the days passed, the team's chatter escalated about not only making some real leaps, but having a shot at the financial windfall that was the Archon Prize—the deadline approaching in just five and a half months. A lighthearted but constant reminder was pinned to the hallway outside their labs, three stories underground—an old-school calendar of cheeky quotes.

The current month, July, featured one by the astrophysicist Neil deGrasse Tyson: *The good thing about science is that it's true whether or not you believe in it.*

The date of December 31 was circled in red, no further comment needed.

On July 6, the date of Galileo's return, the latest results from the karyotyping, microarray, and genetic sequencing of Zoe's DNA came in.

Which was why, when Natalie found him unpacking in his apartment, her palms were clammy with dread.

He greeted her with a friendly but tired smile. "Hey, what can I do for you?"

She stepped inside, waving a hand to indicate that this was no trivial matter to be discussed in the doorway. Through his only window, the late afternoon sun poured a golden dust mote across the floor where his black suitcase lay, half emptied. Outside, she could see the foothills of the mountains clustered tight around them like sentries.

His apartment was smaller than she expected, the same cookie-cutter studio as everyone else's. She wasn't sure why that should surprise her. From the little she did know about him, it was clear that he didn't care much for show. His only luxuries seemed to be the fine suits he wore when he came back, but while he was living on the compound, he spent his days in a tracksuit and sneakers.

Still wearing his fine navy suit, he knelt to flip his suitcase closed. Then he stood, giving her his full attention.

"What's up?"

She wondered how many days he had gone without sleeping this time. In truth, his exhaustion was almost titillating. It was like a dent to the barrier of his professionalism, one notch closer to the real him.

"Tough commute?"

"You might say."

She ignored the temptation to press him for details. "Going to stick around for a bit?"

He shrugged. "I've got a four-day turnaround."

"Practically a vacation for you." She smiled nervously, indulging her desire to delay the news. "I bet you can't remember the last time you took one?"

A flash of what looked like grief crossed his face, so quickly that she barely processed it. Then he was shaking his head with a bemused smile: "Can't say I do."

"Too bad. Hey, you look different. Did you change something?"

His eyebrows raised as if to say, *That the best you can do?* She could tell his patience was dropping off by the second.

"I know!" she exclaimed. "It's your nose! You took off the prosthetic." When he'd come to pick her up from the jail, the bridge of his nose had been high and thin, with a mild bump. Now it was straight and sharp. It made his whole face look more proportional—more handsome.

"Yep. No cameras, no costume. This is me."

"Is it, now?" She crossed her arms, her tone as light as she could manage.

He eyed her before turning to hang up a black suit in the closet. "So what is it you're afraid to tell me?"

I could ask you the same, she thought.

Instead she said, "We got the results of Zoe's genetic analysis today."

His head snapped around to face her. "And?"

"We found something. A weird variant. She has a microdeletion in region q13.3 of chromosome 22."

"Could it be significant?"

"Well . . ." Her eyes roamed around his compact studio—his glass coffee table, black love seat, full-size bed made up with a neat white comforter. The room's only picture was on the wooden nightstand: a framed four-by-six photo of a smiling young girl wearing a pink baseball cap. Oddly, her eyelashes were white, and her skin sagged around the corners of her mouth like an old lady's. Natalie found herself transfixed by the image.

Galileo walked between her and the picture and lowered himself to the couch.

The sudden storm in his mood was alarming—his brows were pulled close together, his lips a tight line, his arms crossed over his chest.

"You were saying? The variant?"

"Sorry, yes." She tore her gaze from the picture behind his shoulder and smiled sheepishly in apology—though for what, she didn't know. "We also found sequence errors in a single gene called Shank3/ProSAP2 associated with an adjacent region that might be related to aging."

He uncrossed his arms, leaning forward. "So what does that mean?"

She took his fascination as an invitation to sit beside him. "We might be onto something. If this is the right mutation, it could be the marker we need to locate the region that causes her developmental inertia. The actual genes in that region would have to be isolated and tested then to see if they're the ones responsible for aging."

"And if they are?"

"Then we run tests to silence the analogous genes in mice. And see if they stop aging."

"Just what the world needs. A bunch of biologically immortal rodents."

She chuckled. "I promise we'd keep them in their cages."

A grin broke over his face, chasing away any lingering darkness. "I always expected you to make progress, but to have come up with a possible marker already, it's—"

"No." She held up a hand. "I wish it were that easy. But we can't be sure that we're starting with the right mutation unless . . ." She trailed off, biting her lip.

"Unless what?"

"Unless we test her family."

He balked. "You're telling me you need DNA samples from her *parents*?"

She held his gaze without flinching. "I know, it's never going to happen. But that's the only way to tell if this is really a weird variant worth investigating or if it's just inherited—in which case, it's not the one we're after."

"Christ. Even Zoe herself couldn't ask them for that. Have you told her?"

"No, I wanted you to know first. The thing is, we really need it to move forward."

"Can't you just assume this mutation is unique to her and keep going?"

She lifted an eyebrow, rebuffing his wishful thinking.

He rubbed his temple as though it ached. "I know what you're going to say."

"What?"

"Assumptions are the death of science. Not to mention a fantastic waste of time."

She gave him a half smile in spite of herself. "Pretty much."

"You're right. I may have an idea. But every time I go back out there, it's a giant risk. I didn't want to upset you, but I heard through the Network that whoever's framing me has struck again. Now the feds' pursuit is hotter than ever. That guy at the top, he's not going to let us get away from him."

"Oh no." Natalie stared at the solemn line of his mouth, realizing how swiftly she had pushed the worry from her mind upon their arrival—not that it made the threat any less real.

"What can you do?" she asked, trying to keep her voice even to match his.

"I've got to be more careful than ever, since my little vacation is up."

"Already?"

"I promised you all the supplies you'd need, didn't I?"

"Within reason—not if it means getting yourself caught—"

By way of answer, he strode back to his closet and lifted the suit he had hung up minutes before. "I leave tonight."

CHAPTER 27

Twenty days after Zoe's disappearance, at a quarter past seven in the evening, Stephen Kincaid heard a knock at his door. His wife was upstairs taking a shower and he was in the den, staring at the distraction of the television without really seeing it.

He rose to answer it, not giving much thought to who could be calling. Probably a neighbor with another fruit basket, another reminder of the most agonizing event of his life. Not that he needed reminding. In his head on a constant loop played every interaction with his daughter leading up to That Morning, as he thought of it.

Where had he gone wrong? By trying to protect her, had he forced her away? There was no doubt in his mind that if he had been more accepting of her choices, she would be here today. At home, safe, where she belonged. But she was as stubborn and determined as he had raised her to be. Since she was a kindergartner learning to count, she had always prided herself on seeing challenges through. He should have known she wasn't about to quit this time.

Overwhelmed with a wave of guilt, he checked the peephole. On the stoop standing before him was a tall, well-built stranger in his fifties or sixties, wearing a crisp black suit and tie, with a briefcase slung over his shoulder. His dark hair was wavy and a smattering of stubble covered his chin. His blue eyes seemed somber.

Stephen opened the door. "What can I do for you?"

"Mr. Kincaid?"

"Yes. And you are?"

"Jonathan Kelp, FBI." He opened his jacket to reveal a gold badge with the familiar open-winged eagle. "I'm on the forensics team in the STB reporting to Bud Pinter and Les Mahler, and I've been sent to tell you about a possible new development in your daughter's case."

"What?" Stephen's heart started to hammer. "Why hasn't anyone called me?"

"This just happened today, sir. My bosses had me come in person because we're going to need your cooperation. I'll explain. Can I come in?"

"Of course." A nauseating dread cooled his skin as they walked inside. Catastrophic visions pummeled him—Zoe's body found, covered in blood, her vital organs removed. His baby's precious body. It was not so long ago, the day that her downy head could fit in his palm.

Kelp was taking a seat on the couch when Stephen clutched his arm, breathing hard.

"Just tell me, is she alive?"

They locked eyes. The other man's gaze was serious, his tone sincere. "We believe so."

"But you don't know for sure?"

"We got a tip today from a woman at a diner in

Omaha, Nebraska, who thinks she recognized Zoe there this afternoon."

He emitted a cry. "Pam!" he hollered. "Pam, hurry!"

His wife rushed to the landing and down the stairs, a blue towel wrapped around her head, nearly tripping over her long black nightgown. "What is it, what's wrong?"

He gestured to their visitor, too overcome to speak. Kelp stood and introduced himself, then delivered the news. Her hand flew to her mouth, tears springing to her eyes.

"Who was she with?" Stephen demanded. "How did she seem?"

"If it was really her," Kelp said. "We don't know yet, but we're taking it seriously. According to the witness, she looked healthy and happy. She was with an older dark-haired woman."

Stephen clenched his fists. "Natalie Roy?"

"That's our guess. But by the time the witness connected their faces to the news, they had already left. The police have dusted their booth for fingerprints and hair and other biological markers, but to confirm that it was really her, we need to test both of your DNA for a match."

"Of course!" Pam exclaimed, almost jumping from foot to foot. "How? When?"

"Now." Kelp leaned over to open the briefcase at his feet and removed two white plastic kits with what looked like toothbrushes and a tube inside. He handed one to each of them. "All you have to do is scrape the inside of your cheek with these swab collectors. Scrape hard for about sixty seconds, so we get enough DNA. Otherwise it could mean a delay."

They took the kits and pulled out the brushes. Stephen inserted its tough bristles into his mouth and scrubbed, rubbing his cheek raw. Pam did the same, wincing. She had always been ticklish.

"That's good," Kelp said after a minute. "That's enough."

They handed him the scrapers, now coated with saliva. He unscrewed the caps on the two plastic tubes and plunged in the bristly heads, ejecting them so that they released into the clear liquid.

"This solution prevents bacteria growth," Kelp explained. "But your specimens won't be in here long. We'll test them right away and get back to you."

He stood to leave, his expression still grave. "Are there any other family members nearby to test? I recall a grandfather? It helps for ensuring accuracy."

Stephen exchanged a look with his wife. *Do you want to explain?*

She turned to Kelp. "Well, there was my father, but . . . but he doesn't live with us anymore."

"He had some cell phone contact with that *woman*," Stephen said, "prior to her arrest. And then he lied to us about the note Zoe left him. We couldn't trust him after that."

"Even though he denies having a part in it," Pam added. "But he moved out anyway. My husband and he just weren't getting along."

"I see. Do you know where he went?"

She shook her head, crestfallen. "We haven't heard from him since."

"Oh." Kelp faltered, seeming unsure how to respond.

"Well, thank you," Stephen said, extending his hand

like a bridge over the awkward pause. "We appreciate your coming all the way here from . . . from—"

"D.C. It's no problem, sir. We just want to get your daughter home quick and safe."

"Thank you," Stephen said again, giving him a solid handshake. "You'll let us know as soon as you know something?"

"Of course. I have a feeling Zoe will come out of this just fine. It's only a matter of time."

As soon as the door closed behind him, Stephen ran to the phone in the kitchen to call Les Mahler, whose number he had memorized weeks earlier. Last they talked, Les had informed Stephen of some promising new intelligence regarding the Network's coded communication with its followers—something about painted mailboxes—but since then, there had been no real leads.

Day after day, they had been coping with the painful rise of hope and crushing disappointment. Now he couldn't wait to rehash this latest, biggest development with the man in charge. Maybe Les would share with them even more details. Stephen wanted to soak up every little one, from the length of his daughter's hair, to the meal she had eaten, to the clothes she had been wearing.

When Les answered the phone, his voice was clipped, as if he were running to or from some important meeting. "Yeah?"

"Les, it's Stephen. Can you *believe* this?"

Pam nudged him aside, pressing her mouth to the phone. "We're freaking out!"

Stephen hit the speaker button. Silence filled the room.

"Les, you there?"

"Uh, yeah, what are you talking about?"

"You know! The witness. In Omaha?"

"What? Who said anything about a witness?"

Stephen wanted to shake him. "The FBI agent who was just here! Doing the DNA testing?"

"The *what?* Who?"

He swallowed past the rise of bile in his throat. "Jonathan Kelp?"

The room was as silent as death. Stephen couldn't bear to look at Pam, even as a low moan escaped her.

"I'm sorry," Les said. His voice sounded strangled. "We have no one by that name."

Stephen sprinted to the front door and flung it open, Pam trailing close on his heels. Outside, the trees were swaying in the warm night. The block was empty, save for a yellow cab rolling by with its light on, waiting to pluck any stranger off the street.

CHAPTER 28

July 11th

Dear Gramps,

    It's been three and a half weeks since I left. I know you're probably worried, but don't be. The people here are really nice and taking good care of me. We had kind of a rough trip, but Galileo got us through it and got me more pills. Since then, I've just been hanging out with my new friend, this guy Theo, Natalie's son. We're about the same age. I mean, in years. I didn't know if we'd get along at first, with all the weird stuff I have going on, but we actually do. He's really fun and down-to-earth, more of a nerd than I thought he would be. I think you'd like him. Natalie's busy in the lab every day, but we see her at night. She's super smart and I can tell everyone really respects her. I think she'll find my mutation, hopefully soon. It's all I can think about. At least I know she's working on it with this whole team nonstop. You're NOT allowed to get any older until then, OK?!

Oh, also, I made some other friends in the hospital center. There's one woman, Mrs. Avalon, she has leukemia and they are trying some radical treatment on her. Sorry I don't know all the medical details. I wish you could be here. You would just eat this place up. I feel like I can barely appreciate it, though. All these ridiculously smart people talk in science language and I can't understand a word. Thank God for Theo. And Mrs. Avalon. She and I have the same favorite books! To Kill a Mockingbird and A Wrinkle in Time and The Secret Garden. I've been reading to her every day, so I feel like I'm still doing something worthwhile while I'm waiting for them to get somewhere. I guess I could go home now that they have my DNA, but I don't want to leave until I know it was worth it to come here. I just have to see what happens.

I'm still lonely, though. I miss you so much. Today especially. No one even knows . . . what today is. I even miss Mom and Dad. I'm a little jealous that Galileo gets to go see you guys without me. Hope Mom and Dad will understand one day how badly we needed their swabs for the research. Sucks that he had to trick them into it, but you know what? If they were on my side the whole time, this wouldn't be happening.

p.s. You would love how pretty it is out here. There are even running paths. Sorry I can't put more than that in writing. It's against the rules. Oh well, you'll get this soon and that will be

*enough. I guess you can't really write back, so
just blow me a kiss. I'll wait for a real one when
I come home. Hope it won't be long.*

> *Love,*
> *Zoe*

She drew a heart around the word *love*, her trademark
sign-off, and stuffed the letter into its envelope, then
stood from her perch on the giant pile of red rocks she
affectionately thought of as her thinking spot. It was
about a mile away from the compound, accessible
through the main hiking trail, and several hundred feet
above the ground. She often scraped her elbows or knees
climbing up by way of precarious stone footholds, but
the beauty and the quiet on top were worth it. Nowhere
else had she found a place so isolated and distant from
the swarming city she knew. Here it was just her and the
mountains and the breeze under a purple-orange sky.
She stretched her arms as wide as they could reach, facing east, away from the setting sun. Toward home.

That was when she heard the rustling noise down
below. It sounded like someone's shoes scuffing the
dirt trail, drawing nearer. Her heart fluttered. Theo. He
was coming to tell her it was dinnertime. Lately he had
been running in the gym six or seven miles in the after-
noons, while she sought out her perch to write and re-
flect. Their routine was peaceful—in her former life
she might have said boring. But in the midst of so
much other tension, she had come to cherish its pre-
dictability, along with his companionship.

She scampered down the cascade of rocks and
hopped to the ground, a grin already on her face. But

the shadow that preceded the person around the bend in the trail was not lanky like Theo. It stretched thicker and longer, with wavy wisps framing the head. The man turned the corner and came into view. It was Galileo, wearing his characteristic nylon track pants, white T-shirt, and sneakers. She brightened at once, surprised and pleased; since he'd returned from New York a few days earlier, she had been desperate for some face time, but he always seemed preoccupied with other people's requests and problems.

"What are you doing out here?"

He smiled. "Coming to find you. Theo told me you'd be here."

"You know I've been dying to talk to you?"

"I know, sorry it's taken me a few days."

She fell into step beside him as they started walking back toward the compound.

"It's okay, I know you're super-busy. You should have, like, a sign-up sheet."

"Not a bad idea. So what's up?"

"I just wanted to hear about home," she said, unable to keep the wistfulness out of her voice.

"Your parents cooperated beautifully."

She tried to imagine her unsuspecting mom and dad doling out their DNA to him. It was a picture that made her want to both laugh and cry.

"How did they seem?"

"They miss you like crazy. It's obvious how much they love you."

A lump popped up in her throat. She realized how badly she wanted to matter, not just as a vessel of cells, but as a person. Who else beside her family could appreciate her for who she was, apart from her genes?

Here she was just a walking experiment. It was cynical thinking, she knew, but sometimes she couldn't help wondering if anyone really cared what happened to her.

"I kind of miss them, too," she admitted. "Are they okay, do you think?"

"They were pretty distraught. I tried to tell them you were safe. But until you get home in one piece, they're going to have a rough time."

She let out a heavy sigh. "I wish we could just tell them the truth."

"I know, darling. But secrecy is the price for the freedom we have here."

"What about Gramps? I wrote him this letter. Can you send it for me?"

He took the envelope without responding right away. Not far above them, a hawk circled, then plummeted to the ground to snap up a snake from a nearby hole. It flew off with its prey wriggling in its beak. She looked away with a shiver.

"I didn't get to see your grandfather," Galileo said. "But I will do my best to get this to him."

Do your best? she wondered. *How hard is it to send a letter?*

They were entering the compound now, crossing through the outer band of apartments and into the quad. It was quiet. Not a single person could be seen dashing to the cafeteria or into the labs, even though the sky was getting dark. Usually at this time people were rushing to get a quick bite before their evening workouts or lab time or hospital duties.

The emptiness was distracting. She turned to see if Galileo noticed it, but he was walking toward the cafeteria, not pausing to look around.

"Wait," she called. "Where is everyone?"

He stopped and shrugged. "Let's go eat."

"I don't know." Her skin started to prickle. "I feel like something's weird."

"Nah, come on, I'm starved." He motioned for her to come along.

She hesitated, but trust in his judgment took over. She was just being hyperalert, probably a lingering effect of their crazy journey. She caught up with him as they reached the entrance to the cafeteria's great hall. He turned to her with a mischievous grin and grabbed the door handle.

Before she could say anything, the door swung open to a boisterous roar from the standing crowd.

"Happy birthday!"

She froze, her heart pounding. It seemed like everyone who lived on the compound was there—Natalie and Theo and Helen, all the scientists she knew from the aging team, along with the other various scientists whom she knew only by sight, plus the lab techs, the cafeteria ladies, the tech guys from the Brain, the hospital nurses—even her patient friend, Mrs. Avalon, was sitting in her wheelchair, grinning. Silver and pink balloons floated up along the ceiling and purple streamers had been hung around the room, dangling from wooden beams.

It took her half a minute to recover her voice. She turned to Galileo, the mastermind, the trickster. He was beaming.

"Now you know where they were."

She stared at the group, feeling a rising sense of betrayal in spite of their goodwill. Her birthday had lost its magic. She had purposely told no one. Before, she used to eagerly anticipate July 11, counting on another year to jump-start her growth. But now—now that she knew it wasn't going to happen—this day felt too strange and disappointing to acknowledge. Especially since it was her twenty-first.

There was a vital mechanism in her that no longer existed. It was like throwing a party for a ghost and pretending it was alive. How could they expect her to participate in such a charade, let alone be joyous? A moment of silence would have been more fitting.

She frowned, surveying the smiling crowd. "But— how did you all know?"

"We had your medical records from Dr. Carlyle," Natalie said. "I noticed your birth date and told Galileo. Blame him," she joked. "It was his idea."

"This has been in the works for a while," he said, turning to the group. "Right?"

They whooped in response. Theo put two fingers in his mouth and whistled.

"Wait," Zoe muttered, thinking back to the other day when they were lounging in the quad, dreaming of Magnolia Bakery back in New York. "Is that why you asked for my favorite cupcake flavor?"

Theo chuckled. "Yup."

She couldn't help feeling touched by his participation. Somehow it alleviated her bubble of angst that was threatening to explode.

"Do you do this for everyone's birthdays?" she asked Galileo.

"No, you're just a special guest." His smile faded as he grew serious. "You know by now this is a pretty intense place. All work and no play. But in just a short time, you've managed to fire up everyone's excitement. And it's not just because of the aging experiments, it's *you*. Your beautiful smile and kind words for all these folks doing such tough jobs, and for the sick patients. This past month can't have been easy on you, yet you don't complain. Age doesn't matter, Zoe. Only who you are. So today, we honor you for being such a remarkable young woman."

It was the word *woman* that clinched her tears. In it was everything she hoped and dreamed for her life—the brains, the curves, the independence, the wisdom. That impossible state all other girls reached without a drop of effort.

They must have thought she was crying with gratitude, because another cheer rose up. Then the crowd parted like a zipper, starting from back to front, as one of the cafeteria ladies emerged with a two-tiered cake and placed it in front of her on the nearest wooden table. She could see right away that it was her favorite, red velvet with cream cheese icing. The circle moved in tighter around her, stealing whiffs of such a foreign delicacy.

"It's not Magnolia," Theo said, coming up beside her, "but I found their recipe online."

She gave a small smile in spite of herself. "Fine, but no singing."

"What the birthday girl wants, the birthday girl gets. You guys hear that?"

"Hurry up and blow it out," someone yelled. "So we can eat!"

Stuck in the center was a single lit candle. She wiped away her tears, wondering how they had decided on the number. Did someone think twenty-one candles might be insensitive? Or just impractical? Would they serve her alcohol? Not that she wanted any—she'd done a few vodka shots at Northeastern and tried to like beer, both without success.

Natalie leaned over and whispered in her ear. "Make a wish."

"I'm the opposite of Peter Pan," she mumbled. "I just want to grow up."

"Hush! Or else it won't come true."

She shrugged. That still wasn't what she wanted most.

Closing her eyes, she chanted a silent wish with all the fervor she could muster.

Let Gramps stop aging.

She blew out the candle and Natalie patted her on the back, while everyone clapped.

"Now where's my slice?" shouted Mrs. Avalon from somewhere in the back, raising a frail hand. "Old ladies first. Right, Zoe?"

A few people chuckled and looked at her, waiting for some kind of response. A response appropriate from the birthday girl.

But she couldn't. She couldn't pretend to be happy or normal anymore. It was too much to bear. Without a word, she stumbled around and elbowed her way through the crowd, ignoring the scattered gasps.

"Hey!" Natalie called after her. "Wait!"

"Zoe!" Galileo shouted.

Too embarrassed to make eye contact with anyone, she hurried to the door and broke into a run. She traced the path they had just taken, rushing past her own apartment, through the hallway, and out into the chilly black night, into the mountains. There was only one place she wanted to be.

*   *   *

It didn't take long for Theo to find her on top of the rock pile. He was huffing like a marathoner on his final stretch as he climbed up to greet her, his feet finding the familiar footholds even in the dark.

"Pretty sure I just ran my fastest mile ever," he announced, plopping down next to her on the uneven stone.

"Great," she muttered, hugging her knees to her chest and looking away. But inside she couldn't deny her happiness that he had come after her. Had she, on some level, run away for this very purpose?

The moon glowed brightly enough for her to see the outline of his face. His frown was a mixture of annoyance and concern.

"So you gonna tell me what that was about? Everyone is totally confused."

A flush of shame crept into her face. She was glad he couldn't see it. "I'm sorry," she snapped. "I just needed to think, okay?"

"Whoa, chill out. No one's angry. Just worried."

"I'm *fine*."

He edged closer so that their shoulders were touching. "I don't think you are."

Part of her wanted to scoot away, tell him to treat her like the capable adult she wanted to be, not a helpless little girl. But she liked the warmth of his body next to hers, the thrill of their forearms grazing against each other. She leaned her head on him.

"I've never been away from my family on my birthday before."

"Do you want to go home?"

"No. I mean, yes and no." She sighed. "It's not like going home would solve my problems anyway."

"What do you mean?"

"Everything just feels so messed up. My parents think I was kidnapped. My body is my worst freaking enemy. My grandfather is getting older every second and . . ." Before she could stop it, her worst fear wormed its way out of her mouth. "I don't know if your mom is going to be able to do anything about it in time."

The thought of losing Gramps—of that possibility being real—made fresh tears sting her eyes.

"But she found that weird mutation already, right? Isn't that a good sign?"

"I don't know," she mumbled, sniffling. "I hope so."

"Hey, look at me," he commanded, turning her chin toward him. The whites of his eyes and his teeth shone in the moonlight, but the rest of his face was shrouded in darkness. His fingers felt icy and she realized they were both shivering.

"What?"

"You've done as much as you could humanly do. I mean, seriously. Taking off on your own to join a secret society, running from the police, having a seizure, surrendering your DNA, all to help the person you love. Who else can say they did that much for anyone, ever?"

"But I'd do anything for him."

"I know. And that's why I like you."

Before she could react to such a bombshell, his lips were on hers. She didn't know what to do—had never kissed anyone—so she puckered her mouth and stayed still, both thrilled and a bit grossed out when their saliva mixed. A second later it was over. He pulled away and looked at her with a sheepish grin. A cold breeze swept by, chilling the wet spot on her lips.

She wasn't sure how to react. Wasn't this exactly what she wanted? What she had been fantasizing about before falling asleep at night? So why did she feel so anxious?

"What's wrong?" he asked, a hint of alarm in his voice.

"Nothing." She ran her fingers through her hair. "I don't know."

"Sorry, I didn't mean to—"

"It's not that. It's just . . . How can you be into me?" she blurted. "I mean, isn't this crazy? I'm like fourteen or twenty-one, who the hell knows—and you're eighteen, and next year, you'll be nineteen, and one day you'll be twenty-five and then thirty and then forty. How can we ever be together?"

"Aren't you thinking a bit far ahead?"

"No!" she shouted, choking up. "How can I ever be with anyone? I'm going to spend my whole life alone! I'm always going to be some weird half-child freak."

"I don't care how old you are."

"Well, I do!"

She was sobbing now, her face in her hands, past the point of embarrassment. He reached for her, but she stiffened. "No. We can't."

"But everything's going to turn out fine. My mom is probably the smartest person here. She's going to figure this out. You won't be stuck like this forever."

Easy for you to say, she thought, standing up. What

would happen to her in five, ten, twenty years, if Natalie didn't get anywhere? What would happen to Gramps?

"Where are you going?" he asked.

"Back. To find your mom."

The lab section of the circle reminded Zoe of an ant farm, with all the underground tunnels and pathways leading to different rooms. With no windows, it was disorienting to find her way around, but she made it down the three flights to the floor devoted to the aging team. Natalie's lab was in a corner, its door partly open.

As Zoe had guessed, she was inside, clad in a white coat and hunched over a microscope, turning its knob back and forth.

"Hi," she announced, not even bothering to keep the desperation out of her voice. The reassurance she needed couldn't come from Theo, Galileo, Gramps, or her parents. It could only come from one person.

Natalie whirled around on her stool with a look of surprise.

"Zoe! Are you okay? Theo promised he would make sure. I thought the birthday thing might not be the best idea, but—"

"It's fine," she interrupted. "I just want to know what's going on. Did you test my parents' DNA yet?"

Natalie pushed a strand of hair behind her ears. "Well—yes. I was just checking the slide again, making sure the report got it right."

Zoe felt her heart rev up like a motor. "And?"

"Unfortunately your weird mutation showed up in

both of them. Just a familial variant you must have inherited."

"So it's not meaningful? It's not the aging gene?"

"No. I'm so sorry."

"So what do you do now?"

"Now . . ." Natalie grimaced, avoiding her gaze. "Now we go back to square one."

CHAPTER 29

In dismay, Les Mahler surveyed the gaggle of reporters seated before him. The press conference was going live in sixty seconds. To his right on the podium stood Benjamin Barrow, patting his brow with a checkered handkerchief. Both were sweating under the hot bright lights in the White House briefing room. When Les caught his eye, a glance of mutual agony passed between them.

After their failure in recent weeks to find a lead from Julian Hernandez's disclosure about the secret signs, and the murder of the prison guard—which was ascribed to Galileo without a blink—the President had insisted that it was time to go public with the Network. His administration felt that Galileo was too dangerous and out of control for his actions to be kept classified.

Les knew that this move would spark a backlash of hysteria and rumors, an endless string of sensational media, and critical commentary from pundits of all stripes. Worst of all, he feared it would cause Galileo to lie low indefinitely, thwarting all attempts at detection. Surely there would be no further outrageous stunts like tricking Zoe's parents—stunts that Les could have prepared for. But he also understood that the President saw an opportunity to politicize the case, demonstrating how seriously he cracked down on bio-crimes. It was a vote grab, and Les had no choice but to go along with it.

"Live in ten, nine, eight . . ." came a voice in his earpiece. The reporters, about fifty representatives of the country's biggest news outlets, were holding out black mini recorders and getting poised to scribble on their rectangular flip pads or type on laptops. Along the back of the cramped, windowless room, a multitude of sleek black cameras were trained on him and Barrow, blinking green. The beady glowing lights reminded Les of staring into the eyes of a cat in the dark, the moment before it pounces.

"Four . . . three . . ."

He took a deep breath, ignoring the sweat pooling at his hairline. He thought of himself being broadcast onto every TV screen in America, interrupting afternoon talk shows and soap operas and weather reports. As much as he despised the reason for his spotlight, the sudden attention—and power—energized him. This debut was going to catapult him into the public eye as much as it would Galileo—but with a crucial difference: He was the hero, and everyone was going to know it.

"Two . . . one . . . And we're live!"

Shoulders down, back straight, head tall. The hot lights from the low ceiling beat down like a dozen suns. He opened his mouth to begin.

"Good afternoon." His voice boomed out of the room's speakers, deep and resonant. He indulged a pause as if to tell the crowd, *I set the pace. You can't rush me.* "My name is Les Mahler, and I'm the chief of the Executive Office for the Committee of Bioethics Enforcement. This is Benjamin Barrow, my second-in-command. We've called you here today to alert you to an important national security matter—one classified until now, but so grave, we've concluded the public has a right to know."

The reporters' pens hovered above pads, their fingers above keys. They stared at him. No one made a peep. Les exchanged a look with Barrow, who gave him a grim smile, then he cleared his throat.

"Ladies and gentlemen, together with the FBI, we have been working for two years to find and uproot an illicit, well-funded criminal organization known as the Network that conducts illegal, unrestricted scientific experimentation somewhere within the U.S. As I'm sure you're aware, all human experiments in the United States must answer to my committee or face federal charges of recklessness and noncompliance. Otherwise, vulnerable subjects stand to be abused and dehumanized—hence our urgency to find the Network and dismantle it as soon as possible. The location of their headquarters is unknown. To date, they have abducted or coerced at least twenty-nine people—scientists, doctors, and critically ill patients—who have vanished into their secret ring."

Hands shot up all over the room. Barrow was about to call on someone when Les pulled the mic closer. It was imperative that he show who was in control.

"The most recent abduction," he said, "was Zoe Kincaid, the little girl who was recently discovered to have stopped aging. As you know, she was kidnapped from her home in Manhattan on June 18 and has vanished. We didn't release it then, but all along we've known that the Network is responsible. We think that her strange condition primed her as the perfect target for exploitation."

A few gasps were heard as the reporters copied down his words.

"Our top priority," Les went on, "is to root out the man we believe is the leader. He calls himself Galileo and communicates responsibility for the Network's abductions by mailing a certain postcard of the solar system to my office. For further details, please see the picture in the press release.

"Like any convincing cult leader, he has managed to recruit a number of susceptible Americans whose homes the Network uses as safe houses. It's possible, though we're not sure, that these members communicate their sympathies by painting a certain sign on their mailboxes—a picture of the sun."

Les slowed down his next words. "It is of the utmost importance that the public be on the alert for these signs and report anyone with suspected involvement. An 800 hotline is now up and running 24/7. No charges will be brought against those who have been suckered into participating, as long as they give us their full cooperation."

"Please," Benjamin Barrow chimed in, "we urge everyone who has any information to come forward. Your fellow citizens' lives are on the line."

"We will now take questions," Les announced.

A cacophony of competing voices broke out. He and Barrow took turns answering as best they could.

"Have any bodies been found?"

"Yes. Two. But we're not at liberty to disclose further details, due to the ongoing investigations."

"What does the leader look like?"

"If we knew that, so would you."

"How many members are there?"

"Unclear."

"What's their motivation?"

"Maybe financial, selling whatever half-baked drugs they develop on the black market. We can only speculate."

"Where does their funding come from?"

"Venture capitalists? Overseas donors? Again, speculation."

Then came the comment that stung Les to the core, from the mouth of a crotchety female reporter who was known for her pointed criticism of every administration since Reagan.

"If this President had any brains, he'd fire all you goddamn bureaucrats and put a real leader in charge. Mr. Mahler, tell us *one* thing you've accomplished since you started this manhunt."

Les narrowed his eyes. *If only you knew,* he thought. The other reporters ceased shouting. Everyone was awaiting his response. Would he chastise her? Be diplomatic? Divert with sarcasm?

Before he could get his thoughts together, a scornful voice to his right spoke into the microphone. "That would be *Dr.* Mahler. And with his double PhDs, FDA and FBI experience, I assure you the committee could have no stronger leader. *Next.*"

Les stared at Benjamin Barrow in surprise. It was true that their rivalry had cooled since their trip to

Ohio, but he hadn't expected anything like loyalty to take its place—especially not such a public display.

The rest of the press conference was short. They answered several more questions, thanked everyone for coming, and hurried into the back room away from the glare of lights and judgment.

Les thanked him as soon as they stepped out of sight.

"No problem," he replied. "We need the country to know we're a united front. Public image rule one, never appear to lack confidence."

But do you? Les wondered. Then he thought of the rule. "Of course. Doubt is weakness."

"That's right. Now we just have to follow through."

Somehow, somewhere, they had to show Galileo what it meant to mess with the U.S. government on its own turf.

Before their credibility expired with a scandalized public.

Before Zoe Kincaid's DNA reached any scientists hell-bent on creating a superspecies out of the human race.

Before his own impatience dangerously spiraled.

From the worried look on Barrow's face, Les could tell what he was thinking. They desperately needed a new lead. And fast.

CHAPTER 30

At 3:30 A.M., holed up in the windowless cavern of her lab, Natalie could not have said whether it was morning or night, a weekend or weekday. Such distinctions had receded from her consciousness, along with other pestering concerns like hunger and sleep. Her world existed solely on the microscopic level. She couldn't hear, smell, taste, or touch her surroundings—the forest of Zoe's genes that she was hacking through, one clearing at a time.

In the silence, her own breathing became a sound track, acquiring musical qualities of pitch and rhythm. Its steadiness lulled her into a deep concentration, beyond recognition of her time and place. She was so "in the zone" that when she heard a sudden loud crack behind her, it sounded like a gunshot.

Without thinking, she dove off her stool, hands over her ears.

An urgent voice shouted at her, "Natalie!"

Crouching under the counter, she turned around to see that her open door had smacked the wall. In her disoriented state, it was difficult to comprehend what else she was seeing. Nina Hernandez, her normally aloof colleague, was running—no, *charging*—toward her with a wild look on her face.

We're being invaded, she thought. *Find Theo.*

"I knew you'd be here!" Nina cried, nearly crashing into the counter. She gripped its edge, panting, her frizzy black hair falling into her eyes. Her lab coat was coming untied and one white string dangled across her chest, rising and falling with her breath.

"What's going on?" Natalie leaped to her side. "Are we evacuating?"

"What? No, I hope not." Her lips spread into a grin. "I think I figured out a new approach for Zoe."

Natalie groaned. "Jesus, Nina. You can't shout like that here."

"Sorry, I'm just excited."

"But you do viruses."

"Yeah, but I've been studying her samples after hours, ever since that weird mutation turned out to be nothing. Think how many more times that could happen! Sifting through her entire genome could take *years*, even if you have a hunch about where to look."

Natalie grimaced. It was the truth. "So?"

"So I thought, rather than spend all that time looking for some random spontaneous mutation, why don't we look instead for an epigenetic cause? Some *external* factor that triggered her genes to change when they did?"

"You mean, like a virus?"

"Exactly. Once you have one, its RNA is in your cells forever. And get this—I've just found a viral strand in her DNA that I don't recognize. I wonder if it's possible she caught some kind of mutated virus around age fourteen that altered the expression of the aging genes?"

Natalie cocked her head, thinking. "If so, we could isolate it and use it to infect mice. Then we examine their genomes and see where the viral RNA shows up. Maybe it could lead us to the right location."

"But in her, the viral RNA shows up across several regions of her genome—not just in one place."

"Okay, we could do knockouts. Silence the different genes in different mice to tease out which ones—if any—make them stop aging."

Nina beamed and held up her hand for a high five. "It's brilliant."

Natalie demurred, raising her own hand to signal caution. "Maybe. Let's not get ahead of ourselves. We don't even know if she had this virus around the right time. What if it was something she caught last year?"

"What time is it?"

Natalie glanced at her computer. "Three forty-five a.m."

"Too early to wake her, you think?"

They traded smiles and dashed to the door. Natalie led the way to the staircase, up three flights, and through the maze of hallways that took them to the residential complex. Outside, through the hall window, the quad was dark and still. It seemed they were the only people awake on the whole compound. Their sneakers scuffed the concrete as they ran past identical door after door. Natalie slowed when they passed Galileo's, but then she remembered he was away again.

Right next to Theo's apartment, they stopped at Zoe's.

"You do the honors," Nina whispered.

Natalie recalled that Zoe was a light sleeper, prone to restlessness and insomnia. She knocked softly so as not to startle her too much.

Almost right away, they heard footsteps padding toward them.

"Who's there?" came her high-pitched voice.

They chorused their names.

She opened the door and gazed at them bleary-eyed, her blond hair mussed on one side. A large cotton T-shirt hung down to her bare thighs.

"Do you guys know what time it is? I was finally falling asleep."

"Sorry," Natalie said. "But we might have a new way to approach your case."

Alertness flashed into her eyes. "Really?"

"We just have to ask you a question."

"A really important question," Nina added. "Your answer could change everything."

Zoe glanced between them, wide-awake now. "Okay . . . ?"

Natalie hesitated. She was startled to realize how much hope she had already built up, against her cautious instincts.

"Did you—do you remember if you got sick around the time you stopped aging?"

Zoe stared at her. "That was seven years ago."

"I know, but try to think back. Does anything stand out—not just a cold, but maybe something worse?"

"Something antibiotics wouldn't have helped with," Nina said. "You might have felt really tired and weak?"

Zoe closed her eyes, frowning. "That would have been around eighth grade. Oh, that was the year I missed graduation, which really sucked. There was a cute guy who was going to a different high school, and I never got to say good-bye 'cause I was stuck at home with a fever."

Nina's eyes widened. "A fever? Did you have any other symptoms?"

"Yeah, I was sick for like three weeks straight. Now I remember. I had a cough. And my fingers tingled. That's when the doctor said it wasn't just the flu."

"So what was it?"

She shrugged. "No idea. It just went away on its own."

"How old were you exactly?"

"That was June, so—"

She broke off, and Natalie watched a jolt of astonishment cross her face. "I was just about to turn fourteen."

CHAPTER 31

Returning to a certain slum in Southeast was a mission Les dreaded, but as he hurried past a group of slouched teenagers, clutching his backpack under his arm, he was spurred on by the thought of that bitchy old White House reporter. *Tell us* one *thing you've accomplished since you started this manhunt.*

If only she could see him now, wearing baggy sweatpants and a muscle T-shirt to blend in with his sketchy surroundings. His last aim was to attract attention. He wondered what Benjamin Barrow and the other committee members would think of this little off-the-record task, one they would never have the nerve to pull off. He could just imagine them squabbling over its consequences, concerned more with matters of irony and principle than real life. *If we accomplish our mandate through less-than-ethical means, would that diminish a future triumph?*

Idiots, he thought. Of course not. Sometimes you had to be pragmatic in life, sacrifice certain standards to uphold bigger ones. That was the way the world worked. Ask anyone who got ahead. There were bound to be indiscretions and concessions along the way. Besides, the answer was irrelevant, since no one would ever find out enough to ask the question.

A beat-up Ford Explorer squealed around the corner, grazing the edge of the sidewalk inches away from him. He jumped, shouting at the driver, "Watch it, dick!" The car zoomed by, a cloud of exhaust floating in its wake.

He cursed under his breath and walked faster. The sooner he got this over with, the sooner he could get out of this hellhole. Grime and rust coated the parked cars lining the block. Torn garbage bags lay on the sidewalk waiting for a collector who never came. The projects looked like jails, crumbling brick buildings with narrow windows. They probably housed more vermin than people. It was demoralizing to picture living here—and worse to remember that he once had.

On the corner, the sight of a middle-aged bum bowed over at the waist, mid heroin bend, brought back memories of his own old neighborhood, the pathetic hopelessness of it, the feeling that he would never amount to anything, shackled by the invisible chains of poverty. Setting foot here felt like a regression, like slipping down a nasty dark tunnel from which he might never emerge. Part of him was filled with compassion for that bum, a reminder of the life he managed to avoid, but mostly he felt contempt.

He remembered how his mother used to light lavender-scented candles during the summer to disguise the foul odor of the trash heap, overflowing with syringes and broken bottles, that backed up to their apartment.

Once, as a kid, he'd asked her who was throwing away all those needles. She'd paused, then responded that a doctor must have been cleaning out his office.

To this day, the smell of lavender filled him with sorrow.

He shook off the memory and averted his gaze from the addict slumping over on the street. As soon as possible, he would hurry back to his gleaming apartment in Georgetown, with its wraparound views of the Potomac thirty stories above the city's filth and pain.

He jogged the rest of the way to the familiar dilapidated building, snarled at a dozing man stretched across its front steps, and marched inside. There was no security, not even a locked front door. The entryway reeked of bile, as though some drunk had gotten sick. Les held his breath and ran up several flights to the apartment he knew, number 317. He knocked, testing the knob. It turned. A voice inside shouted at him to go away, but he walked in, only to be met with the unmistakable skunk scent of marijuana.

Ten feet away, Cylon was sprawled on his couch, a shiny glass bowl at his lips. At the sight of Les, his bloodshot eyes opened wide and he began to cough, waving his arms to clear the smoke around him. Amidst his fit, the bowl somehow disappeared into the cushions.

Les stifled a smile. "Excuse me," he said with exaggerated politeness, "am I interrupting something?"

Cylon straightened, pulling a blanket over his fleshy white belly. "Um, no, sir. What are you doing here?"

"You know you're not supposed to be smoking pot, Cylon." Les crossed his arms and walked closer, putting on his best expression of disappointment. "What would your probation officer say?"

"You can't tell him!"

"Why not?"

" 'Cause I helped you." He pouted, averting his gaze the way he always did during confrontation. "Come on, man."

"Well." Les seemed to consider. "I actually have another job for you. Why don't you see how fast you can get it done and we'll call it even?"

"What is it?"

"I need you to hack the computer of a guy in Ohio. We think he might be helping the gang I told you about."

Cylon cracked his fat white knuckles, looking interested. "How do you know?"

Les gave him a sharp look. "That's not your concern."

The truth was that Les suspected Julian Hernandez's secret signs were a misleading crock of shit, but he couldn't know for sure unless he found some direct proof of dishonesty. What he did know was that the FBI hadn't been able to locate a single sign, even with the post office cooperating and the national hotline running. If Julian really was a liar, what else was he hiding?

"So you wanna check out his hard drive?" Cylon asked.

"Better yet, his e-mail. I want to see exactly who he's talking to."

"You know his address?"

"Julian-underscore-Hernandez fifteen at yahoo."

"Are you gonna pay me again?"

"Jesus, John, not if it's going to drugs." The use of Cylon's real name made him cringe. It was a low blow, ignoring the avatar of the brilliant computer hacker to acknowledge the overweight, ex-con loser behind the screen. "Is it not enough to keep you from going back to jail?"

He frowned, wounded. "Fine. But it might be tough."

"Why?"

"Well, I can try the easiest way first. Send him a link to a virus from a made-up account and see if he clicks. Then I'd have control."

"Sounds easy enough."

"But most people don't click on links they don't know these days."

"It might work. This guy's old and foreign, probably not tech savvy."

"If not, there's other ways." Cylon was staring straight at him now, a look of intense pleasure on his face. The only time he ever made real eye contact, Les realized, was when he was talking about hacking.

"What ways?" Les asked, his voice low, almost seductive. He knew better than to break this trance.

"I just pose as anyone and get the dude to reply to an e-mail. The headers probably'll tell me his ISP and mail server. Then I can find the GPS coordinates of the server and take over his local cable network loop, figure out what OS he's running, and research what bugs exist at that patch level. As soon as I find one I can exploit"—he snapped his fingers with a grin—"*bam*, I'm in. Sucker wouldn't have a clue."

"Great. How long do you think it will take?"

Cylon shrugged. "Depends."

"Come on."

"It's true. I won't know what specific patch level until—"

"A rough guess?"

"I dunno. Remember, he has to reply to my e-mail first."

Les jumped to his feet, unable to contain his irritation. "Then make it happen." He tossed a plastic-encased cell phone onto the couch. "That's clean. Call the minute you have something." He headed for the door, his backpack tucked under his arm. Thank God for the pot; Cylon's mistake had saved Les another two grand in bribery fees.

"Wait!"

He rolled his eyes and turned around. "What?"

Cylon gazed at him with pitiful earnestness. "Did you talk to the President yet?"

Les gave a sardonic smile. "Not yet."

"But you promised."

"Once I crack this case, I can ask him anything I damn well please. Got it?"

Cylon reached for his silver laptop. "Yes, sir."

"And hand over that bowl," he added.

With a look of anguish, Cylon retrieved it from under a pillow and held it out like a sacrificial offering. Les stuck it inside his jacket pocket.

"Don't let me catch you smoking again," he snapped, and walked out.

As soon as the door closed behind him, he pulled out his prize and inspected it. Inside the glass hole were bright green buds, browned on top. He chuckled under his breath, thankful for dumb luck and dumb cons. Now he just needed a light.

CHAPTER 32

The compound was sleeping when Galileo returned after three weeks away. In the predawn hours, Natalie heard a strange crunching noise coming from the quad and bolted up in bed, pressing her nose to the window. But rather than intruders, she saw the silhouette of his tall, rugged figure against the indigo sky. He was pulling a black suitcase over the gravel.

She let out a gasp of joy, threw off her comforter, and stumbled in the dark to pull on her terry cloth robe. As soon as everyone else awoke, a mad dash would ensue to be first in line to speak with him. All the researchers had ongoing agendas competing for his attention. She knew that hers was the most crucial, with the Archon Prize deadline looming closer every day, yet he still didn't know about their new approach with the virus, nor their fascinating results from the recent mice experiments.

She rushed out of her apartment and padded down the hallway toward his, reassuring herself that her visit wouldn't bother him. Of course he'd want to be updated right away on something so important, even if it was the middle of the night. The unusual chance to catch him alone didn't hurt either.

She arrived at his door just as he was approaching from the other direction. His fatigue was apparent in his dragging steps, yet his posture remained erect, his head of black hair held high. He stopped in his tracks when he saw her. She waved shyly, aware of how eager he might be for sleep. Why hadn't she waited until morning?

An amused smile came to his lips, and affection expanded inside her like a balloon. She had to will herself not to ambush him with a hug. Instead she leaned against his door, tucking her hands into her robe pockets.

"Welcome back."

"What are you doing here?"

"Oh, just wanted to catch up. I heard your suitcase outside, so—no, no, it's fine, I wasn't really sleeping, and neither are you, obviously . . ."

She closed her eyes, trailing off. How was it possible that at her ripe age of thirty-seven, after all she'd accomplished, the right man still had the power to reduce her to shaky knees?

But if he noticed, he didn't let on. "Have I missed much?"

"Actually, yes." She smiled, her heart accelerating. "Nina and I stumbled onto something with Zoe. A whole new approach. It's—big."

His tired eyelids perked open. "How big?"

"Major. Groundbreaking."

"Really?"

"Would I joke about this?"

"And you 'just wanted to catch up'?" He grinned. "Why didn't you say so?"

She shrugged. "Let's go in and I'll explain."

When he led her inside, instead of taking a seat at the dining table in the kitchen, she opted for a leather recliner that was positioned at the foot of his bed. It was the only chair in the sparsely furnished room. He had no option but to perch on the bed across from her.

"Go ahead," he joked, "make yourself at home."

She smiled and stretched out her long smooth legs, grateful for having shaved that night. She eyed his wrinkled pin-striped suit and dress socks. It was as though he'd stepped into the desert straight out of a boardroom.

"Don't you want to change?"

He cast a quick glance over the apartment, which was compact even by her Manhattan standards, with its insult of a kitchen—half a fridge, a stove, and two cabinets—and its closet-sized bathroom. Privacy here was strictly meant for one.

"I won't look," she added, with deliberate coyness.

His gaze shifted from her naked legs over her robe-clad curves to her graceful neck. When their eyes met, she could detect some kind of fierce struggle within him, a poorly masked hunger under his sheath of professionalism. She stayed still, staring back at him, as though face-to-face with a rare and beautiful animal. One wrong move might spook him.

He tore his eyes away and checked his watch.

"It's late. Why don't you just tell me your news."

"Fine." She tucked her legs underneath herself and sat up straight, matching his crisp demeanor. Then she launched into an efficient summary of the recent strides in her lab—discovering Zoe's virus, isolating it in her

DNA, using it to infect young mice in an inhalation chamber, and observing their uncanny reactions— stunted growth and seizures.

"It's *just like* in Zoe," she concluded, feeling that familiar chill of awe she had been experiencing for days. "We think the viral RNA causes these maladaptive side effects by inserting its fragments into regions of the genome that control the nervous system as well as aging. So the next step is to tease out which genes are which. And then we should have our answer—can you believe it?" She let out an amazed chuckle. "We're probably just weeks away from unraveling one of the most fundamental mysteries of *life*."

He listened with an expression that was both proud and strangely sad. "I knew you had it in you. I knew it from the moment I met you."

A pang of unease jolted her. "Isn't this what you hoped for?"

"Of course. It's—fantastic." He looked at the floor, his voice quiet. "Better than that. I would say it's a miracle, but that wouldn't be giving you and your team enough credit."

She wanted to jump into his arms and shake him. "So what's wrong?"

He sighed. "I wish we could be as strong as we think we are."

"What are you talking about?"

"Things are pretty dicey out there." He clenched his jaw. "I'm not going to sit here and lie to you. Ever since that press conference, and those two murders that the idiot feds blamed on me, there's been a lot of backlash. I've been out trying to fight it, but popular opinion is just unshakable. It's become 'common knowledge' that the Network is some kind of crazy cult, and our investors are dropping like flies. Plus we've lost about thirty safe houses on our most important routes. So far."

Her mouth dropped open. "It's that bad?"

"I'm afraid so."

"And all this time, I've been thinking of nothing but work . . . But no one knows where we are, right?"

"Only the thirty-eight people who live here. No one else."

"What about the Indian tribe? The Laguna Pueblos?"

"They have no idea we have anything to do with the Network. For all they know, we're just some isolated religious sect who rejects the modern world, not exactly unheard of in the Southwest. But what do they care, as long as they're getting paid."

"And what about you? Those former allies can't turn you in, right?"

He shook his head. "Why do you think I'm so firm about my pseudonym?"

"Does *anyone* know who you really are?"

"This is who I really am."

"You know what I mean."

"No. And no one ever will."

The harsh undertone in his voice took her aback.

"It's a matter of security," he said. "It has to be this way."

"I didn't argue, did I?"

"I'm sorry. I'm just—you don't even know the half of it."

She threw her legs over the side of the chair so that

she was facing him full on, a ready and willing listener. Briefly she was reminded of Helen, and the many times they'd poured out their lives to each other without reservation. She realized he must not permit himself any close friends—if any friends at all.

"Am I allowed to ask?"

"They're coming for us. Maybe not today, or tomorrow, but soon. That guy at the top, Les Mahler, I've gotten my own intel on him and it's not good. He's different from the past chiefs, smarter and meaner, with something to prove. I have no doubt he'll do whatever it takes to track us down."

She stared at him. "But how?"

"I don't know. But it's just a matter of time until he finds a way."

"Isn't there anything you can do?"

"Why do you think I've been away so long?"

"So why come back now?"

"To get our evacuation plans ready."

The anger that came out in her voice surprised her. "We should be giddy right now, not worrying about some government asshole!"

A bitter look darkened his face. "I couldn't agree more."

"So let's not. It won't change anything tomorrow." She leaped out of her recliner and crawled up alongside him on the bed, placing one hand on his stomach. "Just for tonight," she whispered, inhaling his scent of musk and sweat, "to hell with all of that."

His stomach stiffened but he didn't push her away, so she scooted higher and kissed him hard on the lips. His mouth was warm, softer than she imagined, edged with rough stubble. He kissed her slowly at first and then greedily, succumbing as a tortured man to confession.

She started to slip out of her robe, but he drew back. "Don't."

"Why not?"

He eyed her bare shoulder with that conflicted expression of desire and hopelessness. "I don't know—"

"We're both adults. It's fine."

"No, it's not." He ran a hand through his hair and swung his feet to the floor, turning his back to her.

"Oh, so now you're all righteous?" She tightened her robe and angrily retied the sash, feeling like a fool. "Not that I should be surprised—I don't even *know* you."

"No, you don't."

The remark stung. She should have known better than to think she could break through the steel fortress that housed his soul. As she slid past him, about to make a beeline for the door, his hand lurched out and grabbed hers.

"You remind me too much of her."

She whirled around, yanking her hand back. "Who?"

"My ex-wife."

She raised her eyebrows, unsure if she was more shocked by this revelation or his divulgence of it. "Ex?"

He studied her, as though assessing whether she could handle his next admission. She realized his hesitation had nothing to do with her. His face was ashen and he seemed to have trouble forming the words, his mouth silently opening and closing.

"You don't have to tell me," she said, ashamed to have asked.

He pulled her closer, looking her in the eye. "Our daughter died."

Words deserted her. She thought of Theo, and what would become of her if anything happened to him. She didn't know how a parent could go on.

"I'm so sorry," she said.

His voice trembled. "She died of old age."

"What?"

"Progeria. She turned into a little old woman before our eyes, bald with arthritis and wrinkly skin and frail bones that cracked if she kicked a ball. At eleven, she was dead."

Natalie glanced at the framed picture on his nightstand. There was the smiling little girl with her white hair and pinched mouth, and the same mischievous eyes as her father.

"My God. How horrible!" She recalled the cases she'd read in the medical literature about such rare, genetically unfortunate children. Of course, there was no cure for aging as yet, no way to slow its progression. "She must have been the opposite of Zoe."

"In genetics, but not personality. Hallie was spunky and playful and bright, so bright. I think they would have liked each other very much."

Natalie sat down beside him and draped her arm around his shoulders. They sat in silence for a minute until she gestured toward the window, at the sleeping compound beyond. "All this. The research, the hospital center, me and Zoe and the Archon Prize. It's all for her."

"Yes."

But it's too late, she wanted to say. Dead is dead is dead. No scientist in the world could change that.

"Is it all still—worth it?" she asked instead. "If she's not here to benefit?"

"It's her legacy. Remember I told you the Network started out with the vision of defeating aging? I wanted to figure out a way to eliminate it on a grand scale, so this same tragedy stops repeating itself every minute of every day."

"We're going to. We just need more time."

"I believe you. And you need to believe me. You have so much to offer—don't waste it on me."

"Is that why you told me? So I would give up on you?"

He lifted one shoulder, as if to convey the futility of her affection. "You deserve to know it's not your fault."

"Well." She forced herself to stand up and gave him one last squeeze. "I'm always around if you need a friend."

"Thank you." He took her hand in both of his and kissed it. When he looked up at her, she knew she was seeing through every mask of disguises in his arsenal to the real, raw man himself—whatever his name.

"In another life," he whispered, "you would have been it."

She smiled sadly. "Too bad this one's all we've got."

She turned around before he could see the tears in her eyes.

CHAPTER 33

Nervous chatter about the nation's manhunt for Galileo and his so-called victims swelled around the compound like the wave at a stadium, and Zoe didn't like it one bit. The sense of safety she'd acquired over the last couple of months, of seclusion amid the mountains, was beginning to feel like a cruel desert mirage. The hardest part was that no one seemed to have any real facts, not even Galileo himself—or at least, none that he was willing to discuss. All they knew was that he had returned to inspect the compound's secret evacuation tunnel, test the intercom system wired in every room, and host somber test drills.

During one such drill, everyone was called to the quad. "We'll know the moment anyone violates our boundaries," he revealed. "An invisible laser surrounds our perimeter that, if breached, trips on the security alerts in the Brain." He went on to explain that a weapons vault was hidden in the floor there, and underneath that was the entrance to the secret tunnel. It cut a path deep underneath the mountains in a mile-long stretch of blackness, and eventually opened up through a manhole at the Turquoise Trail Campground and RV Park. A fleet of fully loaded RVs was waiting at all times to shuttle escapees to nearby safe houses.

Zoe remembered Natalie once asking him whether he suffered from paranoia. *A hazard of the job,* he had replied. She wondered now, as she made her way alone from her apartment to the Brain, whether these precautions were necessary, or if they were just his way of re-assuring himself that he was still running the show.

She wished she could analyze the situation with Theo, but a strange distance had developed between them since the night of their kiss. They saw each other at most meal-times in the cafeteria, but he refused to meet her eye, turning instead to chat up one of his mom's colleagues or tease the dorky tech guys with whom he'd become friends. Even though Zoe knew she was well liked and had plenty of other people to talk to, there was some-thing to be said for having a peer, someone roughly her own age.

Theo was the closest approximation, and without him, she felt painfully alone. To be fair, their estrange-ment wasn't only his doing. She avoided him, too, tak-ing circuitous paths from the labs to the hospital to the gym so as not to pass through the quad, where he often hung out. They were stranded in the chasm between friendship and crush, with no way to reconcile the two. How could they ever go back to being friends, when their feelings for each other were out? But how could they ever grow as a couple, when she literally couldn't? When she tossed and turned late at night, one thought crept through her mind with the terrifying ring of truth—what if she was not worth loving?

Galileo's return and the community's sense of impending disaster—whether real or hyped—provided a distraction. On the third day of his visit, while everyone else was convening for dinner, Zoe decided to do a little research of her own to see if all the doomsday prep was justified.

Weeks had passed since she'd interacted with the outside. It almost seemed like a distant planet—but not quite. Her acute longing for Gramps brought into sharp relief every last memory of home—the colorful garden they loved in Riverside Park, the sweet smell of her mother's hazelnut coffee, the silver skyscrapers that reflected the afternoon sunlight. Home was waiting for her—her family was waiting for her—half a continent away. How bad could the world be?

There was only one way to find out.

When she reached the Brain, the control tower perched upon the highest peak of the compound, she climbed the winding stairs and pushed open the heavy steel door. Inside, the circular room looked like a lighthouse transformed into a cockpit. A panorama of windows allowed for 360-degree views of the quad, the ring of adobe buildings around it, and the mountains beyond. Computer touch screens and live streaming video were built seamlessly into the walls next to a multitude of levers and red buttons and knobs that reached higher than Zoe could on tiptoes. She didn't doubt that some logic existed behind the impressive panel, but it was beyond her comprehension. All she wanted was to get online, and this was the only place to do it.

She was greeted by Ted, one of the techies who traded shifts monitoring the compound's electronic activities. He was a quiet, thirty-something guy with friendly dimples and thick black glasses. Theo had once told her that he'd gotten his PhD in computer science from Stanford and was practically a genius, but she'd never be able to tell by looking at him.

"What's up?" he asked.

"I want to go online."

"You sure?"

She'd stayed away from the Internet these past two months for fear that it might burden her with a dangerous homesickness and guilt over leaving, but her curiosity had become too powerful to ignore.

"Yep. I'm allowed to, right?"

"Yeah. Just check with me before you send anything so I can anonymize it first."

"I just want to check the news."

"Go for it."

She pulled up a stool to one of the touch screens and tapped out "the Network" into a Google news search. The Internet was lightning fast. In a split second, a long list of blue links appeared, with headlines like *Network's "Galileo" an Avowed Cult Leader* and *FBI Planning Covert Operation to Hinder Network: Source* and *Profile of a Psychopath Through His Victims*.

The last link led to a list with pictures of his thirty-one alleged victims—the two men whose suspicious deaths Galileo had assured everyone that he had nothing to do with, plus the twenty-nine missing people—the researchers and doctors and patients whom Zoe had come to know and admire.

In the last spot was her own smiling face.

It was her high school senior picture. Next to it, in boldface italics, was another link: ***Have You Seen This Girl?***

When she tapped, the page redirected to a number for a national hotline.

She closed the window, then went back to Google and typed in her own name. The first link took her breath away:

Kidnapped Girl Who Can't Age: a Sign of the Apocalypse?

She touched the link and was led to the blog of an apparently popular preacher, whose Twitter handle @TJschurch counted over two hundred thousand followers.

> Zoe Kincaid is Pandora reborn for modern
> times, sent by God as a test of our faith in His
> perfect nature. Experimenting on her to re-jigger
> human longevity would be the same as opening
> that dangerous box and releasing a plague of
> epic proportions . . . It is critically urgent that
> she be found and isolated from exploitation by
> that satanic cult before such tampering unleashes
> His wrath . . .

Zoe stared at the words. She had never given much thought to religion, either positive or negative, but the idea that she was some kind of stealth pawn of God to be avoided at all costs—it was ludicrous, wasn't it? She was just a girl with a freaky condition trying to get by with her dignity intact.

She wasn't a *plague*.

But what if she was?

What if figuring out how to help people live longer really was going to doom the world? Why hadn't she thought bigger than herself and Gramps?

She had to find Natalie. She sprinted out of the Brain, forgetting to say good-bye to Ted, and ran as fast as she could to the cafeteria, winding down three flights of stairs and through the darkening quad, gasping past the fire in her lungs.

Only a few scattered people were still eating. Natalie's brunette bob was nowhere in sight, so she pushed back through the door and dashed to the research center, the likeliest other place Natalie would be—retracing her steps across the quad, down more flights of stairs into the bowels of the compound, then through the ant-farm maze of hallways to Natalie's lab in a faraway interior corner.

Sure enough, she was there, along with Nina Hernandez and a few other researchers from the aging team, all wearing white coats, plastic hair caps, and blue gloves. They were crowded around a counter studying a bunch of slides. When Zoe burst in, they all stopped working and looked up at her.

"Zoe!" Natalie exclaimed. "What are you doing here?"

"I need to talk to you."

"Right now?"

"If you can."

Natalie murmured something to the others and walked toward her, pulling off her gloves. Her eyes carried the dazzled gleam of a miner who's struck gold.

"Get this," she said, putting a hand on Zoe's shoulder and steering her into the hallway, "your virus infected the mice in five different regions of their genomes.

Five! We've gone from about twenty-five thousand possible locations to five!"

"That's great," Zoe replied weakly.

"So that means starting tonight, we're going to start preparing knockouts to deliver to five different mice at the gamete stage, each one targeted to silence a different gene—"

"Natalie," she interrupted. "Do you really think that I know what that means?"

"Oh, sorry." But she didn't look sorry, just impatient. "A knockout is an artificial piece of DNA that we insert to stifle expression of a certain gene. So we're going to silence these five different genes, one in each mouse embryo, to see if any of them is actually the master regulator. If one dies, we'll know we've found it, since living beings are unable to grow without it."

"No kidding."

"Excuse me?"

Zoe glared up at her. "You don't give a damn about me, do you?"

"What are you talking about?"

"I rush here to find you, and you don't even ask what's wrong. You only care about my genes!"

Natalie's mouth twisted as though she'd been stung. "I—that's not true!—wait, where are you going? Stop!"

"Forget it," Zoe called over her shoulder, on her way out. What was the point of waiting around for some forced apology? Her primary concern was clear. For all Natalie cared, she saw Zoe as just another lab rat, only a rarer specimen, a prized capture. The team had gotten what they needed. If she died right now, who here would mourn?

Gramps would. Her parents would. The people who knew and loved her in spite of Syndrome X—not because of it. She thought of something Gramps told her after her diagnosis: *You're destined for greatness, sweetheart—not because of your body, but your mind.* He'd gone on to praise her independence, bravery, and tenacity. What he didn't know was that in her desire to grow into the fine young woman of his expectations, she'd copied the best parts of him.

Missing him was like missing a phantom limb. She ached in a place where pain couldn't be measured, but where it could be felt the most.

Outside in the quad, the night sky glittered with stars, and she remembered the way he had taught her to find her way home if ever she was lost. Just find the Big Dipper, then stretch out her hand wide. The distance between thumb and pinky was about the space between the cup and the North Star.

In New York City, it was practically impossible to see anything in the sky but light pollution, so she'd never tried out his advice, but now she tilted her head to the sky. The number of constellations you could see in the desert was stunning, but the familiar angles of the Dipper jumped out at her like a jigsaw piece. She held out her palm and closed one eye, following the line of her hand to the bright glowing star at her pinky.

"Hey, champ," came a friendly voice behind her, "what're you up to?"

She snatched her hand back and turned around. Galileo was towering behind her, sweating as though he had just worked out. The second they made eye contact, his face contorted with worry and he dropped to his knees.

"What's wrong?"

He reached up to wipe tears from her cheek. She hadn't realized she was crying.

"Are you okay?"

"No," she admitted in a small voice.

"What is it? Can I help?"

She shook her head, unsure where to even begin.

"Come on, there must be something I can do."

A thought as radiant as Polaris popped into her mind. "Actually, remember the letter I gave you to send my grandfather?"

"Yeah?"

"Can you arrange for him to send a reply?"

He let out a troubled sigh and took her hands in his. "Zoe, I didn't know how to tell you this before, but your grandfather never got your letter."

"What? Why not?"

"He's missing."

CHAPTER 34

Injecting the mice embryos with gene silencers was like firing a gun at the start of a horse race—except the winner would be the first to die.

All of Natalie's colleagues on the aging team were crowded around the pregnant rats like spectators—Nina, James, Karen, Susan, Peter, Terrance, Richard, and Gina, as well as Helen, an honorary onlooker. Over the past arduous weeks, a kinship had formed among them devoid of the competitiveness so rampant in academia. In this lab, they shared the goal of advancing scientific knowledge about aging. Period.

If the elusive gene was silenced, the results would not take long to come in, perhaps a day at the most. No living organism, in their hypothesis, could grow without the biological instructions ordered by the master regulator gene that was embedded in all species since the beginning of life on Earth. By switching off its crucial green light in utero, embryonic development stopped short, and death would soon follow.

But if the green light stayed on throughout life, as it naturally did in every animal now, the gene's orders would continue unchecked, even after maturity was reached—eventually leading to the body's breakdown and death. The trick was to find the gene and silence it in young, healthy adults, so that the developmental progression known as aging could be stopped after it was no longer needed, but before it turned lethal.

Natalie wondered if anyone in history had ever been so eager for the death of a mouse embryo. Finding the gene would be no less than paradigm shifting—as consequential in the twenty-first century as Leeuwenhoek's discovery of microbes in the seventeenth, Mendel's laws of inheritance in the nineteenth, and Watson and Crick's DNA double helix in the twentieth.

Now all they could do was wait.

In the fantasies she would never admit, she enjoyed imagining Galileo's reaction to the victory that might be imminent. This project was their baby—the union of their life's missions. She liked to think that its success might motivate him to relinquish his painful past and commit to life in the present. All progress—all survival—required forward motion, but she understood that no doctor or scientist could speed up the healing of a human heart. In that most personal lab, the rules were reversed. Expert opinions meant nothing, persistence could spell failure, and letting go was sometimes the only path to discovery.

Her confusion over Zoe's behavior persisted. That sudden burst of criticism had come as a shock, and even though Natalie knew it wasn't fair, she still felt guilty for whatever she had done wrong. Zoe had turned utterly cold in the days since, so far from her normal self. She wore a permanent scowl and refused any attempts at reconciliation. She even avoided Theo.

Whatever her private struggles, the message was clear—she wanted to be left alone.

The anticipation currently mounting in the lab—Nina's pacing, Helen's wide-eyed glances at the mice, the group's excited chatter—seemed wrong without Zoe there. She was holed up in her apartment for some reason Natalie couldn't understand. The Zoe she knew was as intent on conquering aging as any of them and would have been first in line to witness this experiment. Then again, teenagers were notoriously moody. If the breakthrough happened, hopefully she would come around. And maybe someday, so would Galileo.

One vial of blood—that could spell Les's retirement. He was sitting in his office, reeling from the call he'd just received from the head of a major drug company, one of a dozen just like it in the last few weeks. Zoe's DNA had sparked a gold rush as news of her existence rippled through the pharmaceutical world. The major companies were jostling to be the first to obtain a sample for their own private R&D, and the only way was to cut a deal with Les himself, the frontline of the investigation into her whereabouts.

One vial of blood, that was all they asked, in return for any price he named.

They didn't realize that Les was impervious to bribery. He slammed down the phone on one sniveling executive after the next, relishing his power as much as their defeat. If Zoe was the bubonic plague, these companies were like engines of biological warfare, vying for the opportunity to spread her syndrome to the masses.

Ever the more reason for him to get rid of her. When desperation combined with wealth on a grand scale, the unthinkable could happen. These ruthless men (and they were mostly men) would find a way to grab her DNA if Les didn't eliminate the possibility first—and eliminate the man who enabled it in the first place.

He grabbed his second cell phone and punched in a number he knew well. Illegally hacking into Julian Hernandez's e-mail account remained his top priority, the best chance at a solid lead, albeit one he couldn't share with his colleagues.

Cylon answered in his nasal monotone.

"Yo."

"Yo, yourself," he snapped. "Is it done yet?"

"I'm having . . . technical difficulties."

"What does that mean?"

"Dude won't reply to my e-mails. I guess he's super-careful or something."

"You hacked your way into goddamn Chase *bank*, Cylon. Find another way!"

"I will."

He sounded hurt, but Les hung up before he could get in another word. The problems were piling up on his desk: newspaper editorials calling for his ouster as chief of the Bioethics Committee, memos from the FBI detailing dead-end leads from the national hotline, news magazines stoking fear over the Network's cult leader still at large.

He was about to call back Cylon to issue a new threat of urgency when the desk phone rang. "This is Les."

"It's Bud."

He leaned forward. Bud Pinter only called when he

had news to report from the FBI's end of the investigation. "What's up?"

"A new sun postcard just arrived with Galileo's signature."

"Where?"

"Get this—the office of the President's physician."

"Oh my God. Bainer?"

"Yep."

"Has he—disappeared?"

"I don't know any details. We just found out. Come quick."

Three of the mouse embryos were dead. Natalie stared at the labels on their mothers' feet and compared them to the master chart of gene knockouts the team had prepared. Yes—she could hardly believe it—and each of these three, numbers T3, T6, and T7, had been injected with the same silencer.

It was 6:30 A.M. She and Nina had remained in the lab all night, taking turns checking on the mice, while everyone else had dropped off to bed. Now Nina was asleep on the floor on a makeshift bed of sweaters, her lips parted in sleep, still wearing her white lab coat. Natalie rushed over and shook her.

"Nina! Wake up!"

"What is it?" she mumbled.

"They're dead! We have to do an autopsy right now!"

Nina bolted upright, zero to sixty in a second. Her dark brown eyes were bloodshot, but never more alert. "Did you just say—"

"Wait—before you get worked up—we have to determine what killed them."

"Are you kidding? *Before* we get *worked up*?"

Natalie suppressed a smile. Her skeptical instincts made it hard to trust the first outcome of any experiment without thorough analysis and reproducible results, but it was nearly impossible to deny the weightless, heady feeling consuming her.

"Let's not get ahead of ourselves," she said to herself as much as to Nina. "We have to focus. Get up."

Together they raced back to the petri dishes, where Natalie had placed the blastocysts after surgically removing them from the mother mice. Now, the critical part was examining them to determine cause of death. Natalie wondered if Nina noticed her shaking hands as she slid the first specimen under her microscope to analyze its cell count. But Nina was already preparing the next one to view under her own microscope.

Normally a mouse embryo at this stage would have about 128 cells.

Inhaling a breath, she peered into the lens.

And forgot to breathe out.

Only a few dozen cells—that was all.

"Are you seeing what I'm seeing?" Nina asked. "This one looks stuck around thirty-two cells!"

"Same," Natalie muttered in awe. She couldn't wrench her gaze away. "I've never seen a blastocyst this old—and this young at the same time."

"We must have silenced the gene!"

"We'll have to repeat the experiment to be sure. We'll try the same knockout on ten mice, not just three. On twenty."

"But, Natalie—just freaking admit it—this is huge!"

Natalie found herself pacing, thinking through the next steps—identify the genetic blocking sequence, then create a viral vector to administer it to healthy baby mice. If it made them stop developing, her hypothesis would be confirmed, and the experiment a success of phenomenal magnitude—aging not only demystified, but stifled by a human hand.

Nina stepped in front of her, beaming.

"Hey, slow down. Take this in."

"We have so much still to do," she protested. "The mice—"

"I've never seen anything like this," Nina interrupted. "I think we found it."

"Maybe." She was finally grinning. "I can't wait to tell the team, and Galileo and Zoe and Theo—"

"And my father," Nina said. "He will be so proud."

Natalie thought longingly of her own parents, and how they would have rejoiced in her accomplishment if they could have lived long enough to see it.

"You're lucky to have him," she said. "You know, he can take some credit for this, too. If it weren't for him helping us, we might not have made it here."

"True." The story of their near escape from the feds and Julian's heroism had become compound lore. "I'll tell him. We've been e-mailing, but I wish he could come here in person. Maybe if his back wasn't so bad." She sighed. "He gave up everything to raise me in this country, alone, with no money, without even speaking the language. All I ever wanted was to make him proud."

"You already have. He told us so himself."

The door burst open. They both turned, about to revel in their announcement, but Natalie's mouth closed when she saw her son—panting, sweaty, and disheveled. In his eyes was a look of horror.

Fear sliced through her as she dashed to his side.

"Honey, what's wrong?"

"It's Zoe," he said. "She wasn't at breakfast so I just went to her room to check and . . . and . . . all her stuff is gone."

CHAPTER 35

The moment Zoe entered the tunnel and inhaled its dank, earthy odor, the reality struck her—*I am alone in the world.* She had never been alone before, not really and truly alone, with no one but herself to make all the decisions.

For a few seconds, she stood still, at once relishing her solitude and terrified of it. The passage was pitch-black, a shock to her eyes after stepping out of the glaring early morning light. Her exit had been seamless, weaving through little-used buildings and hallways to avoid detection. The ease of leaving almost astounded her. But no one had a reason to anticipate her departure. She had served her purpose. How long would it take before someone even noticed she was gone?

Her sagging backpack weighed on her as she trudged into the tunnel, traversing its uneven slopes. All she owned pressed down on her spine—two pairs of jeans, three shorts, eight shirts, six pairs of underwear and socks, a size 30AA bra, an iPod, her pill bottle, her toothbrush, and her wallet containing $500, which she'd brought from home but never opened, since there was no money on the compound. Anything people wanted to buy they ordered via aliases online for shipping to the nearest safe house, only a few blocks from the casino.

She wondered if she should go straight to that house for help getting back to New York. Was she still part of the Network's protection if she was leaving it? She felt guilty for ditching the place without saying good-bye to anyone, not to Theo or Natalie, not even to Galileo, who seemed like he did care about her. He would have arranged a way for her to get home without a problem. It's not as though she was being held hostage.

Another part of her felt that she had to go on her own terms. For the first time in her life, she had to assert her independence from everybody and everything. She had to figure out how to take care of herself like an adult. Bottom line, she wasn't going to wait around for some scientific breakthrough that might never happen—a breakthrough with questionable moral implications. She was going to force herself to grow up no matter what biology had to say about it.

She was going to find Gramps before it was too late.

At the thought of him, she broke into a jog. She kept one arm stretched out, awaiting the elevator that she was bound to run into on the other end. It was frightening to be effectively blind, not knowing what was right in front of her face. She slowed down, but not before bumping against a sharp rock jutting out from the wall as the path unexpectedly curved. She grabbed her shoulder with a cry. Now she'd get a nice big bruise. Galileo should have installed a few lights. Then again he knew every foot by heart, and who else had ever made this journey without him? A better question—why hadn't she thought to bring a flashlight?

Just as she was chiding herself for such a basic blunder, her outstretched hand smacked into something cold and metal. The elevator! She patted the side and found the button. It lit up in a circle of reassuring brightness. Real light—the real world—wasn't much farther away.

When the door opened, she stepped in. It looked like a freight elevator, with all-black walls and a silver floor. But she noticed there was no emergency call button. In fact, there were no buttons at all. Just four solid walls tucked into the solid earth. The ride to the top was slow and jerky. When she thought that she might never get out, she remembered how long the descent had taken, a full minute at least. She paced in small circles until at last the car stopped and the door screeched open to reveal a musty carpet smelling of cigarettes. A shimmering garden wouldn't have delighted her more. She leaped onto it, gulping a giant breath like a diver coming up for air.

Muffled sounds of the casino floated toward her— clinking coins, the clapping and whooping of men, electronic beeping noises.

She leaned against the wall, thinking back to the layout. After zigzagging around three or four turns, she'd be smack-dab in the center of the action. She'd need to march straight into the open to reach the door. That meant walking normally, head down, until she got outside. Then she'd head to the nearby safe house.

She remembered the address from the time Galileo had ordered her extra pills. She didn't know who owned the house, but she was sure she could talk her way into getting online and figuring out where to buy a phone. Then she'd map out her route back to New York, using whatever combination of trains and buses she could find. Gramps couldn't have wandered too far from home—where else would he go?

Maybe her worry was for nothing. Maybe he was staying at a hotel, ordering room service and watching old black-and-white movies, having the time of his life. Hopefully he wasn't lonely. As soon as she was on the bus or train, she'd start calling every Manhattan hotel she could think of until she found him. Once she got home safe and sound, she'd prove to her parents there was no reason to be mad at him, and they'd let him come back. It would all be fine.

She tucked her long hair into her shirt and wound her way around the hallway, putting on her best poker face. The beeping and chanting and clinking sounds got louder. People gambled this early in the morning? Who did that?

As she rounded the last corner, she learned the answer—obese cigar-smoking old men. She couldn't have felt more conspicuous on a courtroom stand. Yet nobody was looking in her direction. A bunch of them were standing around a craps table, chanting numbers at a bald guy who was shaking a pair of dice. After he threw them, a raucous cheer rose up from all sides and the dealer started to parcel out chips.

She knew what Gramps would whisper in her ear. *If there's a job to be done, just do it.* The time was now.

Holding her breath, she looked down and shuffled past the table toward the large door a few yards away.

Too fast, not so fast. A tuft of uneven carpet tripped her up and she remembered to slow down.

That was when she heard a gruff voice call after her: "Hey, is that the girl from the news?"

Shoot.

She couldn't help speeding up—the door was so close, she could almost reach out and grab the handle.

"Stop her!"

Heavy footsteps came up behind her and a hand clamped down on her bruised shoulder. She shrieked.

"Get off me!"

The man spun her around to face him. About ten gawkers gathered to watch her squirm. He had the slow eyes and hulking build of a gorilla. Keeping her in place with one fat hand was a cinch.

"What was her name again?" he asked the group.

"Zoe something?" someone suggested.

"Kincaid, I think," another man volunteered. "Damn, she looks *just* like her."

Gorilla refocused his gaze on her, exhaling sweet smoke into her face as he spoke. "Are you Zoe Kincaid?"

"I don't know what you're talking about. Just let me *go*."

"A little girl like you?" His grubby fingers dug into her shoulder. "Where's your parents?"

"I don't have to answer to you," she retorted, and kicked him in the shin.

A few onlookers gasped. The man's lips parted, but before he could scold her, a menacing voice snarled at him from across the room—a voice so familiar that she froze.

"Get your hands off my daughter."

Everyone turned to size up the approaching stranger, a formidable, hard-jawed man whose blue eyes were flashing with rage. Zoe didn't know whether to laugh or cry.

It was Galileo.

She wrenched herself free and raced into the shelter of his arms, pressing her face into his stomach. His shirt smelled of clean laundry, a welcome breath of freshness in the smoky casino. Apologetic voices chorused around them.

"Hey, man, we didn't mean any harm—"

"She looks like that kid—"

"The kidnapped one—"

"Didn't see you there—"

Galileo cut them off, the vibrations of his stern voice rumbling from his chest to her ear.

"I don't know who you're talking about, but *my* kid is not your concern."

"Sorry. She just looked like she was running away."

"With her backpack and all."

Galileo's voice sharpened. "We're about to hike Pajarito Mountain, if you must know." He leaned down to address her. "Now, sweetie, want to get a move on?"

"Yeah," she said, "let's get out of here."

Unsure which direction to go, she waited for his lead. He glared at the crowd, took her hand, and marched outside into the sweltering morning. When the door closed in their wake, she gazed up at him, awestruck.

"How did you—?"

"You crossed the sensor in the tunnel. It set off the alarm in the Brain."

"Oh yeah." She closed her eyes. "You told us about that. I forgot."

"Where were you going? And if you wanted to leave, why didn't you tell me?"

"To find my grandfather. I wanted to do this one thing on my own. You've done everything else."

"But it's not that easy. Especially not for you."

"What's that supposed to mean? You think I'm some dumb kid, too?"

He shook his head with a concerned look that made her uneasy. "I should tell you something, but we first need to get out of here. I don't want any more trouble."

She glanced back at the casino, crossing her arms. "I'm not going back in there. I'm not going back at all."

"Before you decide, hear me out." He tilted his head toward the parking lot, where the morning sunlight was glinting off a few scattered cars. "Let's go for a drive."

She raised her eyebrows, but knew better than to be surprised by anything he said or did. "You're going to steal a car?"

He smiled. "What do you think I am, a criminal?"

He reached into his pocket and pulled out a ring of shiny keys. When he clicked a black button, a silver Toyota Camry in the middle of the lot beeped twice.

"How did you think I come and go?"

She shrugged. In truth, she had never given it much thought.

Once they were in the car—black leather, clean as new—he revved the engine and maneuvered out of the lot onto the open road. The land around them was as barren as New York was crowded. Instead of people, dry shrubs stretched in every direction. Instead of buildings, jagged mountains pricked the blue sky.

"Is the thing you want to tell me about Gramps?" she blurted.

She couldn't stand suspense, especially if the news was bad.

He shook his head. "This is about you." He turned to look at her, his face grim. "I didn't want to have to tell you this, but the guy who's in charge of rescuing you, the guy everyone thinks is the good guy—he . . ."

"He what?"

"He wants you dead."

She was too shocked to respond. Too disarmed by the sudden vision of herself lifeless and limp in a coffin. Underground. Like the elevator in the tunnel, but forever. Forever meant long after anyone had ever heard of her, after the Earth stopped turning and the sun exploded and life went on somewhere else in the universe, she would *still* be dead. Just another piece of galactic debris.

"Because of—my condition?"

"Unfortunately, yes. There are drug companies right now fighting each other tooth and nail to make deals with him and try to get a piece of your DNA, if he ever tracks you down. But he thinks if they mass-produce some drug that mimics what you have, it will wreck the world with overpopulation."

Like a plague, she thought, staring out the windshield. *Theo drops me, Natalie uses me, Gramps is missing, and now I'm a danger to the whole freaking world.*

Anguished words spilled out of her mouth, the admission of a worry almost too horrifying to voice. "What if he's right? Maybe we'd all be better off if I was dead."

"You can't mean that."

"I'm serious! What Natalie's doing back there might help science, but what about the outside?" She swept her arm toward the expanse of ruddy desert around them. "Here, in real life?"

"Think about this," he said. "You take any past era in history, and propose that one day the Earth will sustain seven billion people. They'd never believe you. They'd think everyone would starve and die. And yet the industrial revolution proved that a growing population could thrive. In a scientific world, there's no limitation to how many people can live in it. We'd be able to cultivate it. Look at this empty desert! There are so many unused spaces, vast oceans, mountain ranges, other planets, if we can figure out how to live there. Time and again, people have created solutions to the most challenging problems and generated wealth in the process."

She frowned. "Okay, so maybe more people could find a way to coexist. But that doesn't mean life would be better."

"People aren't irrational. If they get to a point where there's too many, they'd adjust to have fewer offspring. You could offer the same argument against curing *any* disease that kills off a large number of people, but you won't find anyone against cancer research. You know why?"

"Because aging is natural," she replied, thinking of her parents' view. "Aging is part of the cycle of life."

"That's right. That's what people are taught. But just

because something is *natural* doesn't necessarily make it desirable. Aging is natural just as living outside in the freezing cold or dying of an infection without antibiotics is natural. One great legacy of our species is the ability to shape nature to make our lives safer and happier. Aging is the leading cause of death in the civilized world, responsible for the equivalent of six Holocausts every year. But if science could stop it, if we could all stay young like you, think of the possibilities: Whatever values you have or want, there would be almost no limitation on your ability to go after them. You could have unlimited goals, multiple careers, travel everywhere, listen to all the world's music, and read a billion books, cherish countless years with your family across generations. Think of all the wisdom and joy to be gained. Time is the essential commodity of life—and you have it in spades, Zoe. The world is yours to win."

She smiled in spite of herself. "I never thought of it like that. So why don't you tell that to the guy who wants me dead?" she asked, only half joking. "Maybe he'll change his mind?"

"I don't think he really cares about overpopulation. Or even about you. I think you've just become a symbol for something deeper he hates, and so have I."

"For what?"

"I think it has to do with his contempt for humanity, and probably also his contempt for himself."

"I wonder why." Zoe gazed out the windshield at the arid landscape. "I wonder what terrible thing would have to happen to someone to make them so mean."

"I don't know. But one thing I do know is that life is

precious. Life is good. And you can never have too much of a good thing. Which boils down to the bottom line—we're lucky to be alive. And the world is lucky to have you in it, not just because of your DNA. You're much more than your genes."

"Am I?"

"We all are. It's what you do with them that counts. You've chosen to be brave and strong and curious and caring. You enrich the lives of everyone around you."

She gave a snort. "Tell that to Theo and Natalie."

He seemed taken aback. "They're your biggest fans."

She shook her head, and in a few words filled him in on the current state of those relationships. He listened without appearing to judge, and when she finished, he switched hands on the steering wheel and glanced at her.

"First of all, I think you should cut Natalie a break. She owes you an apology, but more for a misunderstanding than any real offense. One thing I know about her is that she thinks of herself as a mother first and a scientist second. And to her, you're family."

"Come on," she groaned, but felt a prick of hope.

"Seriously. After one of the drills this week, she came up to talk to me about contingency plans for you and her and Theo. She's watching out for you, even when you don't know it. When you went to the lab, I'm sure she was just excited and thought you would be, too."

Well, aren't you pulling for her, she thought, but said nothing. It was one thing to share her personal life with him, as to a trusted mentor, but vice versa was quite another. She watched a gas station and a cluster of fast-food chains whiz by next to the side of the empty highway. Every few miles they passed a modest one-story home with acres of barren desert surrounding it.

"As for Theo," he said, "I think you know he's not the real problem."

"No kidding. If I could just be normal—"

"No," he interrupted. "If you could just believe you're worth it. If you push people away, you miss out on life's greatest gift."

She pretended to gag. "That's so corny."

"I know, but it's true. You and Theo need to stop ignoring each other and start communicating. He's a nice kid. I can see why you like each other."

A flush heated her cheeks. It was time to change the subject, stat.

"Whatever," she said. "What are you doing to find my grandfather?"

They were pulling into a trailer park. It was filled with RVs lined up neatly in rows along the sand. No one was outside, and she wondered if they were all empty or if people were still sleeping in them.

"I've put the word out to the Network," he said. "We've got lots of people keeping their eyes and ears open for him. The second we find out anything, you'll know."

"What about calling hotels? He probably couldn't have gone far."

"We're already working that angle. But can't you see it's too dangerous for you to be wandering around by yourself? If you still want to go home, I'll arrange for someone to personally escort you. We also have to prepare you for the media firestorm that will hit when you get there. It will be a big undertaking, both emotionally and logistically, so make sure you're ready for it."

She sighed as her vision of single-handedly finding Gramps and reuniting her family dissipated.

"Let me repeat it," he said. "You'll be in grave danger if Les Mahler finds out where you are. I think you would do best not to take any chances, at least until he gets caught up in another case. Right now, getting rid of you is his top priority—you and me both."

She cringed at the callousness of the words. You got rid of useless things like trash—not human beings.

"What about all the hype with your drills? Is it really safer to go back?"

"Nowhere is completely safe. But at least there, our security plans are in place. We can never be too careful."

"Where are we right now?"

"This is the Turquoise Trail. See that manhole over there? That's the opening to the evacuation tunnel. We can get in through there instead of going back to the casino. Or I can drop you at a safe house until we make proper travel arrangements for you to go home—but remember any travel for you is risky."

She thought of Gramps's unsentimental rationality. For him, the decision would be easy. No amount of longing was worth endangering her life, especially if nothing but chaos awaited her at home. Plus, maybe she wasn't quite ready to leave a certain handsome boy or his mother after all.

"Up to you," Galileo said. "But I can't stick around

much longer. I've got to head out on business this afternoon."

"When will you come back?"

"I don't know exactly. A few weeks, maybe more."

"If I go home, will I ever see you again?"

"Maybe if we both live long enough," he joked, but his playful tone barely masked his sadness.

"Let's go back," she said. "I'll stay."

CHAPTER 36

The newest postcard was more baffling than Les could have anticipated. The President's doctor had not vanished. He was alive and well, tending to patients in his office, and could offer no explanation for why the Network had chosen to send the card to him. Was it a threat? A warning? Some kind of coded message?

Only when Les returned in frustration to the committee's headquarters did he begin to understand. Calls were pouring in with panicked reports of the identical postcard arriving all over the country, from Virginia to New York to Illinois. Each postcard just contained Galileo's cheeky catchphrase: "And yet it moves," plus his signature. No one had gone missing. Les's bewilderment turned to fury when he deduced the common thread among the recipients. It wasn't that they were all men or women, black or white, old or young. It was that they all worked for the FDA.

Les imagined that somewhere in his hideout, Galileo was laughing.

The Network was perpetrating a hoax to mock government regulators—and it wasn't funny. Already the media had broken the story and the committee's PR team was struggling to handle the press inquiries. An emergency press conference was arranged for later that afternoon to mollify an anxious public.

But the stunt that happened next, Les didn't foresee. In retrospect, he realized it was the cherry on top of a psychopath's pie—a madman's sense of poetic justice—and it aroused a nasty and primal urge within him that was always lurking just beneath the surface—the urge to inflict pain.

It started with a knock on his door that interrupted his preparations for the press conference. Benjamin Barrow walked in without a word, his silent rage apparent in his pink face—a strange contrast to his mane of white hair. Through his wire-rimmed spectacles, he blinked at Les.

"Have you gotten yours yet?"

"Gotten what?"

"This."

He held up the iconic postcard for Les to see, pinching it between two fingers as though it might contaminate him. Then he flipped it over and read aloud in a tone of sarcastic disgust.

Hey, Ben, Cool if I call you that? Or might it offend your mock dignity? Don't think for a second that just because you're so senior, you've got what it takes to find me. All you approval-craving, power-lusting, science-fearing committee cows have the same problem, a blindness to your own faults. But I'll give you a

*hint. What drives you forward is exactly what
drives me away.*

*Ever yours,
Galileo*

Les snorted. "Who does this bastard think he is?"

"The master of the universe, apparently." Barrow tossed the postcard onto the desk. "I bet he has a small dick."

"Cowards usually do."

"When was the last time you checked your mail?"

Les stared down at the paper piled high on his desk—reports, speeches, meeting minutes, case files, several days of mail. None of it had seemed like a priority before, but now he riffled through the stack, spreading it into a disorganized mess, until he spotted the innocuous-looking sun postcard wedged between two envelopes.

The date was August 24. Today. The postmark, Washington, D.C. The return address—333 Prospect Street NW. Les felt the hair on his arms bristle: That was *his own address*.

"What does it say?" Barrow asked.

He read the neat handwriting aloud:

*So, Chief. Did you get what you wanted yet? All
the power and the glory? You disgust me, but
probably not as much as you disgust yourself. At
least when you were poor and bullied, your
struggle was honest. Don't spew your 'science as
dehumanizing' garbage when you don't give a
damn about humanity. You don't really want to
protect anyone. You just want to destroy whoever*

*reminds you of your own self-hatred. You think
I'm the bad guy, but what does that say about
you?*

> *Ever yours,*
> *Galileo*

Barrow whistled. "Talk about below the belt."

Les's fists ached to punch something. If it weren't
for his colleague's presence, he might have stuck it to
the nearest wall. How could this faraway psycho have
known about his childhood? And his address? Les was
supposed to be stalking *him*, not the other way around.

The stiff paper crumpled under the force of his fingers.

"This," he said, tearing it into shreds, "never happened. Got it?"

"But it's evidence!" Barrow cried, making a grab for
it. "It has to be analyzed—"

He jumped away, his reflexes quicker. "No way. You
know none of these stupid postcards make a difference."

Barrow crossed his arms. "You're letting him provoke you."

His condescending tone was further incitement. Les
wiped his hands of the torn bits and dug his nails into
his palms, itching to take his anger and humiliation out
on someone—anyone. "That's it," he snapped. "We're
done here."

When Les finally left the office around midnight,
his fury had congealed into hatred. Too worked up to take

the Metro home, he walked. The streets grew darker and emptier as he left the tourist center of the city and headed west toward his own residential neighborhood. In stark contrast to his air-conditioned office, the late summer heat was merciless—a thick, muggy heat that seemed to multiply gravity. Mustering the energy to plow through it left him with pooled sweat under his arms, behind his knees, on his upper lip. His suit and pants clung to the wet spots, stifling his movements.

He was cursing August, cursing the whole goddamn city, but cursing Galileo most of all, when he heard coins clinking in a cup nearby.

"Spare some change?" asked a disembodied voice in the shadows.

"Get a job," Les muttered, without slowing. He noticed he was in a deserted alley between two blocks, a shortcut he'd taken many times, but also a popular spot for vandalism and drug deals because it was so well shielded from the major streets. Graffiti covered the walls on either side, the strange symbols and codes like hieroglyphics to the uninitiated, but Les recognized them as signs of a turf war.

The gravelly voice edged up right behind him. "Bet you wouldn't keep walking if I had a gun."

He turned around and stared down the skinny, vacant-eyed oaf still shaking his pathetic cup. The handle of a revolver was poking out from the waistband of his ill-fitting jeans. Les was not afraid. The sight of it only piqued his fury.

"Back off, asshole. You don't want to mess with me."

"Oh no? You a big bad white boy?"

He rolled his eyes. "I'm going to keep walking and you're going to get lost."

The man cackled, the whites of his eyes glistening with scorn. "G'luck with that."

He was so close that Les could smell the foul odor of urine emanating from his body.

"I'll give you one last chance. *Step back.*"

"Whatchoo gonna do about it?" he taunted, lifting his foot to come closer. But Les was faster. Before the man's foot hit the pavement, Les's fist smashed into the bridge of his nose with an obscene crunch. The man stumbled backward, groping for his gun, dark blood spilling over his lips. Les knocked his hand away and punched him again, this time in the eye, his quickness sharpened by adrenaline and rage, compounded by the man's grunts and groans.

The pathetic whimpers were like a siren song, luring him to greater energy, greater strength, as he pummeled the man's face, neck, stomach, imagining Galileo receiving the blows. The urge to dispense suffering grew so powerful that he craved the bruising of soft human flesh beneath his knuckles, feeling no pain himself, nothing but the craving to split skin and intensify the agony. He didn't know how long he continued to pound his would-be assailant, but before long he noticed that the man was sagging against the wall, no longer attempting to recoil. His mouth was gaping open, dribbling saliva and blood. His eyes were two swollen mounds.

Les grabbed his wrist. There was no pulse.

He jumped back in surprise and stared down at his hands. His knuckles were bloodied and throbbing. The fog of his rage evaporated and a cool pragmatism swept in. He glanced around and was relieved to see that the alley was still deserted.

He had to act fast. Any minute, someone could come walking through, spot them, and call the cops. Thinking quickly, he pulled out a fat black Sharpie from his briefcase, which had fallen a few feet away. After taking a moment to scrutinize the nearby graffiti, he traced a line around the body and drew a giant *MS-13* above it on the wall in thick block text, mimicking the font of similar markings. MS-13, he knew from the news, was the name of a violent transnational gang that had recently expanded to D.C.

Next from the briefcase he withdrew a cigarette and a matchbox emblazoned with the name of a fancy restaurant he'd eaten at the week before. His hands shook as he dragged the match head along the strip, slipping the first few times, but succeeding when a yellow flame bloomed. Its heat jabbed at his fingertips as he lit the cigarette and took a long drag.

Then he tossed the match onto the slumped body and sauntered toward the street, casually exhaling a puff of smoke. He turned the corner before the stench of burning flesh could reach his nostrils.

CHAPTER 37

The mice looked like newborns—salmon-colored, hairless, thumb-sized creatures with toothpick legs barely strong enough to hold up their plump bodies. In a single glass-walled cage, a dozen of them slept huddled together, one on top of the next, the tight cluster almost appearing as a single, pink-blobbed organism. It wasn't much of a show, but that didn't stop the entire population of the compound—all the scientists, doctors, tech guys, nurses, cafeteria ladies, and stabilized patients—from crowding into Natalie's lab for a peek.

Because they weren't newborns. They were twenty-one days old.

Above the heads of the onlookers, Natalie gazed at the mice fondly, as though they were her own children. In a way, she thought, they were—born not of her body, but her mind. The last several weeks had been the most innovative of her life. After determining the nucleic acid sequence of the knockout that had silenced the alleged master gene in the dead embryos, she and the rest of the team synthesized an antisense sequence intended to bind to the gene and prevent its expression in living mice. Next they inserted the sequence into a carrier viral genome—a Trojan horse method of sneaking in biological cues to alter a host's DNA. When these mice were born three weeks ago, they breathed in the specially engineered virus—and Natalie practically stopped breathing altogether.

Would they age normally? Would they get sick? Would they die?

So far, none of the above had happened. In the days since, the mice appeared to be biologically frozen, destined to remain newborns for—well, it was impossible to say how long. The words Natalie kept thinking of, as everyone clamored to get closer to the cage, were *uncharted territory*. As cautious and skeptical as her training had prepared her to be, she knew that this was already a revolutionary moment—even if the mice collapsed tomorrow. She felt closer to her fellow researchers, more permanently bonded with Nina and the others, than she ever had with most of her own blood relatives.

"You should charge admission," Helen joked, coming to stand beside her on the outer ring of the circle as the awestruck crowd huddled around the cage and snapped pictures.

Natalie smiled. "Or we could just submit them to the Archon Prize for a cool twenty mil."

"You're going to win, guaranteed. I don't see how you couldn't."

"Neither do I."

"Will you guys split the money with Galileo?"

"Are you kidding? None of this would have happened without him." She glanced wistfully at the door as though he might walk in. He had been gone for weeks now, with no expected return date.

"What will you do with your share? Nat?"

She tore her eyes away from the door. "Oh, the next phase. I'll have to talk to him to figure out the best plan, but we'll want to test the sequence on primates, and then humans."

"Where do I sign up?"

"That's years off; you know that."

"No, really," Helen said, "you're going to have the entire Network knocking down your door. You should start a list of human research subjects now, with me at the top."

"Oh yeah?" A playful gleam came into her eyes. "What clinical trials do you have for me?"

"Let's see. I could stick you in with my synthetic oil–pooping organisms."

Natalie laughed and was about to reply when she felt a tap on her arm. Zoe and Theo were standing behind her, hand in hand. Since Zoe's return from her runaway escapade a few weeks earlier, Natalie had spotted them a few times holding hands, and it cheered her.

So she was both delighted and chagrined to find Zoe gazing up at her with serious eyes, clutching Theo's hand as if for strength.

"Hi. Can we talk?"

"Of course," Natalie said, excusing herself from Helen. "Where do you want to go?"

Zoe shrugged. "The hall's fine. Be right back," she told Theo, letting go of him. He gave her an encouraging smile, and as soon as she turned her back, flashed

Natalie a secret thumbs-up. The knowing gesture didn't surprise her. He had always been the more diplomatically gifted one in the family.

"Listen," she said to Zoe as soon as they crossed into the privacy of the hallway, "I know you're upset with me, and I don't blame you. That day you came to find me—"

Zoe flicked her hand. "I'm over it."

"No, please, let me apologize. I was totally involved in my work that day and not paying attention to what you needed. It was hurtful. And since your return, I know you've been mad, but to be honest, I've been afraid to hear how much I've disappointed you. That's why I haven't come to you sooner, not because I don't care. I'm sorry. You'd think at my age"—she smiled— "I'd know how to behave."

Zoe nodded, not disagreeing. "I was ready to forgive you anyway, but that means a lot."

Natalie's eyes watered, the full force of her guilt hitting her as soon as she was pardoned. She hoped Zoe wouldn't notice and mistake her reaction for some kind of play for compassion. The truth was that she often experienced distress most acutely after the fact, as though her coping mechanism broke down the moment a threat vanished—when its danger became safe to feel.

"Don't cry," Zoe said. "It's okay. I get it. Anyways, I also wanted to say congrats. I can't believe you guys actually freaking cured *aging.*"

She grinned, wiping her eyes. "Only in mice," she allowed, "and only so far."

Zoe's expression took on a shade of worry. "But you found the gene! Isn't that like the biggest deal ever?"

"Well, yes, but we still have a long way to go. Someday we'll get to human trials and *that*, if it works, will be the biggest deal ever."

"Someday? Like when?"

Natalie hesitated, sensitive to the fact that her deepest hopes rested on the answer, but doling out empty promises would do her no favors.

"Years from now. The next phase will take much longer because primates and humans have much longer life spans than mice."

Zoe's chin dropped to her chest. "Oh." She stepped away, turning to leave. Her lips were pursed tightly and Natalie could see the effort she was making not to burst into tears.

"But you deserve a huge thank-you," Natalie added. "From all of us. None of this would be happening without your bravery."

Zoe paused, looking back at Natalie over her shoulder.

"Or," she replied with startling cynicism, "my DNA."

Those words, that tone—the full kaleidoscope of her anguish shifted into view, the private torment that must have driven her to seek out a kind ear, only to be met with Natalie's blind eye. She hoped it wasn't too late to make up for it.

"True," she agreed, "your DNA helped." Then she crossed the gap between them and placed two fingers under Zoe's delicate chin. "But I'm going to tell you something, and I want you to listen. Because I'm not one to bullshit. I speak only facts. And I know this much. *You are so much more* than some chemical strands. You're a young woman with a heart and a brain and a soul. Don't ever forget it."

At dusk, Zoe and Theo were reclining on their chosen boulder in the mountains, taking a break from the mice mania, when he put a hand on her arm.

"What's wrong?" he asked. "You seem weird."

"Hey, thanks."

"No, like there's something you're not telling me."

She smiled. Since her return and their joyful reunion, they had become comfortable enough to sit in silence, but also close enough to discern when that silence was troubled.

"I'm starting to think," she said, "that you hacked into my brain."

"Apparently not well enough." He leaned over and planted a kiss on her forehead. "But seriously. Don't tell me you're still worrying about our age thing?"

She shook her head. "I've decided I can't problem-solve that one because it's impossible. Whatever happens is going to happen, so we may as well just appreciate each other while we can."

"That's what I've been trying to tell you!"

"I know."

"So what's wrong?"

She sighed. "Everything else. The mice . . ."

He cocked his head. "Let me get this straight. We've just set eyes on the world's first biologically *immortal*—"

"Yeah, yeah. It's a huge deal, but it's not enough. Your mom said so herself. It's going to take longer than my grandfather can wait."

Theo had no response, so she went on. "I was stupid before. I had no idea how science really worked. To think they could come up with some magic cure so fast . . ."

"You weren't stupid," he said. "You were just thinking like a kid. Kids love fantasies. Now you know better. And you really wanted to grow up?" He shot her a look of shocking bitterness. "Growing up sucks. If the person you love is going to walk out one day, or drop dead, all the wishful thinking in the world won't matter. Welcome, your childhood is officially over."

She stared at him, stunned. "Ouch."

"Well, it's true. I don't sugarcoat stuff."

"You and your mom both."

"Yup. We're straight shooters."

"Just like Gramps." It was impossible to keep the wistfulness out of her voice.

"You want to leave?" he guessed.

"I'm dying to. Not that I don't love hanging out with you, but it's killing me not to be with him, now that I know . . . what I know . . . and I still don't have a clue where he is. Galileo's supposed to be looking for him but now they're *both* gone."

"You're not thinking of running away again, are you?"

"I wish. But it's too risky for me."

"How come?"

She couldn't bring herself to tell him about the threat on her life—it was too disturbing—so she just said, "Galileo told me to lie low until the government's investigation dies down. But now with his whole postcard hoax, I don't know when I'll ever get to leave!"

"He was just trying to throw them off."

"But now they're even angrier, so where does that leave me?"

"When he comes back, we'll ask him to figure something out."

"I don't know how much longer I can wait."

"Patience in the face of uncertainty," he said, giving her arm a tight squeeze. "Just one more joy of growing up."

CHAPTER 38

The phone call woke Les at dawn. Startled out of a fretful sleep, he rolled over to snatch his vibrating cell off the nightstand. *The body,* he thought. His heart thrashed in his chest.

"Hello?"

"Yo," came a familiar nasal voice. "You up?"

Les exhaled with a groan and lay back on his pillow. "Jesus, Cylon, can it wait until normal business—"

"I got into the dude's computer!" he said. *"Finally."*

Les bolted upright. "You hacked Hernandez?"

"Yup. I'm controlling it as we speak. Playing solitaire. Ooh, got an ace!"

"I thought he wouldn't reply to your e-mails?"

"He wouldn't. So a coupla weeks ago, I mailed him a flash drive that looked like a Netflix promo with a bunch of free movies on it. Of course my little virus was tucked in, too. And the sucker fell for it."

Les smiled. "I have to hand it to you."

"I know."

"Can you pull up his e-mail?"

"Got it right here."

"And?"

"There's a bunch from someone named Nina. Same last name, too."

"Recent ones?"

"One from yesterday. 5:11 P.M."

So the daughter who had supposedly vanished into the Network's clutches wasn't really missing after all—which meant Julian Hernandez was a liar, exactly as Les suspected. But he couldn't care less about that. All that mattered was a single question—*Where was she?*

"Don't move," he said. "I'm coming over."

The cab hit the early morning rush on Prospect Street, forcing Les into passive consumption of the driver's blaring radio station. He was about to demand a quiet car when three chimes rang and a smooth announcer's voice launched into a summary of the latest local developments.

"News on the hour . . . An unidentified man was found last night beaten to death on N Street near Connecticut Avenue. Police are attributing the gruesome crime to MS-13, a gang notorious for homicides that has recently infiltrated Washington. Commissioner Farley issued a statement this morning vowing to crack down on violence in all districts . . . Congress today votes on the passage of . . ."

Les tuned out, indulging a grin. Things were starting to go his way at last. The rest of the ride seemed to fly by, and soon he was climbing the dirty steps two at a time up to Cylon's apartment.

When he walked in, Cylon was slouching on his

couch in front of his laptop, patchy stubble dotting his double chin, wearing sweatpants and no shirt.

"Check it out," he said, swiping his chubby fingers across the trackpad. "I just won."

Les edged him aside and sat down, shifting the computer to his own knees. A cascade of aces was bouncing across the screen in the solitaire victory dance.

"Get this out of here. Show me the e-mails."

Cylon clicked a few boxes and up popped Julian Hernandez's Yahoo account against a dark blue background—the actual image of his screen in real time. Les scrolled through his e-mails, skimming the subjects and senders. Many of them appeared to be from Nina. He opened the most recent one—dated yesterday, subject line *wow*—and read.

Dad, I so wish you could be here to see this. The mice I've been telling you about STILL haven't aged since we made them inhale the viral gene silencers. This is huge, like 20 million bucks huge. Natalie thinks we'll definitely win the Archon next year, so it looks like my time here is going to be longer than I thought. I can hear you sigh—I miss you, too, but once we get that funding, the doors will open to so many more experiments. We already have a long list of volunteers for when we get to the human trial phase. Everybody here wants to try it, except Zoe of course. Do you want me to put you on the list, too? We're opening it up to family members b/c we're going to need a wide sample size. The thing is it doesn't reverse aging, just freezes you

*where you are. Or you could just come for a
visit! We could get someone to drive you here.
Think about it. I love you. N*

Les stared at the screen, openmouthed. He read the
letter again to be sure he hadn't imagined it. The truth
he'd long suspected was literally spelled out. Galileo's
henchmen were getting away with all kinds of illegal
biomedical experimentation right under the committee's blind eye—in some secret place accessible by car
from Ohio! He felt a tsunami of rage engulf him. A single thought penetrated every neuron. That place—that
man—needed to be found—and destroyed.

"Cylon," he said, "what's her IP address?"

It didn't take a computer genius to know that this
was all he needed to locate their physical coordinates.

"Well." Cylon fidgeted with a paper clip, unwinding
its curves. "First I'd need to figure out her outbound
server. But have you noticed her e-mail address?"

Les returned his attention to the screen. Her address
was nina@heurjgf3n47.com. That was odd. He frowned
and clicked through to another message from her:
nina@doej68sk2n.com. And then another message:
nina@pen68snfje.com.

He turned to Cylon. "What the hell?"

"They've been anonymized. It's a service that ob-
scures the true server so you can't trace it."

"But we need that IP address!"

Cylon sighed. "I checked it out already. Her e-mails
seem to come from a different country every time—
Russia, India, Mexico. Who *knows* how many servers
they've bounced off before they get here? Wherever
this chick is, her tech people know what's up."

"Can't you *un*-anonymize them?"

"I'd have to trace back through however many servers each e-mail pinged to figure out which common one they all originated from."

"So it's technically feasible?"

"Feasible but . . ."

"But what?"

"Superdifficult. And illegal without a warrant."

"I *am* the law. And let me tell you, this is damn well warranted."

"Okay, okay. I think I can do it. But you're gonna need to get me a case of Red Bull because this shit is hard."

"You can do it. I'll get you whatever you need."

"Fine. I'll call you when I have something."

Les snorted. "You think I'm leaving?"

"I don't know how long it'll—"

"Then you better get on it, because an extra ten grand is waiting for you."

"It is?"

"Yep, but every minute you dick around, another buck comes off." Les glanced at his watch. "Starting now."

Cylon grabbed the computer from his lap and pounded out a code language filled with dashes and slashes, as though a stream of gibberish were draining from his brain through his fingers.

Les watched with a tight smile, thinking of how he would explain the imminent discovery to the FBI and the committee. It was simple. After his insistent haranguing, Julian Hernandez had broken down and revealed the location of the secret compound. Once that much was known, no one would care to probe how the information had been delivered—and if they did, it would be Les's word against a proven liar's.

Now it was only a matter of time.

Fifty-seven hours later Cylon shook Les from his bleary stupor on the couch, where his head was resting near a pile of empty Red Bull cans.

"Hey," Cylon hissed. "Wake up."

Les opened his eyes. The room was dark, the shades drawn against the wan light outside. He'd called in sick to work for the rest of the week. What day was it now? How long had he been sleeping? Cylon's bloodshot brown eyes and sour breath loomed above him. "Yo, wake up."

He pushed himself up to his hands, twisting his cramped neck from side to side. His stomach was growling, his bladder straining, his head pounding. He really needed to go home, even though Cylon might slow down without him there, and they couldn't afford to lose a minute, not with those crazy scientists running loose—

"Sixty-seven dot fifty-four dot one four four dot zero," Cylon announced.

It took Les a second to recognize the format—but then he sucked in a breath. It was an IP address.

"You did it?"

"Yep. Haven't slept in two days."

"Amazing. You're a master."

"I know."

"So where is this place?"

Cylon squinted at the screen, reading out the latitude: "Thirty-six dot—"

"In plain English, for God's sake!"

"Pueblo Peak Mountain, New Mexico." He expanded the satellite map and tilted the screen toward Les. "Looks like it's in Indian country, tucked behind some casino."

Multiple to-do tasks barreled through Les's mind at once. Notify Pinter and the FBI and the President, deploy a local SWAT team, prep a jet and a helicopter for immediate transportation, direct his staff to hold the media at bay until the operation was complete, dispatch the rest of the committee, including Benjamin Barrow . . . In spite of their annoying rivalry, Barrow was the other person who wanted this just as badly, so he deserved to be the first to know—and the first to acknowledge Les's triumph.

He dialed his partner, his hands trembling with excitement. After two rings, Barrow answered in a clipped tone.

"Is it important? I'm rushing into a meeting—"

"Drop everything. We're going to New Mexico. I found the compound."

CHAPTER 39

If Zoe ever saw Gramps again, she wanted to set the record straight. She owed him an apology that was seven years overdue. He'd never asked for one, but she'd hurt him once, during a vulnerable time in his life. Apparently he was better at forgiving her than she was at forgiving herself, because the niggling guilt had stayed with her. Now she realized that if you didn't say what needed to be said at the time, who knew if you would ever get another chance?

It happened when she was fourteen—really fourteen, the summer after eighth grade—during a family vacation, an Alaskan cruise. Her mom had billed it as a fun getaway for them all, but Zoe hated the cold and knew the trip was also not enjoyable for Gramps, who was fighting a losing battle with grief over his late wife. On the ship, her parents turned in early every night, leaving her to find entertainment. She was too young to be accepted by the cliquey teenagers and too old to play with the kids. So she and Gramps, the two night owls, were stuck with each other.

She learned that playing gin rummy on the deck

with a cigar-puffing old man was not the way to impress the teens she yearned to join. To this day, she cringed when she recalled how she had rolled her eyes at his jokes when they passed by, even though his light-hearted manner must have taken monumental effort. That whole trip she blamed age for her predicament—he was too old to be cool, she wasn't old enough—and not her own misplaced priorities.

But now, thanks to Natalie and Theo and Galileo, she knew better. Age was never the problem. She didn't need a drug to make her the adult she wanted to be.

All she'd ever needed was perspective.

The things that mattered had nothing to do with whether you were fourteen or eighty-four. A number couldn't reveal how independent your mind, how empathic your soul, how deep your love. No wonder soul mates didn't ask for ID. To judge others on age was to be more shallow than a paper cut. To judge her own value that way was to ignore herself as she had once ignored Gramps. She was too old to make that mistake again.

Even if she still looked like half a woman, inside she felt for the first time more whole than she had ever been. If only she had another week with him to share what she had learned. Wasn't it what he had been trying to tell her all along?

She needed to find him here and now in the only way she could—on the page. So what if no one could deliver her letters? She would write another one, and the words would summon a meeting of their spirits, even if only in her mind.

She was fishing around for paper and a pen when a voice burst through the intercom into her room:

"Everyone report to the quad immediately. This is not a drill. I repeat, *immediately*."

She stiffened, recognizing the throaty bass of Ted, the tech guy. He sounded terrified. Through the window, she could see people streaming outside, emerging from the underground laboratories, the cafeteria, the hospital, gravitating to the quad like iron filings to a magnet.

Someone pounded on her door. She dashed to open it. Theo was standing there, wearing black running shorts, a sweaty shirt, and gym shoes. With a no-nonsense look, he grabbed her hand and pulled her outside.

"Come on!"

"What's happening?"

"No idea."

He ran without letting go of her hand. She sprinted to keep up, running down the hallway and turning the corner a step behind him. Outside in the quad, several dozen people were gathered in a tight cluster of white coats in front of Ted, who was standing on a bench and motioning to the remaining stragglers to hurry.

Natalie called to Theo and they rushed over to her, pushing through the buzzing crowd. She embraced each of them, her face pale and drawn.

"What if something happened to Galileo?"

"No," Theo said. "I'm sure that's not it."

"Why hasn't he come back? It's been *weeks*."

"We'd hear about it," Zoe reassured her. "It would be in the news."

"Maybe not right away."

A blanket of silence descended over the crowd. They looked up at Ted. He was holding his palms out to summon everyone's attention. Despite the warmth of the afternoon breeze, Zoe found herself shivering.

"There's been a major breach," he announced. "Our server was hacked. The feds are on their way. We have to evacuate, Galileo's orders."

A ripple of panicked gasps tore through the crowd. Zoe tried to repeat the words in her head to comprehend them, but they didn't make sense.

"Is he in trouble?" Natalie shouted.

"He's not, but we are. Any minute we could be facing a SWAT team. Everyone follow me through the evacuation tunnel in the Brain. The RVs are waiting for us on the other end to take us to safe houses. Forget your things, we go *now*."

"What about the hospital patients?" a doctor called out. "How can we bring them, if they're attached to oxygen machines—?"

"It's safer for them to stay. They'll be found and transferred to other hospitals. They're not the perps here. All of us are."

He hopped off the bench, ran toward the Brain, and disappeared into the building. Everyone else lost no time stampeding after him. Order devolved faster than Zoe could believe, with the bustling mob of white coats swallowing her into its frantic center and dragging her ahead. Somewhere along the way she was forced to let go of Theo, but fighting her way backward was like trying to oppose a blizzard.

"Just go!" he shouted at her, falling behind.

Zoe saw Natalie back there with him, so at least they were together. They didn't need her to wait. She let the tide steer her into the building and up the three narrow flights of stairs to the Brain, trying to ward off the elbows and knees flying near her face. She made it to the packed control room without injury. At the edge of the room was a wooden floorboard that had been moved aside to reveal the evacuation tunnel. At its mouth, which led underground via a steep metal ladder, a bottleneck of people had formed. Only one person at a time could climb down, as the rest of the anxious group shouted to hurry.

Zoe glanced behind her, where more people were pushing their way into the small room, and felt the rising tide of claustrophobia choke her. There was no way out, except into the bowels of the earth. She marched up to the front of the frenzied line, where Helen had one foot on the first rung. Helen, whom she thought of as a friend.

"Let me go!" she pleaded. "I'll be quick."

Helen took one look at her desperation and moved aside. "Go, dear. Careful now."

She hopped onto the ladder and climbed down, as the air around her grew colder and the light dimmed. The dank muddy scent of earth filled her nostrils. Far below, she could hear the voices of those who had gone first, echoing off the walls and fading away. Around fifty steps down, she hit solid ground and followed the sound of the voices. Though just as dark, this tunnel was wider than the other one that led to the casino. Several people could walk here side by side. Soon, she thought, Theo and Natalie would reach her and they could head together to safety.

Any second they would be coming up behind her if she stopped to wait. She thought of Les Mahler and shuddered, but no one bad was going to find her now that she was hidden. Just then Helen came barreling past her, followed by a blur of other researchers who were difficult to identify in the darkness.

She leaned against the cold wall and waited. People rushed past, one white coat after the next.

Every time she sensed a tall figure coming toward her, she shouted Theo's name, but no one slowed down. The crush coming down the ladder thinned. If anyone noticed her, no one cared enough to stop.

She heard a thump far above, like something slamming. She traced her steps back to the base of the ladder and looked up. The circular hole of light marking the entrance to the tunnel was gone. The wooden floorboard had been replaced over the opening, apparently by the person who was currently climbing down the ladder. When he neared, carrying a flashlight, she recognized him as one of the hospital doctors she knew only by sight. It took another thirty seconds for him to reach her at the bottom.

"What was that?" she demanded, as he hopped onto the ground beside her.

"That's it," he said. "No one was behind me."

He started to run past her but she grabbed his sleeve.

"There's still two people left! Natalie and Theo, didn't you see them?"

"Natalie." He said her name with a shake of his head. "She ran back to the lab. We can't leave the tunnel wide open while she messes around."

"What about Theo?"

"Not my problem. The rest of us have to get out of here!"

He shook her off and jogged ahead, then stopped and turned around.

"Hey, aren't you coming?"

She was already scrambling back up the ladder, fighting past the burn in her thighs as she climbed ten rungs, twenty, thirty. When she reached the top, she pushed hard against the wooden board and nudged it aside long enough to haul her body through the opening. She swayed as she stood up, seized with a rumbling in her bones. But it wasn't just her. The windows were rumbling, too.

That was when she saw the grass down below in the quad lay flat, as though in surrender to the massive black shadow cast across it.

A helicopter was landing.

PART 4

A . . . mortal danger is contained in the now popular notion that a person has a right over his body, a right that allows him to do whatever he wants to it or with it.
—LEON KASS, Chairman of the President's Council on Bioethics, 2001–2005

CHAPTER 40

"**M**om!" Theo screamed. "Where are you going?"

"Just go without me!" she yelled, running too fast to look back. The brisk air whipped at her face as she broke away from the mob of her colleagues charging toward the Brain. Adjacent to its windowed control tower loomed the adobe walls of the lab building, where her life's work lay trapped.

"Stop!" he called, his voice getting closer. "Mom!"

The door to the lab was a yard away.

His footsteps pattered to a stop behind her. "You've got to be kidding me."

She whirled around and stared up into the face of the man who was her son.

"Just go. I'll catch up with you."

He lunged to grasp her arm, but didn't anticipate her reflexes. She plowed ahead before he could touch her, pushing through the door she had entered a thousand times and never would again. For a split second, the abrupt silence was almost disorienting. The emergency seemed unreal, distant—but then he was storming in after her and she was racing down three flights to the precious room nestled in the back where the secret to aging lay captive.

The steps rippled under her feet so quickly that she barely noticed when her sandals slipped off and she was flying down the stairs barefoot, then jogging over the cold floor to the last room on the left. She arrived disheveled, panting, to find the lab in a deceptively normal state, the way she had left it before the intercom announcement. The computer monitors were lit, the mice sleeping, the microscopes on, the centrifuges spinning. Somewhere, on one of the shelves or in a supply cabinet, she knew there was an external hard drive. The team was supposed to be backing up onto it nightly but had gotten complacent, and now she couldn't remember who had used it last or where it was. All she had to do was find it, plug it into her computer, and load up the data. Without it, the biggest breakthrough of her lifetime would be lost—seized by the feds and relegated to some gloomy evidence room, forever buried under a mountain of bureaucracy.

She bolted to the supply cabinet and flung it open as Theo rushed in, his face red with fury.

"I can't believe you! Everyone else is gone!"

"Please, go with them," she begged, flinging pipettes and petri dishes and slides to the floor. *Where was the damn drive?*

"No."

"Don't be a hero, just get out of here—"

"I'm not leaving you!"

She rummaged in the back of the cabinet, feeling nothing but empty space.

"Fine. I'm not going anywhere until I find our hard drive, so you might as well help me look."

He brushed past her to open a nearby closet of textbooks and files. "This is crazy. Do you really want to go back to jail over a science project?"

"Would I leave *you* trapped under the rubble?" She ducked her head into a drawer. "Don't argue, just look!"

He slammed the closet. "It's not in here. We really don't have time for this."

"Keep looking!"

The discarded contents of shelves, drawers, cabinets, and closets piled around their feet as they rushed to excavate every nook and cranny, to no avail. She was about to unbolt her computer itself from the counter when, behind the monitor, she felt a hunk of rectangular plastic and let out a cry of joy.

He rushed to her side. "You found it?"

"Yeah, someone must've put it there so we wouldn't lose it."

She swiftly located the USB jack and plugged it in. The drive's icon popped up on the screen and she dragged over a massive folder that read "Syndrome X." It contained every piece of knowledge from the experiments, from Zoe's fully sequenced DNA and the chromosomal analysis of the master regulator gene to the chemical makeup of the knockouts and the day-to-day records of the ageless mice. The data was priceless— and impossible to re-create from memory.

A blue bar indicated the progress of the file transfer: 15 percent, 18 percent, 20 percent.

"Come on," Natalie muttered. "Go, go, go."

Theo paced, kicking around the debris on the floor— a box of rubber gloves, a spilled tub of mice food pellets, a brick-sized textbook.

"Almost thirty percent," she said.

He stopped and frowned.

"It's going fast," she added. "Relax."

"Did you hear that?"

"Hear what?"

"That noise."

They hurried to the doorway and peered into the hall. Though they couldn't see anyone, there was no mistaking the heavy thud of footsteps coming down the stairs. Many footsteps.

Her breath caught in her throat. "Maybe they didn't want to leave us behind?"

He blinked at her. "Everyone?"

She looked around, but they were at the end of the hallway, with no escape.

"Hide!" she whispered, running to the empty supply closet that stood against the wall opposite the door. It was just large enough to fit one of them, so she shoved him inside and slammed it shut.

There was nowhere else to go. The footsteps pounded in the hall, thundering like a pack of stampeding bulls. She knew she was about to be trampled. Her brain throbbed. Should she give up, or play dead, or try to fight?

The computer gave a cheerful ding. The file transfer was complete.

She leaped toward it as a barrage of voices reached the doorway and shouted at her to freeze. Inches from the drive, she stopped short. It was over. She closed her eyes, afraid to find out what she was up against. Her last fleeting thought was of Galileo—and how he had failed her.

She turned and opened her eyes.

Six masked men in bulletproof vests and combat boots stood facing her with their assault rifles cocked.

CHAPTER 41

The minute their helicopter landed, Les and Benjamin Barrow were ushered by an agent from the SWAT team across a strangely quiet courtyard into a stout beige building and down three flights to a room at the end of a hallway. Every step in this illicit place felt to Les like encroaching upon a spider's nest. His skin crawled with exhilarated disgust, his muscles twitched, his pupils dilated. He yearned to slow down and inspect the web, untangle its intricacy, fumigate its crevices, but a couple of instant snags demanded their attention.

"A young man and a woman," the agent informed them. "Neither will talk."

Maybe not to you, Les thought. But he would grind down the captives until they pointed to the spider himself—and the little girl who was his most dangerous prey.

He noticed as they sped into the hallway that Barrow was scanning the premises, his whole face taut in revulsion and fear. Les suppressed a smirk. His partner could talk an intimidating game in the office, but he was a prissy bitch at heart. Les, on the other hand, was prepared to take on any thug the universe hurled at him. That, more than anything else, made him worthy of being chief. His hands itched for the ultimate fight. A tingling, aggressive energy coursed through his blood.

A woman's moaning trickled into the hall as they neared the door. When they burst through the ring of SWAT team guards, they marched into a messy lab—a lab where Natalie Roy was handcuffed to the leg of a counter, writhing on the floor next to an also-handcuffed, petrified teenage boy. Both were trying to twist out of their cuffs, but when Les and Barrow entered, their bodies went rigid.

Natalie's tear-streaked face paled so fast Les thought she might faint. He waded through the haphazard debris of textbooks and glass dishes and boxes strewn on the ground and spread his arms wide in mock grandeur.

"So *this* is where you've been hanging out! I can't say I imagined it this disgusting, but I guess it's only fitting."

She scowled, yanking her wrists against her cuffs. Red lines cut into her skin where the metal rubbed against it.

"Oh, you're not happy to see me?" He pouted, feigning hurt. "But we got along so well the last time, remember?" He raised his voice an octave, mimicking her. *"The Network what? Galileo who?"*

A ball of spit flew from her mouth and smacked his cheek, warm and gooey, reeking of sour coffee as it slid down his face.

"What the—!" He was about to slap her when Barrow appeared at his side and thrust a handkerchief at him, then glared at Natalie from a safe distance of several feet, as if she were a wild animal.

"Look, lady," he said, "either you help us and we help you, or we lock your ass up for a long time. Which would you prefer?"

She stared at him.

The boy opened his mouth like he wanted to speak, but then closed it.

"What is it, kid?" Les prompted.

"I-I think we should cooperate."

Barrow gave him a tight smile. "That's right. Very sensible."

"No!" Natalie shouted, craning her neck to face her son. "Don't you dare."

"We need you to answer a few questions," Les cut in, ignoring her and addressing the boy. "The quicker you talk, the sooner we can get you and your mom out of here."

"Okay."

Barrow hung back while Les approached him. "Tell us everything you know about Galileo."

"Well, he's about six—"

"No!" Natalie cried, straining against her cuffs.

"About six feet tall," Theo went on, refusing to look at her. "Curly black hair, clean-shaven, superfit but not bulky. He's badass, like I wouldn't want to mess with him, you know?"

"How old is he?"

"Hard to tell. Maybe fifty?"

Barrow approached Theo at a wide angle, careful to keep out of spitting distance from Natalie. "When was the last time you saw him?"

"Not that long ago." He cocked his head. "Earlier today, at lunch, right before you all showed up."

"And then what happened?" Les demanded.

"People just scattered. My mom came here and I followed."

"So is he still on the premises?"

"I dunno. Can't be far. There's a trail that backs into the mountains behind the cafeteria, check that. There's also a tunnel through a door to the left of this building that leads to the Indian casino. Those are the only ways out."

"What about Zoe Kincaid?" Les asked. "Is she alive, have you seen her?"

"Oh yeah, she's around, too. They were both over by the cafeteria like an hour ago. Just go out of this building and make a right, cross the quad, and you'll see the wooden barn. That's it. All the apartments are back there two in a row, hers is number 3 and Galileo's is 21. Doors are never locked around here."

"Theo!" Natalie cried. "What are you *thinking*?"

"I'm doing this for you," he retorted. "You're welcome."

"You heard the boy," Les yelled to the half a dozen agents who were primed near the door. "Let's go!"

They streamed into the hall, as if springing to life at his command. He started to follow them but noticed Barrow shrinking back with a look of apprehension.

"Come on," Les snapped, "what are you doing?"

"We're just leaving these two unsupervised?"

"They're handcuffed."

"But what if someone comes to help them? We have no idea who's around."

You're such a pussy, Les thought. "Fine," he said, "stay here and make sure nothing happens."

He turned and sprinted out the door.

CHAPTER 42

In the Brain, Zoe frantically jabbed a button on the life-size screen that broadcast live footage from strategic cameras throughout the compound. Every time she pressed it, the image changed to a different vantage point—inside the hospital wing, the cafeteria, the tunnel to the casino, one empty lab after another. There were so many labs—where was Natalie's? What was happening?

When the first helicopter landed, Zoe had watched in shock as a dozen black-masked, armed men poured out and scattered like roaches, invading every space they could find. Some had swarmed the lab building, but none had yet broken through to the Brain, whose entry she had secured from the inside by six metal bolts that budged from the outside for only a few fingerprints on earth, the tech guys' and Galileo's.

The men had pounded and shot at the door, their bullets as loud as cannons as she ducked under a stool, unsure whether to climb back into the evacuation tunnel and escape or wait it out. But she couldn't force herself to abandon Theo and Natalie.

Then the ground had started to rumble again, and she heard the men retreat. Outside, in the quad, another helicopter touched down and two stern men climbed out wearing bulletproof vests over their suits. One was gray-haired, bony, and lean, the other white-haired, taller, and more muscular. Another man escorted them to the lab building, into which they all vanished out of sight.

Desperate to follow their path, Zoe had rushed to the video screen that was hooked up to cameras all over the compound—except she didn't know how to select a specific camera, so now she was pressing buttons haphazardly, shuffling through all kinds of useless footage as the minutes slipped away. If only she shared an ounce of Theo's computer savvy—but—*wait*—what was that muffled shouting outside?

She ran to the window and peered down at the quad. Armed men dressed in black vests and black boots were emerging from the lab building and splitting in opposite directions, toward the casino tunnel and the cafeteria. The thin gray-haired man was following close on their heels with an angry expression. Theo and Natalie were nowhere to be seen. She turned back to the screen, jabbing the button again to switch cameras. Up popped the gym, the rehab center, an empty lab, another empty lab, and then—

Zoe uttered a cry.

Both of them were *handcuffed* to the leg of a counter. Natalie's face was contorted in a sob. Theo was shaking his head.

The white-haired man was alone with them, bending over, his back to the camera. She watched helplessly as Theo strained against his handcuffs and appeared to shout something at him, a plea or a curse—it was difficult to tell without sound—and she was too worried about losing the image to press any other buttons.

The man gripped Theo by the shoulders to subdue him, then reached around to his wrists to inspect his handcuffs.

That was when she realized that the man's back was not only to the camera—it was also to the door. Her heart rammed against her chest as a last-ditch plan formed in her mind. It would be risky, but at this point, also their best hope for escape. They didn't have long— maybe only minutes before the other men returned— and no way was she going to let them be captured without a fight. She thought of Gramps. Even if he would try to talk her out of it, he would have to applaud her daring. This was a job that needed to be done.

The weapons arsenal was in this room, under the wooden floorboard that was near the evacuation tunnel. Galileo had mentioned it during one of their drills. She dove to one that seemed in the right location and tried to pry it open, but it wouldn't budge. She moved to the board next to it, barely noticing as a splinter sliced her hand. This one loosened right away and she peeled it back. In a shallow bin was a heap of different-sized guns, some with barrels the size of her arm, others compact enough to conceal in a purse. She selected the least scary-looking one, a small black handgun that was surprisingly heavy. She hoped that meant it was loaded because she wasn't sure how to check.

After listening at the door to make sure no one was there, she unbolted all the locks and swung it open. The stairs were deserted. She raced down them, winding around below the level of the quad, to the subterranean maze of tunnels that connected the entire ring of buildings in the compound. She knew the way by now and could avoid setting foot out in the open. But she concentrated on the map in her mind's eye, creeping through one hallway after another, making a turn here and there, until she crossed into the lab building and descended two floors to the right one.

She crept down the empty hall, clutching the handle of the gun. Her pointer finger smothered the trigger with sweat. She had never shot a gun before or even held one. It felt like metal power in her hand, heady and terrifying.

Natalie's and Theo's voices grew louder as she neared the corner lab. She couldn't make out what they were saying, but their urgent tones compelled her to pick up her pace. How relieved they would be to see her! She lifted the gun to eye level, copying the stance of the armed men she had witnessed prowling the quad.

Her hands were quivering when she reached the doorway. She tiptoed over the threshold before she lost her nerve. One glance across the room confirmed that Theo and Natalie were still handcuffed, and that the official remained bending over them, his back to her. Then she took aim, squinting through the crosshairs at his leg. Right as she was about to pull the trigger, his back shifted several inches to the left, leaving Theo directly facing her. A shriek ripped from his lungs.

"No, don't!"

She stumbled backward, confused, as the man spun around to face her.

The gun slipped from her fingers and clattered to the floor.

In spite of his white hair, spectacles, and strange hook nose, she recognized the fierceness in his eyes.

He was Galileo.

CHAPTER 43

"Zoe!" Natalie exclaimed, yanking her chafed wrists against her handcuffs. "What are you doing here?"

"You should have left us!" Theo yelled. "Get out of here!"

She didn't appear to hear them. She remained gaping at Galileo—stepping toward him, cautiously at first, a smile tugging at her lips. He grinned as only he could—and then, at last convinced, she ran straight into his arms. Natalie couldn't help feeling touched as they embraced, but her desperation was climbing. The men would return before long, and her and Theo's handcuffs were difficult to pick. If Galileo didn't get them off soon enough—

"Come on!" she called. "We need to go."

Galileo released Zoe and sprung to Natalie's side, producing a metal pin that he jammed into her cuffs. His brow furrowed in determination as his agile fingers worked to pick the lock.

"Let me help," Zoe said, crouching next to Theo. "I'll try his."

"I wish I had another pin. Or the key."

"Where is it?"

He sighed, scraping and clicking inside the lock. "With Les."

"I can't believe it." Zoe paced back and forth in a daze. "You've been working with *him* the whole time?"

"Against, darling."

Natalie shook her head. "When you guys walked in together, I thought I recognized you—and then I thought I might be going insane."

"It was the hand signals," Theo said. "When you started signing to us behind the dude's back, that's when I knew."

"Same," Natalie agreed, craning her neck over her shoulder to watch his maneuvering. "I hope we followed them well."

"Perfectly," he said, without looking up from the lock. "Otherwise we wouldn't have gotten rid of him."

"Yeah, but who knows for how long," Natalie said. "Can't you hurry?"

"I'm going—as—fast as I can . . ." She moaned as he tugged against the cuffs to no avail.

Theo cast an imploring look at Zoe, who was still pacing. "You should just go—seriously—get out while you can."

"He's right," Natalie said to her. "Go back to the tunnel, we'll meet you—"

"No," she declared. "I'm not leaving you guys."

As if to cement her point, she went to pick up her handgun from the floor where she had dropped it and then came back and plopped down next to Theo, leaning against his chest. His free arm draped across her in silent concession.

"Damn," Galileo muttered. "I can't pick these. I need the key."

"Keep trying," Natalie begged. "Hurry."

She felt Galileo's breath near her ear. "You don't have to worry, I've got your back."

She turned to look him in the eye, her pulse speeding up in spite of everything. "You do?"

"I was wrong before," he whispered. "But I'm here now." He leaned in and planted a gentle kiss on her lips. The moment seemed to suspend itself in time, but all too quickly he pulled away to refocus his attention on the lock, leaving her stunned—and never more desperate to be free.

"Hey!" Theo shouted. "We forgot the hard drive!"

"Where is it?" Galileo asked.

Natalie lifted her chin toward the counter above them. "Next to my computer."

He jumped to his feet, unplugged it, and stuffed it under his bulletproof vest.

"What about the mice?" she said. "They're our only proof!"

He frowned as he approached the cage, where a mound of tiny infant mice were dozing—at a month old, they still appeared to be newborns, barely able to stand on their toothpick legs. She watched as he stuck his hand in, scooped up five or six, and loaded them into the pocket of his pants. They were still inert enough not to climb out.

She raised her eyebrows. "Really?"

"What else can I do? Smuggle out the cage?"

In the silence before she could reply, they heard the slap-slap of footsteps out in the hallway.

Footsteps getting louder. Closer.

"Get in here!" Galileo mouthed to Zoe as he opened the tall supply cabinet, which had been emptied of all its contents. "Hurry!"

She obeyed, diving inside just as he closed the door behind her.

Natalie caught the look of anguish on his face. It was too late. There would be no rescue. No freedom. No reunion.

There was nothing he could do when Les Mahler walked in, alone and furious, except revert to his erect posture and stern detachment, with his hands clasped behind his back and his feet planted like a guard's. The ease with which he transformed back into Benjamin Barrow took her breath away.

"Did you find anyone?" he asked. Even his voice sounded different—colder.

"No," Les snapped. "No one except a bunch of cripples. We're still searching, but I came to take them away. The helicopter's outside waiting."

He produced the key to the handcuffs and approached Natalie, while Galileo hung back, motioning her to remain calm. She trusted him, willing herself not to struggle as Les squatted next to her and removed the cuffs from the leg of the counter, only to recuff both wrists behind her back.

"Stand up," he commanded. "Now!"

She rose to her feet.

"Take her," Les instructed Galileo, "while I get the boy."

He steered her toward Galileo, who took her by the arm, while Les undid Theo's cuffs and replaced them on both of his wrists as well.

"All right," Les barked. "Let's move out."

One glance at Galileo's ashen face told Natalie all she needed to know.

His bag of tricks was empty. They had no choice but to cooperate, to put one foot in front of the other in an inevitable march toward fate. She couldn't bear to look at Theo. He had been right all along. If only she hadn't been so insistent about the hard drive, they would be far away, tucked into some safe house, probably watching the whole wretched invasion on television instead of—

"Stop!" a girlish voice screamed. "Get your hands off them!"

Natalie turned in disbelief to see the cabinet door swinging and Zoe standing a few feet away, snarling at Les, her gun aimed at his face.

CHAPTER 44

The look in her eyes chilled Les to the core. He had seen it in prisoners of war, in hunted animals, in the face of the man he had beaten to death—but never in a child. It was the kind of frenzied desperation that unravels sanity.

He stared down the barrel of her gun without flinching.

"Well, look who's decided to show herself."

"I mean it!" she screamed. "I'll shoot!"

The gun shook in her tiny hands, allowing him to catch a glimpse of its side, where the safety was still on. He smiled. She couldn't fire on him if she tried. Yet she was handing him the perfect chance to get rid of her and her troublesome DNA forever. No one could blame him for self-defense. But what if she had information about the man he needed most?

"Drop the gun," he said. He rested a hand on his own loaded gun in its holster around his waist.

She gulped a great big breath, her shoulders heaving, her blue eyes wild.

"Drop it!" Benjamin Barrow yelled. "Or we'll have to shoot!"

Les detected a frantic edge in his partner's voice that was galling. If he was scared of a *little girl*, how could he handle a criminal mastermind?

She appeared to hesitate, staring back and forth between them, the gun shaking in her grip.

"You don't want to hit your friend by accident," Les said, jerking Theo's shackled arms in front of his own body like a shield. The boy struggled and kicked, but Les held him in place.

Her lips parted in horror as Natalie let out a cry.

"Come on, Zoe," Barrow coaxed, "drop it and no one gets hurt."

Staring at Les, she lowered the gun.

"Good girl," he said. "That's right, all the way to the floor."

She crouched and deposited it at her feet with a thud.

Les heard Barrow breathe a sigh of relief and half turned to him, keeping Zoe in his peripheral vision. His face was haggard, as if he'd just lived through the world's shortest war. The boy hung his head, no longer trying to resist Les's clutches. Natalie stood slouched in Barrow's grip, breathing hard.

"Take these two outside," Les ordered, pushing Theo to him. "Zoe and I need to have a little chat."

A trace of fear came into Barrow's face. "Are you sure? I might need backup."

Les rolled his eyes. "They're *restrained*, for God's sake. Just walk them upstairs."

He tightened his arms around Natalie's and Theo's elbows so that they formed feeble links on either side of him. "Don't even try to step out of line," he commanded, hauling them out into the hallway.

As soon as they were gone, Les locked the door. He had Zoe alone at last. She was standing erect with her face flushed, her blond bangs matted to her forehead, her fists clenched at her sides.

"So," he said, "you were hiding in that cabinet the whole time, huh?"

"They didn't do anything wrong! It's not fair!"

"They'll be fine." He gave her a friendly smile. "I'm here to help you."

"I don't need your help."

"Don't you want to go home?"

"That's not your problem."

"But it is. I'm here to rescue you."

"Bullshit."

He frowned. This girl was tougher than he expected.

"You're confused, Zoe. You've been through a lot. Why don't we talk about it?"

"No." She crossed her arms and took a step back. He advanced, closing the space between them. She sprinted around him toward the door, but he was quicker; he blocked the way and took hold of her scrawny bicep. She flailed, hollering.

"Let me go!"

"Shut up." He dragged her to a metal stool next to a counter in the back of the lab and shoved her onto it, but she resisted, kicking at his legs and trying to bite him. As he struggled to subdue her, he felt her teeth pierce his hand. He yanked it away with a howl, then smacked her hard across the mouth. She grunted and grew still, cupping her jaw. Bright red blood dribbled down her lip. Tears shone in her eyes. Taking advantage of her daze, he snatched her wrist and cuffed it to the stool, along with her ankle.

"What the hell is wrong with you?" he barked. "Now my hand could get infected."

She glared back. "I hope so." A purplish bruise was darkening her chin.

"You know, it doesn't have to be like this. If you just tell me what I need to know, your friends go free. We all go home happy."

"What?"

"Where's Galileo?"

In her eyes he saw a flicker of uncertainty. "How would I know?"

"Don't lie to me."

"I'm not."

"I can tell. Where is he?"

"I don't know."

"What kind of friend are you? You're going to let Natalie and Theo go to jail?"

"You think I'm that dumb?"

He inched his face closer to hers. "You know what I think? I think you're a liar."

"You would know."

He cocked his head and pulled away. "Listen, I don't blame you for wanting to protect the guy, but you have to realize it's because you've been brainwashed. And it's not your fault. But now we need your help."

"I'm telling you, there's nothing I can do."

"Don't you want to be a national hero?"

She gritted her teeth. "What I *want* is for you to let me go."

"Well, I can't do that. Not until you talk."

"So you're going to keep me here forever?"

"As long as it takes."

The desperation in her eyes intensified. "That's illegal!"

"Says who? I'm the one in charge."

"I'll tell everyone you're a monster! You held me hostage!"

He gave an amused chuckle. "I'll just explain you have Stockholm syndrome and I had to restrain you for your own good. If it even comes to that."

"What do you mean?"

"I changed my mind. Screw waiting. You better start talking." His fingers closed around his holster.

Her eyes widened. "What, you're going to shoot me?"

"In self-defense, of course. I already have witnesses to prove you tried to attack me."

She sneered. "You *are* a monster."

"And you should never have been born."

"Go ahead and kill me, then." Her voice trembled. "I know you want to."

"So you'd rather die than talk?"

"Don't pretend I have a choice."

He sighed, removing his gun from its holster. "You really think it's worth dying for a psychopath?"

He walked around her stool in a circle, purposely letting the tip of the gun skim her knees and drag across her back. She tried to recoil, but it was impossible with her ankle and wrist shackled.

"Help!" she screamed, her blue eyes more terrified than ever. "Help!"

"No one can hear you down here," he said. "It's just you and me."

As he slid his finger to release the safety, an eerily deep voice thundered overhead.

"You sure about that?"

CHAPTER 45

Les froze. Zoe's screams faded in her throat.

They both looked up, as if expecting to see a phantom floating down from the spot where the voice had boomed. Instead, he recognized the circular grates of an intercom next to a black camera bulb.

"Who's there?" he shouted.

The voice sounded too low to be human. *"You don't know me, Les, but I know you. Did you like my postcard?"*

He felt the hair on his neck stand up. "I'm coming for you next, asshole." He aimed his gun at the camera, poised to shatter it.

"I wouldn't do that if I were you. You wouldn't want your partner to get hurt now, would you?"

"Nice try." Les rolled his eyes. "He's right outside the door."

But then the familiar gravelly voice of Benjamin Barrow cried through. "Help! Hurry! I'm in the—"

Static crackled. A smack echoed. Then, silence.

Les's breath caught as he tried to fathom what could

have gone so wrong in a few short minutes. But it meant Galileo was close—extremely close.

"Where are you?" he yelled. "Try to tell me where you are!"

"He's dead unless you uncuff the girl and let her go right now."

Les turned to Zoe. Her expression was blank, as if she were afraid to reveal any stake in the outcome. He twirled the gun in his hand. How could he just let her walk away, knowing the havoc her DNA could wreak on the world? And what did Benjamin Barrow matter anyway? Les didn't need him—unless he could point the way to Galileo, and for that he had to be alive.

A shot boomed through the ceiling, followed by a man's agonized wail. It sounded like Barrow.

"I said now!"

"Jesus, okay!"

He shoved his gun into its holster and produced the silver key from his pocket.

"See?" He waved it at the camera like a white flag.

"Do it!"

He did. As soon as Zoe's limbs were free, she leaped from the stool and scrambled out the door. He had never seen a girl run so fast. Fury overwhelmed him as he looked back up at the camera.

"Happy now?"

"Very. Next I want you to—"

A guttural roar interrupted the voice, and then three quick shots resounded like firecrackers. The sounds of a struggle ensued—grunts, punches, gasps, glass shattering, something heavy falling.

Les stared at the ceiling, transfixed. "Where are you? I'm coming!"

There was no answer—just more sounds of crashing and grunting.

"Barrow, can you hear me? Are you okay?"

The seconds ticked by in radio silence. Just when Les was losing hope that he was still alive, Barrow's breathless voice resonated through the speaker, giddy with shock.

"I knocked him out! Come, hurry!"

"Where are you?"

"In this—lighthouse tower. It's—ah—come outside and look up to the right, up the stairs, the broken window—hurry, my leg is bleeding!"

Les tore out of the lab, sprinted up three flights of stairs and out into the center courtyard, where several helicopters were waiting to take any criminals into custody. It was dark now, but he could see that the squat adobe building next door housed a cylindrical tower on its roof—with one window pane smashed to pieces, its shards of glass glinting in the moonlight. He ran toward it alone. The SWAT team had scattered to the mountains to search. How could they all have missed Galileo hiding just under their noses the whole time?

"Come back!" Les hollered as loud as he could. "Help!"

He couldn't afford to wait for them. He raced into the building and found the stairs, taking them two at a time, winding up and around the flights until he came to a battered door at the top landing and pushed it open, his gun outstretched.

Inside the small tower, Benjamin Barrow was writhing on the floor in the fetal position, clutching his calf. Blood seeped out under his hands, soaking his pant leg. Pieces of glass littered the wooden floor around him. On the wall was a control panel with dozens of buttons and a cracked video screen, as though it had been punched. Two chairs lay overturned, their legs snapped off.

No one else was there.

"What happened?" Les demanded. "Where did he go?"

"Down there." Barrow moaned, pointing to a spot at the edge of the room where the floor and wall met. "He just got away."

Les ran to the spot, where a wooden board had been shoved aside to reveal a hole about two feet across. A metal ladder nailed inside it descended into total darkness. There was no telling how deep it went.

Barrow tried to drag himself over on his elbows. "He can't be far."

"Stay there." Les hopped onto the ladder and climbed down rung by rung, as fast as he could without slipping. It didn't matter that he had no clue where he was going, or where he would end up, or even that Barrow was badly hurt. All that mattered was one man. He couldn't wait to set eyes on the evasive mastermind at last—and then annihilate him on his own turf.

"Wait," came an eerie subhuman voice a few yards above him.

A chill crawled over his skin. He glanced up from the ladder, confused.

Barrow was standing—standing!—over the hole, his tall figure in silhouette. He was smiling, holding a small rectangular device close to his mouth. When Les's eyes widened, he tossed it aside and spoke in his normal voice—a voice that for the first time sounded fearless, steady, triumphant.

"You forgot something," he said. Then he pulled out a handgun and aimed it down the shaft. "This is from Zoe."

Their eyes met over the barrel a second before the shot rang out, and Les understood. Not only was he beaten—he always had been. A bitter cry escaped him, but it was too late to flee, too late to fight back.

The bullet flew at his forehead. He closed his eyes and let go.

CHAPTER 46

Hiding in her apartment, glued to the open window, Zoe watched in horror as Galileo came limping into the quad, his lower right leg soaked in blood. He shouted into the loudspeaker she recognized from their evacuation drills, his voice booming across the compound and beyond.

"SWAT team report back immediately! Man down, perp at large!"

It took only seconds before the men in black helmets and masks streamed in from the mountains—six, seven, eight, nine of them, she counted as they returned and clustered around Galileo, who gestured to the Brain. She craned her head out the window to catch what he was telling them:

" . . . this tunnel, but the perp was hiding in there and shot at us—my partner's dead—he's on the run, I couldn't follow, hurry, go before he gets away!"

In one black swarm, they bounded toward the building that housed the Brain and disappeared inside. As Galileo watched them go, his shoulders appeared to relax. He set the loudspeaker down on a bench and looked around. Two helicopters stood nearby waiting to take away those who would never be found. His gaze swept past them to the row of apartments, darting from window to window, his brow furrowed, until he spotted Zoe waving. Joy lit his face.

She knew her cue. With her backpack loaded to the brim, she ran out the door and into the quad. He stretched his arms out, beaming at her.

"There's my girl!"

She basked in the freedom to hug him—no more disguises, no more acting. Finally they could be real. She detected the relief in his arms as they wrapped around her, and the pain, too. The Network had suffered a wound as crippling as his own. But he would survive—and for that reason, so would it. As long as he was alive, he would rebuild it stronger than before. If she knew the real him at all, she could count on it. He crouched down so they were face-to-face. Already, she could see the undaunted resolve in his eyes.

"Ready to go home?" he asked.

"You might say."

"Then let's go."

She raised an eyebrow. "Right now? You don't need to stay and—pretend to search for yourself?"

He smiled. "I'm chief now, and my priority is getting you home." He started to walk toward the nearest helicopter.

"But your leg! Don't you need help?"

He bent over and lifted up his pant leg, where the blood had soaked through. To her surprise, the skin was perfectly intact, without so much as a scratch. Her mouth fell open.

"Remember the mice I put in my pocket? Turned out I really did need them."

She gasped. "You killed them?"

"I had to," he said. "To complete the illusion."

"But what will Natalie say?"

"There are still a bunch left, and we only need one for proof for the Archon Prize."

She set her backpack on the ground and opened the zipper with a flourish. "Then it's a good thing I went back and got them all."

Galileo grinned in surprise as she lifted up the cage, where at least a dozen infant mice were soundly asleep—perennially stuck in their first day of life.

"I knew you were brilliant."

"You have to promise to get them safely to her."

He put his hand over his heart. "You have my word."

"But can I keep one as a pet? They're the only other living things like me on Earth."

He chuckled. "Sure. I think she'll understand."

"I wish I could have gotten to say good-bye."

"I know. But once we rebuild somewhere else, we can all reunite. It's not over—don't even think that for a second."

"Will Theo and Natalie be safe until then?"

"Absolutely. I made sure they escaped to the RV park, to safety. And you'll be fine, too. Les Mahler will never bother you again."

The words filled her with relief. "I knew you would come through. You always do. But how could you stand working with him all this time?"

"I had to. I had to get myself appointed to the committee and know every little thing they were doing and pretend to agree with it all—it was the only way I could run the Network without them catching on to me."

A feeling of warmth overcame her. It was the realization that he was trusting her—and that she was worth trusting. After all, kids weren't good at keeping secrets. You had to be an adult for that.

"Come on," he said, sticking out his hand. "There's nothing else for you here."

She took it. Then she picked up her backpack and they climbed several steep steps into the helicopter. Inside, two pilots sat waiting in the cockpit. The rest of the interior consisted of six leather seats, barely larger than a van. While Galileo went to talk to the pilots, she plopped down by the window and fastened her seat belt. He came back a minute later and handed her a headset with padded earmuffs and a microphone.

"For the noise," he said. "It's loud."

"So where are we going?"

"To the closest air force base, and then you'll fly with a police escort back to New York."

"You're not coming all the way?"

He shook his head. "I have to come back and take care of the patients that were left behind. You'll be okay without me?"

As usual, he was two steps ahead—trusting her to trust herself. She smiled at the rightness of it. "Of course. It's fine, I'm a big girl."

"You're a young woman."

The ground lurched away and they soared up above the buildings, above the mountains, into the starry black sky. As she watched the compound grow smaller and smaller, she waved good-bye to Natalie and Theo, imagining them tucked into some warm and cozy safe house down below.

Next stop, she thought, *home.*

It was morning when she shuffled up the steps to her family's brownstone on the Upper West Side, nervous and bleary-eyed, with the police escort at her side. She had spoken only a few words to her parents over the phone before boarding the plane, so she had no idea what kind of greeting to expect. Relief? Ecstasy? Anger? Would they ground her for the rest of her life? What had become of Gramps? She was afraid to find out—and even more afraid of the possibility that no one could tell her.

She rang the bell. A feeling of surreal detachment struck her as her parents opened the door, both of them already weeping. They bombarded her with hugs and kisses.

"My baby," her father whispered into her hair. "I thought I would never see you again."

"I'm okay, Dad. It's okay."

Her mother kissed her forehead, clutching her hand. "Is it really you?"

Zoe smiled, seeing she had to be the strong one. "It's me. I'm home."

They looked older than she remembered. Her mother's face was lined and drawn, and the creases around her father's eyes had deepened.

"Thank you so much," he told the cop. "You have no idea how grateful we are."

"Just doing my job, sir," he said, giving a little bow. "You all take care now."

As soon as they closed the door behind him, Zoe turned to her parents in the foyer and braced herself. The truth had to be stated. There was no time like the present.

"I'm sorry," she said. "I put you through hell and I feel terrible, but I chose to go. I was never kidnapped, and I was never harmed. I didn't tell you because I knew you wouldn't understand."

Her parents exchanged glances, and then her father surprised her by taking her hand. "It's our fault, too," he said. "We were treating you like a child."

"That wasn't fair of us," her mom said. "We promised ourselves that if we ever saw you again"—her eyes watered—"well, we'd do things over. We'd let you run your own life."

Her mom's gaze wandered to the stack of newspaper clippings on the hall table, and Zoe inferred from a few of the headlines that they were all stories about her disappearance. A fresh wave of guilt choked her up, but her mom quelled it with a tender smile.

"All that matters is that you're home," she said, as though reading her daughter's mind. "From now on, we *never* want you to feel like you can't talk to us."

She looked back and forth between them, her mouth hanging open. "Seriously?"

They both nodded.

"You're the boss," called a gruff voice behind them.

She felt her heart leap into her throat. Her parents stepped aside.

There, leaning heavily on his cane, stood Gramps. His hair was thinner, the bags under his eyes darker, his wrinkles deeper—but an ecstatic smile was plastered across his face.

"C'mere, sweetheart."

She dropped her backpack and ran to him, choking down a sob. The fresh lemon scent of his soap filled her nostrils as she threw her arms around his gaunt frame. "I thought you were gone!" she cried, then lowered her voice. "I tried to send you a letter."

"Oh, I had quite the adventure myself," he whispered. "Want to take a walk?"

She turned back to her parents, who were holding hands, unable to stop smiling. "We're going to go outside for a bit," she said. "I need some fresh air."

"Whatever you want," her dad said.

She linked her arm through Gramps's. "We'll be back soon."

It took him longer than usual to walk the few blocks to Riverside Park, but she was happy to go as slow as he needed. There was no rush.

"I was worried sick," she admitted once they were outside. "Where were you?"

"That makes two of us. I went after you."

"You *what*?"

"I didn't know if these folks in the Network were safe—I knew you trusted them, but how would I know? The media was making such a fuss about you being kidnapped, so I started to doubt them. Then your parents and I had this big fight—they thought I had something to do with it—so I . . . well, I pulled a Zoe."

"You just took off?"

"Yep. I took a train to Ohio, where your black Civic had been found in a ditch. It was all over the news. I figured I could go there and ask around, talk to the police myself. But when I got there, no one knew anything. I stayed in one hotel after the next for a month, hoping to stumble on someone who was in the Network. But eventually I ended up in the hospital, exhausted. I'm sure all the nurses thought I was losing it." He shrugged. "They called your mom and she came and got me. Your parents figured out pretty fast that I wasn't to blame."

She shook her head. "I can't believe you. And all this time, I was dying to tell you that I was okay."

"It doesn't matter," he said. "We're together now."

They approached a bench that overlooked their favorite garden. The roses and gardenias were in full bloom despite the early autumn chill in the air. Soon only their shriveled stems would remain—but today, they were still beautiful. As Gramps lowered himself to sit, he leaned back and closed his eyes. She admired his restraint in not pressing her for details right away. That kind of respect was a gift. Taking a seat beside him, she lifted her face to the early morning sun. Neither spoke. *So this is peace,* she thought.

"I have so much to tell you," she said. "I don't even know where to start."

"Start anywhere. Or nowhere. I'm just happy to have you home."

"Do you want to see my souvenir?"

"Sure."

She reached into her sweater pocket and pulled out a tiny docile mouse. Gramps gave a start and scooted away.

"What is *that*?"

She stroked its pink back with her fingertip. It shivered with delight and curled into a tight ball, barely opening its eyes.

"It's a long story."

"I've got time."

She bit her lip. Time was exactly what he did not have. Not for much longer—and there was nothing she could do about it. The human trials with the aging treatment would take years to begin, and that was only after the Network could rebuild. But then she thought again—of Theo, of Galileo, of Natalie, even of Les—and realized that there *was* something she could do. If knowing them had taught her anything, it was not to take the present for granted. Because no matter how much time you thought you had, you never really knew.

"You look so serious," Gramps said. "You okay?"

"I think so." It was true. She was.

She looked down at the mouse. Its tiny feet were twitching in dreamland.

"He's just a baby," she said. "He sleeps all the time."

"Does he have a name?"

"Not yet. But he might be stuck with it forever."

"Forever, huh?" Gramps lifted an eyebrow, intrigued. "Then you'd better pick a good one."

The first ideas that came to mind she rejected—no way could she name a mouse after anyone she knew. But it had to be something special, some way to pay tribute to the spirit of wonder and adventure that made his existence possible—the spirit that united her with the people she loved.

"Well?"

Then she grinned. "Your favorite poem. The Tennyson one."

"What about it?"

"This little guy *is* the knowledge beyond the sinking star. Beyond the utmost bound of human thought."

Gramps cocked his head and smiled. "Then I guess we know his name."

The mouse lay in her palm, the picture of contentment. She leaned forward and brushed her lips against his delicate ear.

"Hey, Ulysses," she whispered. "Welcome to the world."

ACKNOWLEDGMENTS

Contrary to popular belief, writing a book is not a completely solitary endeavor. I am grateful to many people whose expertise, advice, and support helped me along the way.

To my agent, Erica Silverman, for her trusted guidance, friendship, and belief in my work.

To my editor, Michaela Hamilton, for her wise insights, dedication, and cheerful confidence.

To Dr. Richard Walker, a leading expert on the science of aging, whose generosity is matched only by the depth of his knowledge.

To the late Dr. Michael Palmer, whose close mentorship I was lucky to receive for three years. He will be forever missed.

To the late Brooke Greenberg, whose mysterious failure to age inspired the character of Zoe.

To Dr. Cristina Rizza and Dr. Michael Peikoff for answering my questions about the clinical signs of aging.

To M.J. Rose, whose creative brainstorming was indispensable in helping me develop the initial premise.

To Brad Garrett, a former FBI agent who kindly found time for a phone call that rescued me from plot gridlock.

To Josh Jaffe, a computer science expert, for explaining the ins and outs of cyber security.

To Rebecca Wallace-Segall of Writopia Lab, for her flexibility with my employment and her enthusiasm for my writing goals, and to my students, for reminding me always to take joy in the creative process.

To my dear friends and my wider network on social media for their interest, encouragement, and word-of-mouth support.

To Andrew Gulli, for the epigraph.

To my early readers: Susan Breen, my classmates at Gotham Writers' Workshop, Jacqueline Berenson, Lisa VanDamme, and my parents.

To my first reader, Matt, for being my favorite inspiration—a triple threat of musician, comedian, and philosopher. All my love, always.

Don't miss Kira Peikoff's next compelling thriller

DIE AGAIN TOMORROW

Coming from Pinnacle in 2015

Keep reading for an exciting teaser excerpt—featuring
the return of Galileo!

1 Minute Dead

Her body undulated in the sea. It swayed with the waves, rising and falling, a rag doll in the froth. Seaweed clung to the dark tangle of her hair. Facedown, she floated on the crest of a swell, then plummeted with the breaker. Her slender limbs splayed out, strangers to pain. She was nothing now but a marionette at the mercy of the tide. White foam engulfed her body and carried it express to the shore.

It washed up on the beach. The tide receded. Her cheek lay against the sand, her eyes swollen closed. Her mouth hung open. Salt water trickled out.

The first person to notice was a little boy digging for crabs. He scooted over and squatted in front of her face.

"Time for wakey," he said. He planted his chubby thumb and forefinger on her eyelid, pried it open, and gazed into her unseeing pupil.

"Wakey," he said, frowning. He poked her limp arm. Nothing happened.

He started to cry. A woman jogged toward him but stopped short.

Then she screamed.

7 Minutes Dead

Two ambulances arrived at the same time. A pair of emergency medical techs jumped out of the first one and raced to her body, where a crowd of about ten sunbathers had gathered. Some were taking turns trying to deliver chest compressions while others stood to block the nearby children from view. The second ambulance waited at the curb; its purpose was to preserve the organs of a corpse for harvesting and donation in case attempts at resuscitation failed. With Key West's popular opt-out program, everyone who died in the city was assumed to be a consenting donor unless indication was given otherwise.

As the two EMTs approached the body, they saw right away that her skin was waterlogged and turning bluish. Frothy salt water spewed out of her mouth as if from an erratic hose.

"Out of the way," the older one commanded. His voice carried an air of authority that matched his jaded expression. The younger tech followed on his heels with a case of equipment slung over his shoulder. He looked to be in his late twenties, about the same age as the drowned woman.

The crowd parted and stepped back.

The first EMT dropped to his knees and grabbed her wrist. No pulse. He flung her disheveled hair off her face and opened her eyelids. Despite the bright morning sunlight, her pupils were fixed and dilated.

The younger tech urgently placed defibrillator pads on her body and attempted to shock her heart. When nothing happened, he switched to giving her chest compressions, hard and fast, about one hundred per minute. Salt water tainted with blood kept dribbling out of her mouth.

"She's flatlined," the older tech said after two minutes. "We should just declare her."

The other man kept on pushing, though his arms were tiring. "No, let's—give her a—chance," he sputtered. "She's so young."

His colleague looked skeptical, but nodded. "Let's switch, you do the line."

The young tech rolled off her chest and tried to inject a peripheral line with epinephrine into her arm, but her skin was so mottled that he couldn't find the vein. He cursed under his breath and moved on to the next last-ditch step.

As the first man continued to deliver fast compressions, grunting and sweating, the other hauled a canister of oxygen and a plastic breathing tube out of the supply bag. Using an L-shaped laryngoscope, he pushed up the roof of her mouth to see down into her throat.

That was when he noticed a piece of what looked like neoprene black cloth lodged inside her cheek. *That's weird,* he thought, and tried to pull it out, but it wouldn't easily dislodge, so he bypassed it. Her throat was extremely swollen and he had to work hard to shove the breathing tube all the way in.

"Should I just put the epinephrine down the tube?" he asked.

"You know—there's—controversy about that," the

other man huffed, still doing compressions. "It doesn't—necessarily—help survival."

"What does she have to lose?"

He seized the drug and pushed 2 mg into her tube. Then he connected her to the oxygen tank, and the men switched positions again so neither tired for too long.

Every two or three minutes, they switched, while one checked her pulse on her neck, her groin. Nothing. Her skin was now a frightening shade of blue.

After twenty-one minutes, the older man pushed on her chest for the last time and rolled off her, sweating profusely.

"We should just stop, I don't know why you want to save the world all the time."

The young man glared, but didn't rush to perform any further compressions. "She had her whole life ahead of her."

It didn't help that she was beautiful: he imagined how her cascade of black hair might have draped across her tanned shoulders, how her green eyes might have lit up when she laughed. She had the athletic figure of a swimmer—flat abs, toned biceps, defined calves. With a body like that, he wondered how she could have succumbed to the waves, even in high tide. Some things would forever be a mystery.

"We have to accept it. She's gone. I'm calling it." The older tech glanced at his watch. "Time of death: 10:12 A.M."

A few of the onlookers turned away. One made the sign of a cross over his chest and bowed his head.

The young EMT sighed and radioed to the waiting ambulance to come claim her body. Then he removed her breathing tube and packed up all the equipment. He tried to think of the bright side: a young, otherwise healthy person was a prime candidate for cadaver organ donation; as many as fifty lives could be saved or improved from her body alone.

Within seconds, two bored-looking EMTs arrived with a stretcher and nodded at the pair who had failed.

"We can take it from here. Thanks."

They lifted her corpse and strapped it in, wasting no time hauling it to their own ambulance. As they tipped the stretcher to load it, her drying hair fell over the edge and glinted in the sun.

Inside an elderly doctor was waiting. He beckoned at the EMTs to hurry. They scrambled in after loading the stretcher, just as the doctor pulled the door shut behind them. Exhilaration radiated from his flushed cheeks, but his demeanor was steady.

He was the famed—some would say infamous—Dr. Horatio Quinn, who had vanished from the public eye seven years prior. Now approaching eighty, his back was stooped, his arthritic fingers gnarled, his white brows permanently furrowed. But behind his tortoise-shell glasses shone an insatiable hunger for truth that kept him as young as the first day he ever walked into a lab.

He placed one hand on the woman's lifeless forehead and smiled.

"Gentlemen," he said, "close the blinds. This is when the fun begins."

33 Minutes Dead

Dr. Quinn lifted a corner of the rubber floor pad and pressed his index finger on a tiny sensor. Together, he and the two EMTs turned to stare at a blank white area on the wall a few inches below the ceiling, near the head of the corpse. They heard a click, followed by a whirring sound. Then four cracks materialized in the shape of a square about two feet across and two feet wide. It was a door. The edges popped out and slid to the left, revealing a secret compartment in the depths.

"Never gets old," muttered Chris, the tech with the best poker face around.

His new apprentice, Theo, rubbed his hands together in anticipation.

The doctor reached inside the hole and extracted an automatic CPR device—a small round machine the size of a helmet. He put it on the dead woman's sternum, securing it around her chest with a band pulled tight. Right away the machine started to deliver perfect chest compressions to the highest standards of timing and force—with no chance of tiring. Next, the doctor opened her mouth and inserted a laryngoscope with an attached camera so he could visualize her trachea.

He frowned; a piece of shredded black cloth was stuck between her teeth and cheek. It had a fraying string wrapped around her tooth. *What the hell is that,* he thought. He yanked it out and flicked it away, then slipped in a breathing tube connected to a ventilator and a portable oxygen tank. He set the CPR device at ten breaths per minute.

"Game on," he whispered near her ear.

At the same time, while Ty connected her arm to a standard blood pressure cuff, Chris retrieved a black circular pad from the secret hole. It looked like an eye patch, but with a narrow blue tube connecting to a digital display: it was a cerebral oximeter that used near-infrared light to measure the amount of oxygen getting to her brain. He stuck it on her forehead above her right eye. The display quickly lit up with a red number: 5 percent.

"Why is it still so low?" Theo asked at her left side. "Shouldn't it be coming up already?"

"It will." Dr. Quinn was standing at her head, twisting his frail body to reach up into the hole. "You'll see."

What he took out next looked like a red gun, but with a long needle in place of a barrel. It was an intraosseous device that could shoot drugs directly into bone, bypassing veins.

"My favorite toy," he declared. He leaned over the corpse, pressed the gun against her left shoulder, and fired. It recoiled as a pin lodged itself in her bone. He shot three more pins—one into her other shoulder and two just below each knee. The techs watched with a mixture of awe and envy at his precision. Then he attached a line into each pin that would serve as a conduit for the drugs.

Chris and Theo moved aside in the cramped space as Quinn positioned himself next to her left shoulder. "Now," he said with relish, "for the moment of truth. I want the X101 first."

"Got it." Chris handed him a tube of chilled clear fluid that had been stored in a container inside the hole.

Dr. Quinn cradled it in his hands with the affection of a father. It was his life's work in a vial—the culmination of decades, the reason he had once been celebrated and then viciously destroyed, accused of intellectual theft by a jealous colleague, driven out of research, driven almost to suicide. If not for the Network's rescue seven years ago, he might very well have been as dead as the corpse before him.

He had designed the drug to exploit the critical time between a person's death and the death of brain cells— roughly a four-to-eight-hour window, maybe even longer. But by injecting an inhibitor of the calpain enzyme—the signal to brain cells that it was time to die— the process could be slowed down, the window expanded, and the brain temporarily protected from damage. One dose of X101 had bought an additional ten hours of brain cell preservation in animal trials, and now at last, he was secretly testing it in humans.

He injected a single dose into the woman's left shoulder. Working quickly, the other men addressed her remaining lines: Chris injected her right shoulder with an icy slurry of water to chill her down rapidly from the inside out. Into her left knee, Theo injected an experimental solution filled with billions of microglobules of fat, each of which contained a dose of oxygen. When released into her body, it would provide a welcome gush to her brain and other organs. In the last line, her right knee, the doctor injected one final trial drug, this one developed by his colleagues within the Network: coenzyme Q. It was meant to protect mitochondria, the energy-producing part of brain cells, from decaying.

All the while Theo got to work using the ultrasound machine installed in the ambulance to locate her carotid artery in her neck, then he inserted a thick catheter with two separate tracks, pushing it down near her heart.

"Nice work, Theo," the doctor commented.

He took over and connected the catheter to a portable

machine called an ECMO that pumped blood in a loop outside the body, infusing it with oxygen and cleansing it of carbon dioxide, before cycling it back into the dead woman.

At the same time, Chris inserted a catheter into her groin to start a drip of epinephrine to bring up her blood pressure.

"Hey!" Theo exclaimed, pointing at the cerebral oximeter on her forehead. "It's already up to forty-five percent."

"Told you," the doctor said. "But it's still got a ways to go. We want it at seventy percent. Now ice her."

Maneuvering around the stretcher in the tight space, Theo reached into the secret hole and loaded his arms with nearly a dozen artificial ice packs. Together, he and Chris covered her arms, legs, and stomach to cool her down quickly from the outside, in addition to the inside. A thermometer indicated that her current temperature was 95 degrees, but the ice would bring it down to 70. Cold was key: it slowed down decay, snatching back time from the impending claws of irreversible death.

"Excellent, gentlemen," the doctor announced. "Let's hit the road."

Chris hopped out and took his place up front in the driver's seat. The curtains remained closed, the sirens off. As the ambulance started to roll out of the beach's parking lot, Dr. Quinn fitted an EEG skullcap over her head to measure her brain waves. The monitor lit up with a low, sustained beep.

Theo's freckled nose wrinkled. "Shit. She's still totally flatlined."

"Because we shut her down," the doctor said. "We've hibernated her."

The engine whirred and the ambulance sped up. He and Tyler settled into straight-backed seats with their knees butting up against the stretcher, holding the black straps dangling from the ceiling. With each turn, the woman's head lolled from side to side. Her bluish lips were slack around the breathing tube and her puffy eyelids were sealed shut.

Dr. Quinn inched aside a curtain to peek outside. He saw the hospital and morgue pass by, a cluster of old beige buildings as desperately outdated as the medicine that was practiced there.

"What about her organs?" Theo asked. "Isn't the hospital waiting on the body?"

"Not for long. Chris should be calling it in now—he'll tell the morgue that we were able to resuscitate her after all, and he'll tell the hospital that her organs were too damaged for donation. Drug addiction or some excuse."

Theo smirked. "Way to honor the dead."

"The trick is to get her lost in the system. The hospital will think we're taking her to the morgue and vice versa. Trust me, once organs are out of the question, no one cares about a corpse."

"What about her family?"

"We don't know who she is—yet. Let's hope we get the chance to find out."

2 Hours, 6 Minutes Dead

The ambulance approached a port where a 440-foot cruise ship was docked. On its side in flowery script were the words *Retirement at Sea*. It was a stately white vessel with five decks, all but the top one lined with rows of circular windows.

Chris navigated onto a wooden pier parallel to the ship and drove several yards until he reached a certain threshold. As soon as he crossed it, a loading ramp yawned out of the side of the ship and flattened onto the pier. It was lined with seven-foot-tall opaque white panels, ensuring the privacy of all who came and went.

Chris backed up to the ramp and killed the engine. That was their cue: Dr. Quinn and Theo popped open the back door, now shielded from onlookers, and quickly hoisted the dead woman's stretcher up the ramp and aboard the ship, accompanied by the equipment on poles: the blood-pumping ECMO device, the cerebral oximeter, the still flatlined EEG monitor.

A tall, square-jawed man in his late fifties was waiting for them on the deck, where a dozen people were bustling about carrying charts, conferring with one another, striding purposefully in and out of adjacent doors. All were clad in medical scrubs or white coats. Though the man was the odd one out in black sweatpants and a gray T-shirt, his erect posture lent him an air of dignity. He had the sculpted muscles and wavy dark hair of a man half his age, but the face of a commanding officer—an alert stare, a hard mouth, a defiant chin. But there was a hint of mischief in his light blue eyes that softened his intensity. One felt in his presence that nothing could faze him, nor should it.

"Galileo," Dr. Quinn greeted him with a respectful head tilt. "We need an OR."

"It's ready and waiting." Galileo stared at the corpse

with the resolve of a doctor confronting the world's sickest patient. "What's the prognosis?"

"Iffy. Her lungs are a mess, still no pulse. But the good news is she's cooled, brain oxygen's up to seventy percent, and the drugs should have bought us some time."

"She looks too young to die." He pressed his lips together, unable to look away from her bone-white face. The black hair plastered to her cheeks made the contrast even starker. "Go. The nurses are already scrubbed in."

After following suit at a station of sterile sinks, the doctor and his two techs took the elevator down to the lowest deck. The wide-open space that was once a luxurious restaurant with seating for 120 had been entirely transformed. Three opaque partitions separated it into several state-of-the-art operating rooms, each stocked with the surgical tools of a world-class hospital. The only hint of the deck's past life was a gold, crystal-encrusted chandelier still hanging from the ceiling.

They hurried into OR 1, where two gray-haired intensive-care nurses were gloved, masked, and standing by. Though only their eyes were visible, Dr. Quinn was pleased to recognize that they were Annie and Corinne, the Network's most experienced gems. They flashed him smiles with their eyes, while Chris and Theo laid the corpse flat on the table. The techs were careful not to disrupt any of the tools tethered to her, including the ice packs keeping her cool and the CPR device that was still delivering compressions to her chest in quick bursts.

Then the two men got out of the way while the others converged around the dead woman in choreographed posts: the doctor standing behind her head, the nurses on either side of him, extending his reach to the various shiny tools on trays nearby.

With them responding rapid-fire to his commands, Dr. Quinn was soon gripping a heavy silver drill with both hands. Steadily he punctured a bolt into the back of the woman's skull. The noise of grinding through bone always made him wince, though he knew she could feel no pain. A sensor attached to the bolt sat on the surface of her brain to measure intracranial pressure.

"Good to go," he said. "Next up, a bronchoscope, please."

The nurses moved with the swiftness and grace of dancers. Within minutes, the doctor had inserted a smaller tube with a camera into her breathing tube, sucked out salt water, washed out her lungs with a sterile solution and given her a dose of antibiotics.

All along the nurses took turns reading out numbers to keep him informed of her oxygen, carbon dioxide, brain pressure, and blood pressure. It was no simple task to maintain the ideal balance of each number: to maintain the goal of 70 percent brain oxygen, they had to pump it into the bloodstream at 95 percent and no further. Oxygen itself was toxic to cells if too concentrated, and dangerously deficient if not enough. Right now she was at a perfect 70 percent and 40 mmHg of carbon dioxide; they just had to keep her there.

"Okay, now bring her blood pressure up, up, up!" the doctor commanded, lifting his hands. The key was to maintain a higher-than-usual arterial pressure—90 instead of the usual 65—to pump the blood back into her brain. Careful monitoring of the bolt sensor would ensure that the brain wasn't getting crushed by the pressure.

Annie was leaning down to check on the bolt when she caught sight of something strange: a bald patch the size of a thumbprint on the woman's head, near her right ear.

"Did you see this?" she asked the doctor. He shifted his gaze from the blood pressure monitor to the patch and shrugged.

"No, but she's got more to worry about than a bad hair day right now."

"But isn't it—"

She was cut off by the sudden angry beeping of a monitor.

"O_2's spiking!" Corinne yelled. The cerebral oximeter was jumping up—80 percent, 85 percent, 87 percent.

Dr. Quinn leaped to the ECMO machine that was pumping oxygen into her blood through the tube in her neck, and adjusted the output. When the percentages started dropping back down, he exhaled a breath. He didn't look away until she was stable again at 70 percent.

"Okay," he said at last. "Lungs are clean. The numbers look good. You know what to do."

The nurses removed the ice packs lining her arms, stomach, and legs, as the doctor set the temperature regulator on the ECMO to gradually rewarm her body at a rate of 0.25 degrees Celsius per hour. The thaw out of the cold state was precisely calibrated—if it happened too quickly, intracranial pressure could spike and cause permanent death.

When there was nothing left to do, the doctor gazed down at the intubated, catheterized, machine-addled corpse on the table. It was difficult not to think of her as his *patient*, even though—by definition—she was still as dead as ever. No heartbeat, no respiration, no brain waves.

He looked up at the nurses with a hopeful smile.

"Now," he said, "we wait."

15 Hours, 20 Minutes Dead

"Quinn!" yelled a familiar husky voice into the intercom. It was Annie. Her words blasted through his wall and woke him with a start. It was after 1:00 A.M. His fitful dream evaporated like vapor as reality hardened around him: he was in his compact box of a room on deck two, gently rocking with the ocean's waves. Frustration nettled him. Where was his patient? Why was he in bed?

Then he recalled keeping vigil next to her body for nearly twelve hours before falling asleep on the floor. Someone must have moved him here.

He jumped up and crossed the three steps to his intercom. "What did I miss?"

"Come fast. There's a flicker on the heart monitor."

He felt a joyous bubble rise in his throat, somewhere between a laugh and a sob. Ten seconds later, he was back by her side in the operating room. Her pulse was erratic, to be sure. A shy beep could be heard at jagged intervals, persisting for several seconds and then disappearing altogether. Her temperature had climbed to 86 degrees Fahrenheit. A pinkish smudge was returning to her ashen cheeks.

"Come on," he muttered. "Come on."

Within minutes the flicker became a sustained line and the beep, a steady rhythm.

"That a girl!" he cried. "Isn't that the most beautiful music you ever heard?"

Annie stood behind him, her hazel eyes bloodshot and weary. "But she's still flatlined. What if her brain doesn't come back?"

"It will. Give her time. I'll take over. You go to bed."

For three more hours, he waited. As the rest of the ship slept, he kept an obsessive eye on every number that could be measured. No matter how many times he had gone through this process—she was the twenty-second patient in his clinical trial—he became awestruck witnessing the retreat of death. It was the stuff of the supernatural, the holy grail sought across all of time—yet it was real. It was happening in front of him.

Only in the last decade had pioneers in cardiac resuscitation made it possible to revive people hours after they'd drawn their last breath, and now his drug X101 was lengthening that window. So far it had worked every time to limit brain damage and restore patients to their full selves, even up to twenty-four hours after their deaths. He was confident it would work again on this Jane Doe, yet he still felt a desperate yearning bordering on despair with each minute that ticked by.

What would he do if he actually did bring her back to life, but brain-dead? Could he ethically just pull the plug without consent, if he didn't know her identity or her family? Or was he bound to keep her on life support indefinitely? It was a dilemma he had never faced, but he tortured himself with its plausibility as the night wore on.

At last, when her temperature reached 91 degrees, he saw it: a spasm of electricity on the EEG. He jumped from his chair and stared, captivated, at the monitor. The previously flat line transformed into spiky bursts of peaks and valleys. They stabilized over the next six hours as her temperature rose to 98 degrees. The doctor oversaw every moment, talking to her gently in case she could hear him. She was in a deep coma, but she wasn't brain-dead. Now she wasn't dead at all.

1 Minute Awake

Her eyes opened. They roamed back and forth, squinting under the fluorescent lights. Her face scrunched up as if she were about to cry. Instead she groaned past her breathing tube and thrashed her legs, her heart rate skyrocketing: 132, 140, 147.

A petite young nurse, who was covering the morning shift, cupped a hand over her mouth and gasped. At the bedside, Dr. Quinn clutched the woman's warm left hand in both of his. He had been awaiting this moment all night.

"You're okay," he said softly. "You're just waking up from a bad accident."

Her head rolled back and forth. She moaned louder.

"I'm going to take out your tube now. This'll be quick. There we go, see, no problem, easy does it—and it's out."

She immediately coughed. "Wa—" she started, then choked and coughed again. Her hand flew to her throat.

"Right here." The doctor lifted a white paper cup to her lips. He cradled her head and she sipped greedily, spilling much of it down her neck. When he pulled back her paper drape to blot her collarbone dry, he noticed a row of deep purple bruises. How could he not have seen them at first? But then he realized that would have been impossible; they could have shown up only after blood was reintroduced into her body.

"Boy," he said, "you really got tossed around in those waves."

"Won't . . . pay," she mumbled, her eyes blinking rapidly but failing to focus on anything. "Not got. Me no."

"What's she saying?" the nurse asked under her breath.

"She's just confused," the doctor whispered. "It's the drugs. Don't worry—it's normal at first."

"Me!" the woman exclaimed with a sudden loopy grin. Her tone was gleeful. "Me! Mama." Her eyes darted around the room, then closed. In a minute she was asleep again.

The nurse raised her eyebrows. "Imagine what her family must be going through, wherever they are."

"We'll get her back to them soon enough." The doctor stroked his patient's clammy forehead. "Once her delirium wears off and she's stable, we'll give her a mild tranquilizer and transport her to the real hospital. She'll think she was there the whole time, in a coma, and the staff will conclude that some embarrassing miscommunication caused her to get lost in their system. They'll do everything to cover it up, but if any investigation is opened, our ally on the board will shut it down. All that counts is that she's reunited with her family alive and well. Her death will be nothing but a forgotten footnote in her life."

48 Hours Awake

She spent two days in a blur of intravenous feedings, babbling, sleep, and agitation. Once her vitals stabilized, she was moved up to deck three into her own private recovery room, with a porthole that let in abundant sunshine. Its morning rays now bathed her skin in a healthy glow, no signs of her earlier pallor. She was sleeping, but Dr. Quinn knew that when she awoke this time, the effects of the drugs would be over. She'd be herself again—whoever she was.

He grinned at the report in his hand from the recent MRI of her brain: normal. Completely, beautifully normal. The X101 had once again proved its efficacy, in combination with the oxygenated fat globules and the mitochondria-protecting enzymes. Part of him wanted to just call off the clinical trial and make the whole protocol available stat to every hospital in the country, hell, in the world—but he knew it was too risky to blow the Network's cover over such preliminary results. If they got to five hundred patients and the percentages held, then he and Galileo would have some serious decisions to make. Would the U.S. government forgive their transgressions of illegal human experimentation if the peace offering was a way to reverse death? He liked to think so. But if not . . .

He brushed those concerns aside, gazing down at the woman's face—her sloped nose, her chapped pink lips, her arched brows. Each steady breath she inhaled was an affirmation of his own reason for being. He memorized the moment, knowing she would soon be leaving his care. It was hard not to get attached to the patients whose lives he had saved, even if they were mysteries as human beings.

"We did good," he said, standing over her. "It was rough for a while there, but you pulled through."

Her lids twitched at his voice, then fluttered open. She stared up at him blankly.

"Well, look who's awake! Hello there," he said, watching her expression transform into curiosity as she took in his white coat, wrinkled hands, and kindly face. "What's your name?"

She cleared her throat, keeping her intelligent eyes on him. "Isabel. Where am I?"

"Nice to meet you, Isabel. I'm Dr. Quinn, and you're in a hospital. You had a bad accident a few days ago in the ocean. Do you remember?"

"No." She shook her head with surprising exertion.

"You don't remember?"

"No, I do." A fierce glare narrowed her eyes.

"You do? Then what's *no*?"

"It wasn't an accident." She fingered the bruises at the base of her neck. "I was murdered."